FALLING
FROM THE
MOON

PRAISE FOR *FALLING FROM THE MOON*

Falling From The Moon is a dreamlike invitation into a counter-culture ritual of peace, love, community and nature that exposes the imperfect humanity of the seekers drawn together in the redwoods while illuminating their yearnings for understanding and forgiveness. Sapphire's story reminds us that our own stories hold the power to both wound and to heal. Our stories are not just our own."

—Mary A. Wood, Ph.D., Co-Chair Engaged Humanities and the Creative Life, Pacifica Graduate Institute

Falling From the Moon kept me engaged from first to last page. [Karin Zirk] poetically explores two characters, Lauren and Sapphire, when they both attend a Gathering in Plumas National Forest in California, a mini-Woodstock, for two weeks. There both wrestle with their own dark night of the soul and learn in the process the liberating joy of self-forgiveness. Both deeply travel the mythic path of the heroine's journey that draws into their sufferings a host of fascinating characters to both help and hinder their destiny."

—Dennis Patrick Slattery, Ph.D., Emeritus Professor, Mythological Studies Pacifica Graduate Institute Author of *Riting Myth, Mythic Writing: Plotting Your Personal Story* and *The Wounded Body: Remembering the Markings of Flesh.*

"I fell in love with *Falling From The Moon* by Karin Zirk; it has everything I want in a good read: compelling characters, an exotic setting, a story that keeps me turning pages and writing that bids me linger to savor the language. Set against the Gathering for Peace and Healing of the Planet in beautiful

Plumas National Forest, this timely book reminds us of our need for environmental consciousness, and that love for one another and peace for the world are still ideals to strive for."
—Judy Reeves, *Wild Women, Wild Voices"*

"Falling from the Moon is more than a tale of a Sapphire, a woman endeavoring on a quest to find her long-lost father while ultimately discovering herself. The true star of this book is the canvas upon which the story is drawn. Exhibiting the keen eye of an ethnographer, Zirk's writing conjures a world, brutally honest and rich with detail, allowing readers to travel through time and space not to any specific place, but to a temporary utopian moment."
—Michael I. Niman, Ph.D. Professor, State University New York, Buffalo, *People of the Rainbow: A Nomadic Utopia*

FALLING FROM THE MOON

a novel

KARIN E. ZIRK, PH.D.

Talk Story Publishing
Albuquerque, New Mexico

ISBN 13: 978-1-7340446-0-7

Published by Talk Story Publishing, Albuquerque, New Mexico.
The Hawaiian phrase "Talk Story" means to connect by sharing stories.
Through story we share our histories, what inspires us, what we're
passionate about, and who we are. We help writers get their
stories out into the world.
www.TalkStoryPublishing.com.

Cover and layout design by Tony Bonds
www.goldenratiobookdesign.com

First Edition, January 2020
Printed in the United States of America

*To the indomitable Drusilla Campbell (1940-2014)
for teaching me that bones hold the story together*

PROLOGUE

"Peace Prevails in the Woods"
By Alana Roscoe
(*Quincy Herald,* July 1, 1990)

WE LOVE YOOOUU! COME HAVE SOME PANCAKES

It is morning at the Twentieth Annual Gathering for Peace and Healing of the Planet, and the kitchens have been cooking around the clock for the last two weeks. Echo Mine Road billows with dust, as new arrivals in multi-colored Volkswagens, fuel-efficient Toyotas, and rusty pickup trucks navigate the mountain roads and wedge their vehicles in between the Giant White Pines. I saw license plates reflecting almost every one of the fifty states, as well as Canada and Mexico.

United States Forest Service Ranger Leon Vale told me that ten to fifteen thousand people from around the world are camped at McGriver's Gap in the Plumas National Forest, about thirty miles east of Quincy. More people arrive hourly in anticipation of the gathering's main event: a silent prayer for world peace and planetary healing, scheduled for Wednesday.

Many of the campers told me they have been making the annual summer pilgrimage for ten years or more, participating in this ongoing experiment dedicated to creating peace on Earth and a leaderless society. Along the way, music is played, children are conceived, spiritual wisdom from Buddhist texts to the Torah is debated, and the late-night drum circles are fueled by large amounts of marijuana.

Dressed like gypsies in their tie-dyed t-shirts and bold Guatemalan fabrics, underneath these flamboyant exteriors are teachers, electrical engineers, military veterans, political activists, and runaway teenagers. Some people have even discarded their garments in an attempt to shed the trappings of "Babylon," or mainstream society.

According to longtime gatherer "Grizzly Bear Garth," preparations started in early June. "We build it all ourselves. Kitchens and community workshop spaces. First Aid stations and fire pits. Last year we even had a nine-hole miniature golf course."

A huge concern among the local residents is the lack of sanitation facilities, but Garth told me, "We dig military-style trench latrines in the woods and use bleach water for sanitizing hands and cooking equipment." The camp has medical doctors, registered nurses, herbalists, massage therapists, and healers of all types who look out for the health of the community. A crew of volunteers patrol the woods at night to ensure that all campfires are built in safe locations and have the required five gallons of water and shovel nearby, to quickly put out any escaping flames.

The kitchens are constructed from dead trees and scraps of plywood salvaged from dumpsters. Mud stoves and ovens abound, and blue tarps serve as makeshift roofs. A circle of tepees creates a camping area for the elders, and the center space hosts sunrise yoga and late-night storytelling.

At the two-story stage, built by the 411 Anarchist Performance Collective, "Try Again" said, "We're just a bunch of street kids trying to awaken the environmental consciousness of America and create a family together. Come back tomorrow for *Romeo and Juliet*."

I missed the anarchist version of this classic play but did meet PS, who looked the part of the drunken Mercutio and shared his vision of the gathering. "The gathering is equal parts community and individuality, teetering on the verge of eruption."

The closest eruption I encountered was at Kid Korral. Dozens of children galloped through the woods and drove Tonka trucks through makeshift racetracks. My attempt at interviewing some parents was squelched by the shrieks of a toddler, whose bunny fell in the creek, and the excited shouts of the crew of eight-year-olds, who orchestrated a daring and successful rescue. On my way out of the gathering, Sapphire gave me a hug and invited me to return with my family for the peace ceremony.

If history repeats itself, after three weeks of celebrations, hundreds of meals, and thousands of "Oms," the entire village will disappear and *gatherers* will return to "Babylon." In a year, only the most experienced naturalist will be able to tell that ten thousand dreamers gathered in Plumas County to create peace, but participants will never forget their new perspectives on love, life, and community.

THE CALM BEFORE THE STORM

Thursday, July 5, 1990
McGriver's Gap, Plumas National Forest, California
(Day Ten of Sapphire's Gathering)

The big drum only sounds well from afar.
—Persian Proverb

SAPPHIRE

The fire-glow ricocheted off the drenched and gleaming flesh of the dancers. The drums pulsated around the circle: *Boom, thump thump, boom. Boom, thump thump, boom.* First, the deep vibrations of the dununs, and then the *slap* and *wap* response of the djembes. Drummers hunched over the drums strapped to their chests and hanging between their legs in prayer, forearms and biceps taut and flexed. Sweat and fire smoke mingled with the pungent aroma of burning weed. Jutting chins and bouncing heads keeping a beat. Outside the circle, the meadow receded into the darkness and the cold and everything else beyond.

Sapphire dissolved into the *boom, thump, rumble* of a hundred throbbing drums. Her hands wove the rhythm into the bonfire, while she joined hundreds of voices chanting, "Hey yanna. Ho yanna. Hey yan yan." Her heart reverberated, and the thunderous roar of the drums compressed her lungs.

He had vaporized fifteen years ago, leaving faint traces of patchouli on her stuffed panda, the echo of an acoustic guitar in the hallway. Sapphire had painted him, twenty times or more, a pagan Jesus dancing barefoot in the park.

Her tombstone canvases stacked up in her mother's garage gathering dust and spiders. Her failed attempts to conjure his flesh had brought her to this gypsy gathering of ten thousand or more, tucked away in this isolated valley in the Sierras. For days, she had wandered the cobalt green meadows, speckled with golden wildflowers, and she'd struggled to recognize his smile on faces hidden behind beards, age, sorrow.

The tingling in her bones convinced her that her father would be here, somewhere. The drums mimicked his late-night storytelling voice. A sound so old, it reached beyond recorded history, beyond anything she could articulate. *Foommm, bloop, foommm, bloop.* A knowing that started in her feet and climbed up her body in waves. Fire, drums, hips moving. Her fingers flirted with the sky above: black canvas speckled with glitter.

Beside Sapphire, Lauren's left hand rubbed her own rounded belly.

"Hey, little one, do you like this?" Her right fingers kept the backbeat on a djembe. "Hey yanna, ho yanna, hey yan."

Sapphire tapped her fingers on Lauren's djembe. *Bump, slap wap, bump.* Lauren looked at her, laughing. Sapphire shrugged her shoulders. She felt easy with Lauren, even though they had only been friends for a few days. Different beats flowed together and made one groove that she wanted to stay in forever.

"The earth is our mother, we must take care of her," Kalmia called out.

They all responded, "The earth is our mother, we must take care of her."

Three sisters danced together in a bronze shimmer of moist skin; hips undulating in unison, fingertips touching, and breasts swaying. "Hey yanna, ho yanna, hey yan yan."

First, they teased a blonde drummer into a frantic beat and then a redhead into a languid rhythm.

Compared to the topless women in batik sarongs, Sapphire blended into the background of any situation. She tugged the rubber band off the end of her braid and swung her hair loose, fluffing it with her fingers. She shook her head—long, brown, white-girl hair. Around her, women had dreads wrapped in colorful ribbons. She tried to sway her hips, to be tribal, more mystical. More like Kalmia.

Kalmia, embodying Sapphire's image of an ancient goddess, undulated her hips to the music. Her purple robes shadowed her movements; her face and hair, the color of burnt sienna. The drummers' arms sped up. Harder, faster, louder. *Thump, slap, rumble,* blending to a frenzy. The voices grew silent, unable to keep the pace. The frenetic pace made Sapphire's body jerk as she tried to keep up. Heart pounding. Short gasps of air.

BOOM! The drums stopped in unison. The crowd shouted, screamed to the sky.

In the moment of stillness that was not quite silence, Sapphire saw her mother clutching a bucket of white paint, slashing a brush against the canvas of her sixth-grade attempt at his portrait, in her mom's mistaken belief that she could whitewash a thousand memories and erase his blood from her daughter's body. Sapphire had run crying to her room, slammed the door shut, and hid in the closet, muttering. *You're not my real mother.*

Sapphire yanked her mind back to the fire, and her father, and the drums. She planted a big kiss on Lauren's tummy.

"I love you, baby Lauren."

The conga to her left called out: *Pop, pop, rap, pop, rap.* The djembes responded: *Slap, bloop, slap.* The conga repeated:

Pop, pop, rap, pop, rap, and then the dununs joined in: *Boom, thumb, boom.*

Kalmia added her voice, "Earth my bo-o-dy. Water my blo-o-o-od."

As a flute warbled behind her, Sapphire sang, "Air my breath."

Maracas rattled and bells clanged out, ringing high on top of the drums. Around her, djembes, doumbeks, and tambourines wove layers of rhythms on top of each other.

"And fire my spirit."

Their voices rose across the meadow, like Tule Fog rising up from California's Central Valley. In front of her, a bearded man slammed his palms onto the tightly wrapped skin of his djembe.

Lauren called out, "Earth my bo-o-day. Water my blo-od," and rubbed her belly with both hands.

Sapphire smiled. "Air my breath, and fire my spirit."

The circle spread backwards from the firelight. Flushed faces fixed their eyes on the sound that rumbled across the meadow to the white-trunked aspens levitating in the distance. Hundreds of voices, even more ecstatic bodies, flowed in harmony, oscillated in unity.

Sapphire imagined the moment she would find him, when her heart would recognize the man who was once her father. She danced alongside Lauren; her hands reached for the djembe, reached for the rhythm, four hands sharing a heartbeat on one drum. In her mind, she painted the scene: two women dancing under the stars by a fire. Two women and one drum. Faces lit from below by the golden light of the flames. Their bodies, dried leaves glued to the canvas.

She wanted to stay here forever, grooving inside the music, reveling in the sense of oneness she had experienced during her childhood in Griffith Park—Mom in a long lavender cape and tiara of daises, swirling with Dad to the music, while Sapphire banged on a beaded tambourine. When the sun began to set, they headed for Olvera Street. They ate cinnamon churros that left sugar on her face, while the Mariachi bands sang songs of lost loves and family in faraway lands. A place and time both near and incredibly distant, she thought.

A lanky man wiggled past her into the center of the circle, his long brown hair streaked with silver. Sapphire studied his features. He offered hands to the flames and swayed. Hundreds of bells on his pants jingled, as he stomped his feet.

"Earth my body. Water my blood."

His face was too round for her father's.

Sapphire grinned at his outfit, and the beat tugged at her. She rotated her hips to it, to the fire, and the night sky overhead. No past, no future, just oneness, until a poof of cold air slithered across her face. She looked up.

Engulfed in a black trench-coat, a kid in his late teens stared into the fire; yet his eyes, reflecting the dancing flames, saw horror instead of harmony. Sapphire had seen him at Dinner Circle a week ago, looking out of place. Beside her, Lauren danced, eyes closed. When Sapphire glanced back towards the fire, the kid was gone. She was not much older than him, but at the gathering, "kid" was more of a culture tag than an age. After all, at twenty-five, she was a kid to the older folks. And he was maybe twenty. Maybe younger.

Across the fire, the three bronze sisters continued their devotion. The drummers continued to pound their instruments, and their thunder roared into the ground and the sky above the treetops. The jingle-bell man continued hopping, and Sapphire wasn't even sure she had seen black-trench-coat kid.

FINDING THE YELLOW BRICK ROAD

Wednesday, June 20 to Monday, June 25, 1990
San Francisco and Santa Cruz, California

Environmental Groups Oppose Logging of Dead Trees

A coalition of radical environmental groups filed suit in Federal Court yesterday to stop the logging of dead trees. Their argument is that standing and fallen dead trees provide habitat for the Spotted Owl, which was recently placed on the federal list of "threatened" species. They argue that dead trees are the most important parts of a healthy forest, as they anchor soils and thus prevent erosion; shade new seedlings from intense sunlight; and provide habitat for scores of insect-eating bats, birds, and small mammals. *(San Francisco Daily News,* June 20, 1990)

SAPPHIRE

Sapphire got off the #22 bus at De Haro Street and started up the hill. A pack of motorcycles rumbled past and the stench of burning oil rose through the warm afternoon, reminding her of the dust in the crumbling cardboard box of old letters she had found in her mother's basement last week, words that told a family story she had never heard. Hand-scrawled letters and typewritten artifacts had revealed her mother's financial ties to her father, and left the taste of half-spoiled milk in her mouth.

Sapphire recited the words he supposedly had written to Mom on a piece of yellow construction paper fifteen years ago. "The universe has other plans for me. Tell Sapphire I love her very much. Divorce me if you wish."

Taking a deep breath, she ran two blocks up the hill, to the ten moss-stained granite steps leading to her mother's front yard. Rolling back her shoulders, she climbed the stairs, unlocked the front door, and entered, hoping that her mom was by herself, or maybe not there at all.

"Mom?"

The silent house ignored her. She peeked into the kitchen and then wandered into the backyard. Her mother's garden, a jumbled mix of sweet-scented roses and pungent white sage, contrived to hide the shady stench of the past.

She found Mom kneeling in front of a tangle of peach-hued roses, trowel in hand.

Mom glanced up, flashing green eyes as she smiled.

"Hi, sweetie."

"Are the guys at the game?" Sapphire needed to have this conversation without her stepdad and half-brother here. This discussion was about events that happened before her mother started her new family.

Mom set down the trowel and brushed the soil off her freckled hands.

"Where else would they be?" She stood up and headed toward the house. "Are you thirsty?"

Sapphire followed her mother into the kitchen, noticing the faint streaks of gray in the long pale hair cascading down Mom's trim back. The odor of garlic and yeast, woven into the wood furniture, reflected childhood memories that Sapphire had reworked with oil paint on canvas for years.

Mom half-skipped across the room towards the refrigerator, opened the door, and grabbed a gallon jug of apple juice. Sapphire took two glasses from the cupboard and set them on the counter. Mom poured. A dance of familiarity between mother and daughter, the tasks completed in harmony.

Sapphire sipped the thick juice while she rubbed the knot in her right shoulder. On the wall by the sink hung a childhood photo of her on the Santa Monica Pier Carousel—the frame covered in dried bunches of basil, sage, and mint. In the picture, a tie-dyed kid with tangled brown hair galloped across the ocean on a carved wooden horse. She remembered waving to her parents and the salty smell of deep blue sea and French fries, and the gold and green mane of the horse. When she had dismounted, she told Dad how fun it was to ride a wild horse across the sea, and he believed her. He always believed in her, then.

She looked at Mom across the kitchen counter, noticed the crow's feet around her eyes, the creases between her eyebrows. Sapphire faltered. A touch of vertigo swirled through her head, and she grabbed the counter to steady herself. She took a deep breath and knew she was finally ready to freefall through whatever happened next.

"I want to find Dad."

Mom smacked her glass down on the counter.

Startled, Sapphire backed up, her right eye twitching. "You don't have to see him."

Mom rubbed her head, tangling her short hair then smoothed it back down again. "It's not that simple."

"What's not simple?"

"John. You."

"He's my dad."

"I know that, sweetie. But," Mom shook her head. "Why now?"

"Why now?" *Because now I know you lied to me.* "You could have told me when I was a teenager, or anytime during the last fifteen years."

"I was just trying to protect you."

"From what?" Sapphire sputtered. "Finger-painting with Dad?"

Mom lowered herself into an oak chair by the window and pressed the glass against her cheek. "He was in love with being a father but not parenting."

"What's that supposed to mean?"

"It's complicated."

"I'm twenty-five!"

Sapphire knew that if she failed to find her father now, the rest of her life would consist of dead-end jobs and painting images of a world that no longer existed. She drew herself up, as tall as her five-foot-four-inch frame could muster, keeping her focus on the box of letters that unraveled Mom's story.

"I have a right to know why my own father abandoned me." She paused. "Or were you going to lie to me forever?"

Mom pulled out the chair next to her. "Sit down, Sapphire."

"Just tell me." Sapphire paced between the table and the counter. "I need to know what happened and where he is now."

Mom leaned into the table, elbows and hands pressed into the dark worn oak, and she buried her head in the crook of her left arm.

"I don't know," she mumbled.

Sapphire wanted to rip the scab off her mother's wounds and let the blood spill on the floor to clean out her own invisible lesions.

"I know the money you give me every month isn't from Grandma Johnson. It's from Dad."

Her mother shook her head. "That's not true."

"Don't lie to me!" Sapphire yelled. "Not anymore."

Her mother stared at the floor.

"That box of my old college papers I took from the garage last week. Some of your old letters were in there as well."

Sapphire gazed out the window at the downtown skyline, the sharp lines of skyscrapers helping her stand tall. She would not back down now. When she glanced back at the table, the woman was pale.

"It's Dad's residuals I get every quarter. Why would you hide that from me?"

"It was child support."

Sapphire shook her head. "I was ten years old when he left. I'm not a child anymore."

"I know. John must have put you as the payee. It's your money not mine."

"Why did you tell me it was from Grandma?"

Her mother stared at the wall.

Sapphire turned away and walked towards the kitchen counter. Holding onto the countertop, she touched the things she had known all her life: Aunt Lena's copper pot, the birch ladle Great-Grandmother Johnson brought on the boat from Sweden. She wondered if the ladle really came on the boat. With all the lies in this family, it probably came from an antique store in Santa Monica.

Mom said, "Even John's former agent doesn't know where he is." She paused. "The money comes from the Screen Actors Guild, not from your dad."

Sapphire paced in front of the window. Staring at the things in the kitchen, she tried to process her mother's words.

"I was only nineteen when you were born. John was twenty-three. Everything changed so fast."

Sapphire collapsed into a chair. "I know. You dropped out of college and Los Angeles was overwhelming. You've told me that stuff a million times. But you never tell me why he left us. Why he left me. You never tell me the truth."

Her mother took her hand. "Sweetie, I love you so much. All I've ever tried to do is what's best for you."

"You pretend like he never even existed." Sapphire yanked her hand away. "Why don't we ever talk about him? Why aren't there any pictures of the three of us together in this house?"

"What about Brandon?"

"He's your husband. Not my real dad."

Mom stood up and shuffled toward the window, clutching her glass of juice. The apricot glow of the sinking sun enveloped her.

Sapphire crossed her arms across her chest and waited.

"The times were different back then. And, your dad… Well, he and I had different ways of dealing with it."

The hum of the refrigerator reminded Sapphire of staying up late with Dad, drinking hot chocolate in a silent house when everyone else had gone out for the evening.

"I was tired of everyone else. I hardly saw him. He spent his days with Ananda or Spirit or Mary, and I spent mine wondering how much longer he was going to come home at night."

"Dad was great to me."

Her mother turned around, her downcast eyes glistening with moisture.

"He was sleeping with them, Sapphire. Sleeping with all those young girls, who were like I was when John and I first met. Girls who worshipped him. I could only take it for so long."

Sapphire shook her head and her eye twitched. "You loved him."

"I couldn't handle having him around. Or them. It was the best thing. For both of us."

Then, Sapphire saw it on her mother's face—the love still there, the longing.

"You're just afraid." She held her breath, afraid to release the words, but now that she knew the truth, she needed to say them aloud. "You're afraid that you still love Dad."

Her mother shook her head. "You're getting it all twisted. I got full custody to protect you."

"You did it to protect yourself. I was a child; what did any of that matter to me?"

Mom's hands shook. Drops of juice hit the floor. She tried to set the glass down on the windowsill, but it tipped over, making bright beige splashes against the dark oak floor.

Sapphire stood up.

"What about the note?" She could have handled the truth back then, but fifteen years of her mother's lies betrayed everything. "You told me he couldn't handle fatherhood. You made me think it was all my fault. Did he really write it?"

Mom shook her head. "I love you," she whispered. "I would do anything for you."

"You preserved me." Sapphire turned away from the woman. "Like strawberry jam."

She ripped the carousel picture from the wall and flung it against the cabinets on the other side of the kitchen. The glass shattered, and bits of dried herbs floated back toward her. She watched her mother bend down to pick up the broken shards.

It was too late for any of that now.

Sapphire retched in the gutter to the thumping beat of lowriders cruising at dusk on Mission, the cookies long gone, and nothing coming out but the truth. The contractions in her stomach kept coming; she stumbled around the corner and up the stairs to her studio, where she curled up on her futon and wailed, choking on her tears. Mom's confession had been a blow to her heart that even reading the letters a few days ago had not created.

Dad was not the villain Mom had imagined. He loved his daughter. Sapphire's so-called mother had kept them apart, her mother who only cared about her own feelings. Sapphire blew her nose into her t-shirt, her eyelids swollen from the tears. She grabbed a beer out of the fridge and watched the full moon rise over the old Wonder Bread factory, while the light flooded her studio.

She mixed Grumbacher Thalo Green with Green Light and a touch of Payne Gray. On her palette, she took a scoop of the mixture and added in some Titan Yellow for the foreground. The moon she left off, but she imagined it about a foot above the top right-hand corner of the canvas. She painted the reflection of the light against a pine forest, long dark shadows hiding creatures in the woods, and the tips of the trees bright green in the luminous light. Then, she mixed Cobalt Blue with Sepia and dabbed it on the spots between the trees, creating a woman's robe. She squeezed drops of Cadmium Red Light, Cadmium Yellow Medium, Yellow Ochre, and Burnt Sienna onto a piece of cardboard and mixed it with a small palette knife. Using the knife, she sliced a half circle into the trees and filled the spot with paint. On the face, she dabbed Titanium White fangs that glistened in the moonlight. One hand of the woman reached out in front of the trees with long fingernails that dug into the bark, the hand larger in proportion than the rest of the body.

Halfway through the night, Sapphire's period came the way that it usually did under the full moon when she painted murky images and the reflection of what might be true. In spite of all the pain and confusion she felt, hope began to take shape in yellow and gold stars on the canvas. If her mother couldn't or wouldn't help her, she would do it on her own. Find Dad. Find the life she was meant to live. When she finished, she drifted to sleep in the worn velvet armchair under the last traces of moonlight.

In the morning, the light on her answering machine flashed. She pressed *Play*, and when she heard the sound of her mother's voice, she pressed *Delete*. Five messages, all from her mom. Sapphire deleted them all. She had been listening to her mother's version of reality for fifteen years now. She was done.

She dressed, went out, and wandered the neighborhood while her mother's words echoed in her head: *protect, sleep, love.* Sapphire sat for a long time at Sixteenth and Mission watching the parade of people swarming around the Bart Station. Short and tall, dark- and fair-skinned, everyone had a secret. The red-haired reverend stood on an overturned five-gallon bucket preaching about the apocalypse.

"Sinners think they know the truth; nevertheless, when Judgment Day comes, all will be revealed. Those who walk with Jesus have nothing to fear."

Every afternoon, the reverend preached about hell, damnation, and traveling with Jesus. Some days, Sapphire thought he was a wingnut, some days a man with purpose. She had seen that man a hundred times, but now that her own judgment day had come and gone, nothing in her life had changed. She remained in purgatory, and he still lectured the passing crowds on the coming apocalypse.

Sapphire ached for Dad, longed to hear his voice, to feel his presence. She remembered how it felt to sit on his shoulders, taller than anyone else in the crowd. The coconut smell of his head, his silky brown hair against her cheek. His hard shoulders, a foundation to her life that falsely promised he would always be there to hold her up.

For believers, Judgment Day would separate the faithful from the sinners, but she was tired of eternal limbo. Hell would be better than not knowing, not understanding why he never contacted her or came to see her on her birthday like Latisha's dad.

The Reverend babbled on, "The Bible is the only word of God, the Great and Glorious Creator of the World. Ye, who seek knowledge, pray to God the Almighty. The Bible is the word, the source of all knowledge. Immerse yourself in the Bible. Learn the truth lest you be left behind on Judgment Day."

Mom only knew half the story; Sapphire knew even less. The only way to learn the truth was to find Dad. The path ahead of her was murky, but anywhere was better than here.

☮ ♥ ☮ ♥ ☮ ♥ ☮ ♥ ☮ ♥

On Saturday, Sapphire took the bus to Santa Cruz to see Uncle Paul, Dad's younger brother. After describing the old letters and her blowout with her mother, she told him she wanted to find Dad, that she was tired of her father being a memory. She needed him to find her place in the world. She needed to know why he allowed himself to be separated from her.

Uncle Paul withdrew to his study and came back a few minutes later carrying a photo that he handed to her.

"John and I by the Peace Pole, at the World Peace and Love Gathering in 1980." He stroked his jaw and stared out the window. "He loved those gatherings."

"How long has it been since you've heard from him?"

Uncle Paul shrugged. "He disappeared about a year after we took this picture."

She stared at the photo. Uncle Paul, a lanky young man with curly locks exploding from his head. Dad with flowing brown hair, a long beard, and a drum slung over his shoulder—the wise man come down from the mountain.

"I've always wanted to go again," Uncle Paul said. He disappeared into the dining room for a minute and then returned with a crumpled flyer in his hand. "Found this at the food co-op last week."

Plumas National Forest. World Peace and Love Gathering, June 21 to July 10. All peaceful people welcomed. The pen-and-ink drawing showed a forest with a rainbow overhead.

"He probably still goes," Uncle Paul said. "He really was happy there."

Uncle Paul remained the only person in Sapphire's life who acknowledged Dad's existence, but he only talked about the past, about his childhood and hers. She wandered around the living room, looking at photos of her cousins playing on the monkey bars and a shot of a Thanksgiving dinner from her high school days, when she wore heavy eyeliner and everyone gathered for the holiday, everyone except Dad.

With her back to Uncle Paul, she said, "Do you know why he left me?"

All she heard was the sound of Paul's breath, slow and heavy.

He put one hand on her shoulder. She turned to look up at him.

"Sapphire, I was sixteen when your parents broke up. By the time I was old enough to understand, he was gone, and you had a new life."

"You knew?"

"Knew what?"

"That Mom kicked him out."

Uncle Paul nodded. "I figured it out much later."

"Why didn't you tell me?"

Perched on the arm of the couch, he took off his glasses then put them back on, slowly hooking them over his ears. "It was your mom's decision. I know you don't understand, but she thought what she was doing was right. I had to respect that. Once you're a parent, you'll understand."

No way. That made no sense. Sapphire didn't understand how they could all lie to her for so many years. She choked down a scream. Their conspiracy of silence seemed to condemn her as the problem. And Uncle Paul functioned more as her big brother than an uncle; she'd expected he'd take her side, not theirs. She picked up a purple-framed photo

25

of her parents on the beach. Their wedding photo: her mother in a long gown and pregnant. Dad with short hair and a tuxedo jacket over swim trunks. Uncle Paul, at six-years-old, the ring bearer.

Paul sighed. "They always seemed so much in love." Rubbing his short beard, he said, "He loved her. In his own way, he loved her very much."

"What about me?"

"You were everything to him when you were born."

None of this made any sense. If Dad loved her, why did he leave? If Uncle Paul and Mom loved her, why had they betrayed her? She no longer knew what love meant. Uncle Paul was Dad's brother after all. He should have stood up for Dad. For her. For them. "Why didn't you tell me?"

Uncle Paul hung his head.

She set the picture down and walked over to the window. She stared at the golden retriever in the neighbor's backyard chewing on a bone, trying to get to the marrow.

"John would tell me these crazy stories of movie stars and poolside parties with girls in bikinis. I knew Hollywood was only seventy miles from Riverside, but it seemed like another planet."

When Sapphire looked at Uncle Paul, he seemed lost in a dream, with the same expression her dad would have when he played guitar.

"As a kid, I wanted to be just like him when I grew up."

"I did, too," she whispered, trying not to cry.

Uncle Paul took her into his arms. She pressed her face against his nubby blue sweater and cried, tears for all that had been lost. They stood that way until her tears turned to sniffles and she pulled away, wiping her eyes.

"He changed after you were born. He really started getting into meditation and Buddhism. He wanted to make sure the world you would inherit was special."

She pulled away from Uncle Paul, sat on the couch, and wiped her nose on the sleeve of her sweatshirt. "I just want to be with him," she said. "I love him so much."

He sat on the chair across from her. "Me too."

For a moment, her uncle stared at her. "I used to lie to my parents as a teenager," he said. "Tell them I was spending the weekend with Bobby or José. Then, John would come get me. Spending the weekend in Hollywood with my big brother. Wow. All my friends were jealous. And you always wanted me to do some crazy art project with you, when all I wanted was to be John's little brother."

She remembered how religious his parents had been and all the arguments between her parents and grandparents. "Grandmother Larson never believed you could be a good person and not be a Presbyterian."

"John was so focused on astrology by then, she said he was going straight to hell."

They both laughed.

"I still have that photo from when you came with us to see Neil Diamond at the Greek. Remember? We danced on the grass and Dad painted our faces."

He nodded.

"I never liked going to your house, though," Sapphire said. "We always had to be quiet and ended up sitting in the backyard while your parents argued about something."

Uncle Paul laughed. "The neighbors would peer out their windows and, once you left, they would come over and tell my parents to get rid of the heathens. Then, Mom and the old lady from next door would pray for your souls to be saved."

"Dad hated going to Riverside. He always said the only reason we went was to save you from growing up to be a Bible-thumper."

Uncle Paul sighed. "John has a knack for making you believe anything is possible. Sometimes though, his dreams get the best of him."

⊛ ♥ ⊛ ♥ ⊛ ♥ ⊛ ♥ ⊛ ♥

After the long bus ride from Santa Cruz back to the city, Sapphire walked home from the Transbay Terminal. The deserted warehouses South of Market suited her mood perfectly. Shabby buildings covered in ornate carvings loomed over her—no object could escape a past brilliance. Exhausted, she climbed the steps to her studio. On the door was an envelope with her name written on it in her mother's handwriting, and on the floor, a pie tin covered in foil. She unlocked the door, picked up the envelope, entered, and kicked the door shut behind her.

After she set water on the stove for tea, she opened the envelope.

> Dear Sapphire,
>
> I know I haven't been the mother you wanted me to be. You're right. Part of me still loves John and always will. He is an amazing man and is willing to take more risks than I can handle. If there's anything I can do to help you find him, I will help. But please, please call me. I need to know you're okay.
>
> Love,
> Mom
>
> P.S. I'm sorry.

Sapphire tore the note in half and tossed it in the recycle bag. After pouring herself a cup of chamomile tea, she wandered around her small studio. All the paintings hanging on the wall were of her childhood-self reaching out to him, but he was never there. She had been naïve. Believing that your dad would return at twelve and make your life wonderful was one thing, but doing it at twenty-five put her in the same league with the delusional Bart Station preacher.

Tuesday morning, Sapphire opened the pine crate she had taken from her mom's basement and pulled out his old wool sweater. She picked at a dark brown thread from the hole on the right elbow, unraveling the stitches. When she hugged the sweater, she remembered Dad's patchouli and tobacco scent and his arms around her even in their absence.

Setting the sweater aside, she reached into the crate and pulled out a stack of drawings bundled in a purple paisley sarong, which she unwrapped, placing her art on the wicker chair. Kneeling on the floor, she examined the first drawing: a pen and ink wash of Dad with no beard. Next, a pastel portrait on watercolor paper of Dad bent over his guitar with his hair covering his face—the second-place winner in her tenth-grade art fair. Her fingers stroked the pebbled surface she had created from paper fragments and leaves.

She grabbed a medium-sized sketchbook and a charcoal stick. Her hand knew the shape of his eyebrows the way it knew her own, and he came to life on the rough surface. His hair had been golden brown then. She had no idea what color his hair was now, but her hand drew a ponytail with gray-streaked hair and then attempted to draw her stepdad's salt-and-pepper look. While she worked, she felt Dad's presence in the room. He stared back at her from the paper and seemed wiser than he did in any of the older pieces that reflected her longing for what existed once upon a time. She set the drawing on the bookshelf under the window, placing it next to the flyer for the World Peace and Love Gathering, and then she dug her backpack and tent out of the closet.

On Wednesday, Sapphire left for the gathering. Hitchhiking from the Interstate 80 on-ramp, headed toward the Sierras, her backpack felt heavy on her shoulders and her heart pounded. Uncle Paul's flyer tucked in her back pocket. She had the photo of him and Dad safe in her pack. For the first time in a long while, her life felt full of possibilities. She could start a new relationship with her father, free from her mother's meddling.

ON THE FRONT LINES

Wednesday, June 20 to Sunday, June 24, 1990:
Samoa and Ukiah, California
Redwood Summer Clashes Continue

Radicals Rally in Samoa

Later-day hippies and backwoods-loving
rednecks have joined forces for what is being
called Redwood Summer. This is not your
grandmother's environmental movement. Earth
First! espouses in-your-face attempts to protect
the last remaining old-growth redwood trees and
the ecosystems surrounding them on the North
Coast of California. While bulldozer sabotages
and tree-sits often take place in the neighboring
hillsides, tomorrow's Redwood Summer kick-off
rally features folk music by *Back to the Way Before
Band*, t-shirt sales, and speeches by prominent
activists. However, Redwood Summer's founders
will be noticeably absent, following a bomb
explosion in their car in Oakland, California, while
they were promoting Redwood Summer on college
campuses. (*Ukiah Standard*, June 19, 1990)

LAUREN

Lauren danced with River on the hard-packed sand, while
the funky folk band played on a homemade stage, overlooking
the ocean, built with mismatched wood. The sky was gray, but
a few patches of blue shone through to the east. Overhead,
the sun fought to break through the fog, even though it was
already past noon. The wind blew in off the ocean. Lauren

31

shivered in the thin windbreaker she was wearing over her blue skirt, but her tie-died leggings kept the goosebumps to a minimum. She had dressed lightly with no jewelry in order to be able to move freely when the time came, dreadlocks tied back so they would stay out of the way.

On stage, the band plucked and twanged a slow and mellow haze that floated across the crowd, with the wail of the harmonica weaving in and out. The guitar player wandered around on stage, but he too seemed to be waiting. Lauren took on the persona of a blissed-out hippy at a Grateful Dead show, swaying and whirling, in a fake trance, arms flailing to the invisible lightshow that her fingers and arms were pretending to catch.

River's stiff arms and legs failed to follow the melody or the beat, and Lauren laughed to herself. His wooden dance, an echo of the lumber he used to cut at his Uncle's sawmill in Louisiana. Every so often he would glance at her and grin, totally clueless about his awful dancing. He tried so hard to be a hippy in his handwoven multi-colored Guatemalan pants and the green tie-died t-shirt with holes in it. His black dreadlocks had just started to set after months of twisting them, and even his beard had started to dread a bit. He was looking the part. However, he came from a logging family in western Louisiana, and Lauren fretted that he would return to his family and marry a local church-going woman who wanted five kids.

As she twirled around slowly, she peeked to the other side of the highway to see what was happening. A row of maybe fifteen police officers stood casually in front of the lumber company offices. The band ended the current song with a *clang! crash! bang!* of the drums and then started up the simple chords of Dylan's "Tangled Up in Blue."

Lauren's stomach twitched and rippled, and excitement sparked in her heart. Her mind repeated the mantra, "Great red woods," as she swayed to the melancholy song. River slowed his dancing, moving side-to-side, just swinging his hands aimlessly. He mouthed, "Great red woods."

Lauren glanced across the highway at the police and the low-slung building, weathered by the constant wind off the ocean. Corpses of ancient redwoods surrounded the building, victims of the current genocide on old growth and the life forms these once majestic trees had supported. The music swelled, the thunderous drums consuming all, and then *bam,* the instruments grew silent.

The vocalist sang, "I got a gig in the GREAT RED WOODS!"

River grabbed Lauren's hand and half-dragged her along after him, with the roar of the ocean overshadowing their voices, and their feet slapping on the asphalt highway. A tall man with a white shirt bumped into her, and River's hand slipped from her grasp. Lauren fell sideways and someone grabbed her hand, which was enough to steady her. She kept running. River disappeared into the crowd. Then, the pace slowed, with the crowd packed in tight, and Lauren wedged herself into the throng. After a brief pause, a small opening formed and she wiggled through it. Indomitable. Her body tingled. She felt strong enough to leap over the damn lumber company and land in the bay beyond. She inhaled the pungent blood of the redwoods, which mingled with the salty spray from the breaking waves until she could taste it.

The sweet smell of coconut oil on the dreadlocks in front of Lauren and the scent of her own sunscreen mingled into a Caribbean holiday. She wasn't sure where she was going. The crowd had become one ponderous pre-historic animal moving together, and all she could see were the heads and shirts in front of her. Someone stepped on her heel, and her shoe disappeared. Then, she felt the unevenness of one shoe hitting the ground and her bare foot hitting a rock. Sharp pain shot up her leg. She hopped on the shoed foot for a step or two, until the push of the people behind her forced her to keep moving.

The pressure from behind pushed her forward into the people ahead of her. Then, the crowd was at the entrance to the mill, spreading sidewise, and police had disappeared. Someone handed Lauren a sign, and she held the wooden handle and bounced the sign up and down while singing along with hundreds of others.

"Redwoods and spotted owls, humans and salmon; together we stand, divided we fall."

She looped her arms through the arms on either side of her, gripping the sign steadily now that space materialized around her. Meanwhile, a huge line formed across the front of the transfer station, where these majestic trees would be shipped overseas to some country that had already decimated its own forests.

She could see the highway now, with a dozen or more people dancing on the asphalt, the same hippy hand-waving dance. The stench of diesel smothered the salty smell of seawater. Then, a logging truck littered with the murdered bodies of giant redwoods swooshed and hissed to a halt on the highway. The truck was two or three times wider than she was tall.

People swarmed onto the truck, monkey-people going to their trees, climbing up the sides. The police circled around the truck, batons up, helmets on. Lauren dropped her sign, pulled away from the people on either side, and bolted for the back of the truck. She slipped between the police as they tried to form their barrier.

She stretched her arm towards a raven-haired young woman, perched on a log with her left arm through the logging chain. The raven-haired woman leaned down to grab her hand. They gripped each other, forearm to palm, and Lauren leveraged the help to pull herself up off the ground. With her barefoot toes, she grabbed onto a metal lip on the truck bed and pushed herself up.

Someone grabbed under her arm and hauled her up, until she could stand with her right hand grasping the binding chains. Her shoed foot pressed against the tree's thick bark, which crumbled under her foot. The acidic blood of dead trees clogged up her nose. Her heart drummed a *thump whomp* in her head. In the bright blue ocean, marshmallow waves broke along the peninsula. The band looked small, and only a few people remained in front of the stage.

Below her, the police struggled to grab the people scrambling up the truck. A couple of officers grabbed a red-headed, dreadlocked guy by the legs. They dragged him off the truck and let him plunge to the road, where he bounced when he landed. They flipped him over and handcuffed him.

Lauren crawled up one more log until she sat on the top of the heap, surrounded by the activists she had been working with for the last month. Pumped, she high-fived the woman closest to her.

"Bam."

"Outrageous."

"We aced it."

The music came across the highway in the manner of gusts of wind coming off the ocean, and the whitewater salt-spray coupled with the redwood smell reminded Lauren of the morning she and River had spent entangled in a tent at Gold Bluffs Beach, naked and sweaty. Outside their tent, Roosevelt Elk snuffled through the bushes, their gentle footsteps tiptoeing around like voyeurs trying to avoid detection. One beautiful moment gone wrong.

Sara pointed to the side. "Here they come!"

Lauren turned around on the log. A wall of police advanced on the truck. Their numbers had tripled since the action started—thirty minutes, an hour ago? She had no idea. Voices started to chant, "Earth First! Profits Last!"

Immediately, after the police reached the truck, Lauren crab-walked sideways on the top of the trees, towards the back of the truck. People were climbing down and running back towards the band. She stood on top of a dead tree, both fists in the air, shouting, "Save the ancient redwoods."

Two police officers reached the top of the trees at the front of the truck and started advancing. A few people scrambled down the side of the truck, away from the police. Below Lauren, people on the ground were yelling at her to come down.

"You've made your statement."

"Don't get hurt."

"They will knock you off."

She glanced down. Mandy waved at her and yelled, "Don't risk it."

Feeling strong as Hercules fighting the demons of his day, Lauren wanted to stay on the trees, fight the corporate machine that tried to destroy the planet, the redwoods, the very air she breathed. She teetered just a bit and her legs trembled. She rubbed her belly.

Grabbing ahold of the binding chain, she half-slid, half-scrambled down. When she was a few feet off the ground,

Mandy and a brother caught her and lowered her to the ground. Holding hands, Lauren and Mandy darted across the highway to the stage and dissolved into the remaining dancers. Legs shaking, Lauren tried to dance, tried to will herself to appear relaxed.

She searched the crowd for River and spotted him lying on the cab of the truck. Two officers had his feet, pinning him down, while the officer on the cab of the truck held his arm. The officers slid him over the truck's edge like a huge sack of soil. She held her breath, her heart drumming against her chest. River flopped onto the officers below him. All three crumpled to the ground.

River lay on top of an officer, unmoving. Lauren's stomach clenched and she darted towards him, the asphalt hot under her one bare foot.

River burst out laughing and rolled off the officers, who sprang to their feet and grabbed him under his arms, yanking him upright. The officers dragged River's limp body towards the police van. Lauren clenched her fists and felt her face flush. She took two steps into the highway and then stopped. The police also had Sara and Ed, plus others she knew vaguely. Everyone seemed calm and focused, one by one, climbing into the police van. She clenched and unclenched her fists, frozen on the edge of the highway.

"He'll be fine."

She turned to see tall, scrawny Dave approaching her.

"I know," she muttered.

"He won't be alone." Dave smiled. "Think of it as a slumber party with no party favors."

Deflated, Lauren's muscles grew weak and she felt so incredibly exhausted. She wanted to lie down until every shameful muscle in her body touched the earth. She was a complete failure. Lauren turned back toward the police van.

"It should have been me."

"You'll get your chance next time." Dave patted her on the shoulder. "And speaking of next time, Sunday at the Center. I hope you'll be there. You have great ideas."

Lauren nodded. "See you Sunday."

Lauren looked out the bay windows of the Center onto the courthouse across the street, while Dave reviewed what had happened in Samoa a few days earlier. Around her, people were sitting on cushions, rugs, and the window seat. Next to her, River perched on an upturned five-gallon bucket taking diligent notes.

"I'm mad about the charges being dropped. Like we all got arrested for nothing."

A woman with tattoos covering her arms responded, "Redwood Summer is not one single action. It's the combination of all the actions that matter. Besides, the photos of the arrests make great news. Even the *Los Angeles Times* covered Samoa."

Lauren spoke up. "If the actions are going to build on each other, then how do charges being dropped create a step up to the next action?" She glanced around, and people were nodding their heads. She stood up. "I don't think it's enough to shut down operations for an afternoon. How can we shut things down for good?"

A multitude of voice shouted out. "Right on." "That's the spirit." "It's about the trees, man." "And the owls, don't forget the owls."

The tattooed woman asked, "What are you proposing?"

"A mass tree-sit. We get two hundred people to go up and stay up all summer," Lauren said.

The red-headed dready guy said, "Hey, I was one of the guys who went to jail, and I am happy to be out. It's not so glamorous as y'all is making it out to be."

Lauren sighed. The fight to save the redwoods had given her a purpose, shown her a life of cooperation, sharing, and environmental stewardship; she could not have imagined this life growing up in suburban Denver. The mainstream world was behind her: the world of golf club memberships and society events, where all that mattered was how you looked and what kind of car you drove. In her new life, growing food and protecting wild places mattered more than your clothes. She had embraced the movement, volunteering to work in order to have the other activists accept her as more than an outsider dilettante. She had just started feeling included, but the baby was slowly pushing her out again.

A gray-beard said, "It's not about the most extreme action; it's about what will save the trees. I think if we do actions where we can meet the loggers and their families, we might get more support."

Dave nodded. "Great idea." He turned towards Lauren. "I'm not opposed to your idea, but tree-sits do not get people on our side."

Lauren met his gaze.

He continued. "Look around this room. These twenty-five people need more people to care. We can't save the trees on our own."

In the redwoods, Lauren felt the hushed voices of people long gone whispering to her in the filtered light of trees— three hundred feet high or taller and wide as a semi-truck.

The big trees were saplings before the American Revolution. In the redwoods, she felt humbled by trees, by the unseen hand of nature creating majesty. A cathedral more sacred than any medieval church in Europe, the universe had created this special place for the planet to pray. It was a miracle, which men—corporations really—wanted to destroy for money. Popularity wasn't the point. The trees mattered. Standing up for the trees made her matter.

A middle-aged woman said, "I would like to focus on the plan for Fort Bragg next month." She spoke about logistics, getting the word out, safety monitors, music, and First Aid crew.

River whispered in her ear, "Even if we did a huge tree-sit, you couldn't be up there."

Lauren rolled her eyes. "What? I'm not free to make my own decisions anymore?"

River stood up and motioned towards the door. Lauren kept trying to listen to what the others were discussing.

"Lauren, we need to talk." River's whisper echoed throughout the room.

Lauren touched her inflamed cheeks and forced a smile. She whispered, "Can't this wait?"

The middle-aged woman stopped talking.

Dave said, "Can you guys be quiet or take it outside?"

Cheeks burning, Lauren stood and picked her way through the people sitting on the floor towards the door. The door let out a loud creak when she opened it, and she felt the faces of everyone turn towards her. River let the door slam behind them.

Lauren turned to face him. "What's your problem? We were in the middle of a planning meeting. A meeting that Dave said he wanted me at."

River replied, "You know exactly what the issue is. You're having a baby." He stroked her head and his voice softened. "Our beautiful baby."

Behind River, a cockroach crawled up the wall, its antennae wiggling, as if bating Lauren to scream. She squeezed shut her eyes, covering her face with her hands, as if what was upsetting her was the insect.

She knew other women in the movement who had kids and made the marches and rallies, but what if she became the type of mother whose love only rained down when her child was winning the spelling bee, or playing Cinderella in the school play, like the perfect princess in the fairytale her mother had woven around her life as a child. What if she became her mother? Lauren wouldn't return to that world where appearances mattered more than feelings. In her new life, she was drowning in quicksand, slowly being sucked down to an unknown world, where she would cease to exist before she had even had a chance to find her own path in the world. Dropping her hands, she gasped for breath.

"Lauren, you're so concerned about the trees; well, what about this baby? Doesn't this baby deserve your love and care?"

Lauren choked on her breath and broke out in a sweat. For seconds, she stared at her boyfriend's feet. "River. Listen to my words carefully. I'm not sure I want to have this baby." She glanced through the windows of the Center, where the meeting was still in progress.

River put his arms on her shoulders and stood face-to-face with her. His beard tickled her chin, and she turned her head away. He reminded her that they had discussed this in April when he first found out she was pregnant, and they agreed to have the baby, that she would move into his tepee near the Mattole River during the summer. "We had a plan."

"April was a lifetime ago." Lauren's stomach churned, like a blender trying to break up chunks of carrots, the vibration working its way up her throat. She swallowed multiple times. "Now, we're in the middle of Redwood Summer and I want to be part of the action, not sit on the sidelines and watch what will go down in the history books. Do you even realize how huge this is going to get? I want to be in the middle of everything, so when I'm old and look back on my life, I will know I helped to create extraordinary changes."

River sighed. He clasped her hand and pulled it to his lips. "You are beautiful. I love you and I love our baby. Everything will work out."

Lauren yanked her hand back. "Don't manipulate me."

River glanced back to the meeting. "We're just going through a lot of changes now, and Redwood Summer is blowing my mind. Hell, I used to be a logger."

"I don't think this is the right time, the right decision to keep this baby."

River's eyes narrowed, forming deep grooves between his eyebrows. Lips pressed together, he crossed his arms over his chest. "What are you saying, Lauren?"

"You keep talking me into doing things I don't want to do."

"Like what?" he asked. "Having this baby?"

"Exactly. Tamara told me about a clinic in San Francisco that will take me up to twenty weeks, which only gives me a week or two if this is what I want to do."

River turned and put his hands up against the wall and hung his head down. The muscles in his arms quivered, and his back heaved with his heavy exhalation.

Lauren held her breath and her hands quivered; she waited for an explosion and for him to make a scene in front of all the other activists—in front of the people who had faith in their power to save the trees. The people she had not told about the baby, but who probably knew, because this was a small community and everyone knew everyone's business. "River," she pleaded. "I'm only twenty-one and still in college. I think I love you, but this is too fast; it's too soon."

He turned around and walked towards her. "You know if we were in Louisiana, you would want to get married. You would be happy to have a man with some money in his pocket and a couple of acres of his own."

Lauren wanted to scream at him that they weren't in some backwater southern town. This was California. Women have rights in California. She had rights. This was her life too. She was still figuring out her own dreams. The only thing she knew was that Redwood Summer was her chance to become someone that did things that mattered, and she was gripping onto it with all her strength before she faded into oblivion. "I am trying to figure everything out and your pressuring me is not helping."

River stood silently in front of her, arms at his sides.

"What do you want from me?"

River smiled and told her Redwood Summer was her baby too, and he wasn't going to take that away from her. She could be a speaker, travel to college campuses, and teach nonviolent direct action, speak to the press.

"Well, that's not always safe either," she said. "Look at what happened to Judi."

His face crumpled. "True words."

They stood there staring at each other. She wanted to go back to the meeting, pretend the baby didn't exist, and reclaim the exhilaration that had coursed through her veins last summer, during the showdown between the loggers in Osprey Grove. She didn't want to be some knick-knack on a shelf gathering dust.

River brought up the World Peace and Healing Gathering taking place in the Sierras, and he stroked her hair. "We could go for a week, like we planned this winter. Take some downtime. Get into a better headspace, so we can come back here stronger."

"Only if I don't go to San Francisco," she said.

TAKING THE ROAD LESS TRAVELED

Tuesday, June 26 to Wednesday, June 27, 1990
San Francisco to McGriver's Gap,
Plumas National Forest, California
(Day One and Two of Sapphire's Gathering)

The sun, the sister of the moon, from the south,
Her right hand cast over heaven's rim;
No knowledge she had where her home should be,
The moon knew not what might was his,
The stars knew not where their stations were.
—"Voluspo," *Poetic Edda* 4:5

SAPPHIRE

Two days after leaving San Francisco and seven rides later,
an old rancher picked up Sapphire on County Road 223 and
offered her a ride to the gathering. By the time the truck left
the blacktop for Forest Service Road 257, the sun had set and
the sky was orange-gold flames.

"Now what?" he asked.

"The flyer says to go 13.3 miles from the turnoff, and
then left just past the big boulder," Sapphire said.

"The odometer reads 257,321 now."

"Okay." She did the math in her head. "That's about
344."

"334." He shifted into gear and drove.

The truck clattered over the washboard road at a furious
pace and she gripped the door handle. The headlights lit up
pine tree sentries where the road curved, and she held her

45

breath, waiting for a deer to jump out in front of them. When she peeked at the instrument panel, the speedometer wavered around twenty.

The old rancher asked, "Are you sure we're going the right way?"

The muscles in Sapphire's shoulders knotted up and she gripped the flyer, hoping it would provide some guidance, but she couldn't read the directions in the dark. This was the road she was on now for better or worse. "This is Forest Service Road 257, isn't it?"

"Yup."

"There," she pointed. "There's the boulder."

He downshifted, grinding the gears, and swung into the dark parking lot, his headlights illuminating rows of haphazardly parked cars. She held on while he pulled up next to an idling van.

A man with a flashlight yelled, "Ten-minute parking."

Shouts of "Welcome Home" rang out, and a dog barked.

Two haggard men stumbled past the truck; Sapphire opened the door, and a blast of cold air hit her face. Her left eye began to twitch. She wondered why she had come on this crazy journey to these remote mountains with no friends and no sense of what to do next.

The old rancher asked, "Are you sure this is where you want to be?"

She glanced at his weathered face, before anxiously surveyed the dark parking lot, confused about what to do next, but she had come too far to abandon her mission. "I'm going to be fine."

He leaned towards the passenger side. "You could always spend the night in my bunk house, and I could bring you back in the morning."

The offer was tempting, but she wanted the worried face to be from her own father, not some old guy who picked her up hitchhiking. "Thank you so much. But really, I'm going to be fine."

She piled her gear on the side of the road and waved while he drove off, leaving her alone again. Around her, people unpacked cars and stacked camping gear on the ground. The smell of wood smoke and tobacco drifted from a nearby fire.

A group of young men tromped past and called out, "Main Gate's that away."

Whatever Main Gate was… Everyone seemed to be heading in that direction. Sapphire hoisted her backpack and followed the others, hoping to find the bathrooms because she really needed to pee. A few minutes later, she paused next to three scruffy guys lounging against a pile of backpacks, sharing a peppery-smelling joint.

"Where's the bathrooms?"

They exploded in fits of choking laughter. After hacking and spitting, the youngest one snickered, "If you gotta take a dump, there's a trench by Main Gate. Otherwise there's plenty of trees."

Her face flushed, she scurried away and wandered around trying to pick the proper place before she squatted behind a giant cedar. Then, she lugged her gear around the beat-up vans and rusty school buses, trying to figure out where to check in, until a bunch of drunks laughed at her.

A burly man with a booming voice, named Grizzly Bear Garth, intervened. "What camp you looking for?"

When she didn't know, he said he was heading into the gathering and he would help her find a spot because, "It's next to impossible to find anything in the dark without already knowing where everything's at."

He tramped off down a sliver of a trail into the darkness and Sapphire scurried after him, trying to keep up. Her pack hung heavy on her back, and she stumbled through the dark. She didn't care where she pitched her tent; she desperately wanted to fall asleep in her trusty sleeping bag.

Camping, she knew. At seventeen, she had traversed the Santa Rosa Mountains with her mother, hoping to spot bighorn sheep clinging to the cliffs. At twenty, she had done Mt. Whitney with a group from college. Two years ago, she spent two weeks in the Desolation Wilderness, hiking with her once-upon-a-time boyfriend.

"What do you do with yourself?" Garth asked, tugging on his long brown beard.

"What do you mean?"

"Job, school? What do you do?"

"I paint. Work stupid jobs to pay rent."

"Do you paint houses, or you one of those so-called artistic types?"

"Artistic, I guess. Oil and watercolors mostly, but I'm starting to get into mixed media. Using plant materials to add texture."

They walked in silence through the darkness, before Garth started a story about a friend named Mike, a pickup truck, and a black bear on the roof, but his story was interrupted by a young woman who danced up to Sapphire and hugged her.

"Welcome home, beautiful sister."

Sapphire embraced her, inhaling the familiar musk of patchouli embedded in the fuzzy fleece pressing against her check, amazed that a stranger would be so happy to see her.

Grizzly Bear Garth muttered, "This Welcome Home crap just keeps a person from getting where they're going."

The hugs kept coming: a woman on crutches, a teenage boy, a grandfather. Sapphire hadn't felt this much love since her childhood in the little house in Hollywood, before her father disappeared.

Garth grumbled, "Don't let this love crap fool you. There's always a creep or two in the crowd."

She savored the crisp scent of fir trees. The trail zigzagged downhill. She slowed down, afraid of losing her balance. Garth plunged ahead of her and was waiting when she hit the bottom. They turned right.

A shirtless brother with gorgeous pecs called out, "Welcome home sister." He stopped to hug her.

She pressed her check against his cold chest and inhaled the smell of fresh mountain night on his skin.

He said, "Jah love," and kept going.

Garth continued his lecture. "You need to camp at a kitchen. If anyone fucks with you, yell 'Peace Patrol' as loud as you can."

"I'm looking for someone."

"Good. I don't like it when young sisters are alone. Where's your friend camped?"

"I don't know yet."

Two men interrupted Grizzly Bear Garth to tell him they were going up to Main Gate for the rest of the night.

Sapphire and Garth resumed walking, and he said, "In the morning, go to INFO and post something on the board. Around six or so, go to Dinner Circle. Listen for the conch shell."

Sapphire repeated his words in her head. *Notice at INFO. Dinner Circle at six.* "Where's INFO?"

"We're on the Main Trail here. Ten more minutes down the drag, you'll see it."

They turned onto a smaller footpath and started climbing. He deposited her next to a kitchen called Lost Souls. "There's a lot of young sisters camped here. Put your tent close in."

Exhausted, Sapphire pitched her tent by the light of the waning moon and collapsed on top of her sleeping bag, the rumble of drums in the distance her lullaby.

Sapphire woke to a baby's hearty wail. Outside her tent, people chatted. She heard the country western twang of an acoustic guitar playing some Grateful Dead tune she couldn't name. The clang of metal against metal rang out and then mellowed into a *whap, whap.* Underneath the morning sounds of camping was the distant thunder of African style drumming. Then, it registered: she was searching for her father at the World Peace and Love Gathering, the perfect place for a reunion of hearts.

Her stomach trembled with anticipation for the reunion that would be, if not today, then soon. Proud for having jumped off the cliff, she was going on faith now, hoping that her ability to take action would make her welcome in his arms. She had drawn their encounter for years. Dad pulling up in a limo to pick her up after school, or his face beaming with his hand outstretched—the watercolor on plain white paper all puckered. She unzipped her sleeping bag. None of this was going to happen outside of her artwork until she got out of her tent and found him.

After she dressed, she checked the side pocket of her mauve daypack to reassure herself that Dad's old publicity shot was tucked away, in case she needed it to identify him. She grabbed some of the flyers she had made in San Francisco. In ballpoint pen, she added, "Find me at Dinner Circle."

Sapphire climbed out of her tent. Two naked men smoked hand-rolled tobacco in front of a couple of tents draped with damp sleeping bags. She gasped and turned the other way, where there were more tents with people sitting outside in various stages of waking. Amazing. To the west, the sky—cerulean blue, sharp, and brilliant in the warm dry air—silhouetted a silver craggy mountain. Joy swept across her heart, joy for the sky and the mountain and the beautiful morning. She wanted to grab her oils and paint the tents, and the mountain, and even the two naked men in the morning light. Such crisp light this morning; at home, the fog diffused the colors. Mountains reached towards the sky in every direction. Rows of hills covered in evergreens marched off into the distance, reminding her of the mountains in Metro-Goldwyn-Mayer's *The Wizard of Oz,* which didn't seem real either.

One of the naked guys called out, "Good morning sister."

Hoping to appear casual, Sapphire gazed at the mountain floating behind his head. "Beautiful day." Then before he could say anything else, she called out, "See you later," and headed toward the pungent pine smoke and the rich aroma of wood-fire coffee.

She ended up at the ramshackle wood-and-tarp structure called the Lost Souls' Kitchen, which she vaguely recognized from last night. In the daylight, it looked lively and huge. Laughing people sliced potatoes, and the smell of cinnamon wafted from the stove.

A girl with red pigtails called out, "Oatmeal in twenty minutes."

Sapphire stopped for a moment. She walked up to the counter. "How much does it cost?"

The girl giggled. "Oh, sister. Nothing costs money at the gathering."

"The food is free?"

"Everything here is free and made with tons of love."

"But who pays for it all?"

"We brought a lot of food in with us. The Piggy Bank kicks in some supplies." She shrugged her shoulders. "People bring us food to cook."

It was so random, yet when Sapphire looked into the kitchen, potatoes were being chopped. Onions were piled on the counter next to a huge bag of carrots. It was amazing. "The Piggy Bank?"

"Cash donations to the gathering. Green energy," the girl smiled. "Or people just smoke us out, and that helps too."

A man in the back of the kitchen called out, "Hey, Pippi! You going to Supply Council, or what?"

"In a minute," Pippi shouted back. Then, smiling, she asked, "What's your name, sister?"

"Sapphire."

"I'll catch you later, then."

Sapphire nodded at Pippi, who disappeared into the trees behind the kitchen. A couple of dready guys stoked the fire. Curious, Sapphire stared at the giant pots of oatmeal bubbling on the grill, finding herself drawn to helping out, but that was going to have to wait until she found Dad.

She followed the trail down the hill, listening to the thunder of drums coming from somewhere below her and boldly echoing off the rocky hillsides. When she reached a much larger trail, a huddle of grungy teenagers sprawled in the sepia dirt around a tiny orange kitten.

A purple-haired girl called out, "Will trade rocks for candy."

Sapphire lifted her empty hands. The trails seemed to run off in multiple directions, but one was much larger. This must be the Main Trail, she thought.

The kids called out, "Go this way."

When Sapphire glanced back at them, they were pointing in all directions and laughing. She felt bewildered. She wasn't sure if she was at the World Peace & Love Gathering, or if she had dropped into a rabbit hole with Alice.

"Which way's Main Gate," she asked.

They pointed to her left. She chuckled at the thought. She was now part of the Lost Souls' Camp, despite having not met anyone in the kitchen except Pippi and the people camped around her tent. Once Sapphire found Dad, she would move to his camp, but until then, she liked the location and the vibes.

She took the trail to the right, past the huddles of kids her own age on the side of the trail getting high under purple streamers hanging from trees. She passed a dripped-mud castle, an image that conjured up her family trips to Santa Monica in the summer, and she felt the far-away vibration of drums sliding through the trees and into her step.

Ahead of her, two women lugged a sack of flour between them, weaving through the crowd. Two men strutted toward her, schlepping a huge drum decorated in red, green, and gold ribbons.

"Excuse me," Sapphire said. "What kind of drum is that?"

One of the men responded, "A sogo. From Ghana."

"Is it heavy?"

"Check it out."

He handed Sapphire the drum. She wrapped both arms around its carved wood barrel. Surprisingly light for as big as it was, but more than she wanted to lug for miles. "Thanks." She returned the drum and continued on her search for INFO.

Last night, Grizzly Bear Garth had told her INFO was on the Main Trail, about ten minutes past the turnoff where she had camped.

The trail was crowded with people, old and young. Children and dogs raced happily back and forth across the trail and through the woods. Women her own age wore flowing scarves and beads. It was the chaos of the kindergarten playground, and the glee was infectious. She felt a smile come across her face, and at that moment, a man spoke to her.

"Hey, little sister. How are you today?"

Sapphire looked up at him, at his eyes the copper-tinged hazel of her own. At the graying hair and the long beard. She stopped. Dad? "Okay," she said haltingly. "How are you?" The simple question could be a daily exchange spoken in passing or a deep soul-searching conversation with someone you had not spoken to in fifteen years.

"I'm having a great day," he said.

Her stomach flip-flopped and she studied his body language, looking for a familiar gesture.

"Do you live in California?" he asked.

She nodded. "And you?"

"Michigan. This is my first visit to the Sierras. It's different than I thought. Much browner."

Holding her breath, she slapped the side of her head. Dad wouldn't be the first man she met, or the second, and it couldn't be this ordinary. Finally, she remembered to breathe, and responded, "I've never been to Michigan."

"Well, you should come some time," he said. "Hey, I'm off to a drum-making workshop, so I'll catch you later." He strolled off in the opposite direction and disappeared in the trees.

Sapphire's stomach cramped, and she collapsed onto a tree stump, horrified by her outright flakiness. She had no idea how to start the crucial first conversation. "See ya later," she called out to his disappearing back. She wanted Dad to be impressed by his daughter, to think she was creative and his heir in myriad ways. No crying. No blame. No guilt trip.

Resuming her journey to INFO, Sapphire ambled down the trail, playing with ways to impress him. *I'm painting professionally, Dad. I have a degree in Fine Arts from UC San Diego. Where are you living these days?* A few minutes later, she glanced up and spotted a rainbow-striped flag with the word "INFO" hanging from a blue tarp, which had been stretched between two giant Douglas Firs.

She wormed past a circle of scruffy young men sitting on the ground smoking cigarettes. A woman with a baby in a snuggly talked to her friend. Three young men loaded down with packs, shovels, and picks chatted with an old woman. Friends greeted each other with hugs and squeals of delight. Sapphire hesitated.

This looked a lot more ad hoc than what she expected. Glancing at the people around her, she realized most of the people were white. Very weird. Living in The Mission, she wasn't used to be surrounding by white people. In San Francisco, her neighborhood was a diverse mix of colors and accents. Hoping that hippies still welcomed people of color, she dawdled among the sheets of plywood mounted on stakes in the ground, ignored by the people around her.

A hand-painted map, which depicted pine trees, flowing blue water, and miniature white tepees, covered an entire sheet of plywood. Camp names were labeled with words and icons: Kid Korral—a wood fence with children climbing on it; Mad Hatter's Tea Party—a guy in a huge striped hat sipping tea; and Main Meadow—on the other side of the trail beyond the stand of white pines with little yellow flowers.

The more Sapphire studied the map, the more paralyzed she became by the enormousness of the gathering. Only slightly aware of others trying to view the map, which covered two square miles, she struggled to take deep breaths and felt her chest rising and falling. She struggled to focus on the map. Days. Maybe weeks. She gulped air. He had to be here; she needed him. *What if they could not find each other?*

She had to make decisions about which camp screamed essence of Dad: The Karma Wheel Kamp, or the Whole-in-One Miniature Golf Course? She needed to get a better grasp on how things functioned, to figure out her strategy. She shuffled away from the map and made it to the message board, hoping for ideas on how to find someone.

Kalmia needs a ride to Miami on July 7th. Find me at Trade Circle.

Sunrise Yoga every day in Main Meadow.

Bob from Austin. Sally and Piper are camped at Blue Moon Bakery.

Lost dog—Misty, a black lab with purple collar. If found, bring to Kid Korral and ask for Sara.

Rap 101: Please protect this Beautiful Land. Harm no living thing. Harmonize—Blend in. Use only down, dead wood.

*Preserve the Meadows… Camp in the Woods. We are caretakers
of this land. Everyone sharing makes a strong human tribe!*

Rap 101 contained echoes of Mom's "leave no trace"
ethic, the same scheme Mom had applied to Dad and would
probably apply to her too.

Sorrow dripped from Sapphire's heart at her now-broken
relationship with Mom. She tried to recall any situations that
would prove her mother's accusations about Dad's infidelity,
but she could only really remember the last couple of years
when she was in school, the years when people packed the
house. She tried to imagine having sex with anyone in a
small two-bedroom house crawling with people. Mary Moss
had been around a lot back then, but the way Sapphire
remembered it Mary Moss had spent more time with her than
Dad.

Sapphire pulled a few "Dad Wanted" posters out of her
pack and posted them on the message board. She tacked one
in the upper left-hand corner, the second one just below it to
the right, and the other two continuing at a downward angle.
She stepped back and the diagonal line of cadmium yellow
paper created movement and drew attention to her message.
The collage of notices on the board contained not only her
dreams, but also other wishes large and small.

For a few moments, she eavesdropped on a conversation
between two sisters her own age. They were talking about
going on Dead Tour, not that Sapphire had ever been on
tour, but no one grows up in San Francisco without seeing
the Dead locally and being a minor expert on Dead lore. She
stepped toward them. "Do you ever make New Year's Eve in
Oakland?"

One woman said, "I was there two years ago."

"Me too," Sapphire said. "Didn't they play for like four hours?"

The woman said, "Oh, I didn't have tickets."

The other woman said, "I have to show you my stencils."

They disappeared down the trail, leaving Sapphire standing there bummed out at not being included. A young man asked her for a cigarette, and when she didn't have one, he moved on quickly. She felt stupid standing there not talking to anyone, so she moved off to the side and sat down.

For a while, she observed the comings and goings of the crowd, and then noticed the big tarped structure to the right. With counters of lashed branches that resembled a ship's prow, it seemed capable of parting the trees on the hillside as the entire structure sailed off through the mountains. The counter was piled with pamphlets. Sapphire decided to get up and check it out. She flipped through a newsletter from Greenpeace, before picking up a tiny pamphlet called The Gathering Guide. She opened it and read:

The Gathering is a completely free event. All supplies are donated or paid for with money donated to the "Piggy Bank." There is no admission fee. All food and medical care is free.

Springs are marked off with strings or ribbons. No campsite or latrine should be located above or within 300 feet of these springs. Never pour liquid wastes into or near a water source or on the ground nearby.

The Gathering works because people take responsibility for doing what needs to be done.

We are all teachers. We are all students. Share the knowledge with those who need it. Be a student of all things.

Our Gatherings are open to all peaceful people. There is no membership, no administration. There are no leaders. Walk the path of peaceful respect.

The voice of Sapphire's father resonated through the
words in the pamphlets. She remembered him sitting cross-
legged on the wooden bench—a crowd gathered on the front
porch, and the guitar in his lap. "Be a student of all things,"
he had said. The women in long skirts held hands, and men
wearing beads smoked. The strangers standing on the lawn
listened from below, and Sapphire sat on the porch railing
with Mommy. When Dad spoke, they nodded their heads
in agreement. He didn't feel like Sapphire's very own daddy,
but like someone important in the world, even if she hadn't
always understood what he meant. But at night, when he
tucked her into bed and she read him a bedtime story, then he
was her daddy and she didn't have to share him with anyone.

As Sapphire browsed the guide, she peeked at the circle
of people behind the counter sharing a joint. A pregnant
woman, in her early twenties, perched on an upturned
bucket, thick clumps of caramel blonde dreadlocks hanging
down her back. A couple of old hippie men with long gray
beards lounged in beach chairs, and a few older women about
her mother's age sat cross-legged on the ground. The pregnant
woman laughed and passed a bag of nuts to the woman on
her right.

Sapphire pretended to read while she eavesdropped, not
wanting anyone to realize how totally alone she felt. One
of the old men recounted the passing of the Piggy Bank at
last night's Dinner Circle, and the others agreed there wasn't
enough green energy to buy food for all the people arriving as
well as batteries for the radios. A blonde woman pointed out
that Kid Korral needed fruit, and First Aid wanted electrolyte
beverages.

A woman with shriveled-apple skin leaned across the counter and called to the pregnant woman, who then stood up and came toward them.

The pregnant woman's red and orange sarong hung low, exposing the tanned swell of her tummy. "Hey, Manzanita."

Sapphire tried not to stare at the pregnant woman, her tanned belly bulging, her back and shoulders straight and strong over her long legs.

"Lauren, we need some volunteers over at First Aid to build a hand wash station."

"Everyone here seems pretty busy already," the pregnant woman answered.

Sapphire couldn't imagine being pregnant and being out here in the woods all serene and beautiful.

"Main Supply has the fixings. First Aid needs someone with the know-how and the labor," the older woman said.

"I can provide the brains, but I can't do anything heavy," Lauren said.

Sapphire edged towards the railing, while keeping her gaze towards the ground to hide her curiosity. Mom had been miserable before Sapphire's little brother was born. Tired all the time and covered in baggy clothes, making Sapphire do all the housework. Lauren's supple body radiated vibrancy, the two women's pregnancies as distinct as the seashore and the mountains.

Manzanita said, "I've got to run. We're doing a grandmother sweat and I don't want to be late."

Sapphire had never heard of a grandmother sweat before and tried to imagine a bunch of gray-haired, saggy-breasted women in a sweat lodge.

"I need two volunteers to help me build a hand wash station," Lauren announced, before sauntering among the people congregated around the message boards. "I need two volunteers," she called out, while rearranging the posted notices, revealing thick muscles in her arms and shoulders. Her long silver earrings caught the sun and flashed sunbeam signals against the blue tarp.

Sapphire couldn't take her eyes off Lauren. She was beautiful and seemed so in her element. They were about the same age, but Sapphire was a disorganized wreck compared to that woman. Even on her best days, Sapphire felt too frumpy to be friends with someone that beautiful. She stared, rebraiding her hair, and then, buckling her daypack around her waist, she approached Lauren.

Sapphire inhaled the rich scent of cocoa butter and sunshine on the woman's skin. "I'm willing to help, but I have no idea how to build a hand wash station."

Lauren laughed. "First rule of Gathering: no experience necessary."

Sapphire nodded. "That's what the guide said."

"Is this your first gathering?"

"It is."

Notices cluttered the board, and someone had partially covered one of her flyers with a cardboard sign offering a ride to Reno. Sapphire rearranged the cardboard so it didn't cover any part of her dad's face. Then, she moved some other notices so everything could be seen. "How many gatherings have you been to?"

"This is my third," Lauren said, and then she called out once more for help, without success. "I guess the two of us will be able to handle this." She grabbed her bag and told the others she was off. "First, we need to swing by Supply and pick up the raw materials we need."

"Cool." Sapphire trailed after Lauren down the path, feeling a bit less hesitant now that she had a traveling companion.

MAKING FRIENDS ON THE JOURNEY

Wednesday, June 27, 1990:
McGriver's Gap, Plumas National Forest, California
(Day Two of Sapphire's Gathering)

Gathering Kitchens Receive Passing Grade from Health Department

The Plumas County Health Department reports that out of the ten kitchens inspected, they were pleased to see most sanitation standards were being met. Their only concern was that not all the kitchens had a sanitary handwashing station, with one of the kitchens relying on hand sanitizer and bleach water alone. The Health Department recommends soap and water handwash followed by the use of a hand sanitizer or appropriate bleach water solution. All kitchens used the three-bucket dish wash system, consisting of hot soapy water, clear rinse water, and a light bleach water solution. Most of the kitchens also included either a compost bucket or compost pit near the dishwash station. (*Quincy Herald*, June 26, 1990)

SAPPHIRE

Sapphire followed Lauren along the big trail toward Main Supply, trying to hide her nervousness. People called out to Lauren, stopped to hug her and ask about the baby. Every time they did, Lauren repeated, "Do you know Sapphire?" as though Sapphire was a long-time gatherer who everyone should know by now. The number of introductions made Sapphire's head spin.

By the time Rainbow and Peace Noodles hugged her and welcomed her home, Sapphire got with the program and hugged Wednesday without hesitation.

"Love you, sister."

Wednesday asked, "Who are you, sweet sister?"

Lauren said, "My friend's name is Sapphire."

Sapphire beamed and her shoulders relaxed a bit. *She was Lauren's friend.*

The trail cut through a stand of lodgepole pines. They passed a sign pointing to the Blue Moon Bakery, and Sapphire caught a whiff of charred flour and yeasty wood smoke. "Are they baking bread up there?" she asked.

"Rolls, sticky buns, pizza, cookies," Lauren replied.

"No way!" Sapphire blurted. "How?"

"I'll show you later."

As they continued down the trail, they passed a camp with all manner of hammocks and swings. Further up the trail, a torn tarp floated over a pile of sleeping people sharing one sleeping bag, the kind she took to slumber parties at thirteen, when she could still remember the way her Dad smelled.

Lauren asked, "So, where are you from?"

"Hollywood. But I've lived in San Francisco since I was eleven."

"Talk about moving from one extreme to the other."

The empty trail wound through the woods full of birds chirping. "We left Hollywood when my mother remarried," Sapphire explained.

"Do you know any movie stars?"

She told Lauren that her dad was a working actor—not a star—but when she was four, she met Robert Redford at the premier of *Butch Cassidy and the Sundance Kid.* "Dad played one of the horsemen chasing Redford and Paul Newman through the desert." She paused. "Have you seen it?"

Lauren shook her head.

Sapphire didn't share the memory of watching Dad up on the screen, bigger than life, galloping across the desert on a horse trying to catch Butch and the Kid, and at the same time huddled in the dark with her eating popcorn.

"What other movies was your dad in?" Lauren asked.

"A couple of those Annette Funicello beach movies and some B-rated horrors."

"That's so awesome. No one in my family does anything creative. My dad pushes paper," Lauren said.

At least Lauren knew where to find her dad when she needed him, Sapphire thought silently, willing to let someone else be impressed by her life, even though she viewed it as a muddy watercolor.

Ahead of them, the woods opened up, revealing a small clearing where a dozen trucks were parked, along with two school buses with a tarp strung between them. An old bedsheet, painted with the word "Supply," hung from one of the buses. Calls of "Welcome Home" rang out, and Lauren hugged quite a few people before introducing Sapphire.

A short man with mutton-chop whiskers and the funk of beer on his clothes stood up and offered Lauren his upholstered dining room chair.

Lauren sank into the chair. "Thanks, Kyle."

Sapphire perched on a pile of tarps and listened to people talk about the afternoon's supply run, the price of watermelon, and the equity of buying sugar for the kitchens to use for late-night cookie baking instead of greens for dinner.

A voice boomed out, "Well, if it ain't my painter friend." Sapphire turned to see Grizzly Bear Garth approaching. "Do you know each other?" Lauren asked.

A scrawny man sitting on a folding chair stood up and handed the chair to Garth, who grabbed it and sat down next to Sapphire. "Well, hell," Garth said. "I've known Sapphire since yesterday. We're old friends."

She could smell Garth's leather jacket, the stale odor of cigarettes and the bitter pinesap on his hands. He smelled good and bad at the same time, much like the movie theaters of her childhood, filled with the same contradictory smells of tobacco and popcorn, or hugging her dad in the park when he smelled of patchouli and day-old sweat.

Lauren said, "Hey, Kyle. Manzanita sent me for some three-quarter-inch plastic tubing, twine, and bicycle inner tubes."

"I think we've got all of that."

Lauren followed Kyle behind the rusty school bus.

Garth leaned toward her. "Did you find your friend?"

"Not yet. I did put up some flyers at INFO."

"What's her name?"

"It's not a her. It's a him." Sapphire felt embarrassed and afraid of sharing her secret with Garth. Very few people knew she hadn't seen her dad in fifteen years. In high school, she made up trips to visit him and then hid out at home or said that he came over and they painted together in the garage. *Only for a few hours because he was so busy.* "My dad."

Garth leaned back in his chair and tugged on his beard. Before he had a chance to speak, the radio in his front shirt pocket went off.

She couldn't hear the words clearly.

He jumped up and started barking orders into the radio about not touching anything, before disappearing down the trail.

Stunned, Sapphire glanced around, but no one else moved. The older man puffed on his cigarette. A twenty-something guy drew on his jeans with a ballpoint pen. She wondered if anyone else had noticed Garth rushing off and thought it odd. After a few minutes, Lauren returned with her arms full of clear tubing and black rubber.

Lauren asked, "Can you carry this?"

Sapphire took the stuff from her. "Garth just got a call on the radio and ran off."

"Grizzly Bear Garth is one of the old time Peace Patrol crew. There must have been a fight or lost child or something like that."

Sapphire wrapped the rubber around the tubing to make an easy to carry bundle. She didn't understand why no one else seemed concerned. It seemed to her that if there was a serious problem, everyone should help.

"Thanks again, Kyle," Lauren said.

"No worries. You just take it easy. I don't want nothing to happen to that little guy."

"I don't know if I'm having a boy or a girl," Lauren said.

Kyle laughed.

Lauren turned to Sapphire. "Ready?"

They headed back toward INFO. At the stand of aspen trees, Lauren turned left and continued about fifty feet, passing through a pile of boulders. She called over her shoulder, "We're entering First Aid camp now."

At least a dozen tents were set back twenty feet from the perimeter. Lauren found the spot marked "Hand Wash

Station Here" and sent Sapphire off to find three branches, about five feet long and two inches in diameter.

Lauren called out, "And a couple of shorter pieces."

Sapphire had to move further into the trees behind the First Aid clearing, in order to find much in the way of sticks. After rummaging through branches too rotten to hold their own weight, sticks too short, and sticks too thin, she had an armful of solid sticks. She returned to find Lauren sitting on the ground, surrounded by three two-and-a-half-gallon water jugs with plastic tubes tangling from their spouts and their tops cut open.

"How's this?" Sapphire dropped her take on the ground.

Lauren asked for help standing up. Once on her feet, she pointed to the longer branches. "We'll make a tripod out of these using twine."

Sapphire grabbed the big sticks and leaned them against each other. "Like this?"

Lauren nodded and pulled off a length of twine. "You hold it, and I'll tie it up."

Sapphire grasped the stick and tried to think of something to say. "Where did you grow up?"

"Englewood. It's a suburb of Denver, but I've been going to school in Arcata for the last couple of years."

"Are you going to Humboldt State?"

Lauren nodded.

"Studying to be a Forest Ranger?"

Lauren shook her head and laughed. "No. I save trees. I'm majoring in resource protection."

They secured the tripod, and Sapphire lashed branches together. She held the shelf in the center, while Lauren wrapped rope around the large poles, looped the ends, and hitched it between the three poles.

Lauren pushed down on the platform to test its strength. "We'll put the jugs here. One with a mixture of soap and water. The other two will be rinse water."

Sapphire said, "We need to secure the ends of the poles, or the whole thing will blow over when the wind kicks up."

"The weight of the water holds it in place."

"Only as long as the jugs are full." Sapphire grabbed the shovel and dug three holes about six inches deep. She set the posts in the ground, filled the gaps with small rocks and dirt, and poured water on top, before tamping it down with her foot. "Backcountry cement."

"Nice." Lauren arranged the jugs, each one facing a different direction and tied them in place. "Now, all we need to do is add foot pedals."

"Foot what?"

"You make a pedal out of wood and attach it to the pipe with the inner tube. The inner tube is the poor person's bungee cord. Then, you tie a string from there to the pedal, so when you step on the pedal, it lowers the pipe and the water comes out."

"Gravity."

"Exactly," Lauren replied.

Sapphire grabbed her sketchpad, outlined the tripod, and blackened out the stripes of old inner tube. She drew the half-hitches and Lineman's loop that held the tension at either end. "If we wrap the rubber like this, it won't slip off when the plastic tubing contracts and expands."

Lauren peered at the sketch. "That way the leverage of the rope is working against the rubber."

"And keeping the tension reinforces the knot."

Lauren nodded. "What else is in here?"

"Just some sketches I've been working on."

"Can I see?"

Sapphire passed Lauren her sketchbook.

Lauren turned the pages. "Who's the man?"

"My dad."

"He looks like he has the secret of life wrapped up in his eyes." Lauren glanced at Sapphire. "Did you do this from memory?"

Sapphire nodded.

Lauren flipped the page. "What's this?"

"Sutro Baths. It's an old salt water pool on the cliffs in San Francisco—just ruins now."

"You're good."

"Not good enough to make a living at it," Sapphire said. "In the meantime, I'm sort of in advertising. Or at least I was until two weeks ago."

"And then?"

"Got fired, decided to change my life. Pretty cliché isn't it?"

"Not if you're following your heart."

Sapphire turned towards Lauren, who stared just past her at nothing, eyes unblinking, head tilted slightly. Sapphire shrugged her shoulders, but Lauren ignored her. Finally, Sapphire picked up a stick and threw it into the bushes before getting up to retrieve it.

Without looking at Lauren, she asked, "Who organized the gathering?"

Lauren laughed. "It just happens. People put out the word and everyone shows up and here we are."

Sapphire turned around and pondered this for a moment, not understanding how it all worked. She thought back on all the strategy meetings her mom and stepdad held for rallies and marches and how many meetings it took to make anything happen. She grabbed the old inner tube and twisted the rubber around the top of the poles. The chalky black powder rubbed off on her hands. "My dad's name is John Larson. He goes to gatherings all the time." Although she really wasn't sure.

"That's so rad."

"Do you know him?"

"He sure looks like old time family, but hardly anyone uses their real name here, so it's hard to say."

She wanted to play it cool. "If you see him? I'm looking for him."

"Of course."

The words vomited out of her mouth. "I haven't seen him since I was ten. He was there when I went to school and gone by the time I came home."

Lauren exhaled, "Wow."

"All these years my mom told me he left because he couldn't deal with me, and I believed her. I believed he didn't love me." Believed that there was something so wrong with her that her own father hated her.

"I'm sure that's not true."

Sapphire tried to stop her mouth but failed. "My mom lied. For fifteen years, she let me think it was my fault. But it wasn't, you see. It was her. She divorced him because she thought he was sleeping with our roommates. I don't know if he was or not, but she wouldn't let him see me because"—she sobbed—"my life"—hiccup—"is such a mess."

"You haven't seen your dad in fifteen years?"

Sapphire picked up the rubber strips and plastic tubing, letting them dangle from her hands. "No." She waited for Lauren to say or do something, but Lauren just stared at her.

Not knowing what to do next, Sapphire held her breath while the seconds awkwardly passed.

Lauren said, "When did you learn all this?"

"A week ago." Sapphire sniffed.

"I don't know what to say."

She was such an idiot. She should have kept her mouth shut; now, Lauren thought she was a fruitcake. "Me either." Poking a small hole through the opposite end, Sapphire slid the plastic tubing through the hole and tied off the rubber tire strip with a half-hitch.

"Are you sure you haven't done this before?" Lauren asked.

"Blurted my life story out to someone I just met?" Sapphire turned her gaze towards the plastic tubing in her hands and fussed with the knot.

"No." Lauren shook her head. "The hand wash station."

Sapphire cheeks burned and she poked at the dirt with her foot. Digging herself in deeper. Stop, stop, stop. Breathe. Wait. "My family makes things. No big deal."

"If you saw my family, you would realize how amazing you are. When I went off to college, I didn't know how to do anything. I ruined all my new clothes in the dryer, because I'd never done laundry before. We had people who helped around the house."

Sapphire gawked at Lauren. "Servants?"

"Just a maid and a gardener."

Sapphire pictured one of the fancy houses in Pacific Heights, all glass windows and people driving Mercedes past the gardeners working on the lawn. She pictured her Mom's house on Potrero Hill with the peeling paint. "We had activists or their lawyers sleeping in the living room, and usually a few musicians thrown in for good measure. We all cooked and cleaned up together."

Lauren flipped her dreads back and sauntered around the hand wash structure, her belly leading the way. "That's how I want my baby to grow up, around art and music and people who are real." Her pupils large and glimmering, she paused and rubbed her abdomen with one hand. Holding onto the tripod, she squatted down and picked up one of the short pieces of wood Sapphire had collected. After standing up, she tied the end of the rubber tube around it.

Sapphire stared at Lauren, so at ease in her actions. Sapphire wondered why she felt so awkward before turning away, glancing at the people moving around the large canvas tent on the other side of the campfire.

"We did a great job," Lauren said.

We, Sapphire thought. *We did it.* She asked where the outflow would discharge.

Lauren explained they would hang an old tarp underneath the tripod to funnel the runoff into a graywater hole fifteen feet away.

Sapphire pointed to a clump of green feathery bushes. "How about if I dig the hole over there. Thorn bushes can suck up a lot of water."

"Where'd you learn that?"

"Camping trips with my mom. She's really into plants." Sapphire grabbed the shovel and cleared away the thick layers of decomposing leaves and crumbling bark that covered the chocolate soil. She dug a small hole in the center, inhaling the rich sweetness of the mulch. Would she ever garden with Mom again? Once she had dug down a few feet, she filled the hole with the mulch she had just cleared.

"If it's full of duff, where will the water go?" Lauren asked.

"It leeches through. The leaves filter out the gunk."

"Impressive," Lauren said.

A bellow ricocheted through the trees.

"What's that?" Sapphire asked.

"Conch shell. It's the call for Dinner Circle."

Tiny ants on roller skates etched circles on the inside of her stomach. *Dinner Circle. Dad. This is it.* It was time to fulfill her destiny.

TRIPPING ON ROCKS AND FALLING INTO POTHOLES

Wednesday, June 27, 1990
McGriver's Gap, Plumas National Forest, California
(Day Two of Sapphire's Gathering)

Hot, Muggy Weather Expected for the 4th of July

...weather will remain sunny and clear for the next few days, with highs in the upper eighties in Quincy, and in the seventies above six thousand feet. Storm clouds expected to move in for the Independence Day holiday, and then rain is on the horizon for the middle of next week. (*Quincy Herald*, June 27, 1990)

SAPPHIRE

The conch shell bellowed again, and Sapphire and Lauren headed for Dinner Circle. The trail curved between white pines and granite boulders before it popped out into a large, bowl-shaped meadow. Along the northern perimeter, skinny white trunks of sentry aspens guarded a stream. Sapphire studied the colors in the sky, a shimmering blue like newly polished steel with snippets of gold. The sun leaned toward the west and slowly sank into a slate thundercloud over Rattlesnake Peak. Clusters of people rested on the ground, and others wandered the meadow, where the olive-green bunch grass had been trampled down in the center of the field. Tons of people pouring into this space—Sapphire had no idea where they all came from.

Lauren wandered through the waves of cobalt green and ochre plants at the edge of the meadow, and Sapphire trailed after her, not a hundred percent certain she had been invited along or if she was being a pest. The urge to excuse herself rose up in her throat, and the excuses started to swell in her mouth. Sapphire could pretend she needed to hook up with friends or connect up with someone at Lost Souls' Kitchen, despite knowing that if she left Lauren, she would be on her own again, at least until she found Dad. She paused and glanced around at the endless expanse of humanity drifting into the meadow.

Lauren said, "It'll be awhile before we eat, but I love visiting with my friends."

Sapphire pointed to a small huddle of people in the center of the field. "What's happening over there?"

"Announcements. Workshops, lost kids, prophecies."

"Prophecies?"

"The gathering is full of people who believe we are some kind of lost tribe that has come to save the earth."

Sapphire smiled. No doubt, her dad believed in the prophesy. In front of her, people hauled white five-gallon buckets, which she guessed were full of food. One of the bucket carriers set down his load to stretch his back. She stared at him. Blue eyes. Short gray hair. He could be her dad. Then, the bucket carrier picked up his load and headed toward the huddle. Too short. Dad towered above her at almost six feet tall. Oh well, she thought. It didn't mean he wasn't here. People were still arriving. She had to stay positive.

A shaggy border collie laden with nylon saddlebags trotted past three naked men chanting in a circle, their hair hidden under green and black tams, their long beards covering their chests. On her left, a sister in a ripped magenta

t-shirt and ragged jeans lugged her djembe and a gallon jug
of water toward the food and plopped down next to a man
reading aloud from the Bible. A juggler wearing a chartreuse
jester's hat tossed five hacky sacks into the air and struggled
to keep them aloft. The shiny bells on the points of his hat
jingled along with his exertions.

Sapphire smiled and half-closed her eyes, until she
imagined herself at a Griffith Park happening in the late
afternoon, letting the past and present blur together. Worn
out from a day of dancing, her parents had transformed into
blissed-out children. At dawn, the bleary-eyed grownups
sprawled on the front porch, watching the sunrise over the
Capitol Records building, and Sapphire climbed from one
lap to the next, feeding everyone strawberries like an angel
rewarding the true believers.

Here in the meadow, the keepers of the dream lay
scattered about, as if waiting for a call to action—Dad hidden
in a sea of graying hippies. Trying to paint this scene would
be impossible without a canvas the size of a warehouse. Even
if it had only been fifteen days instead of fifteen years since
Sapphire had seen her father, he would be hard to find in the
middle of thousands of people.

Lauren lowered herself to the ground, and Sapphire
collapsed in exhaustion, staring hopelessly into the crowd, not
sure where to begin. A willowy guy looped toward them, with
short black dreadlocks, naked from the waist up, and wearing
a turquoise sarong. He flopped down on the ground and
kissed Lauren.

Lauren introduced River. "Sapphire's an awesome artist."
She urged Sapphire to show River her sketchpad.

They flipped through her drawings, their bodies
intertwined until they created one body. A stroke on the arm,

a brush of hair, a kiss on the cheek. Sapphire's skin yearned for that touch. She inhaled their love and wished that someone was thrilled to see her at the end of the day. Her parents had loved each other in this way, but she had never witnessed this kind of intimacy between her mom and stepdad.

"Hey, sister, these drawings rock." River flipped through them while talking about their tepee on the Mattole River, where they would have the baby—just them, a midwife, and a couple of close friends.

Lauren leaned into River and he caressed her stomach. She said, "We're going to have a naming ceremony when she's three months old."

"What are you gonna call her until then?" Sapphire asked.

Lauren and River exchanged glances. River said, "Chipmunk. It's a family thing; we call babies Chipmunk until the naming."

A couple of River's friends joined them. "Redwood Summer" was all they talked about. The first direct action had taken place a week earlier, and River had been arrested for climbing on a logging truck.

River hugged Lauren. "As soon as the gathering's over," he said, "we'll be back on the North Coast for the Fort Bragg action."

Lauren puckered her lips, sighed, and dug around in her bag.

A couple weeks earlier at Rainbow Grocery, Sapphire had seen flyers for Redwood Summer, which had raised her curiosity, but she was afraid to join in the discussion and show her ignorance. The sounds of the crowd slid past her, happy voices shouting unintelligible words.

FALLING FROM THE MOON

A call for "Circle" rang out, and Lauren said, "This is my favorite part of the day." The crowd stood, and River pulled Lauren to her feet.

Lauren clasped Sapphire's left hand, and a teenage boy took hold of her right and tugged her in his direction. Lauren pulled Sapphire one way, the boy the other. They inched backwards and then shuffled to the left. The chain of humans formed a gigantic circle. The loop curved around a young man in a black trench coat, who stood frozen among the brightly colored sweaters and Mexican serapes.

Sapphire shivered in spite of the warm sun on her back. The circle tugged them north, and the black trench coat disappeared in the crowd. She calmed down when the circle formed, telling herself a black trench coat only signaled the bad guy in a second-rate horror film, such as when her Dad played a zombie dad in *Beach Babe Zombies*.

Lauren pointed toward a short gray-haired woman entering the circle, her peasant dress bright white, in spite of the dusty trails and patches of mud. "There's *La Abuela*."

The Grandmother. Incredulously, Sapphire pondered the idea of her own grandmother at the gathering, or in any part of her life for that matter. Grandmother Schmidt appeared at funerals and graduations wearing a dark suit and complained about the food, the music, or whatever Sapphire wore. And Grandma Larson despised her. Dad had been gone for a year the last time Sapphire had seen Grandma Larson, when the woman emerged from the trees at her birthday party, pointed her finger at Sapphire, and screamed, "It's your fault Redford got the lead in Butch Cassidy. You and your chickenpox left him too tired to audition properly."

When La Abuela reached the center of the circle, she raised her hands to the sky, then bent over and pressed her hands into the ground. Straightening, she spoke about the Aztlan ways, about the Sun God, about the Conquistadors who had killed her grandmother's grandmother's grandmother. She spoke about identifying patterns that had created unhappiness in the past and about consciously altering them in the present. She lifted a yellow flower in the air. "Watch your footsteps my children: *Mis amigos son pequeños.* Please don't crush them."

Sapphire lifted up her left foot to discover a mangled flower. Dropping Lauren's hand, she tried to stand the flower upright, but it kept crumpling. Her hand dangled at her side in remorse. Then, she felt Lauren's hand clasping her and lifting it up. The crowd was silent except for a baby crying in the distance. Sapphire closed her eyes, concentrating on the stillness. The peace sank into her bones, and the sound of her breath felt like fighter planes screeching overhead.

In the distance, a vibration swelled and rolled toward her, until she realized that people were Om-ing like in her yoga class. All around her, voices oscillated at different frequencies. Sapphire shut her eyes and allowed the surge to massage her chest, thighs, lips. The Om rolled in fuller waves and then ebbed until silence remained. She wanted to paint this experience on a large canvas. The Om would be apricot swirls coming out of the center, twirling its way across a steel blue sky. The mountain would loom over them, dark and foreboding in gray-cloaked mystery.

Cries of "Rainbow!" filled the air, and the crowd burst into a roar of joy.

"Praise Jah."

"Goddess has given her blessing."

Sapphire opened her eyes and spotted a faint rainbow draped across the top of the mountain. Thousands of people whooped and hollered, stretching their clasped hands toward the sky. Sapphire's body turned to jelly, and she floated above the meadow, while squeezing Lauren's hand and that of the man on her other side. She couldn't imagine a better reunion than hugging Dad in the meadow, surrounded by thousands of people.

A voice from the center of the meadow bellowed, "Four concentric circles!"

Chains started to form.

Someone called out, "If you want to get fed, we need concentric circles five feet apart."

The crowd jostled and reformed before people started to sit down. In awe of the manner in which the crowd broke one large circle and started to form many smaller circles, Sapphire followed Lauren's lead, trying not to be a complete dork.

After they had situated themselves, River and Lauren pulled out bowls, and Sapphire followed their lead.

A young man, carrying a white bucket, approached her. "Pinto beans with rice?"

"Yes, please."

He scooped out a solid clump of brown rice and beans, careful to not touch his ladle to her bowl, serving, as Lauren said, in the Gathering tradition of not sharing germs. With a slight shake of his hand, the clump broke loose and fell into Sapphire's bowl.

Sapphire shivered, amazed by the bellow of the conch shell beckoning the people to the community womb of their ancestors, perplexed by the circle's formation. The people milled about in peaceful chaos, responding to a cellular memory of gatherings embedded in human genes. "Thank you," she said. She wondered if the first gathering twenty years ago had been this way, or if the evolution had created the deceptive chaos of a fractal.

"Hot sauce? Spike? Tamari?" asked a woman wearing a kitchen apron with multiple pockets. "We've got Louisiana fire sauce and Thai peanut sauce." She paused for a moment. "The peanut sauce isn't vegan; it's got honey in it."

Sapphire laughed. "Fire sauce, please."

The sauce woman sprinkled some of the fire sauce in Sapphire's bowl.

"Thank you." Sapphire dug into her clump of beans and rice.

Opposite her, a gray-haired woman ate while five dogs drooled next to her.

"Salad?"

Sapphire held her bowl out and a small scoop of shredded cabbage and carrots landed on top of the beans. She savored each bite, enthralled by the food, the woman eating beans with chopsticks, the coral sky melting into raspberry sherbet overhead, the wind sinking down the ridge and tickling her face.

☮ ♥ ☮ ♥ ☮ ♥ ☮ ♥ ☮ ♥

The night before, Garth had made finding someone seem easy, but now, surrounded by a few thousand people, Sapphire felt overwhelmed. How could she find one middle-aged, longhaired white man she had not seen in fifteen years in a sea of middle-aged, longhaired white men sitting in concentric circles, munching on vegan stew and chewing whole wheat bread, while music and conversations flew at her from all directions? Paralyzed by the sheer magnitude of the gathering, she ate, chewing and swallowing to the *wap bap* of a pair of bongos—a ready diversion from finding Dad. There were thousands of men who weren't her father. And one who was.

After a while, people started breaking up the rows, grouping themselves in smaller circles and passing joints or leaving altogether. Sapphire put her bowl into her daypack and stood up, "Hey guys, I need to go look for someone."

"Your dad?" Lauren waved her closer.

Sapphire squatted down. "Before everyone's gone."

"Good luck. Don't stress too much. If he's here, you'll run into him eventually."

In spite of her uncertainty of how it would all work out, Sapphire nodded.

"Let's hook up tomorrow at INFO in the early afternoon?" Lauren asked.

Ecstatic and her stomach tingly with joy, Sapphire sprang to her feet. "Sounds like a plan."

She hunted the crowd, looking for men with gray or brown hair—tall men—trying to catch a glimpse of faces without appearing to stare. She stepped around three people sharing a Tupperware container full of food. Beyond them were two guys playing djembes with synthetic heads, the twang in sharp contrast to the deep-throated bongos behind her.

"Yo, sis." A guy with long black hair held out a joint. "Want some of this?"

Shaking her head, Sapphire said, "I'm looking for someone."

A man ahead of her appeared to be searching the crowd. His long hair was light brown. He was tall. Sapphire passed him, catching a quick glance at his face when she passed, but he turned out to be a woman with dark eyes and dimples.

A short man waved a peace flag. Sapphire tried to step around him, but he blocked her path.

"Don't you believe in peace, beautiful sister?"

"Of course."

"Then, give me a hug."

She lightly draped one arm over his shoulder for two seconds before escaping from his stinking body and resuming her search. Two crying children and one dogfight later, she glimpsed a man with grayish-brown hair, pale blue eyes, and a beard, who was cuddling a small girl in his lap. Stunned, Sapphire gawked at the girl with long blonde hair and slanted blue eyes, as his new daughter giggled. The new girl that Dad adored, the one who cuddled in his lap, listening to the echo of his acoustic guitar in the hallway.

Sapphire watched him scoop pasta out of his bowl with a wooden spoon, and the little girl opened her mouth. When the girl spit out the pasta, he laughed a big laugh, baring buckteeth. Sapphire's shoulders relaxed and she exhaled deeply. It wasn't Dad! Those weren't Dad's teeth. That girl was not her half-sister. The realization smacked her in the face. She had never even considered he might have a new family, a new daughter he could shower with affection and dreams, as he had once done to her. What if he didn't need her anymore, or even worse, what if he never did?

Sapphire picked her way through the now-ragged circle and dwindling groups of people, while the daisy sky glowed with the last traces of the sun, and her opportunity to find her dad that night grew dim. She wandered through the clusters of people lounging around the meadow, deep in conversation or song. Then, she spotted a pair of fringed buckskin chaps on a lanky middle-aged man heading toward her. The man carried a carved staff decorated with dangling dream catchers and beadwork, and he sauntered toward a huddle of guitarists, then sank down until he sat cross-legged on the ground. She followed him and parked herself near him. He had butterscotch hair streaked with gray, hazel eyes, and a long beard. She retrieved Dad's photo and held it up in the dying light. Their noses matched.

Grabbing her sketchbook, she roughed out the man's face, her arm following the angle of his jaw, reliving all those wretched nights when she had drawn him, a pagan Jesus dancing barefoot in the park, hoping to resurrect him with her pencil and erase the pit in her gut. Now, she drew him with his shoulders touching both edges of the paper and his arm stretched toward the corner of the newsprint, where she sketched the moon somewhat small and light, keeping the thick lines on Dad.

Sapphire added details: a beaded headband, a ring with three stones. Drawing the details kept her from jumping up and hugging him. She took a deep breath, tried to slow down. He wouldn't know the lies she had been fed. He probably thought she didn't want to see him.

A woman passed the man who could be her father a bowl of food, and Sapphire watched him eat rice and beans—such an ordinary thing to watch your father eat. Then, watching herself from outside her body, she stood up, stepped toward him, and offered him her drawing. He scrutinized it and then grinned at her, comfortable with his missing teeth. She shuddered. He looked old and worn-out and gazed at her without a hint of recognition.

She stammered, "This draw-drawing is of my da-dad when we lived in Hollywood."

"One of these days I'm going to see Hollywood for myself, maybe meet a movie star. Clint Eastwood. I'd love to meet him."

Frozen, she stared at the drawing he held out, until she realized that this man did not know her. He was a stranger and she was an idiot. She scuttled away, so shrunken within herself that her arms disappeared into the hollow of her stomach, suffocating under her embarrassment, which covered her face like a plastic bag.

Sapphire stumbled toward the ridge, tripped on a rock, and crumpled against the rough red bark of a downed pine. Inhaling the pungent sap, she choked on her sorrow and burned with shame. She couldn't even identify her own father. Her own father. She had forgotten the man who had taught her how to dream. She struggled to remember his flesh-and-bones body, but her portraits had replaced his living presence. From her pack, she removed his acting headshot and held it in her trembling hand, while she scrutinized the photo. His hair cropped short, head tilted to the side; he had just the hint of a smile around his eyes and mouth. Eyes with flecks of dancing copper. Dad posing for his audience.

Leaning against the log, she clutched a charcoal pencil in her right hand and with quick lines created Dad with short hair and crow's feet around his eyes. Crumpled up the drawing and tossed it on the ground. Then, she drew him balding on top with long hair on the sides and no beard. She flipped the page. Slowly this time, she drew him with short hair, a long beard, and a bald spot on the top of his head. Then, with no teeth and smiling. For fifteen years, she had been drawing echoes of him from childhood memories. Would she be doing the same for the next fifty?

"Are you okay?"

Lauren stood in front of her.

"It wasn't him."

"Who?"

"My dad," Sapphire said. "I was so sure it was him."

Lauren lowered herself onto a rock. "People change."

Sapphire picked up twigs from the ground and broke them into smaller pieces. "I can't even remember what he looks like."

Lauren laughed. "My dad has a huge belly that spills over his belt and is completely bald. But in his college photos, he was a skinny string bean and had a greased-up flattop."

Sapphire tossed another crumpled-up sketch on the ground and kicked it down the hill, before picking up a pinecone and throwing it at the tree.

Lauren said, "Things will all work out. You'll see."

Sapphire wiped her sleeve against her nose. "But what if it doesn't?"

Lauren rubbed her belly and remained silent.

DREAMS AND RE-MEMBERING

Wednesday, June 27 to Thursday, June 28, 1990
McGriver's Gap, Plumas National Forest, California
(Day Two and Three of Sapphire's Gathering)

"Seeking and learning are in fact nothing but
recollection."
—Socrates

SAPPHIRE

The stars sparkled overhead as Sapphire lumbered back to
her tent. After sunset, the temperature had dropped rapidly.
Lauren and River had invited her to go to storytelling at the
tepees after Dinner Circle. Not planning to be out after dark,
Sapphire had begged off to get warmer clothes. Truthfully, she
was humiliated by crying in front of someone she barely knew
and wanted the privacy of her tent to finish her meltdown.
She shivered as she wove her way through the people on the
trail, who blinded her with their flashlights. Finally, fed up,
she blurted, "Can you please shine your light on the trail,
instead of in my face? You're blinding me."

The current offenders turned their light towards the
ground, but the next group shone the light right into her
eyes, turning the trail black and creating floating white discs
in front of her face. Stumbling, she blinked and struggled to
regain her vision. She crashed into a tree branch and gripped
it, the rough bark scraping her hands. "Whoa."

She was an idiot. Finding Dad wasn't going to be as easy
as when she was six and had lost her dad at a Griffith Park

Love-In. Then, all she had done was stand on stage and said, "I'm Sapphire. I lost my daddy," to see him running out of the crowd towards her. At six, she had held it together and never burst into tears, even though she was scared. Sapphire sighed. Of course, at six, she had no clue what losing her dad meant nor the dangers that were facing her. Back then, everyone had stopped what they were doing to help her. Now, people nodded or shook their heads, but they didn't really care. She had met other people at the gathering whose dads had disappeared years ago, and they didn't seem to think it was that big a deal. At six, the fear had been acute. Now, she suffered chronic heartache.

Finally, arriving at her tent, Sapphire unzipped it, changed into her thermals, and slipped into her sleeping bag, with a shiver. She figured it probably wasn't much after ten yet. She was cold and exhausted and grateful for her warm bag. Lilting laughter and belly chortles danced through the air around her tent, as happy people laughed and talked about their day and their evening plans. Snuggled in her sleeping bag, she conked out quickly, exhausted from the last few days. Her body melted into bliss and dreams of happier days.

Perched on her daddy's shoulders, six-year old Sapphire pretends she is a giant. She waves to all the colorful people and they wave back at her. A lady with a unicorn on her shirt twirls in the grass. A guy with no shirt but lots of scribbles on his back kneels in the dirt playing with a rock. Across the meadow of heads and hats—from the black stage that's decorated with miniature people in purple, gold, magenta—music spreads through the crowd.

A clown walks by in long purple shoes and orange hair that sticks out in clumps. Sapphire leaps off Daddy and runs after the clown.

The clown stops and smiles. "I make magic bubbles." He pulls a huge metal bucket out of his pocket. His hand grows into a wand and he dips it in the bucket and blows, releasing giant bubbles into the air. The bubbles rise over Sapphire's head. She jumps, trying to grab them, but they float towards the sun. The most ginormous bubble pops, and a parrot flies towards them, landing on Mr. Clown's head. Two little boys with blonde hair clap.

Ananda Rose sleeps on a yellow blanket with their picnic basket. She jumps up, and her hips started to wiggle. Her hand dances in the air like a snake. Her silver bracelets jangle.

Dancing. Her and Daddy and Ananda Rose, with a skirt that billows as she moves. The grownups pass the cigarette back and forth between them. Dancing in a cloud. A man with a huge smile twirls by, trailing the scent of patchouli in his wake.

Red and orange circles float in the sky, beaming warmth on her face. The circles bob up and down. People float through the sky, dancing sunbeams, twirling to the music Sapphire can still remember. Not the melodies—she forgets those—but the mood, the joy in the air. The smiles on everyone's faces.

Then, the sunbeams are dancing with her and Ananda, singing the song, that one she tries to remember but that's always floating just out of reach. Songs of love and hope: the only two emotions anyone ever needs to grasp.

Sapphire yawned and pulled the sleeping bag up over her head. She tried to go back to sleep, back into the dream, back to the Love-In, when she was six and life was a kaleidoscope of dancing with the other kids and the clown making magic. That pure joy felt like she was floating through the sky in a soap bubble. She forced herself to think of the real moments, of the two blonde boys she danced with, surrounded by majestic oak trees. She remembered how it felt when Dad still loved her, and they danced in the park with joyful people, who were creating the world the way they wanted it to exist.

Sun shone through the trees and warmed her tent. She floated with a smile on her face, full of the bliss that had encompassed everyone in her father's presence. She never wanted to leave the joy of that day, of all those days with Dad. She closed her eyes, willing herself to fall asleep. The sensation of cold damp wind blew across her shoulders, which made no sense in her sleeping bag. She turned onto her side and drifted back to the world of her dreams.

Broken yellow daisies lie in the dirt.

A lavender sweater drags on the ground.

A young woman suckles her baby at her white breast. Sapphire uncovers her other breast and drinks the warm milk. At the same time she drinks, she is also watching herself dribbling milk on her brown-and-yellow-flowered dress.

Daddy and Ananda Rose wiggle their arms and bodies as they dance. Grownups block Sapphire's view of the stage.

A voice bellows, "Please go home everyone. Please go home."

Daddy yells, "This is our park. You can't make us leave!"

Ananda Rose lies on the ground with the yellow blanket pulled up over her head.

A golden woman hugs Sapphire and sprinkles gold glitter on her head. "We don't need music to dance; just listen to the sounds floating around you. Dance is our collective energy."

Sapphire runs through the crowd, gasping for breath, trying to find Daddy or Ananda Rose. She trips over a man sprawled on the ground. He laughs.

Mr. Clown jumps in front of her, with makeup dripping down his face. He bares his teeth. He waves his hand in the air, and it's covered with blue and red paint.

On stage, everyone stares at her. They have torn jeans and headbands, cigarettes hanging from lips. They laugh and joke. Daddy's gone like a bubble, leaving her all alone. Sapphire's body shakes with fear. Fingers point, reaching towards, wanting to grab her. One man pulls her towards him.

People huddle near the microphone. Sapphire stands in front of the microphone and stares at the flower field that waves and dances to the music. Loud sounds hurt her ears, poking holes in her head. Black yarn hangs from the dark clouds.

Then, silence.

Sapphire holds the microphone, looking out at the people. She sees herself standing there, scared and alone, whispering into the microphone that she lost her daddy.

He runs toward her, but he's running in place. She stretches out her arms and tries to move, but her feet are glued to the stage. She yells as loud as she can, but no sound comes out.

Sapphire's eyes burst open. She gasped, heart pounding. Confused, she tried to figure out where she was. Red fabric. Sun. Sauna. T-shirt wet. She wiggled her feet, moving them up and down, before realizing she was no longer in Griffith Park. No longer six years old. She slid out of her sleeping bag and unzipped the door of her tent to let in the breeze. The darkness swallowed her every time he disappeared.

The moments of perfection were too fleeting, like the day playing pirates in Danielle's backyard, when everything had flown magic, their laughter soaring through the air. They had planned to do it the next day, but by then the radiance had vanished, even though they were the same people, playing in the same overgrown yard, wearing the same outfits from the same big chest in the basement. She wondered how Dad had managed to create so many electrifying moments, day after day.

Sapphire grabbed her sketchpad and drew Dad as a
racehorse and herself as a donkey running down the track.
The racehorse on the left had legs stretched straight and long
in galloping diagonals, and the donkey trotted slowly along
in ninety-degree angles. Tripping and falling was how she
pictured the donkey. She tried to remember that quote that
she liked. Something about making paths instead of following
them—in the act of creation, the creator and the destination
are changed. She wrote down what she could remember.

She flipped the sheet over and started again. This time,
she drew the donkey trotting next to the racehorse, leading it
to the gate, while the racehorse nuzzled the donkey's chunky
mane.

After only three days, she still hadn't walked the entire
gathering. Too soon to quit. Setting the sketchpad down, she
got ready for the day, stuffed a stack of "Dad Wanted" flyers
in her daypack, and headed out to post a flyer at every camp.

Sapphire gazed up at the sun high in the sky. Late
morning. Already, Main Trail teemed with people who
ambled along, greeting long-lost friends with a hug and
a shriek, or a slap on the back and a "Sup brother." She
wandered into one camp after another, staying long enough
to exchange a few words with whoever was there and then ask
if she could post a flyer. Most people were friendly, helping
her post a flyer by the bliss rails or on a tree somewhere
prominent.

At the No More Faith Camp, she ran into a bunch of
teenagers who were dressed in plaid flannel shirts over ripped
jeans. Boys and girls wore heavy eyeliner and dark purple

lipstick. She could have been looking in a mirror, circa 1981, when she drew black lines around her eyes and tried to hide what she felt behind her makeup. She asked if she could put up a flyer, and one of the guys said, "I'm trying to get rid of my dad. Why you lookin' for yours?"

She laughed, remembering how she felt the same way at their age. Mom had already left for work on that Friday morning when Sticky had come by and they had split in his rusty '65 Ford Fairlane, headed for Sears Point. Twenty-five bands on two stages, and Mom had refused to let her go, said sixteen was too young to be gone three days with boys, and she didn't even know Sticky. Sapphire paid her own way in and even gave Sticky some cash for gas. When they walked over the hill and she saw the stage laid out at the end of the field, she'd felt light and airy. A condor riding the currents, she floated through space, free, and trying herself on for size. She drank piss-water American beer with Sticky and Bill and some other blokes from the city. All the guys had worn black denim and torn flannels.

"I know what you mean," Sapphire said. "I was the same way at your age."

The guy shook his head. "No way. You's just trying to get us to go home."

"Are you parents here?" Sapphire asked.

"Don't fuckin' know. Don't fucking care."

Sapphire shrugged her shoulders. Their parents were probably here, since the teenagers refused to acknowledge their parents' existence. She couldn't change their perspective. When she had been determined to split, nothing could have stopped her. Probably not the best decision of her life, but at the time, she had loved it.

FALLING FROM THE MOON

Jilly had cut Sapphire's hair and dyed it red, and the guys had loved her. Loved her dancing topless. Loved to kiss her. Loved to pull down her pants and make her squirm. Sticky seemed proud to share her. Maybe, he was proud he had something someone else wanted for a change. Zach promised to call her when they made it back to the city. Sapphire was golden, popular. She was the chosen one. And it felt good. On the drive back, she told Sticky she wanted to stay with him, ready to throw off school and family. Nothing would have stopped her then.

She paused her memory, watching one of the girls light up a cigarette. "It's cool," Sapphire said. "Ya gotta do what your heart demands. But you have to be prepared for the consequences."

"What's that supposta mean?"

"Figure it out." Sapphire turned around and walked out.

The kids' pigsty camp reminded her of Sticky's squat in the old shoe factory, with extension cord juice from the auto shop next door. They had crashed shows at the Deaf Club and snuck into the Mabuhay to slam dance to the Dils and the Avengers. After a couple of weeks, Sticky had brought home a tall blonde girl from Walnut Creek, who had a car and a credit card, and Sapphire became their go-fer. She and Zach and some other kids tagged along with them, living off their takeout leftovers. By then, it didn't really matter. Sapphire was cold at night, hungry during the day, and the only decent part of life was the burn of whiskey on her throat and someone's hands caressing her breasts. She had been no more prepared for life then than these kids were now.

She glanced back at the No More Faith Camp, shaking her head as she headed up the trail, cringing at her own teenage behavior. She wasn't the same person who thought letting random guys fuck her was cool. Dad must have changed as well. Her eye twitched. Suddenly hot, she slipped off her sweatshirt. Things were getting more complicated instead of less.

Sapphire remembered that cold summer night when Sticky and the gang had gone to China Basin, and she had played an old recorder against the moan of the fog horn. Sitting by the docks, drinking cheap white wine and waiting for the Third Street drawbridge to rise, or for their lives to begin. Wallowing in the dark gray abyss of her life, the fog swallowed up the streets of San Francisco and silenced the tears of the destitute gold-diggers and straggling flower children shivering in their frilly dresses like ghosts from the past. Sapphire was wise beyond her years, or so she had thought then.

Sticky had yanked half a dozen spray paint cans from his pack and passed them around. He screamed, "Anarchy." They would show the staid businessmen and flower-loving hippies what anarchy was all about. And it felt good, good to be using paint and creating an idea on a steel girder that others would see and then know that Sapphire existed. She had begun to miss painting; she longed for her corner of her garage, where the light came in through the window and she had painted past dark, painted past dinner, and the world.

When the cops arrived, everyone ran; only she wasn't fast enough. Not knowing what else to do, she called home and her stepdad Brandon picked her up from the Valencia Street police station. He had cross-examined her about where she had been for the last five weeks, but her mind had been a gray abyss, where sound had reduced itself to a low moan that had rumbled in her low belly. She had only admitted to spray-painting the bridge.

Every time she thought about that mess, she felt queasy, like there was something she needed to vomit out.

"Love you, sister."

She smiled at the old man. "Beautiful day."

After the man had passed by, she noticed the fork in the path. The tree in the middle was plastered with signs. Blue Moon Bakery and Rasta Pasta pointed to the right. At least ten camps had signs pointing to the left. She took the left branch, following the trail to Yogi Magic, Blind Wizard, Chi Town, and the rest of the camps.

Sapphire's relationship with men hadn't evolved much since her time with Sticky. Men were either adventures or worshipers. In a less flamboyant manner, she was repeating that pattern. "Serial monogamy" her friends called it, but when each relationship only lasted a few months, she knew she was the problem.

The narrow and crowded trail dropped down through granite boulders before opening onto a small clearing. In all these years, she had never talked about the Sticky weeks with her mom or Brandon. Shame ran deep in her veins, and she wasn't sure if she or they were to blame. Maybe, if they had included Dad in the family lore, Sapphire wouldn't have felt so alienated. Maybe, if she had seen him a few times a year, he wouldn't have become a golden idol in her life, forever caught in those sparkling days of her childhood, frozen in time like James Dean and Marilyn Monroe.

At the bottom of the small hill, she found a flat rock to sit on. From her pack, she grabbed water and a snack, enjoying the dappled light through the trees. As cold as the nights were, the days sure warmed up. In the clearing below, a few people were playing frisbee, and dogs tumbled happily with each other.

Dad had auditioned to be a rodeo cowboy in *The Misfits* and saw Marilyn on the set during his audition. Sapphire's bedtime stories had included Dad's acting adventures and movie studio gossip. If Marilyn had lived, she would be old by now. Maybe in her sixties. Sapphire wondered if Marilyn would have become a renowned actress like Katherine Hepburn, instead of a sex symbol. Or even in old age, would Marilyn's image be frozen in time like Dad's, always young, charismatic, playful?

She tried to imagine Dad as he might be now at the age of fifty. Gray-haired and overweight, or trim with close-cropped hair. For years, she had followed the movie tabloids looking for a reference to him or a recent movie starring him, but she always came up short. The tabloids never covered extras.

Finishing her apple, she headed towards a rainbow banner hanging from a tent. Beyond that, a row of Tibetan prayer flags hung along the tree line. Off to the left, a black flag with a white skull and crossbones hung from a pole over a firepit.

Thud.

"Ow!" She stumbled, staggering to catch her balance from the impact to her shoulder that sent her spinning. Her flyers rippled through the air like confetti in slow motion. "Damn it."

"So sorry, sister," exclaimed a tall older man who was already lowering himself slowly to the ground, reaching for the "Dad Wanted" flyers scattered in the dirt.

A pack of muddy dogs thundered towards them, knocking the man to the ground. Muddy prints covered the scattered, and now somewhat crumpled, flyers.

For a moment Sapphire hesitated, wondering what had just happened. The man, her flyers; she glanced in the

direction the dogs had disappeared. "Duh. Let me help you."
She reached out her hand.

As the man slowly stood, she stared into his face, looking
for traces of her father, trying to manifest their reunion out of
thin air.

THE CULT OF MOTHERHOOD

Sunday, July 1, 1990
McGriver's Gap, Plumas National Forest, California
(Day Seven of Lauren's Gathering)

World Peace and Love Gathering Full of Contrasts

...After spending an entire day exploring the World
Peace and Love Gathering, this reporter will be the
first to acknowledge there are many "gatherings."
From defiant activists to spiritually-centered
yogis, the miracle of the Gathering is that diverse
groups of people seem to get along, despite
differing beliefs about child-rearing, dietary habits,
relationships, and work. I observed a heated but
peaceful discussion over a late-night fire between
Hari Krishna devotees and Jewish believers over
the form of the sacred and the nature of the
universe. When the "zu-zus" (sweet treats) showed
up, accompanied by a wrinkled guitarist playing
Joni Mitchell's classic song "Woodstock," both
Krishna and Jewish voices sang together. While
no consensus was reached during our visit to
this campfire, I have faith that the discussions
continued until dawn. (*Quincy Herald*, June 30,
1990)

LAUREN

Lauren pressed her back against the rough bark railing that
separated people engaged in gathering with those sharing
information. She sighed. A tired looking woman with two
mud-spattered toddlers asked her where to find Kid Korral.

Lauren pointed to her right, her brain tightening. "Did you see the map over there?"

The woman shook her head.

Miffed, Lauren pointed to Main Trail, going south of INFO. "That's okay. It's not far from here." She waited impatiently for the woman to turn in the direction she was pointing. "Follow that trail a third of a mile, then turn right at the Kid Korral sign, and go up the hill."

"Why is it so far away?"

Lauren shrugged her shoulders. "If you're coming in from the far end of the parking lot, it's only half a mile, but INFO is at the center of the gathering, and Kid Korral is at the back side of the gathering."

The woman thanked her and turned back toward Main Trail. As Lauren watched the woman wearily trudge down the slope, her face flushed with shame at her curt behavior. The old Lauren would have been more empathetic, but for the last two months, her conflicted feelings about her own pregnancy popped out of her mouth, despite her positive intentions. She stared aimlessly at the people checking out the INFO boards.

Her friends from Arcata were building a stage out of logs and tree branches at the 411 Anarchist's Collective performance space. Lost Cause and Volkswagen Willy said they were going to put on *Romeo and Juliet* the night of July 4, "hippie-style" according to Willy. Lauren could help them make costumes, but Willy was still upset with her for climbing onto the logging truck at Samoa while pregnant, and she didn't feel like facing him. River had left on a supply run yesterday, and she had no idea when he would resurface.

Instead, she plugged in at INFO, watched her belly grow, and rubbed the knotted muscles in her neck, caused by the constant fuss from random strangers. Even first-time gatherers, who needed help finding their way around the gathering, gave her unwanted advice on "the baby." Despite being four and a half months pregnant, she felt great. Mornings, she rose with the sun and hiked around the gathering. The crisp air energized her, and she would ramble for at least two miles before the day warmed up and her feet started to swell. In the early morning, when most people were still asleep, birds dashed past her, trilling their displeasure at her intrusion on their pre-human day. The tangy sap of pines filled her nostrils, reflections of Sequoia sempervirens, the Coast Redwoods, where her heart had found a home and more importantly, a voice. In the morning stillness, tenuous links connected the abyss between humans and trees. Only then, when she could hear the trees sing, could she even acknowledge the joy and sorrow, excitement and anger dancing in her heart.

An older couple approached the counter. The man said, "Do you know where the Kundalini yoga workshop is happening?"

There were fifty to a hundred workshops every day, some advertised, some more private. "I don't know, but check the workshop board," she said. "It's the one with the blue border." While they wandered off, she noticed a large circle of guys her own age near the trail getting high and kicking a hacky sack. She so wanted a hit off that joint.

Two older women carrying shovels marched down the trail past INFO. Lauren guessed they were off to dig a new trench latrine, a task she had loved to do in the morning chill. When done sans men, there were no egos, no trying to show off, just honest sweat and sharing stories. Once the men showed up, they strutted, discounted the work of the women, and one-upped everyone with their stories, until the man who insisted on swinging a pick non-stop collapsed in the dirt exhausted and dehydrated.

A skinny man pushed a wheelbarrow piled with sacks of flour, rice, and beans—one of the few men she saw working. A man carrying a drum strutted past her. His white tank top shimmered on top of his dark sculpted pecs. The tug in Lauren's groin made her yearn to saunter up to him and smile. Flirt a little perhaps. Rub her hands across his shoulders and inhale the sun and sweat on his back. She took a deep breath and sat down.

River acted as if they were already married because they had conceived this baby. She wasn't sure what she wanted from him, but for now she needed the physical and emotional support he provided, even if it got on her nerves. In fact, the more she needed his help, the more she resented it. People stayed together for many reasons, most of which had nothing to do with love. Lauren's parents were a perfect example. Her mom flourished at the golf club parties. Her dad's ego required a pretty wife, believing her beauty enhanced his net worth. Sometimes, she thought her parent's marriage was as much a business contract as love.

When Lauren had first met River, the adrenaline rush of being chained to a bulldozer and trying to save the redwoods had taken over her life, and he became an integral part of the experience. When they started dating last year, a family was just some fuzzy future thought with a man she would meet years down the road. The family part of her life had crashed into her future, like a chain-sawed redwood crashing to the ground. Now, River would be in her life forever. She sighed.

"Hey, Lauren."

Sapphire ducked under the rear railing of INFO. The best part of Lauren's gathering so far had been meeting Sapphire, who was the only person who didn't treat her like a pregnant woman.

"How's it going?"

"I just had the best walnut waffles." Sapphire smiled. "I'm fueled up and reporting for work."

"Great. We need signs directing people to the latrines." Lauren pointed to the pile of cardboard by the railing. "You can use those. There's a bucket of crayons in the supply tent on the right."

Sapphire disappeared into the tent. Lauren climbed onto the bench, her belly protruding under her cropped Bob Marley t-shirt; she rubbed her swollen ankles and rotated her stiff neck.

Sapphire sat cross-legged in front of piles of cut-up cardboard and a worn sheet of paper with phrases for the signs: *No pee in the pooper. Wash your hands. No poop in the woods, Poopers.* She looked happily engrossed in making latrine signs; no doubt the thrill of a lifetime. Sapphire had a childlike quality about her. When they had first met, she seemed so wise, so cool with her stories of concerts in Griffith Park and hiking the Sierras, but when Lauren had gotten to know her better, she began to realize how immature her new friend was. But Lauren could either hang out with Sapphire or drown herself in the cult of motherhood at Kid Korral, and anything was better than that. Besides, Sapphire wanted to hang out with her, which is more than Lauren could say of most of her so-called friends, even River. He wanted her to hang out at Kid Korral and take it easy, while he ran around the gathering being Mr. Important. Although it was his first gathering, she did want him to have fun, even if she resented him for it.

With a pencil, Sapphire sketched out the letters on the signs. "How many should I make?"

Lauren shrugged her shoulders. "It's up to you."

"I'll make three of each to start."

A young girl ran up and peered under the counter at Sapphire. "Can I color too?"

"Can you stay in between the lines?" Lauren asked.

The child jumped up and down. "Yes."

"What's your name?"

"Dakota," she said, ducking under the counter. "That's my mom over there." She pointed to a short, round woman with long ebony hair.

Sapphire said, "See these signs? We just need to color inside the letters."

The child selected a red crayon and, with immense concentration, proceeded to color.

"My name's Sapphire."

Dakota asked, "Where's your mommy?"

Lauren sighed at the cutesiness.

Sapphire said, "At home."

"Your mommy let you come here all by yourself?"

Sapphire said, "I'm a grownup."

Lauren looked away, trying to smother a laugh.

The child brushed her hair out of her face. "Then, why are you coloring?"

"Coloring isn't only for kids," Sapphire said.

Dakota looked up, her eyes squinting. "My mommy never colors."

"Well, maybe she's saving the crayons for you." Sapphire said.

If Lauren had to spend the next few years having conversations that never exceeded endless discussions about crayons, her brain would explode. Sapphire and Dakota huddled in the dirt, coloring furiously. Dakota colored a "P" in red, an "O" in green, and an "E" in yellow. Sapphire colored all her letters in yellow. Lauren tried to imagine herself coloring with a five-year-old, but the image was alien. Had she ever colored with her mom?

Dakota dug through the tub of crayons and pulled out a bright pink one.

"Dakota," yelled the ebony-haired woman.

A voice from behind Lauren said, "Excuse me."

She turned to a gangly man with bronze skin and long black hair, standing in front of the counter. "How are you today?"

"I have a question."

"I have some answers and can invent more if you like." She tried to be silly, but he looked so serious, she had no idea if he got the joke or not.

He blushed.

"Is this your first gathering?"

"It's not what I expected." He picked up a flyer. The purple one with *Ferndale. Redwoodstock. Labor Day Weekend.*

By Labor Day weekend, Lauren would be seven months pregnant and humongous. She wanted to do the five-mile march through Ferndale to the headquarters of Northwest Lumber, before Redwood Summer ended and everything she had worked for would be history. If she kept walking a few miles a day between now and then, she would be able to make the march.

"So, I'm here with my girlfriend," the gangly man said. "She needs…" He moved flyers around on the counter, then leaned toward her, and whispered, "She's having her period and…"

Lauren giggled. "My apologies. I don't mean to laugh. I just. Oh, never mind. First Aid has tampons, pads, and painkillers too, if she uses them."

The gangly man started to walk away. Lauren asked, "Do you know where First Aid is?"

He looked at his feet and shook his head.

Lauren felt bad for him. Truly, she wasn't trying to embarrass him, but it was so easy, and he was so bashful. She gestured toward Main Trail. "Go left until the fork; then, veer left and walk about five minutes."

As he walked away, Lauren turned to Sapphire, who stared at her. They held each other's gaze for a few seconds and then burst out laughing.

Lauren said, "He was so red."

"You were mean."

"I wasn't even." Lauren laughed at his embarrassment. Men ought to feel stupid about being so ignorant of women's bodies. Once she caught her breath, she heard a woman scream. The sound came from near the ride-share board.

The ebony-haired woman ran toward her, yelling, "My daughter's been kidnapped."

That woman breathed hysteria. The night before at Dinner Circle, she had freaked out about her lost dog that turned up five minutes later. Lauren rolled her eyes at the drama queen and pointed to Dakota coloring in the dirt. "Is this your daughter?"

The ebony-haired woman ducked under the counter and set her hands on her hips. "Dakota! You promised to stay with me."

"No worries," Sapphire said. "We've been coloring."

"Moonchild." The round woman reached out her hand to Lauren.

Lauren shook it, passing on the usual greeting hug, afraid that scatterbraininess and flakiness were catching. Moonchild rambled on about her day. No toilet paper at the latrine, and she lost her bag, but really only left it at the kitchen.

Moonchild disgusted her, and at the same time Lauren worried that once she gave birth, she would end up a slightly less spacey version of her. She knew not all mothers acted like Moonchild, but which type would she become, and if she turned into a flake, how would her child survive?

After rambling on for another five minutes about diaper rash and the alignment of Saturn, Moonchild said she had to go to Kid Korral, and she left with her daughter.

"Thanks for helping," Sapphire called after them. She glanced up at Lauren. "That's a neat kid."

Lauren shrugged her shoulders. She wasn't a big fan of children, and her mother hadn't been either. By the age of four, Lauren had been in school, camp, afterschool activities, or anything her mother could dream of that would require someone else to take care of her. That wasn't going to be an option for her. A few people approached the counter with questions, and she explained Dinner Circle, where to find a doctor, acupuncturist, herbalist, etc., and reminded everyone to take their trash home with them.

No one had told Lauren that she would feel the pregnancy everywhere: the heaviness in her limbs, the aching in her back that never seemed to go away; even her fingers felt fat. If she hadn't understood the implications of gravity before, she knew now. The earth pulled her toward its core with a grasp she had never imagined possible. The scholars said a man discovered gravity, but she knew it was a cover-up. Women discovered gravity so far back in the annals of history that its discovery predated fire or the wheel. No one who had ever been pregnant could be ignorant of gravity.

"Do you see anyone who looks like my dad?" Sapphire asked.

Lauren shook her head, imagining River reading bedtime stories or changing diapers. Jobless, he was the complete opposite of her workaholic dad, who only made appearances when she won awards or graduated. She had no idea how River was going to help her support this baby, when he lived off dumpster diving and whatever he made trimming weed in the fall.

A man with a heavily wrinkled face and straight gray hair approached the counter. "Is this Lost and Found?"

Lauren said, "It sure is. Did you lose or find?"

The man placed a small beaded bag on the counter. "I found this in the meadow earlier."

She thanked the man for returning the bag, lumbered over to the supply tent, and tossed the bag in the plastic barrel, and then lowered herself into a chair next to Sapphire.

"Remember Chiquita?"

"Is she the one you're planning the tree-sit with?"

Lauren nodded. "She doesn't want to anymore."

"She's backing out?"

"No," Lauren said. "She doesn't want to do it with me."

"Why?"

Lauren looked down at her stomach, brown and round, an unwelcome guest sitting in her lap. The guest that chased away everyone. "She found a new partner."

Sapphire kept coloring in the letters on the word "Pooper."

"Aren't you going to say anything?"

Sapphire stopped drawing but didn't look at her. "Chiquita's right."

"What do you know, anyway?" Lauren heaved herself up and returned to the counter.

Sapphire followed her and started stacking pamphlets on the counter. "I mean, really. What happens if the cops start beating on you?" Sapphire turned toward her. "You don't know what will happen."

Lauren ignored her. Sapphire wasn't the one giving up her dreams or getting unwanted advice on breastfeeding from every joker in camp who stroked her belly. She wanted this summer to be wild and free, standing up to the government, the loggers, her parents. She wanted to shout from the tops of the trees: "We are here. We are strong. We are the future!" Instead, she and River had run out of condoms that one day when they couldn't get a ride back from Gold Bluffs Beach, and the elk wandering through camp made her and River snuggle under their thin blankets, while the fog lay down around them. Her dream had evaporated, and in its place, her belly bulged; her swollen fingers stiffened.

"Are you oaky?" Sapphire asked.

"I'm fine." Lauren turned away to watch the people reading the INFO boards and tried to ignore Sapphire. After a few minutes, Sapphire resumed her coloring. Lauren leaned back against the branch railing, her monumental breasts lying against her ribcage. She had no idea where these breasts had come from. And to think that in high school, she obsessed over having small breasts. The skin on her belly began to itch and she ran her fingernails over her skin, enjoyed the prickle of her nails. She gazed out at the crowd milling about and pointed to a man standing by the one of the boards. "He's looking at your flyer."

Sapphire jumped up and leaned across the counter to get a better look.

"Go talk to him."

"I should."

As they stood there, he approached the counter.

Lauren nudged Sapphire. "He looks about fifty. Isn't that how old your dad is now?"

He set his right arm on the counter and leaned toward them.

"Hello, ladies." He brushed his long brown hair out of his eyes. "So, you are the INFO booth?"

Lauren tried to put a smile in her voice. "Do you need information, or do you have information to share?"

He said, "I reckon I'm looking for someone. Her name is Charlyn. Charlyn Pauley."

"And you are?" Lauren asked.

"Well, forgive me my manners. My name is Bill. Bill Hudson." He paused. "I'm a patient of hers. At the VA hospital in Decatur, Georgia. She said I should look her up iffin' I made it."

Sapphire said, "Is that your real name?"

"Yes, ma'am. That's the name my pappy give me."

"What does Sharisha look like?"

"She's a black woman, close to fifty."

He must be seeking Bumblebee, Lauren thought. There weren't too many African-American women at the gathering, and even fewer older ones. "Is she a nurse?"

"Yes, ma'am. She took mighty fine care of me after I busted up my leg." He scratched his head. "Hell, she even came to see me on her day off, 'cause she knew my boy wasn't coming around."

"Are you okay now?" Sapphire asked.

"Rightly so. Excepting I limp when it rains."

Lauren nodded and told him the woman he was looking for went by the name of Bumblebee at the gathering, and the best place to hook up with her was at First Aid.

Sapphire shook her head as he walked away. "Not him," she said.

"I figured. His name was Bill, not John," Lauren said.

"I should know my own dad, don't you think?" Sapphire pressed the crayon into the cardboard, and it snapped into pieces. "But Dad's not southern. He grew up in L.A."

Lauren nodded. She was trying to put distance between the life she grew up in and the new one she was embracing.

Sapphire dug another crayon out of the bucket and continued coloring.

Lauren refused to let her child grow up in a fancy McMansion on a golf course that felt more like a hotel lobby than a home, with hired help doing the housework, managing the garden, and sometimes even the driving, if her parents were too busy. Determined to provide the type of hands-on parenting she had lacked as a child, her child would be raised with family dinners and the freedom to express herself. Of course, lacking any income, Lauren had limited options.

She giggled. Housekeepers for a tepee? No way. She wanted a kid covered in mud, climbing trees, and splashing naked in the river. She wanted a wild child. River wanted these things too, or at least that's what he told her now. They would be different from their parents, he said. But she knew that old patterns were hard to break. "I worry sometimes," Lauren said, "about River. About him going back to Louisiana and marrying some blonde, who makes blackberry pies and pops out babies in the same breath."

Sapphire glanced up. "Have you talked to him?"

"Like this is all playtime, and when he gets tired of saving the redwoods and being arrested, he'll go back and work at his daddy's mill."

"He loves you, Lauren. He loves the baby."

Lauren rearranged the pamphlets on the counter. "I think he's in love with the idea of having a baby." But she didn't tell Sapphire that River was the one who was truly excited, not her. He was the one talking baby names. All she could see was what she was losing.

"It's going to work out," Sapphire said. "You guys are so awesome together."

Lauren detested the platitudes. Life didn't just work out, and she knew Sapphire didn't believe that either or she would have accepted her dad's absence. Lauren had never been a go-with-the flow sort of person. She made goals and then lists of action items that would help her achieve her goals. That's how she made captain of the cross-country team in high school. That's how she got her parents to accept she wasn't going back East for college. She had planned to write her senior honors thesis on defending the redwoods, and now she had nothing. "This summer wasn't supposed to be like this."

"Like what?" Sapphire asked.

They had been meeting, planning, trying to figure out a way to turn their isolated actions into a big event that would draw attention to the slaughter of the old-growth forest and the destruction of the entire ecosystem, including owls, salmon, and the Mattole tribe. They organized, built coalitions, and prepared workshops, while holed up in Ed's ramshackle living room at two in the morning. Night after night, they discussed strategy and how to train hundreds of inexperienced people in the tenets of nonviolent direct action. Back then, she had imagined herself leading hundreds of people to the logging sites, chaining herself to the equipment, and daring the loggers to resume destruction of the forest. "I was going chain myself to a grapple skidder," Lauren said. "Get arrested. Stop them from destroying the redwoods." From destroying the rhythms of the earth, she thought.

"But you're still one of the organizers. You're still involved," Sapphire said.

Lauren turned toward Sapphire. "At the Spring Equinox campout, I thought my missed period was due to the stress and late nights, but by April I had a sinking feeling, and by May, before the first action, everyone knew and I was branded. Then, they wanted me to take on media work or design t-shirts. They told me I couldn't be on the front lines anymore. 'Because of the baby,' they said."

"There'll be other summers." Sapphire looked at her belly.

The hair on Lauren's head prickled at the manner in which her dreams were so easily dismissed. No one cared that she could not do one, let alone thirty, pull-ups anymore or climb a tree. Her friends were moving on without her, and she felt excluded from the actions into which she had poured her heart and soul. Left on the sidelines to welcome newbies and fax press releases. She didn't want to be the secretary.

A gray-haired couple approached the counter, and Lauren choked back her tears.

"Is there someplace that sells food around here?" the old man asked.

Lauren stared for a moment, trying to steel herself against tears and what-ifs. This was her life now. "You'd have to go back down the mountain for that. Up here, people share what they have with each other."

"Then, where do we get food?"

She glanced up at the sky—still early afternoon. "You might want to check with some of the kitchens; sometimes they have food midday. Otherwise, Dinner Circle starts about two hours before sunset in the large meadow over there." She pointed through the birch trees to where River approached, his ripped jeans and unbuttoned shirt covered in mud. "Make sure you bring a bowl and a fork."

River jumped over the INFO railing and placed his hands on her belly. "Hey, Mama."

She pulled away from him and forced a smile at the couple. "Where you all from?"

"Walnut Creek," the woman said. "We just got in today."

Lauren gave her the five-minute Welcome Home rap: Do your number two in the latrines. No ground scores. Check the board for workshops. Camp with other people. Yell "Peace Patrol" for emergency help. First Aid is that way.

River swatted her behind and collapsed onto an upturned five-gallon bucket near Sapphire. "I keep telling her to go play. Go hang out at Kid Korral. Visit with the other moms. But she's stubborn."

Sapphire shrugged her shoulders. "She's gonna do what she's gonna do."

"It don't work that way anymore," he said.

Lauren seethed at how easy River dismissed her as anything more than the person incubating his baby.

She turned and saw River's mouth close to Sapphire's ear.

"Why would she listen to me?" Sapphire said.

River rubbed the stubble on his face. "'Cause she admires you."

"Me?"

"Hell yes." River rubbed his hand across his bare chest.

Lauren lumbered toward them. "Are you talking about me?"

Sapphire coughed.

"Hell yes," River said. "I was just telling Sapphire how beautiful you are."

Lauren raised her eyebrows.

"A total goddess," he said, before winking at Sapphire.

Sapphire grabbed another crayon.

Exasperated, Lauren turned her back on them and returned to the counter where at least people pretended to appreciate her.

"See," River said. "She's totally hormonal."

"I can hear you," Lauren called out.

Sapphire followed Lauren and hugged her from behind. "Maybe you should let her be pregnant the way she wants to be."

"You're taking her side?" River said.

In spite of how ignorant the girl was, at times she knew exactly what to do and why. Lauren moved a jacket off the bench to make room for her.

Sapphire sat down and tried to help. The INFO questions were endless.

Where's the nearest bathroom?

Are there showers?

What kitchen is serving?

I'm looking for Elvis Camp. Ding-a-Ling Camp. Jesus Camp. Whole-in-One Camp.

Every time River came near her, Lauren busied herself talking to a first-time gatherer, explaining the peace prayer or giving directions to the nearest latrine. Finally, River disappeared down the trail. He didn't even say goodbye. Her back ached, and Sapphire asked as many questions as she answered. There was no time for personal conversations. People expected her to know everything.

The Dinner Circle menu? – "Whatever the kitchens cooked."

Where to find a needle and thread? – "Barter Circle."

The afternoon dragged on, and La Abuela showed up in a pale blue dress of crinkled cotton.

"Oh, *mi hija,*" she exclaimed. "How are you this magnificent day?"

"I'm doing okay."

"Well, dear, I wanted to invite you to *mi casa este noche.* After dinner. A circle for the mamas to be *con las abuelas.* With the grandmothers."

Lauren shook her head. "No, thank you." They were body snatchers, trying to convince her that having a baby was the most important thing in the world. Everywhere she went, they tried to suck her into the cult. She wasn't ready to let herself or her dreams vanish. Not now. Maybe never.

La Abuela continued. "The shadow follows you, my child. You must come. Birth is a journey, very hard. *Muy dificil.*"

A woman approached the counter and said, "Excuse me. I'm looking for a wallet."

Sapphire asked, "What's your name?"

"Sylvia Marken."

"Hold on a second."

Lauren said, "Grandmother, I appreciate your concern. I'm just not ready."

"My daughter. Of course, you have not prepared. It will be a few months before you need to be ready. We will help you."

"Maybe another time."

"Oh, child. There is no other time. *Tenga miedo.* Feel the shadow of death knocking at your door. It is so for all women."

Lauren had no intention of becoming a bread-baking, supermarket-aisle, breast-feeding woman. Yet to disrespect the grandmother was not an option. "When is it?"

"Tonight, after dinner. The lodge with the black roadrunner, in the circle of the tepees belonging to the elders, *las ancianas.*" The grandmother took her hand. "We are here to help you, *mi hija.*"

Sapphire rang the brass bell and yelled, "We have a winner," before handing the wallet over to Sylvia.

"Thank you so much." Sylvia left with her friends.

"This night," La Abuela said, before she meandered up the trail toward Dinner Circle.

Sapphire asked, "Are you going?"

Lauren felt out of balance, as if tipping over, a feeling that had been with her since she had found out she was pregnant. She had no interest in hearing glowing stories of the spiritual side of pregnancy or being made to feel abnormal for having more interest in monkey-wrenching a Knuckleboom Loader than discussing birthing music. She had no urge to stockpile baby clothes or even search for names, and she was sick to death of discussing parenting.

"It would be good for you to hang out with pregnant sisters," Sapphire said.

"How the hell do you know what's good for me?"

Sapphire stepped back. "I'm not trying to tell you what to do."

"Then, you're the only one," Lauren snarled.

THE STORM LOOMS

Thursday, July 5, 1990
(Day Ten of Sapphire's Gathering)

Thousands Pray for World Peace

Yesterday was the main day of the World Peace
and Love Gathering that culminated in a morning
of silent prayer for world peace. While many
people are leaving the gathering, I spoke to many
others who would be onsite through the official
end of July 7. So far, no major incidents have been
reported. This reporter, and photographer Sandra
Weis, were onsite for the silent prayer and the
celebration afterwards, enjoying the never-ending
drum circle, the children's parade and much
more. Look for our Sunday feature, "Celebrating
Interdependence Day in the High Sierras." (*Quincy
Herald*, July 5, 1990)

SAPPHIRE

A hundred throbbing drums roared around the bonfire,
keeping the dancers enthralled in a call and response between
body and rhythm. Sapphire danced blissfully under the star-
speckled night sky in a *boom, thump, wap* trance, the thunder
of the drums reverberating through her chest. The conga
to her left called out *pop, pop, rap, pop, rap.* The djembes
responded *slap, bloop, slap.* The conga repeated *pop, pop, rap,
pop, rap* and then the dununs joined in *boom, thumb, boom.*

Beside her, Lauren chanted, "Earth my bo-o-dy. Water
my blooood. Air my breath, and fire my spi-ir-it." Others

joined in until they were all singing the now-familiar chant that wrapped them in the arms of ancestors long gone. The drums slowed down to match their voices. Sapphire closed her eyes and tapped the ground with her feet, the chant slowing down her breath until her body melted into sound and the trees beyond. She exhaled into the unity of voices, "Earth my bo-o-dy. Water my blooood."

The shrieking crackle of a handheld radio cut through the crowd, and the drumming disintegrated into fractured banging.

Startled out of her trance, Sapphire stumbled and opened her eyes.

Grizzly Bear Garth pushed his way through the circle, gripping his long beard in his left hand; his cowboy hat tipped forward across his forehead.

Sapphire laughed. It didn't seem to matter what was going on, when Garth arrived, he was always louder than anyone else. Everyone mobbed him, asked questions, and wanted his opinion.

Garth bellowed into his transmitter, "Hold on a minute 'til I get the thumpers to stop. Ten-four." He looked around. "Hold up, folks."

The dancers' movements evaporated. Most of the drummers stopped, but a few kept furiously slapping, oblivious to the changes taking place around them. One by one, they lifted their heads and then their hands.

Garth waited until all the drums were silent. "We're looking for a missing kid. Five-year-old girl named Dakota. Dark brown hair, and she's probably carrying a stuffed green turtle."

A man's voice rang out from the far side of the circle. "Bro, you're ruining the vibe." He stepped into the center of the circle, stroking his chunky dreads. "We're here to drum."

Lauren called out, "No, brother, we're here to be together in body and spirit. Let's find our sister. Let's find Dakota."

"Let Peace Patrol deal with the problem," the man shouted, thrusting his naked chest towards Lauren. "That's their job."

"Brother, get a clue. We're a family. We dance together, work together, and pray together. You and I and everyone here are Peace Patrol." Lauren shook her head.

Garth stepped towards Lauren, his burly frame blocking the firelight. "You listen to me, punk. I don't know what parking lot you crawled out of, but around here, family comes first. I'm asking you nicely to shut your mouth."

The man stepped backwards and glanced around as though he expected backup. The crowd backed away from him.

Lauren turned to Sapphire and thrust her fist into the air. "Family first!"

Sapphire shouted, "Family first."

Garth said, "Dakota was last seen two or three hours ago when her mom put her to bed."

Kalmia called out, "Where are they camped?"

"By the tepees!" Garth replied.

"Let's spread out across the meadow and find her."

Garth shouted, "Before you all go running off, anyone who finds her should take her to First Aid. Use the buddy system. We don't need any more folks lost tonight."

"Ho." The voices from the circle rose in unison. "Ho." The bodies moved away from the fire. "Dakota, DA-KO-TA," the cries rolled out.

Sapphire gazed at the forest ridges surrounding the meadow. Hundreds of miles of wilderness. Coyotes and bears.

"It must be forty degrees out here." Lauren started into the darkness, her body straight and her shoulders back. "We don't have much time." She marched off, abandoning her drum.

Sapphire grabbed their daypacks. "DA-KO-TA," she yelled and hurried after Lauren. The *thumpety thump whump* of the drums started up and she glanced back to the fire. Only a few people remained.

Sapphire trailed behind Lauren, her shadow licking at Lauren's feet. She searched the sky for traces of the moon. The moon's arrival would have been heralded by a glow over the eastern horizon, but the purple-black of the night sky remained an even color, broken only by thousands of sparkling stars.

The valley echoed the charge, "DA-KO-TA. DA-KO-TA. We LOOOOVVVVE You DA-KO-TA."

Lauren paused, "What do you see?"

Sapphire gazed at the beams of light passing back and forth across the meadow. To their right, the woods loomed dark and dense. "Dark woods. Flashlights in the meadow."

"Exactly."

"And?"

"No one is heading towards the creek."

"It's dark and isolated."

"Kids love water," Lauren argued.

"She'd head for a fire."

"There's five hundred people looking near fires and only us over here." Lauren placed her hands on her waist. "What if she came this way and we didn't?"

"We don't got the gear for this."

"Does she?"

Sapphire rocked back and forth on her heels. Her mother's voice buzzed in her head, *compass, tarp, waterproof matches, map.* They didn't have any of it. "Let's find someone else to search the creek, and we'll hit the area between the tepees and Kid Korral."

Lauren marched down the trail, ignoring her completely.

"Weather in the Sierra Nevada Mountains can change in an instant," Sapphire shouted after Lauren, when the faint line of her body disappeared into the woods.

Once Lauren got an idea in her head, changing it was like trying to stop the mosh pit at a Chili Peppers show. Sometimes, Sapphire admired her tenacity. "Not too far," she said.

Sapphire followed Lauren on the trail away from the valley, away from the gathering, away from where her own father might be sitting around a fire telling stories. She took the trail without knowing where it went.

Lauren's faint voice drifted through the trees, "Daa…"

Sapphire searched for the path that Lauren would have taken and squeezed her eyes shut, hoping to erase the firelight from their memory, trying to adjust to a world of darkness, and when she opened them, she thought she could see the plumes of goldenrod and the clumps of False Hellebar along the footpath, which wound down the slope toward the creek. The chatter of water on rocks and the faint rasping of wind in the trees beckoned from the spirit world, issuing warnings or invitations—Sapphire couldn't tell the difference. Ahead of her, beams of light pricked the darkness, and soon she caught up with Lauren.

Lauren swept her flashlight from side to side, the beam of light illuminating and obscuring the creeping wild orchid, covered in dark-colored flowers.

Sapphire said, "If you turn the light off, your eyes adjust."

"To darkness?"

Sapphire shrugged. "See the shadows."

"Light on, I see things. Light off, darkness."

Sapphire shook her head and dropped behind Lauren. The trail shrunk and curved around granite boulders, where it paralleled the creek before winding through a stand of giant white pines.

Lauren trained her flashlight on a faint path that disappeared into a thick tangle of dark green Saskatoon, intertwined with the low-hanging branches of a willow bush. "I bet five-year-olds love magic tunnels."

Apprehension filled Sapphire's chest and she tapped the ground with her foot: hard-packed soil. Lots of use; it must go somewhere.

"It's a trail." Lauren ducked her head and disappeared into the brush.

Sapphire picked up a couple rocks and stacked them by the trail. Leaving a cairn would help them find their way back to Main Meadow. Mom had taught her to respect the wildness of the mountains, starting that first summer without Dad, when they had stayed at a friend's cabin in Big Bear and gone hiking every day and never once saw a black bear. Glancing up, she realized Lauren had gotten too far ahead. Sapphire hurried after her, hunched over to keep from banging her head on the living canopy. "Think Dakota's dad is here?"

"I doubt it."

"The moon will be up soon."

Lauren pushed branches aside and pushed her way into the tunnel.

Sapphire grabbed the branches before they swung back and smacked her in the face. "Do your people camp?"

"My people?"

"Your parents."

Lauren chortled.

Sapphire took her reaction as a no. "Her dad would be looking for her."

"If he cares about her."

She always wondered about other people's fathers, what they were like: old, young, gray-haired, or red-headed. Maybe Dakota missed her dad too. The trail swung to the right, climbed out of the willows, twisted around a granite boulder, and took them up onto a narrow bluff. It dipped to the left and they followed. She trained her eyes on the vague shapes lurking in the shadows, hoping to see something familiar.

"How far can a five-year-old walk?" Lauren turned her face toward the sky.

"Twenty feet in the grocery store."

Lauren shone her light on the rocks, revealing jagged edges. "What about the cliffs?"

"Most everyone survives childhood."

"And the rest?"

She heard Lauren's heavy breathing and felt her own heart beating. This was the story of a huge mountain, looming high above the patchwork of farms in the big valley eight thousand feet below, and two women searching for a child and tomorrow.

She had hiked this type of terrain with her mother a few years ago, over by Redding, where her mother identified every tree and every bush, while writing notes in a journal. Grateful for the skills her mother had taught her, Sapphire tried to commit the details to memory. The trail dipped down, and scrub oak thickened around the pines. Sapphire sketched the surroundings in her head, trying to create a mental map to guide them home: short water birch trees nestled at the feet of the willows. Gnarled, red manzanita twisted around a huge rock at the base of a sugar pine. S-shaped creek below. Six black cottonwood trees on their left. The woods hemmed them in, and they struggled through the thickets until the trail squeezed between the rocks and the water.

The trail oozed a dangerous mixture of algae and mud and disappeared into ferns. Her foot hit a slick spot and she slipped. She tried to regain her footing, while fending off branches that slapped her face. Twigs jabbed into her cheeks and bounced off her eyebrows.

"Are you alright?"

"I almost lost an eye!"

"You were grunting like an ape."

Sapphire stomped past Lauren until only the sounds of the forest remained, hushed voices whispering sinister thoughts in the rattle of leaves. Then, another sound. She heard crying in the distance. Turning away from the creek, Sapphire stepped up onto a boulder. "DA-KO-TA," she yelled. "Dakota, if you hear me, yell as loud as you can." She held still. Her ears strained to hear every rustle.

"What are you doing?" Lauren asked.

"I hear someone crying."

"Are you sure?"

"I think so."

Lauren caught up with Sapphire, where the trail opened onto a rutted dirt road and what seemed to be an old vehicle turnaround. "Dakota could have wandered down there."

"Why would she have gone that way?" Lauren asked.

"Well, it's not any crazier than climbing through that brush. It's an easy trail."

"I'll wait for you here."

"We have to stay together."

"Go a couple of hundred yards up that trail and then come back." Lauren held her lower back and wobbled toward a fallen log. "I need to rest a minute."

The only thing they had done right so far, Sapphire thought, was to stick together. "You're pregnant."

"I'm not helpless."

Torn between respecting Lauren's autonomy and staying together, Sapphire heard a voice. A voice crying. Overhead, the clouds rolled toward them. "Once the rain hits, we'll never find her," she muttered and inched up the old dirt road, listening for Dakota. "I'll be right back."

After twenty yards, Sapphire stopped and shouted, "DA-KO-TA." Nothing. Thirty more yards. "DA-KO-TA." The trail hugged the butte, and a short way up, the brush disappeared and the trees thinned. She walked across dying wildflowers that snapped under her feet. Not a person in sight.

Her shoulders slumped and her feet grew heavy. She plodded back to Lauren, scared that no matter how long she searched, she would be lost forever.

The clouds erased the last threads of light. Sapphire smelled the rain welling up. A cold shower would push them from chilled and tired, to hypothermic and dead. "We need to turn back now."

"You're quitting?"

"You don't even have rain gear."

"Dakota doesn't have a jacket."

"People die in the Sierras every year," Sapphire said. "People who aren't prepared."

"She's close. I can feel it."

"No five-year-old would trudge up here by herself."

"I can sense her like I feel my own baby—like she's grabbing at the end of my umbilical cord."

Sapphire rolled her eyes. Lauren wanted them to risk their lives for a vibe. "We can't stay out here any longer. Think of your baby."

Shrugging her shoulders, Lauren marched up the trail and disappeared around the bend.

Sapphire waited for her to return. "Lauren," she yelled. "We have to go back."

Slivers of light snaked across the sky. Sapphire counted. *One thousand and one. One thousand and two… One thousand and ten.* The metallic crash of thunder roared through the night. She screamed, "Lauren, wait up," and darted up the trail until she caught up with her. The thunder detonated again and rolled through the mountains before bouncing back at them. "Storm's moving fast." The wind jangled through the aspens and ripped through her flimsy sweatshirt.

"What's that?" Lauren pointed.

"The creek."

"There's something on the sandbar."

SOMETIMES THE END IS JUST THE BEGINNING

Thursday, July 5, 1990
(Day Ten of Sapphire's Gathering)

You will find something more in woods than in
books. Trees and stones will teach you that which
you can never learn from masters.
—Saint Bernard

SAPPHIRE

The wind overhead whipped the trees back and forth; they
crashed and smacked against each other, showering the
ground with leaves. Sapphire peered at the banks of the creek,
searching for any sign of a child. Sand. Rocks. Tree branches.
That was it.

Lauren shone her light on the thin strip of sand along the
bend of rushing water, fifteen feet or more below where they
stood. "Climb down there and see what that is."

"What what is?"

"That oval thing."

"Driftwood."

Lauren glared at Sapphire. "I'll do it myself."

"Stay right there!" Sapphire twisted through the dense
shrubs, slipped over the boulders, banged her knee with a
thud, and landed on the sand. The creek snaked through the
ravine. Bits of light shimmered on the cobblestone water,
burnished brass specks on gunmetal gray, the color of the ice

in her veins. The howl of the wind through the trees echoed in her ears. She slugged through the sand toward the bend.

Lauren's voice tumbled down the embankment. "Is ... stream ... under?"

Lightning exploded. *One thousand one, one thousand two. CARUUMP*—the thunder broke, and a few fat drops of rain splattered Sapphire's face. She wiped her cheeks with her sleeve. Her eye twitched.

In the moment of lightning-bright night, she glimpsed a body. A child's body lying on the sand, alone, curled up against the wind and the cold. Sapphire faltered, squinting her eyes against the raindrops, and held her breath. With a shallow exhale, she slogged toward the body lying in front of her. Afraid of what she might find, she averted her gaze toward the creek.

Kneeling, she pressed her hand against the tiny back that twisted beneath her touch. Sapphire gulped and stroked Dakota's back, her tiny ribs expanding and contracting. Sapphire gulped oxygen.

The girl rolled over and sat up. Streaks of mud covered her face, and her sweatshirt was ripped halfway up the middle. "Where's my mommy?"

"Dakota," she coaxed. "Remember me? Sapphire."

"No," the child said, rubbing her face with the back of her hand.

"You helped me color at INFO."

The tiny mouth melted into a smile for an instant. "Oh yeah. I like coloring." Then, she wrapped her arms around Sapphire's neck and squeezed.

Sapphire clutched the child to her chest. The girl's rapid heartbeat tugged on her own, and soon the beating of her own heart was louder than the wind. Dakota began to sob;

Sapphire clutched the shivering girl to her chest and rocked her. Dakota could have died. They all could die, Sapphire thought, her arms and legs beginning to shake. Thus far, they were still alive, and if she fell apart now, they wouldn't be for long.

Rain splattered across Sapphire's face. Removing her hoodie, she slid it over Dakota. "We need to go now." Overhead, the clouds swallowed the last sliver of starlight, leaving them in darkness. Sapphire turned on her flashlight and searched the area. She spotted a stuffed green turtle on the sand and picked it up. "What's your turtle's name?"

The little girl hugged the stuffed animal to her chest. "Joey."

Joey. Joe. JoJo. She had been this age when her turtle, JoJo, had died. Dad had been there that day when her heart broke, and he understood. She shook her head, trying to chase away the ghosts of the past and stay focused on present dangers.

Lauren's flashlight flickered above the creek. When Sapphire trained her beam up the hill, Lauren's red sweatshirt stood out in the bushes. Sapphire followed the beam of light that was guiding her out of the ravine. She scrambled up the bank, scraped her palm against the rough bark, and rubbed the blood off on her jeans. Trying not to drop Dakota or slide back down into the creek, she grabbed at another branch and clambered up until she reached the top.

Lauren hugged them both and smiled at Dakota. "Baby girl. How are you, baby girl?"

Dakota's wet hair hung about her face. "I'm on an a'venture."

"Well, I think you've had enough adventure for tonight." Lauren said. "Let's go find your mama."

Trying to protect the girl's face from the fat drops of rain, Sapphire shifted Dakota to her right hip.

Lauren hissed, "Why didn't you answer me? You just vanished."

Sapphire hugged Dakota close, trying to warm the child's body with her own.

"You can't just disappear on me like that."

The clouds, dark with heavy tendrils, stretched toward the spot where the creek dropped off the mountain. Sapphire's heart thrashed about her chest. Her legs shook so hard, she didn't know if she could walk.

Then, the storm hit.

Two women, a child, and a baby yet-to-be huddled under the low-hanging branches of a Dogwood Tree and watched sheets of rain convert the trail into mud; the storm raged above their heads. Sapphire had been trapped in storms far worse than this, but each time she had the gear for it and had pitched her tent and gone to sleep until morning or the storm let up.

Sapphire set down Dakota on a carpet of withered ivory petals, yanked her 99 Cent Store rain poncho out of her pack, and gave it to Lauren. "Wrap her up."

"You're soaked." Lauren pulled a plaid wool shirt out of her pack and tossed it to Sapphire.

The plaid was musty and rough, but dry and maybe warmer. She shoved her wet t-shirt in her pack and peered out at the storm, her left eye twitching. Beside her, Lauren worked to untangle Dakota's hair, and the child chattered on about colors and finger paint. If they had been hanging out under a tarp at the Lost Soul's Kitchen listening to a harmonica wail, the rain would be awesome—but out here ... She shuddered at the thought. All three of them were wet and cold. Eventually, hypothermia would set in and they would lose their ability to think clearly. In the end, cold-induced stupidity would kill them.

As if responding to her need for a sign, swatches of stars appeared, and the rain turned into scattered drops rolling off trees—*plop, plop*—voices falling from the sky. *Breathe. Believe. Be Brave.*

Now, they had to get moving, head toward camp, wherever that was. Sapphire whispered, "Thank you, Dogwood." Then, turning toward Lauren, she asked, "Ready?"

Lauren tried to hoist Dakota onto her left hip and groaned, letting the girl slide down her leg.

Dakota giggled and hung from Lauren's arm.

Sapphire grabbed hold of the child and pulled her away from Lauren. "Are you okay?"

Lauren rubbed her lower back with both hands. "I used to hike with a forty-pound pack."

"You weren't pregnant then," Sapphire muttered. "Or exhausted."

Dakota pulled on Sapphire's arm. "Are you going to carry me?"

"That's right, sweetie." Sapphire swung the child onto her right hip and asked Lauren, "Can you walk?"

"Are you going to carry me if I can't?"

"I'll help you," Dakota said.

Lauren smiled. "Thank you, sweet pea."

"We'll take it slow." *A journey of a thousand miles,* Sapphire thought and took a few small steps, struggling to keep her balance on the muddy trail that, with a bit of luck and a bit of skill, just might take them home.

Lauren tottered after them. After only a few minutes, Dakota's head sagged into Sapphire's chest. She pushed the fine strands behind the girl's ears and stroked her cheek. Lauren and Dakota were depending on Sapphire to get them back to camp and she wasn't sure she could do it. It wasn't far, but she was exhausted, Lauren kept stumbling, and Dakota grew heavier with each step.

"Daddy, please find us," Sapphire whispered to herself. "I need you now." She had not been in his arms since she was ten.

⊛ ♥ ⊛ ♥ ⊛ ♥ ⊛ ♥ ⊛ ♥

Sapphire and Lauren labored along the trail, avoiding the muddy patches where the tree cover was thinner. Even without the rain, Sapphire's clothes soaked up raindrops from the bushes she rubbed against in passing. Blasts of wind bent the groaning trees. Fatigued, she searched the terrain for the trees and rocks she had mentally noted on their way out, but nothing seemed familiar.

Lauren groaned. "How much farther do we have to go?"

"I'm not sure."

Ahead of them, the trail curved around the twisted trunk of a pine tree and then six black cottonwoods. Sapphire's feet sprung from the ground in elation. The mental strain melted from her shoulders, and she sighed with heartfelt relief. "We passed these trees on the way out."

"How do you know these were the trees?"

"I counted them. Six in a row. This is the way back."

"I know the gathering is over there," Lauren pointed. "Let's cut through the woods to save time."

"It's safer to go back the way we came."

"I don't know if I can."

Lauren's pallid cheeks drooped, and it was the first time Sapphire had ever seen her mouth down turned. What a mess. Lauren should have stayed behind, kept track of who went where, not plunged into the backcountry. "Strap your pack to mine."

Lauren buckled her pack onto Sapphire's and even though it wasn't much more weight, Sapphire's legs quivered and her right shoulder ached.

Lauren groaned, "My hips feel like they're about ready to pop out of my joints."

Despite the momentary elation of finding the trail back to camp, and exhausted by slogging along the muddy trail, Sapphire searched for something to anchor her. Unsteadily, she sang, "The earth is our mother; we must take care of her." She trudged on, half-singing her feet forward. Left foot, "The sky is." Right foot, "Our fa-ther." A moving meditation, the chant pulling her home. They lumbered on, passing a sugar pine with a huge rock at the bottom of its trunk. Then, the cairn she had built. Recognizing where they were, her voice grew stronger as they approached the tunnel of trees.

Lauren swung the beam of light from side to side, until it revealed a cardboard sign painted in glow-in-the-dark yellow: "To Dinner Circle." She collapsed against a rock, her shoulders dropped, and she wheezed, "At least we know where we are."

"You and Dakota wait here," Sapphire said. "I'll go for help."

Lauren rubbed her belly and took a couple of deep breaths. "I can make it." She stood up and plodded toward Main Meadow.

Sapphire shifted Dakota's limp body to her opposite hip and followed Lauren. Finally, the moldy smell of dying grass embraced them, and she gazed across the empty meadow. Sapphire's legs trembled. Relief overwhelmed her. Dakota could be dead. She could be lost in the woods in a hypothermia-induced stupor. The odds of a successful conclusion had been slim. On the far side of the clearing, the First Aid lantern glowed.

Lauren picked up her pace. "We can take it easy now."

"I'm fine." Sapphire knew how she would paint the three of them, soaking wet coming down the trail. One wet and confused artist, one pregnant warrior, and one magic kid. Coming out of the slate gray squall and living happily ever after. Her seventh-grade art teacher had lectured the class on the importance of placing three objects off-center, so the focal point of the space would be on the edge. Their bodies would be in the right-hand third of the canvas; the wilderness occupying the remaining space on the left. A low horizon line would divide the bottom third of the canvas, where they poised in the meadow, against the chocolate brown trees and purple sky. Three survivors united forever. "Hold up a minute, Lauren."

Lauren paused.

The packs cut into her shoulders, and Sapphire tried to adjust them as best she could.

Lauren stroked Dakota's forehead. "She's so peaceful."

"All kids look like angels," Sapphire said, "when they're sleeping."

Lauren nodded, rubbed her belly, and whispered, "Hi, baby. How are you?"

Sapphire shouted out, "We found her; we found Dakota!" The sound flopped in the deserted meadow.

"Okay, on the count of three," Lauren said. "One, two, three."

In unison they shouted, "We found DA-KO-TA!" Their voices rolled across the meadow toward First Aid. A cheer burst out, and a small pack of bodies bounded toward them.

THE CHILD WITHIN

Thursday, July 5, 1990
(Day Ten of Sapphire's Gathering)

The songs we sing
To our children
Reveal our own fears
And fail to address theirs.
—Karin E. Zirk

LAUREN

Lauren's abdominal spasms had begun on the far side of the meadow, causing her to collapse against a rock. Twinges had darted through her midsection while she lumbered over the dried grasses. If Sapphire had noticed her struggling, she had given no indication, which made her new friend either insensitive or reticent. She had seen evidence of both. The girl was at once annoying and supportive, leaving Lauren in the strange position of dependency and irritation. An intense cramp grabbed her side and she exhaled away from it, pressing her fingertips along the tight skin of her belly in clockwise circles. From the corner of her eye, she observed Kyle and Rich studying her as if she were a laboratory specimen. Kyle was always in the midst of the Peace Patrol movies, telling everyone what to do.

"Lauren!" Kyle said. "What the hell are you doing?"

"Standing here."

"That's not what I mean," he said. "What were you doing out there?"

Frustration filled her chest and exploded. "Airhead mama spaced-out her baby, and someone needed to find that child." They should be angry with Moonchild, not her. The woman was a complete and total flake.

Kyle sputtered, "Cut the crap."

"I wish you would," Lauren said. "Or at least drop it in a latrine where—"

"Guys?" Rich interrupted.

"Since when do I need another middle-aged man dispensing cheap advice?" Lauren blurted.

"Well, at least I've got sense in my noggin," Kyle said.

Sapphire stepped between them. "We're okay. Dakota is safe. Let it be."

Kyle turned toward her. "What the hell did you think you were doing, dragging a pregnant sister into the woods?"

"We didn't go far. Just past the creek and—"

"Shut up," Lauren interrupted.

"Come on," Rich said. "Let's all calm down."

"You're pregnant," Kyle said. "You can't be acting like Daniel Boone."

"My pregnancy is not a public works project."

Kyle tugged on his gray beard and sighed. "That ain't just your baby, you know."

Rich handed her a blanket and she wrapped it around herself, as if in hiding her belly, she would be safe from their judgment.

Moonchild said, "Sister, you need to take it easy."

Bumblebee strode toward them with her rolling gait, close-cropped hair, and dangling silver earrings shimmering against dark brown skin. Lauren breathed a sigh of relief at the appearance of an ally, even one in purple sweatpants and a down parka. Bumblebee usually listened instead of spouting assumptions and proclamations.

When Bumblebee reached them, the first words out of her mouth were, "Y'all stop arguing."

Lauren shut her mouth and turned away from the men, not wanting to be chastised by the older woman.

"Let me see that child and them," Bumblebee said.

Moonchild clutched her daughter but let Bumblebee touch her.

"Dakota, honey, show me your tongue?" Bumblebee trained the flashlight's beam into Dakota's mouth.

Dakota responded by sticking her tongue out.

A jolt of pain shot across Lauren's back and bit into her spine. She moaned and kneaded her lumbar with her fists. The spasms were stronger than they had been yesterday. The harder she tried to escape her pregnancy, the more it inserted its dominance over her life.

Kyle barked at Rich. "Get Doc on the radio. Tell him we got a woman gonna have a baby."

"Calm down," Bumblebee said.

"I'm fine," Lauren muttered. "Just fatigued."

Rich stepped away from her and Kyle followed, haranguing him to call for a doctor on the radio.

"Lauren," Bumblebee asked, "how far along are you?"

"Twenty-two weeks."

"Dakota needs a checkup after being out in those woods," Bumblebee said. "It would please me much to make sure your baby is doing fine, too."

Lauren wished she had handled her pregnancy differently. She should have kept it a secret from River. Had an abortion. It would have been just her again. She could have chained herself to a bulldozer and gone to jail. Now, it was too late, and she was hurtling toward a future she could not fathom. Lauren clenched her shoulders and exhaled. She pressed her fingers against her midsection, softly at first, then with her palms harder. "It's nothing. Just Braxton-Hicks."

"Or preterm labor," Bumblebee said.

"You're having the baby?" Sapphire gasped. "Now?"

"No," Lauren said. "I am not having this baby." No one understood the convoluted ways her life had been transformed into that of "generic pregnant woman," and her survival depended on reminding herself of who she was, deep down, in the core of her cells. She needed to keep being Lauren.

Moonchild asked, "What about my little girl?"

Bumblebee put her hand on Moonchild's arm and told her she knew three excellent doctors at the gathering and not to worry herself.

"I'm going to bed," Lauren said, and lumbered toward the Main Trail. She heard Bumblebee rushing after her, the rustle of nylon against nylon, and paused.

Bumblebee caught up. "I'm worried."

"Well, you're worried. All I need to do is get something to eat and go to bed. I'll be fine in the morning."

"What about your baby?"

"What about me?" Lauren said. "I'm not dead, you know. And last time I looked, this was still my body." But it didn't feel that way to her. She felt like some strange space alien was colonizing her body, and everyone expected her to be excited about the invasion.

Bumblebee pulled a knit cap out of her pocket and put it on Lauren's head.

Lauren tried to find the words that would make Bumblebee understand. She couldn't tell Bumblebee that she wasn't sure she wanted this baby, that she wanted her old life back. "I'm sorry," she said. "I'm tired of everyone telling me what to do."

"I hear you, sister. Them men need to be getting their noses out of women's business."

She nodded.

"Y'all know I don't make anyone do anything they don't want to be doing. All I'm saying is, it wouldn't hurt to make sure you are doing okay."

Lauren cradled her belly in her arms. She struggled to keep from breaking into tears. "I don't know what I want."

Bumblebee wrapped her arms around her, and Lauren felt the older woman's soft abdomen pressing against her own taut one. Then, Bumblebee nodded toward First Aid and started walking. Lauren hesitated for a moment. If she went into preterm labor, she might lose the baby. Depending on the hour of the day, she would accept that as a positive or negative turn of events.

Sapphire stood there looking at her, waiting with that dreamy expression of longing on her face. She was so pretty, nothing but muscles and curves. Damn. Sapphire always wanted something she didn't have, when she had everything.

Overhead, the stars were sparkling reminders that life existed in her womb, as well as on some long dead planet whose light had been traveling since before she was born, to show her an image of what it once was. Not that the stars cared about her. She was just a random speck of dust in a universe that erupted volcanic ash over entire villages and smothered them in molten lava. To the cosmos, she functioned solely as a channel to future generations.

"Are you coming, Lauren?" Rich called out.

She shuffled after Bumblebee. Sapphire trailed two steps behind her like an eager puppy, while Rich and Kyle brought up the rear, arguing about strategy and debating if there had been enough radios for people out on a search and rescue mission. Obviously not, Lauren thought.

Lauren trailed Bumblebee and Moonchild into the large, faded green tent. A Coleman lantern hung from a pole, and Lauren collapsed into a chair. She rubbed her ankles and calves and then, leaning back in the chair, pressed her spine into the canvas and rested her head against the backrest. Her eyes closed. All the energy drained from her body; she felt like a used dishtowel. She half-listened to Moonchild's fearful worries and Bumblebee's calm responses. Lauren wondered what type of Mom she would be—hysterical or grounded. If only River were here to rub her feet. He was never around when she needed him. She had thought she could do this alone, but now she was no longer so sure.

Bumblebee grabbed a jar from the shelf overhead and shook out a few pills into a small bag. "Lauren. You're overdoing it."

Lauren was too tired to respond, so she ignored Bumblebee.

"Are you listening to me?"

The only way to get Bumblebee off her back was to play along. She nodded. "I promise to rest more."

"I know you, girl, and your idea of easy is a ten-mile hike up the mountain."

"I'm hardly doing anything."

"Just being here is work enough for you." Bumblebee handed her the small bag. "Take two before bedtime."

"For what?"

"It will help you and that baby get some rest."

"I'm fine."

Bumblebee shook her head. "You the sorriest looking person I seen all day."

Lauren was tired of being under the spotlight. In the other corner of the tent, Moonchild cradled her sleeping child, stroked her hair, and gazed into her face. Lauren watched her. She looked entranced, probably thought Dakota was a miracle. "Why did you leave her behind?" Lauren asked.

Moonchild lifted her head.

"Dakota. You left her alone."

"She wasn't alone. She was in the tent and I wasn't far."

"She almost died."

"Kids are always one step away from catastrophe. Why, just the other day I heard about a baby that fell out a second story window and landed on a bush." Moonchild smiled. "Babies bounce."

"That's not the point."

"My dear beautiful sister, you will learn."

"I think I already know enough not to let a five-year-old wander around in the woods at night."

Moonchild wiped tears off her cheek. "I'm not perfect, Lauren. I never said I was. I'm doing the best I can. On my own." She snugged the blanket around Dakota. "You'll see."

Bumblebee hugged Moonchild. "Of course, honey. Doing a fine job. Look at the beautiful child. She's tough, alright. And smart."

Moonchild rocked forward and back, humming a lilting tune.

"That child's not going to survive if Moon Mama doesn't get her act together."

Bumblebee said, "And you're not one to talk. You should be taking it easy, not crashing through them woods late at night, or that baby's not going to make it into this world."

"I thought you were on my side."

Bumblebee said, "Now, Lauren. Calm down. Both you and that baby need some rest."

"Don't even tell me what to do." Lauren pushed herself up out of the chair, trying to make a quick exit, but, failing to get the momentum, she sunk back into the chair. "This is my body. My baby." Rocking herself forward, she stood up and pushed out of the tent and headed down the slope toward the Main Trail.

Sapphire chased after her. "Wait."

"Leave me alone." Lauren said.

"What did I do?"

"You had to open your big mouth, and now everyone's butting into my life."

"Your life?" Sapphire grumbled. "I'm the one everyone's mad at for dragging you out into the woods, and it wasn't even my idea."

Rich and Kyle caught up with them. Rich lowered his voice. "Lauren, I'll walk with you to your tent."

"Fuck off, all of you," Lauren hissed. "You don't even get it."

"Yeah, I fucking get it," Kyle said. "I get that you think you have the right to judge Moonchild 'cause you're pregnant." He paused. "Moonchild needs healing. She needs help. Isn't that what we're here for?"

Lauren shook her head. Crossing her arms, she rested them on top of her stomach and planted her feet on the ground. "How many kids do you have, Kyle?"

Sapphire blurted out, "Dakota was found. Why are you all arguing?"

Rich sighed. "Chill out. When you've been to as many gatherings as I have, you'll get used to all the bickering."

Kyle leaned toward Rich and muttered, "Another newbie who thinks she knows it all."

Sapphire shoved her hands in her pockets and looked at the ground.

Lauren saw the look of chagrin on Sapphire's face. People had said she was a clueless newbie when she first came to the gathering, and it had stung. She should tell Rich and Kyle to back off, but part of her was happy to see Sapphire taken down a notch.

Sapphire looked at her as if expecting support. Lauren shrugged her shoulders.

"What's wrong with you all? Standing there like a bunch of angry dogs." Bumblebee walked up with Moonchild and Dakota. She said Dakota would be just fine.

Kyle harrumphed and started to hack. "Moonchild, aren't you going to tell us what happened?"

Lauren sighed. Moonchild was one of those women who held people hostage to her birthing story and enlightened others to the fact that her perineum had not ripped, and now the story of Dakota's disappearance would be added to her arsenal of weapons used to subdue unwilling subjects into extreme boredom.

Moonchild explained that she had been thirsty and wandered over to the campfire near her tent for a cup of tea. The short tea errand stretched into an hour visit with friends, and when she returned to her tent, Dakota had vanished. "I love her. I'd never do anything to hurt her."

"You can hurt someone without meaning to," Lauren said.

"Back off, Lauren," Sapphire said. "It could happen to anyone."

"Quit making excuses."

Kyle muttered, "Life ain't just black and white, Lauren."

"If you think life gives you second chances, you might want to think again." Lauren frowned.

"Enough," Bumblebee interrupted. "One of you men help Moonchild and Dakota back to their tent."

Kyle offered to carry Dakota, and together, he and Moonchild departed for Tepee Circle.

Sapphire glared at Lauren. "What was the point was of upsetting everyone?"

"You were just worried I was going to ruin your happy ending."

"And what's wrong with things working out?"

"You're living in a dream world, Sapphire. You think all your problems will go away when you find your father," Lauren said. "Get over it."

"You don't even know me."

"I know enough." She was weary of Sapphire's clutching onto the past like last year's shoes. She just needed to grow up but could not get it through her thick skull. Lauren sighed. She had only known Sapphire for a few days, and already the emotional drama was grinding her down. They only met because Lauren was supposed to be taking it easy, avoiding heavy lifting or other strenuous activities. Otherwise, she would have been out digging latrines or chopping wood instead of hanging out at INFO. Fed up with everything and wondering where River was, she turned around and headed for the trail back to camp. Rich trailed along beside her without speaking, and she ignored him.

Sapphire shouted after her, "Someday, Dakota will remember the magic of the World Peace and Love Gathering, and she'll spend the rest of her life trying to recreate it."

SYNCHRONICITY SAVES THE DAY

Thursday, July 5, 1990
(Day Ten of Sapphire's Gathering)

We are going to the moon—that is not very far.
Man has so much farther to go within himself.
—Anaïs Nin

SAPPHIRE

The crescent moon hung above the tree line on the ridge, illuminating the deserted meadow, which reeked of molding hay. The meager moon commiserated with Sapphire, or so she imagined. Even the drum circle had disappeared, with the people she had thought were becoming her friends. In pagan lore, the waning moon was the realm of the dark goddess, the one leading toward death. The domain of Kali, the goddess of destruction, whose eyes glowed in Rose Madder and sparked flames at the unwary.

Sapphire heard footsteps behind her and turned.

"Why you still out here?" Bumblebee asked.

Sapphire glanced up at the tip of the moon just now visible through the trees and sighed. "I don't know."

"We're all tired," Bumblebee said. "Things will be better in the morning."

"Define better."

Bumblebee draped her arm across Sapphire's shoulder. "Will you be at Womyn's Healing Space tomorrow?"

Sapphire shrugged.

"I'll be stopping by your camp on my way."

Sapphire groaned as Bumblebee left. In this moment, she would paint herself as an unwanted and rusty spoon lying in a far corner of the yard, under a Blackberry bramble that was holding up the fence, if she had the emotional energy to paint. Lauren was mad at her. Kyle blamed her for endangering Lauren's unborn child. She had met hundreds of middle-aged men who turned out to be random strangers, and each time she failed, a sliver of rusty steel pierced her heart. Existing only in her art, Dad was just as gone as he was two weeks ago, when she found out why he had really disappeared.

Around her, everything was silent. There was nothing left to do now but go to bed. Sapphire shuffled down the trail and into the trees, completely alone. The only signs of life were the endless dome tents nestled under the pines and an occasional scattering of wet clothes hanging from a tree branch. Echoes of drums from Main Meadow floated up the hill. A dog barked in the distance, and the glow of a flashlight or candle in one of the tents silhouetted the inhabitants. She smacked her head on a tree branch and bounced back, colliding with a young guy who had not been there five seconds earlier.

He asked, "Are you okay?"

"I'm fine." He probably thought she was a freak, and she tried to explain her actions. "I was looking for the Tea Kitchen. It's along here somewhere."

The young guy, with short blonde hair, wearing a flannel shirt and carrying something black, kept walking, ignoring her completely.

Embarrassed, she brushed by him, hurried down the trail until it swung up through a stand of pines and into the narrow clearing of the Tea Kitchen. She entered, as if that had been her plan all along. The hiss of Coleman lanterns lit up the night. Weary, she staggered past two people cuddled on a log bench, talking and smoking hand-rolled cigarettes, their tattered backpacks at their feet. They turned to look at her, and she forced a smile at them; then, she stretched her hands toward the mud-and-rock stove to soak up the heat. The dreadlocked Rasta man asked, "Tea, woman?"

"Yes, please," she replied, digging through her daypack until she found her cup.

He dipped a ladle into a gigantic pot and scooped steaming tea into her cup.

Peppermint, the tea of staying home sick in bed and Mom making her tomato soup. "Thanks."

He nodded and slid a few twisted branches into the fire, poking it with a long metal stick.

In spite of all the mistakes she had made that night, she thought they had done the right thing by rescuing Dakota. Made it back to camp. Reunited mother and child. Yet, she felt no pride. She was not any closer to finding Dad, and everyone hated her.

The Rasta man asked, "So how's your gathering?"

If he had asked her this morning, she would have replied, "Magical, amazing. Like arriving at the Emerald City." Instead, she replied, "It could be better."

He grabbed some cut wood from the pile at the back of the kitchen and stuffed it into the fire. "Well, sister. Sometimes you can learn a lesson from the bad. Go with the flow and see where it takes you."

"Things aren't always that easy."

"The more you try to focus on the pot of gold, the less likely you are to make it over the rainbow." He dipped the ladle into the pot and lifted it toward her. "Let's fill it up."

With her cup full, she drifted toward a log and collapsed. Her memories of Dad faded into the background, like unvarnished paints faded into gray. His slate face vague under smoky purple hair. He was fading from her memory, but if she could just find the exact pigments, she could hold on to him. Turquoise and jade and fuchsia seemed so far away, and his image no longer glistened in front of her. Only his eyes matched hers, hazel eyes that gazed back at her in the mirror.

She had no idea what lay in front of her anymore. All she could do was keep her last shred of hope tucked safely in her pocket, beckoning her on, holding her hand until she could find Dad. When she drank the last of her tea, she felt ready to slide into her sleeping bag and conk out until the sun warmed her tent and she could crawl out into sunshine. "Thanks for the tea."

"Goodnight," Rasta man called out behind her, as she wandered out into the late-night silence. The moonlight on the trail guided her.

The bottoms of Sapphire's feet felt bruised and she stepped carefully, trying to avoid rocks and sticks on the path. Exhaustion seeped into her bones. Lost Souls' Kitchen and her tent were on the opposite side of the hill, which was a half-mile or more, following the trail around the hill. Searching for a shortcut, she found a few strands of rainbow-colored ribbon tied to a tree branch and followed the yarn up the hill.

The trail led straight up, and Sapphire felt guilty about taking a shortcut after her speech to Lauren on wilderness safety. But, she rationalized, this was a completely different situation. She figured the worst thing that could happen was she ended up at the wrong kitchen. Hardly dangerous. Halfway up, she lost the trail but kept climbing until the green forest gave way to blackened trunks jutting into the sky. She picked her way through the scattered debris—a morgue of fallen trees, with a few corpses still standing—strikingly beautiful. Remnants of a lightning strike. The highlights and shadows created by the crescent moon depicted nature's chiaroscuros and created what appeared to be a three-dimensional painting. She studied the way the moonlight shaded the burnt wood for some future painting, exploring shades of gray, and wondered how she would capture the moonlight-saturated soil.

Crunch.

The sound rolled across the ridge. She swerved toward it. Caught a flutter of movement. Heard nothing but the click of her eyelids opening and closing. She stared at her burnt surroundings. Searching for an animal or …

She tiptoed through the rubble, kicking up acrid cinders and sneezed. Something rustled. She whirled around hoping to catch a glimpse of a raccoon, but the moonlight revealed nothing. She froze. Then, she heard the rasp of paper against paper. Panicked, she bolted toward the green trees. She tripped and fell into the green-needled boughs. Gasping, she grabbed a limb. The pungent smell of pinesap burned the back of her throat.

Grunts and wheezes in the shadows. A bear? She froze. Held her breath. Glanced to her right. Her left. Swallowed. There he was. She pressed her back against the trunk behind her.

A torn black trench coat hung off his shoulders. "This guy wanted me to go to Bus Village and kill dogs."

Sapphire slunk behind a tree. Peered through the branches. Her legs trembled. Oh boy! Her palms pressed into the trunk and when she finally let go, bark was embedded in her palms. That was the weird guy from the drum circle. "Kill dogs?"

He stumbled toward her. "It freaked me out."

She sidestepped around the tree, keeping the trunk between them, the wood her only protection.

"I wanted to stay with the sister. It was nice with her. They wouldn't let me. They made me leave. I don't like them."

Frozen in place, she listened.

"Then, it got too weird and I wanted to go to sleep." He rubbed his forehead. "Why do people kill dogs?"

"Who kills dogs?"

"This dude in a long red cape. I couldn't see his face, but he had a shovel."

Sapphire glanced around, hoping that someone else had been stupid enough to take the shortcut, but it was just the two of them on the top of the ridge under the dying moon.

He turned around. "I lost her."

"The sister you came here with?" she asked.

"My mother."

Killing dogs. Mother. Red cape. Red dogs. Cape. The words rattled through her brain.

"Why do people kill dogs?" he muttered.

"I don't."

"Mr. Zachary killed all of Brownie's puppies when I was six."

She searched for an escape route. "Were they just born?

"When I was in the hospital, they told me it's bad to kill dogs," he said. "And people too."

She felt ill. *And people too,* she thought, wanting to yell, "Peace Patrol," but no one could possibly hear her.

His long black trench coat swung as he stumbled in circles, kicking up ashes and pine needles.

She had seen him before, somewhere, and his presence had given her a chill even then. She needed to get down the hill to the rest of the gathering.

He grunted, ran toward her, and crashed into the tree. The thud rattled her bones, knocking pollen onto her face. She stumbled backwards and sneezed.

He exploded. Fists in the air. Yelled, "Don't fuck with me!"

She froze. "Did you ever kill anyone?" The words hung in the air. She wanted them back. Her left calf cramped, and she reached for the muscle, rubbed it.

He dropped his arms to his side. "Jesus says turn the other cheek."

A beam of moonglow shone on his face, and she could see the drool beaded up in the corner of his mouth and dripping down his chin. She inched away. Her left calf crumpling under her. Trying to be silent. Right foot on the ground. Felt the branch too late. It snapped. *Crack!*

He spun around. "Where are you going?"

She stopped. Pictured her lifeless body tossed in the burnt debris. "You can't see it from here, but if we go down this hill, there's a fire and we'll be warm." She headed into the living woods. Turned left past one tree. Turned right past another, pine needles crackling under her feet.

He trailed behind her with thuds, thumps, and the air groaning in and out of his lungs. He couldn't have been more than nineteen or twenty, and even at this elevation, he was too young to be huffing heading downhill.

"That's what the guy tried to do. He tried to make me go with him. I don't want to kill dogs," he said.

She choked for just a minute: no one would find her. Dad would never know it wasn't her fault that he had been exiled. Mom's last memory of her would be that last hateful day when they fought over Dad. Lauren would never know what became of her. Maybe in death, her paintings would suddenly be deemed the brilliant beginnings of a star that burnt out too young.

The crazy kid tailgated, and she could smell the dried sweat on his clothes. Stale beer and something else that was rank. Dog shit. He must have stepped in dog shit.

"Are we almost to the fire?" he asked, his voice friendly, like they had just been out hiking and he was tired.

She stopped, listened. Hoping to hear a voice instead of his labored breathing. A faint rhythm, soft, echoed up the hill. Drums. People. People and drums had to be around a fire. "We're almost there," she said. "Do you hear the drums?"

He shook his head.

Traces of wood smoke drifted up the hill. The *bong, boom, bang* of the drums in the distance calling the faithful to Sunday worship. "Don't you want to sit by a fire?"

"They won't like me," he said. "Nobody likes me."

That's exactly how she felt, but she'd much rather be lonely with other people around than alone with him in the woods. She hurtled down the hill, slapping her feet against the ground, her pack bouncing on her back. A moment later, she spotted the faint glow of the fire. She stopped to catch her breath and pointed at it.

"I don't wanna go there."

"You know what I want to do?"

He shook his head.

"I want to roast marshmallows."

"I love marshmallows," he said.

She pointed. "See that campfire."

He nodded.

"I'm going to walk down there and roast marshmallows."

"My mom used to let me roast them on the stove."

"I like sitting around an open fire."

He scratched his head.

She started walking and he followed. "What's your name?"

"Mole."

"I'm Sapphire." They approached the small fire with a few people huddled around it, stretching their fingers and toes toward the heat. A sister and an older man played a meandering rhythm on their djembes. A dark-haired man lazily toked on a joint.

"Hey, sister."

"Come warm yourself by these kind flames."

Should she tell them that Mole was crazy high and he almost killed her, and she was scared because she didn't know what to do, and somehow they ended up here, and she still didn't know what to do with him? Instead, she said, "We've come to roast marshmallows."

"Awesome."

Mole tromped around the fire.

The dark-haired man held out a joint.

She shook her head and squatted down beside him. "I just met this brother on the trail. I think he tripped too hard."

The man nodded, and it seemed to Sapphire that he was experienced in these matters. "Hey, brother, have a seat."

Mole said, "I want a marshmallow."

A longhaired brother said, "Sounds awesome, bro. Anyone holding?"

This was the moment of reckoning. There wouldn't be any marshmallows and Mole would flip out; but at least now, there were five other people to help.

Mole paced around the fire, swinging his arms violently from front to back. "Marshmallows. You promised me." He stopped next to Sapphire and peered down at her. "Where are they," he yelled.

The kind brothers at the fire sat up from their sleepy conversations.

The male drummer switched his rhythm and called out, "Fanga alafia."

The sister responded, "Ashe, ashe."

The men joined in, "A-she, a-she."

Sapphire took a deep breath and exhaled, channeling energy the way her dad had taught her all those years ago, in that world then struggling to emerge. *Marshmallows, come home to us. Snowy white pillows, we need you here to bring peace.* Her dad reflected in the fire, legs crossed, Om-ing the cops away. She closed her eyes and opened them again. This time, she saw crimson, ultramarine, and lemon sparks dancing, and Mole pacing. Following her breath, she inhaled and exhaled, letting all thoughts disappear from her mind, except the image of marshmallows. *Marsh* (inhale), *mallow* (exhale), *marsh* (inhale).

The drums thumped out the call, "Ikabo alafia," and she joined in the response, "Ashe, ashe."

A voice called out, "Hey, folks, anyone want marshmallows?"

Everyone at the fire grew silent.

Sapphire opened her eyes and beheld a grizzled old man hobbling along on a walking stick and swinging a bag of marshmallows in his left hand.

When he reached the fire, he held up the bag. "They're not vegan."

Sapphire doubled over in laughter and wasn't sure Mole even knew what "vegan" meant, but the irony wasn't lost on her. She didn't ask the universe for vegan. The others stared at her. When she tried to explain her delirious state, she choked on her laughter and knew they had no idea what was so amazingly funny.

Mole grabbed the bag out of the old man's hand. "I love marshmallows." He clutched the bag to his chest as if it were his beloved teddy bear.

Finally catching her breath, Sapphire peeled a sliver off a skinny stick. "Mole. Can I have the bag?" She ripped it open, grabbed three marshmallows, and pushed them on the wood. Handing the stick to Mole, she said, "Why don't you sit down."

"I love roasting marshmallows." He kneeled and held the stick with both hands, the end dangling over the flames, where they browned and billowed quickly. Pulling a marshmallow off the stick, he popped it in his mouth, the melted sugar sticking to his lips and cheek. He seemed to relax, licked his fingers, and rubbed them against his jeans.

Sapphire ate one cold and then passed the bag around the circle, and soon, everyone was roasting. She leaned against a log surrounding the fire. The joint made its way around the circle again, and this time she took a hit. The sporadic talk wandered from the journey home to the Mayan calendar. She drifted in and out of the conversation, watching Mole, half-waiting for an explosion, but he seemed calm now. She giggled at the thought of vegan marshmallows. The scene at the top of the ridge had made her think of B-rated horror flicks and young women murdered in the midst of escaping—always when the audience thought they had made a clean getaway. Around the fire, Mole was more like a puppy that had been kicked too many times than a killer. From time to time, he made a comment and the other brothers laughed.

She took another hit off the joint and passed it to her left. Listening to the voices and the crackling of the fire, she watched the firelight dancing on the nearby trees. Her body warmed up, muscles melting, her fear dissolving. She began to nod off. Jerking herself awake, she realized everyone was half-asleep or stoned. The sky began to lighten, but the moon held its ground. "Is it okay if Mole stays with you? I'm exhausted."

"Sure."

"No problem."

Sapphire nodded. "Then, I'm going to bed." Standing up, she tried to get her bearings. "Where's Main Trail?"

The older brother pointed. "Just past those aspens. INFO is to the right, Krishna Kamp on the left."

Her camp was near INFO. Dragging her worn legs down the trail, she felt satisfied. She had handled the situation the way Garth would have. Tomorrow, she would find him and tell him the tale of Mole and the magical appearance of marshmallows, at the juncture between her hyperactive imagination and the serenity of the campfire. Now, she had her own gathering story to tell.

LESSONS ON METTĀ

Friday, July 6, 1990
(Day Eleven of Sapphire's Gathering)

The universe speaks to us in moments of gentle
stillness. Only then, can we be fully conscious of
the hearts in our midst.
—12th century yogi

SAPPHIRE

*At Dinner Circle, a tuxedo-clad waiter served her goat cheese
pizza and raspberry iced tea, while people faded in and out of the
pink-tinted fog pouring out of a metal barrel. Lauren and River
rambled on about Ferndale's refusal to grant a permit for the
march to North Coast Lumber. A clean-shaven man took shape
in the mist, his heavyset body filling out slowly like a blow-up
toy. He wore beige canvas pants and a plaid flannel shirt, and
there was something about his eyes that seemed familiar. Lauren
held up a sign reading, "Lost Fathers Court," and River practiced
Lamaze breathing: pant, pant, exhale.*

*The man squatted down next to her. "Is your name
Sapphire?" He ruffled the bristle-brush hairs on his head, fluffing
them up. "Sapphire Larson?" He handed her a business card:
John Larson ~Actor .. Prophet .. Lost Soul ~*

*Intense joy bubbled through Sapphire's veins, permeating her
body with a sense of lightness, and she floated effortlessly towards
a rainbow-colored sunset. She grinned so hard, even her ears were
smiling.*

"Hey, does anyone have any TP?"

After all this time, Dad was asking her for toilet paper, and it made no sense. Lauren disappeared, and Sapphire peered into the pink fog, looking for her father or the waiter. Gradually, her eyes started to open, and the pink fog transformed into sunlight shining through the red nylon of her tent.

"Here you go, bro. Just bring it back when you're done."

Sapphire looked around, hoping the part about Dad was real, but she was alone in her tent.

Outside, her neighbors engaged in their typical morning conversations: "What's for breakfast," "What'd you do last night," and "What are you doing today." The responses generally ranged from pancakes, drumming, and pizza, to poetry reading or barter circle, in no particular order. Normally, waking up to their morning conversations made her feel part of their family; today, she wanted them to be quiet so she could fall back asleep and re-enter the dream where Dad's eyes sparkled.

When that failed, she imagined a dream, complete with pink fog. She said, "Hi," to Dad, and before she had the opportunity to say much more, he pulled her toward his chest, wrapped his arms around her, and hugged her so tight, her face smashed into the buttons on his shirt and she could hardly breathe. She choked on the aroma of patchouli and clove cigarettes. After a few moments, he rocked her from side to side, and she felt the tickles of his tears on her cheek. She couldn't envision what happened next. Maybe nothing would change after she found Dad. Or she would start spending Thanksgiving at his house and Christmas with Mom, like Latisha did.

By the time they had been in high school, Latisha was on her second stepdad. He was a really nice guy and took them ice-skating and to the horse show and Latisha liked him, sort of, but Sapphire wanted someone who would be there forever, or at least that's the way she imagined fathers were supposed to be.

She had no idea what Dad had wanted. At her age, Dad had been an actor, a husband, and a father with dreams for a future starting to unfold, and he must have been hoping to pass it forward to his progeny, like a gift from the City of Angels. She had done nothing with her life but create a basement full of paintings no one wanted and dream about the life she could have had—if only. No wonder he wasn't in her life.

She perched in the doorway of her tent, hoping for a breeze. On the slope below her, the tiny ivory wildflowers, which had looked wilted yesterday morning, seemed to have sprung back from last night's rain.

"Howdy, neighbor."

She smiled at Mikey.

"You missed a kick-ass party last night. We baked brownies and a couple of dudes threw down some killer twelve-bar blues." He picked food out of the bowl he was carrying and laughed. "Those brownies were strong."

She sniffed the garlic and fried potatoes he was eating, wishing she knew Mikey better so she could ask him to share.

"So, what did you do last night?" he asked.

"Lauren and I went to the drum circle. Then, we ended up on this totally insane search for a lost kid."

"Yeah. We heard about that. We looked around for a while but didn't turn up anyone."

They had only been in the woods for a couple of hours, not long really, but last night had been an eternity. "Yeah. We found her. About a mile down the river." Treacherous. Out there, it had been just the two of them, and Lauren had been fearless. She admired that about Lauren, the way she seemed to jump feet-first into every situation, while Sapphire hung out in the background trying to make everyone happy.

"No shit. Hey, did that rain get you?"

She nodded. Even now, her bones felt weary.

His mouth full of home fries, he mumbled, "I left a window open on my tent. Soaked a bunch of clothes."

"Bummer." She was glad she'd left everything zipped up and her gear in the center of her tent. "Where did you get the potatoes?"

"Our kitchen."

"Are they still serving?"

He nodded. "Hey, thanks for your help last night. I'm really glad the kid was found."

Wouldn't have been found, if it were up to her. Sapphire grabbed her wooden bowl and stood up. "I'm starved," she said and stepped gingerly on the bark- and twig-covered ground with her bare feet. She headed toward the kitchen, where the sweet smell of fried onions and garlic mixed with the earthen smell of the potatoes. Her stomach growled. Food went fast around here and if she didn't hustle, she would miss out. She joined the line of eager people hovering around the kitchen with their bowls. There might even be ketchup.

"Well, if it ain't Sapphire."

She knew Garth's voice anywhere. "Hey."

He bulled his way through the crowd of hungry hippies that swarmed between them. "What are you up to this morning?"

"Trying to fill my belly."

The sun shone through the trees and the air was warm and dry. In the kitchen on her left, the cooks sweated around the fire, while they flipped potatoes with giant spatulas. Grizzly Bear Garth, oblivious to the heat, wore a heavy denim jacket and cowboy boots.

"Did I ever tell you about the guy we yanked out of the creek?"

The line inched toward the cookie sheet heaped with home fries, and the sweet smell of braised onions made Sapphire's mouth water. She shook her head and stepped forward, right eye twitching. She knew if her dad was here and she didn't start asking for help, she was never going to find him. "Remember when I told you I was looking for someone?"

"Yeah. The night you arrived." Garth looked around. "You know, the road into this gathering is just as crazy as the road into Colorado in '83."

Suffocated by the cheerful voices chattering on about mundane issues, she tried to tune everyone out, to tell Garth the truth about her life as a fatherless child. A truth she had never told anyone. "You probably don't remember that I'm looking for my dad. What I didn't share was that I don't know if he's here. I haven't seen him since I was ten..." There, she had said it. Aloud. She'd told Garth, who knew everyone, why she was here, and now he could help her find Dad. Maybe saying it aloud was an accomplishment, after spending fifteen years hiding Dad's absence in her life from everyone she knew. She wasn't ready to confess how many lies she had made up about her Dad.

"It was raining cats and dogs, and me and Vince were sitting up at Main Gate drinking coffee. Weren't no cars coming in." Garth stepped out of line and lowered himself onto the log. He pushed his gray, felt cowboy hat back on his head and rubbed his forehead. "I started to get real worried."

Garth couldn't care less about her; he just wanted an audience. The food line swung away from the log, giving Garth room to stretch out his legs and lean back against the stump of a branch, and Sapphire was left standing next to him. She could see the potatoes on the counter and was so hungry she felt her stomach pushing against itself. Hoping the food would hold out for another fifteen minutes, and wanting to find out if he knew Dad, she sat down next to Garth and placed her bowl on the log. "I haven't found him yet."

"Are you sure he's here?"

"No," she whispered. "But I was hoping."

"Got a picture?"

"In my tent."

"We'll get it in a bit."

She wanted to tell him everything about Dad and Mom. About Mary Moss and Zach and her fears about never being good enough at anything. She wanted to confess it all, and she wasn't even Catholic.

"My gut was telling me there were people stranded on the road, so we borrowed this guy's jeep without asking permission." Garth burst into a deep-rolling man-laugh that drew the attention of the cooks and the half-naked people loitering in the sun. "Man, was he pissed when we returned it—seats soaking wet, and everything covered in mud and blood."

Legends about the mighty Grizzly Bear Garth echoed the tales of the Lone Ranger. Grandiose tales of hunting down criminals in snowstorms and rescuing small children from the jaws of vicious dogs. Outlandish stories were recited around campfires, and when she asked for details, there were none, as if the legends were made of celluloid not human flesh. Even so, if anyone could help her, it was Garth.

His brown beard glistened with silver in the sunlight, and he pulled the gnarly hairs down, stroked them. "It was four-wheel-drive all the way, and even then the tires spinning, going up the hill, and when we popped over the crest of the ridge, the damn thing fishtailed so bad I thought we was going off the cliff."

"Were you scared?"

"You think a little rain and mud is going to scare me, little sister?"

Little sister. And Sapphire didn't feel quite so alone.

"So, we drove real slow. Kept stopping and turning off the engine."

"What were you looking for?" Sapphire said, trying to be the person he thought she was.

"That's the thing. I had no idea. Just had a hunch something wasn't right. But Vince says he sees a light."

"A light?"

"Yeah. An orange light down in the creek. So, we get out the rope we brought, tied one end to the winch and the other around my chest."

His performance an echo of her father's, his arms conjured up the images that accompanied his words. Others started to gather around. A couple of young guys with dreadlocks stood a few feet away, arms crossed, listening intently. An older woman wandered up and sat down a few feet away on the log. An old man shuffled toward them and wheezed out, "Hey, Grizzly Bear." A bunch of guys her own age sat cross-legged in the dirt, studying his every move.

Garth's voice swelled. "I tried to take it real slow, but there was so much mud coming off the road, I slid down a ways, and then I could see the overturned car in the creek." Garth took a pack of Marlboros out of his pocket, tapped the pack on the palm of his hand, and pulled out a cigarette. He lit it and inhaled slowly. The smoke plumed from his nostrils and he checked out the scene.

Sapphire could picture the night. A night of rain and mud and not knowing where they were going.

Garth leaned toward her. "The driver was suspended upside-down by his seatbelt. Windows cracked and water rushing through the car."

Someone called out, "Was the guy dead?"

Sapphire held her breath.

"Grizzly Bear Garth!"

Kyle stalked up the trail. "We've been trying to reach you on the radio for the last twenty minutes."

The smile disappeared from Garth's face, and his growl returned. "What's up?"

"The Forest Service Commander is at the Main Gate, demanding to talk to you."

Garth pulled his radio out of his vest pocket, turned it on, and bellowed, "Grizzly Bear to Main Gate. Grizzly Bear to Main Gate, come on back." He held the radio to his ear.

The device crackled. "This is Main Gate."

Sapphire grabbed her bowl and stood up, straining to decipher the transmission, but she couldn't understand a word.

"I'm on my way. Give me thirty minutes." Garth turned to Kyle. "Go to INFO and find Cowboy Ken and send him up."

Kyle lifted his radio to his mouth.

"No," Garth bellowed. "Stay off the air. The Forest Service could be listening."

Kyle nodded and headed down the hill. Garth marched after him. Sapphire followed.

"Can I help?" she asked, jogging to keep up with Garth.

He glanced at her and kept going. "It's no big thing. Ken's a lawyer so I need him there." He pulled the brim of his hat down over his eyes. "I'll catch ya later."

"What happened to the guy in the car?" she asked, not wanting to hear that he died.

"He ain't going nowhere. Remind me later." Garth marched down the trail, took the turn to the left, and disappeared behind the trees.

Sapphire threw her bowl against a pine. It bounced off and rolled down the hill for a bit, before it hit a rock and stopped, covered in dirt, with no place to go from there. Good, it could sit there for all she cared. Garth wasn't the sort of person Dad would hang out with anyway. If her needs were so inconsequential that he didn't have time to help her, she would work things out on her own like she always did, with the same pathetic results.

At the kitchen, a voice called out from behind the counter, "Hey folks, we'll have oatmeal in an hour." The kitchen crew, backs to the serving counter, scraped pots into compost buckets.

Sapphire collapsed on the log. It was her own damn fault she had missed breakfast to hear Garth's story. Of course, she was to blame.

In front of her, an older man said to his companion, "Shall we wait, or do you want to try to find food at one of the other kitchens?"

The woman replied, "The same thing will probably happen. I don't know why the kitchens don't plan their meals better. This is ridiculous; this is the third kitchen we've been to."

Sapphire blurted out, "If you're so concerned about getting fed, why don't you go to a restaurant? No one's in charge here. Do you know who pays for all this food?" She paused for a moment and then launched into them. "The kitchen crew. They worked for two months to buy food to feed people. What did you contribute?"

The woman started to open her mouth, but the man put his hand on her arm. "Sister, we know that all the food is created by love. Don't take out your hurt on others."

"You know nothing about me," Sapphire snapped before she stomped off. Forget this. She was sick of people who knew what she was feeling, when she wasn't even sure herself. She retreated to her tent and collapsed in front of the screen door flap. Every time she turned around, some do-good cosmic healer was telling her how to feel.

She struggled to open her tent and a piece of the nylon flap stuck in the zipper; her arms trembling, she yanked at it until it finally wrenched open. Groping around, she pulled everything out of her big pack, tossing it on the floor of the tent, threw the shiny metallic wrappers of already-eaten chocolate in the corner. She shook out her shorts and, finally, at the bottom of her tote found a small bag of shelled sunflower seeds. Ripping off the top, she poured half the bag into her mouth, chomping the food and swallowing. She swore she could feel the kernels bounce when they hit her stomach.

For a few minutes, Sapphire hunkered down half-inside and half-outside her tent, not sure what to do next, half-hoping for the kitchen to call out, "Oatmeal." She pulled out her sketchpad and grabbed a piece of charcoal from her pencil box. Quickly, she sketched a witch on her broomstick, her long cape wings floating around her. Her pointed hat tilted sideways, and her long hair streamed across her face. Mouth open, teeth bared, she screamed curses in a dialog bubble that melted into stars. Sapphire shook her head at the drawing. Melodramatic at best. At worst, a stereotype. She ripped the sketch off the pad and tossed it aside. She tried to take some deep breaths but couldn't get her breath out of her chest.

On the path below, travelers journeyed with friends. Two women, walking arm in arm, laughed; one in a long skirt and topless, the other in jeans and a t-shirt. Two guys carried a stretcher loaded with sacks of something, while a third guy walked alongside, helping to balance the load. From the opposite direction, she saw a man and a woman holding hands, dressed in tie-dyed clothes from head to foot.

She drew the couple linked together, arms crisscrossing between bodies, with hair that grew from two heads to one mane. She penciled in a tall man with a little girl on his shoulders, even though she didn't see any such thing. The people she tried to capture on paper disappeared before she had more than a faint sketch. Quickly, she drew a woman, who appeared to be singing, with two kids walking hand-in-hand. Sapphire caught the faint threads of a song up the hill that carried echoes of her childhood, so she added music notes about their shoulders.

Below her on the trail, the mystical gypsy ladies with bells on their feet jangled down the trail, so confident and beautiful in their macramé and sequined tops, their hula-hoop hips swiveling. She had never felt that womanly or sexy in her life.

A middle-aged couple with daypacks, in matching shorts and sandals, could have been bird watching. Big olive-green canvas hats. She assumed the shorter one was the wife. Is this how her parents would have been in another fifteen years, if they had stayed together? Looking alike, dressing alike? She worried about how drab she would be at that age, if she was already this boring.

Everyone else had begged through India, hitchhiked through the Amazonian rain forests, and been arrested for civil disobedience, but she had stayed home painting and perfecting her technique. She lingered in galleries and gazed at other people's art, other people's lives, other people's creations. But living—that's what she had done with Dad. Living was messy and unpredictable.

Nine days of searching in this chaos, and still she hadn't found him or even anyone that knew him. Maybe Uncle Paul was confused. If he wasn't here, she had no idea were to even look for him. She drew a couple: one in a wheelchair being pushed by the other. Life was messy; she drew a child stepping in a pile of dog poop and holding his foot up.

Both Mom and Dad were striving to create a better world, but Mom organized charity events for battered women's shelters, while dad took the people off the streets and installed them in the living room. Sapphire had no idea where that left her. Playing it safe hadn't filled the emptiness inside her, and now, she was out here floundering in deep water, and that wasn't working so well either.

She drew herself on the trail, Dadaist style, the left half of her body ten feet in front of the right half. The left half of her was in a batik sarong with bare feet, her chest covered in African trade beads and hair wrapped in a scarf. The right half was on crutches, wearing jeans and a t-shirt. The lines on the first image loose and almost not there, mere suggestions. The lines on the second one stiff, cautious, clearly showing the knuckles on her right hand, her shoe laces, and the tongue of the boot sticking up just a bit. The rubber tip of her crutch.

"Hi, Sapphire."

She glanced up. "Hi."

Bumblebee tossed her bag on the ground, gathered her long blue skirt in her hands, pulling the fullness in front of her, and smiled as she sat down on the log next to the tent. "I went to see Moonchild and Dakota this morning, and Dakota was running around pretending to be an airplane."

Sapphire wished she had dropped Dakota off at First Aid and then gone straight to bed. She didn't want to remember any of it. Not Lauren, not Mole. Not even the Tea Kitchen, where she always felt idiotic.

Bumblebee asked, "Do you want to go to Womyn's Space for the circle?"

"I don't feel like it." For sure, Dad would not be at Womyn's Space.

Bumblebee took the paisley scarf off her head and ran her hand over her close-cropped hair. "My first gathering was five years ago in Vermont."

Sapphire wanted to roll her eyes. She had heard too many stories of first gatherings—all Bible-thumping to her. She was tired of having everyone else's lives shoved down her throat. She wished they would all just leave her alone to find her own way.

"I'd just left my husband. I was living in Florida and didn't bring warm clothes or decent shoes. Three days of solid rain." Bumblebee laughed. "I was cold, and my feet had blisters from walking around in sopping wet tennis shoes. Every day, I complained about being cold and wet. On the fourth day, I spent the morning digging a pooper in the rain, and a brother gave me a pair of hiking boots and a yellow rain poncho. Then, that evening I was sitting around a campfire singing, and a sister gave me a pair of heavy wool socks."

Sapphire watched a spider crawl up the log. It tumbled backwards until it caught the strand of the web it was spinning. It climbed up the web and fell again.

"The point I'm trying to make is that this is a hard family. But we are a forgiving family, and if you stick with us, this family will teach you more about yourself than you thought possible."

Sapphire smirked. More sage advice from the wise old elders. The spider reached the summit and scurried across the log, leaving her wondering if it was succeeding or escaping.

Bumblebee wrapped the scarf around her head and pulled two apples out of her bag and offered her one. "Hungry?"

Sapphire salivated and took the battered apple. "Thanks." Avoiding the bad spot, she bit into the juicy apple.

"I always keep a stash of apples in my tent. It's important to share, but keeping yourself nourished matters just as much."

"I made the mistake of sharing my granola bars with everyone. Seems like I hiked in ten pounds of them and ended up eating three."

Bumblebee smiled. "First gathering crushes."

Sapphire savored every bit of the apple. "Boyfriends are like that. When you first fall in love, he is always so perfect, good looking, intelligent, sexy, but then after you've fought over cleaning the kitchen or how to celebrate Christmas, he starts looking tarnished."

"A relationship is a relationship. Only here, you inherit a bunch of crazy-ass relatives all at once." Bumblebee stood up. "If we're going to make the circle, we best get started. You coming?"

Happy to have someone else take charge of her life for a little while, Sapphire stood up. "Let me grab my stuff." She followed Bumblebee down the hill and onto the Main Trail. They turned east, toward the far reaches of the gathering, walking in silence.

A pack of teenagers on the side of the trail yelled, "Weeeee looooove youuuuuu," to the sky. Sapphire smiled at Bumblebee. They clasped hands and sang back, "We love you too!" The sky overhead was steel blue, and every individual Sapphire passed had a smile to share. Bumblebee hummed as she sauntered along. They turned left at the fallen pine and crossed over to the north side of the meadow, where Sapphire heard angry voices rumbling up through the grove of trees to their right.

As they climbed higher on the ridge, she could see the crowd in the clearing ahead, and the clamor dissolved into distinct cries. "No guns in the church!" "Walk in peace." "Six up!" About fifty people flanked the men in green uniforms, who marched along the tree line in a tight bunch, looking straight ahead and seemingly oblivious to the screaming, angry people. A man in an apricot robe dashed in front of the procession, dropped to his knees, and pressed his hands together.

Bumblebee shook her head at the spectacle. "You'd think they'd just give up, accept the fact that we gather, we cook, we drum, we pray, we clean up, and we go home. I never can figure out what is such a big deal that they have to recruit every available law enforcement officer to baby-sit a bunch of pot-smoking hippies."

Sapphire laughed. The Krishnas in their apricot robes chanted, "Krishna, Krishna Hare Hare, Hare Rama." They trailed behind, mourners following the casket of their leader, but instead of a military drumbeat, they danced to their accordions and cymbals—trying to infuse Krishna consciousness into Forest Service cops.

Sapphire spotted Grizzly Bear Garth walking alongside the cops.

She said, "Should we help?"

"And do what?" Bumblebee replied. "Besides, they do this every year, at least twice, and everyone yells and screams, and the Forest Service still keeps walking through, and we keep gathering."

Sapphire turned to Bumblebee. "Then, why do they do it?"

"Politics. If they didn't march through here like they owned the land, then they would think we'd have won, and their egos be way too big for that."

"I think they need some peaceful people down there. We can always go to Womyn's Healing Space afterwards."

Bumblebee stopped. "Girl, you still ain't figured out that one simple task turns into an endless movie. If we get ourselves involved, we'll be lucky if we make it back in time for Dinner Circle."

"Maybe that's where we're needed."

"You a direct action junkie?"

She shrugged her shoulders, afraid that if she didn't start taking risks now, there was no hope for her.

Bumblebee said, "Direct action isn't always the best solution. Sometimes, creating peaceful vibes changes reality."

Sapphire heard the echo of her father in Bumblebee's words. *How can we create peace, if we can't feel peace in our hearts? Brothers and sisters, it all starts with what's in our hearts.*

Bumblebee put her arm around Sapphire's shoulder. "I know you had a rough night. Perhaps the sisters will help you put it in perspective."

Sapphire glanced back at the Forest Service and then took the trail to the left, toward Womyn's Healing Space and her sisters.

Bumblebee sang, "We are the daughters of the moon, we are the sisters of the sun...."

FINDING THE INNER GODDESS

Friday, July 6, 1990
(Day Eleven of Sapphire's Gathering)

And you, O Blessed Goddess, a smile on your
immortal face, asked what had happened
this time, why did I call again, and what did I
especially desire for myself in my frenzied heart.
—Sappho, "Hymn to Aphrodite"

SAPPHIRE

Sapphire and Bumblebee left the sun-strewn ridge and the yelling behind them, as they dropped into Goddess Glade. The trail twisted between the fluttering silver-green of the aspen trees and the powder-blue columbine, dancing in front of granite boulders. It was cool here. A circle of women in multi-colored skirts held hands in a small glen overlooking the creek. Bumblebee headed toward them.

Lauren, her brown dreadlocks cascading down the back of her vermilion shirt, stood next to a short-haired girl in cutoffs. Sapphire wobbled, not ready to see Lauren after their fight last night. She should have kept her mouth shut instead of letting herself be dragged into arguments with people she barely knew. Now, she needed to apologize, or at the very least acknowledge her harsh words; that is, if Lauren was even speaking to her anymore. Friendship no longer seemed possible.

Bumblebee said, "Aren't you coming?"

Sapphire wished she could stay planted in the soil like the trees surrounding her, their pale linen bark growing out of the ground with endless patience. A hawk circled over the little valley, its flight path shifting north with each revolution, until it disappeared over the dark green ridge and left her there alone to face her demons.

"I'm coming."

When they reached the other women, Sapphire slid off her pack and dropped it on the ground. She stepped toward the circle and stopped behind a woman with long gray hair, who was holding hands with a redhead. Gently, she placed her hands on theirs, and they opened up and drew her into the circle. She inhaled slowly, taking the Om deep into her lungs, her chest expanding until she was dizzy with oxygen. She exhaled from her belly and felt the breath vibrating in her throat, as she joined the other women in Om-ing.

The earth moaned through her legs and up into her stomach, and then her heart and lungs; the vibration ran off her lips and mingled with the sound of the universe. The reverberation floating into the air after the hawk. The creek, the trees, and the wind sang out to her in language she no longer understood, even as she remembered that as a child, she could hear the earth singing in her chest. The blessing complete, one by one the voices dropped off, until the brook chattered solo from behind the granite boulders. Sapphire inhaled deeply, and the crisp, fresh air rose up from the running water to soothe her nostrils, laden with dirt and wood smoke. She opened her eyes.

The circle was a painter's pallet: magenta, Prussian blue, and malachite green. Scarlet and golden ocher mingled and melted into each other on the canvas. A woman with short blonde hair stood across from her. She looked amazingly neat in her clean, white shirt and spotless hiking boots. Next to her, a Japanese-American woman whose dreads, more rats' nest than cords, cascaded down her naked chest. Toward the creek, a teenager in ropes of necklaces and bangles and a purple skirt with a peace symbol made of sequins. And then a woman with clear skin and freckles, wearing a tan Sierra Club t-shirt and blue jeans. A convergence of dreams and desires and possibilities. Dried mud decorated a few of her sisters, as if they had wallowed in the nearest puddle for pure pleasure. Sapphire admired their joyous spirit.

One dry hand she cradled was warm, dark from soil and sun; the other, a cool mottled beige hand with cords of twisted blue veins. The woman turned her head and smiled, her green eyes just visible within folds of flesh. Sapphire gave the worn hand a gentle squeeze.

A voice began to sing, "We are an ancient people; we are a modern people."

Lauren's strong deep voice echoed off the rocks. "We are the same people, loving all the time."

Other women joined in. "We honor you, empower you, live from your heart." The refrain thundered through the miniature valley. "We honor you, empower you, live from your heart."

Sapphire joined in. "We are an ancient people; we are a modern people. We are the same people, loving all the time."

Inside the circle, a couple of toddlers stopped laughing and gazed around, as if they had suddenly noticed the presence of the adults. Their eyes were full moons, their bodies still and quiet. A little girl in purple pants pranced along the edge of the circle. Her chest was bare in the midday sun. Sapphire's mind caught an image of herself dressed in harem pants, dancing with Daddy, when she was the most important person in the entire world. She couldn't remember if it had ever really happened. The child started to twirl with her head cocked to one side and her arms outstretched, spinning faster and faster, until she collapsed on the grass, giggling. Manzanita stepped toward the children in the center of the circle, and the kids ran toward her, and they hugged.

Two evenings ago, Dinner Circle had been winding down, and the Piggy Bank Council had been at wits' end trying to decide which function should receive their desperately needed supplies, and who had to do without. Food versus medical supplies. Manzanita had walked into the argument, sat everyone in a circle, and asked them to write out what they needed to get through the next two days. When the totals came up a thousand dollars short, she organized a crew of musicians and dancers to do a Piggy Bank Parade through the gathering—sending them into every camp, to every fire, to every group of Krishna chanters—to sing a song about feeding the pregnant women and nursing mothers. Sapphire had heard they collected almost two thousand dollars.

Now, Manzanita worked her spell on this group of women who, in another place and time, would never have met each other, let alone be about to reveal their most intimate thoughts and memories.

A little girl pointed to the dragon on Manzanita's t-shirt, and two toddlers hid behind her skirts and ever so briefly peaked up at it. They stood in the center—three at the beginning of their lives, one at the end—until the circle grew silent. The old woman pointed to her pack, and the girl ran over and brought back a stick adorned in beads and feathers.

Manzanita turned to the east. Grasping the stick, she raised her hands to the sky. "To all my relations in the East, the sun rising and the grass growing in the spring, thank you for giving us this day." She gave blessings to the South for ripe fruit, the West for peace, and the North for rain, before handing the stick back to the girl, who set it gently on her blanket. Manzanita returned to the circle of women and lowered her body toward the earth. One by one, the others sat down.

Bumblebee took a feather off her backpack and offered it to Manzanita.

Manzanita shook her head. "We can circle without the feather, if we can show respect for each other."

Sapphire waited for the now-familiar argument to begin: Should the circle pass the feather to ensure that everyone had the chance to speak, or should people speak freely and respectfully in a dynamic conversation.

Lauren's voice rang out. "Honor the Grandmother's wisdom."

Sapphire couldn't believe how hypocritical Lauren was. When Manzanita wanted Lauren to participate in a mother-to-be circle, she tried everything she could to get out of it.

Bumblebee lowered her head for a second and then turned slowly, gently pressing her bare feet into the grass, as she returned the feather.

Manzanita spoke, "In this family, we have much to learn." She looked around the circle, slowly resting her eyes on each of the women. Heads nodded in agreement. "The brothers need healing. The sisters need healing. Even our children need healing." She inhaled deeply, her spine straight as the aspens surrounding them. She exhaled loudly. "We are all of us children inside." Manzanita rocked ever so slightly forward, pressing the palms of her hands into the ground, and then she rocked back until only the tips of her fingers touched the soil.

"When a two-year-old child runs into the street," she said, "we rush after her and snatch her from harms' path. Then, cradling her in our arms, we carry her, kicking and screaming, to the safety of the sidewalk. And while we carry her, she cries and screams, 'I hate you, you're mean.' And while we are carrying this wiggling, struggling bundle of life, our hearts are full of love, and we kiss her forehead."

The circle was silent. Even the dog stopped panting and pricked its ears at Manzanita. Awed by the simplicity and depth of Manzanita's words, Sapphire closed her eyes and tried to sear the delicate wisdom of loving in her heart.

"And this is how we must be with our brothers and sisters." Manzanita pulled her hands out of the grass. On them, greenish-yellow splotches mingled among soil smudges: the hands of a farmer or a planter of seeds. She turned to her left and bowed her head.

The woman to Manzanita's left said, "You have spoken the truth. It is time we became our sisters' keepers. It is time we stop turning our heads, stop ignoring the pain we see around us, stop blaming each other."

Sapphire choked, struggling to swallow, to get beyond her anger, to find a way to let it all go, but at the moment, her past was suffocating her. Her mother had been wrong to let her live all these years thinking that she was so awful, even her own dad didn't want her.

The redheaded sister spoke. "It's very easy for keepers to turn into jailers. What about when I walk down a path that has not been walked before? I'm tired of trying to fit into what other people see."

There was truth in her words as well, so Sapphire spoke up. "I respect the words that Manzanita has shared with us here today. But there are many ways of living in this world, and if we go around stopping others from living their true nature, how can that be loving? How can I judge if my sister is walking in danger, or just walking a different path than the one I know?"

Manzanita nodded her head.

Across the circle, a girl spoke up. "Last night, I heard a kid got lost. This morning, the word is she is found. But what about the kid's mom? Maybe that kid's mom needs some love."

Sapphire replied, "Just because Dakota was lost, doesn't mean her mother is at fault."

"And did we find the mother as well as the child?"

Bumblebee said, "Both mother and child are doing fine."

Lauren cradled her belly. "Where was Dakota's father while I was out looking for his kid?"

Frustrated by Lauren's censure, Sapphire defended the poor man. "What's that supposed to mean?"

Lauren glared at her. "It was a rhetorical question."

Sapphire remembered the time she and her dad had gotten separated when she was in first grade. But that was completely different. They were in a Los Angeles park in springtime; it was the afternoon, and there were other people around. "Seemed more like an accusation of guilt," she said. Everyone was so quick to judge the minor mistakes and overlook the major joys a parent created in a kid's life. "Does one mistake overshadow all the wonderful times?"

"Ladies, please."

The grandmother on Sapphire's left said, "Will one of the women here visit with the mama? Perhaps take the little one for a few hours?"

"Lots of people don't have their dad around. I don't. What's the big deal?" Sapphire said.

The blonde woman said, "No one is attacking you, Sapphire. We're just trying to talk about how to help each other heal, and to keep each and every one of us safe."

"Sister, we're not criticizing anyone's parents," said the redhead on Sapphire's left. "But it's hard to be a positive parent if you weren't parented positively yourself. Growing up for me was 'Do what you're told, or else.' We are trying to find a new way of creating family, a way filled with love and respect, not fear and isolation."

The woman next to Manzanita said, "Let's try to focus on the issue. What happens to our children when they aren't cared for?"

"Children need love. They need someone watching over them, and they need help when they take a wrong turn," said the blonde.

"Parenting takes all forms," Sapphire said. "My father included me in everything he did. So what if sometimes he got a bit overwhelmed. I think that's a whole lot better than some dad who goes to work every day at a job he hates and watches football on the weekends."

"You don't understand," a woman shouted.

"Just 'cause I disagree with you doesn't mean I don't understand," Sapphire said.

"We're arguing about how to love each other, and we can't even love each other while we are arguing. Can we please show some love?"

Another voice said, "Let the sister speak."

"Focus," cried the circle. "Focus!"

"We need a feather."

"Love all our relations."

"Focus."

Bumblebee stepped into the center of the circle, picked up the feather, and handed it to Sapphire.

"Fuck the feather," Sapphire said. "You all are talking about love, but you're all so judgmental. There's more than one way to love and more than one way to live, and who are you to put Moonchild or anyone else down for living differently." She turned around and stalked out of the circle. She had repeated last night again, only this time in front of more people. Humiliated, she climbed toward the ridge, trying to escape their judgment. She needed to get out of there.

"Sapphire," a voice called out behind her. "Wait up."

Sapphire paused and saw Bumblebee following her. "What?"

"Stop for a second."

Sapphire paused, kicked a rock, and swallowed her feelings. She wasn't going to give anyone the satisfaction of knowing how upset she was.

Bumblebee caught up with her and asked, "What's eating at you, child?"

"Nothing."

"Lauren and them was just blowing steam. They weren't talking about anyone in particular, just talking about how to love the child in each of us."

Sapphire crossed her arms in front of her chest. "I was just trying to point out that we all have different ways of living, and what works for one of us doesn't work for all. We need to be careful of laying our judgments on others." As the words escaped from her mouth, she realized her own hypocrisy in judging the sisters.

"Girl. You sure see what's up. You've got a way."

Sapphire unfolded her arms. "I don't know how it got blown up into such an argument."

Bumblebee said, "You got hooked into reacting to their words, instead of staying focused on what you was trying to share."

Bumblebee embraced Sapphire, who stiffened, her arms frozen at her sides. Other sisters skipped up and piled on her, brushing her hair, embracing her back, rubbing her shoulders. They smelled sweet and stale, of sunscreen and wood smoke, peppermint and sage. Long hair tickled her nose. Someone's arm smashed her breasts down. She tasted the salty dried sweat of a bare shoulder pressed against her lips. Jewelry pressed into her cheek, and she could barely breathe.

She didn't know how to respond. They should have left her alone. Let her go. Given her time to calm down. The heat of their bodies choked her, pressed into her, and the more she struggled to breathe, the less oxygen she got, until finally she surrendered to the pulsating sweaty bodies. All the pain of being cast aside broke loose from its mooring in her lower intestines and lurched toward her now-defenseless heart, before the tears poured down her face.

"Cry, sister. Let the tears come out."

She melted into the bodies around her, the tears draining from her body and into the ground underneath her feet, her breath jagged and wet.

The women tangled together, laughing and crying and hugging each other. "We love you."

"I guess I overreacted," Sapphire sniffled, as the circle began to break apart.

"It's okay, sister."

"Was I really being that intense?"

"Think Marxist Mel."

Sapphire flushed with embarrassment at the mention of the angriest punk rapper alive. "I'm so sorry."

A sister got into a Mel squat and started rapping, "I'm so angry, you're so mean. I'm so angry."

Sapphire squealed at the sister's zany performance and leapt towards her. "No thoughts. No words. No gun big enough can blow these troubles away."

Others joined in, until everyone was rapping over everyone else, and they started laughing. Sapphire fell on the ground, her stomach muscles spasmed from laughter, and soon, other girls were lying next to her in the dirt. She gulped to catch her breath and inhaled a clod of dirt. As she coughed, a sister rubbed her back. "We love you. You'll find your father."

"Of course you will. Just another miracle at the gathering."

Her body tingling, Sapphire truly believed anything was possible.

"So, ladies," Bumblebee asked, "are we going back to the circle?"

"Yeah."

"Let's go."

A cloud of butterflies, the sisters sprang up and fluttered back down to the glade.

As Sapphire stood up, she realized that, as much as she had painted Mom, there wasn't a single portrait of a woman with a heart hanging outside her ribcage, dripping blood on the wood floors, as she struggled to clean the house of dust balls and old memories.

LAUREN

On the far side of the brook, the hills rose quickly with red firs and some ponderosa or Jeffrey pines serving as sentries to the north. Lauren squinted. Hard to tell the difference between ponderosa and Jeffrey from this far away. Not one hundred percent certain that the hill was not old-growth forest, although the lack of diversity in species suggested second growth. Plus, an old-growth forest would have more variety in tree height and trunk diameter. She searched for white firs on the hillside and mountain alders and black cottonwoods along the creek, indicating old growth. No alders or cottonwoods lined the creek. The stream's banks covered in wildflowers grew happily, untrampled by the thousands of people in the larger valley where they camped. The grass rippled as the wind blew off the water. She wondered if there were native rainbow trout in the stream.

How personally people took things. Lauren knew it was hard to bare one's soul, feel safe, and protect one's innards from being trampled, because she felt unable to open up anymore herself. Anything she said made her sound like a bitter woman, and that was not at all the image she wanted to project. Instead of sharing, she remained silent, mysterious, languishing and slowly sinking in a pool of muddy water, which was dragging her down to some place she had never been before, nor wanted to visit. The huddle around Sapphire dissolved. That girl was really into all the woo-woo stuff. All the older women were sitting in the circle talking, as if nothing had happened. Lauren was the only woman under thirty left there.

"They needed that."

Lauren nodded at the woman next to her. "Things had gotten way too serious."

The woman laughed. "You got that right, sister."

"How has your gathering been?"

"Lovely." The woman smiled. "This is my first time in the Sierras, and it's just breathtaking."

Breathtaking in a forlorn way, Lauren thought, and sighed. Even the scattered patches of old growth looked sad, as if they knew their days were numbered.

The woman's name was Penelope, and she had two kids in their teens. She had come to the gathering to keep an eye on them—hadn't really wanted to but was afraid they would come on their own—and she was having a great time, learning yoga, meeting amazing people. She had never done it before, and everyone was just so nice.

"I just love that there's so little undergrowth under the trees. I'm from Ohio and the underbrush is always a tangled mess. It's airy in these woods."

Lauren nodded, distracted by her frustration with Sapphire. "Come up to the North Coast. There's enough moisture up there for ferns." All Sapphire would do was talk about last night, and that was over with and it was time to move on.

The woman smiled. "Have a beautiful afternoon." And walked off.

Lauren watched Penelope float toward the creek, as if her bliss were a cloud on which she was riding. She had felt that way last year when the gathering was in Montana. Today, she floundered in a strange 1950s sitcom, only no one had given her the script. She stared for a while at the women playing without a care in the world, women who believed they had the power to change the future rather than be consumed by it. She lumbered toward the altar, looked at the trinkets placed with faith on the pile. And where does faith come into it? It's funny, but when she was on the line, police pointing guns in her face, she felt hope for the future. For all that could be changed. But now. Alone. The hope evaporated. She crossed her arms. She was stuck in between.

She sulked around, waiting for the circle to start up again, upset that Sapphire's drama had wrecked it for everyone, when she glanced up and saw Sapphire approaching her. Her brown hair was loose for a change and floated ominously behind her head. She had this funny look on her face, as if she were in trouble or trying to apologize for something. Lauren shrank away from the emotional vampire's advance. She turned and started to walk toward the creek.

"Lauren!"

She paused for a moment, and then Sapphire was in her face, again.

"I'm glad you're here," Sapphire said.

"Why wouldn't I be?" she asked.

Sapphire rubbed her hands on her pants and fiddled with her hair, sucked on a strand. "I'm sorry."

"What the fuck are you sorry about now," Lauren blurted out. "You're always sorry about something. Why don't you get a spine and do something." Feeling as if she had just kicked a puppy, she felt ashamed of her outburst.

Sapphire turned away and took a couple of steps. Then, she turned around. "I want to be more like you. Confident. Strong." She poked her toe into the ground. "You believe in yourself." She just stood there with her hands in her pockets and her shoulders hunched in over her chest.

"Why would you want to be like me?" Lauren rubbed her belly. Fat, pregnant. A failure.

"It's not an insult." Sapphire wanted to be the person Lauren had once been.

Well, Lauren had news for Sapphire; she wanted to be that person as well. "Why don't you go hang out with your new friends?"

Sapphire glanced over her shoulder. "I thought you were my friend?"

"If you think I'm so mean, then why are you talking to me?"

Sapphire threw her hands up in the air.

"Oh, yeah. You're full of it. Blabbing about your perfect childhood. You're not a kid anymore, so get over it," Lauren fumed.

Sapphire glared at her. "I don't need you." She turned and stomped off. "I don't need any of you."

Lauren's lower back ached. Damn, she just wanted to make the girl start living in the present, not chase her off. At least Sapphire didn't seem to trip on her being pregnant. The girl was the only one who just let her be herself, and now she had blown her off. Lauren was tired. Wanted to lie down. Her stomach rumbled and she could taste the pancakes she had for breakfast.

"Circle." The call rose up. "Circle."

Lauren joined the reforming of the circle, gripping the hands of the sisters on either side of her, gripping hands tightly.

A small boy ran around the circle laughing, and a dog galloped after him. The circle was more oval than round, and the women were scattered a bit.

The song started up. "Mother, hear our songs. Trees, feel our hugs."

Lauren joined in. "Stars shining overhead, sending us messages from the ancient ones." She glanced up the hill, and Sapphire stood on the ridge. Lauren yearned to go after her, to apologize, but she couldn't. Didn't know how. Her rage at the baby building up. Her life had always been so easy before; she decided what she wanted and went after it with checklists and tenacity. She imagined handing Sapphire an oar. "We are born of love. We give birth to love."

The singing grew silent and they all sat down to continue the circle.

The women decided to honor someone in their lives who had nurtured them and provided love; they sang their praises.

"My grandmother spent every Sunday with me. Telling me stories of her grandmother and life in the old country."

"My third-grade teacher tutored me in math."

"My mother is always there for me; even though she's seventy-two, she still brings me soup when I'm sick."

"My father and I spent two years restoring a '66 Mustang from scratch that he gave me for my sixteenth birthday."

"When I got divorced, my baby brother and his boyfriend took me in and nursed me back to love, a job, and a new life."

Fatigue dripped from Lauren's bones. All she wanted was for every molecule in every filament of her body to be touching the ground, spread out horizontally like spilled milk. The positivity fest rankled her nerves, creating the sense that she was huddled at the bottom of a dark muddy pit in the middle of the wilderness, and no matter how hard she screamed, no one could hear her.

SEEKING PEACE IN YEAST

Friday, July 6, 1990
(Day Eleven of Sapphire's Gathering)

Bus-loads of Food Arrive at the Gathering

"Free food in the woods" is a commonly heard
refrain at the gathering, as kitchens serve up
buckets of oatmeal, stir-fried vegetables, pasta,
and the infamous "zu-zus," or sweet treats.
The food arrived in converted school buses that
had gone out on "supply runs" to purchase
food in bulk, using funds collected by the Piggy
Bank. Local farmers drove up with crates full of
tomatoes and apples to donate. As the gathering
winds down, gathering participants vow to donate
non-perishable food supplies to the Farmer's
Friend Pantry in Quincy. Locals are worried about
the safety of the incoming food, but pantry
volunteers vow to inspect all donations carefully.
(*Quincy Herald*, July 5, 1990)

SAPPHIRE

Sapphire stormed down the ridge, leaving the Womyn's
Healing Circle behind, and burst through a clump of
goldenrod, leaving broken stalks in her wake. Ducking a
Frisbee, she ignored the cries to walk gently on the land. The
bile rose up in her throat and she choked on it, sucking the
bitter aftertaste of betrayal into her stomach, where it sank.
Despite all the loving words, the sisters had been just as

judgmental as a group of Bible-thumping Baptists. Maybe not all of them, but definitely Lauren.

Lauren, in her dreads and prayer beads, was a hypocrite. She wanted a crew to bow down to her and her idea of the way things should be. Sapphire blazed down the trail, fast approaching a woman, hair wrapped in a green turban, clasping the hands of two toddlers. Sapphire swung off the trail and trampled through a patch of blue flax, before she cut back onto the trail ahead of them.

The woman called out, "Sister. Please stay on the trail so the flowers don't get hurt."

Sapphire ignored her and stomped through dirt that bounced up and covered her already-grimy boots. Swerving to avoid a man carrying a huge drum, she sidestepped an elder talking, and she exhaled loudly. All these people were in her way.

A cluster of spastic dancers blocked the trail; their bodies jerked and shimmied, and drums throbbed and shook the trees around them, exploding in sound: *boom, crack, bellow.* Every mountain lion within earshot must have split to the high country. She glared at them, snaked through the crowd, past a woman smudging the dancers with dried white sage, and she choked on the entire stinky mess of it all.

"Sapphire!"

She stumbled on a backpack lying in the dirt, and then River was dancing in front of her. He totally fit Lauren's ego trip. Not strong enough to challenge her, but enough in love to take everything she said as gospel. His purple Guatemalan pants hung low on his skinny hips.

"Long time, no see." He hugged her.

"Later." Sapphire ducked behind a startled woman, but River followed her.

195

He reached for her arm. "What's bugging ya, sis?"

Sapphire pulled away from him and yelled over the pounding drums, "I just need to sleep."

River leaned towards her and said, "I know you're looking for your dad, but it's not everything."

"I know. I know already." She kept going until she was clear of the damned dirt storm, but River was still there.

"My biggest problem in life was getting away from my dad."

"I'm sorry for you. But can I go now?"

"Sapphire," he pleaded, "just chill for two minutes."

She stopped, hoping it would be quick, so she could get back to the semi-privacy of her tent and escape the endless sermons.

"I grew up with all my family 'round me. Six brothers and three sisters. Mom and Dad. Aunts. Uncles. Grandparents. Cousins. Second cousins. And everyone expects you to be that way."

"What way?"

"Get married, build a house. Have babies. Cut trees."

"Where'd you grow up?" she asked.

"Louisiana—but the point is my people smothered me. Never could hear myself think or figure out what I was looking for, with my people telling me what I wanted."

At least he wasn't lonely. Her relatives were scattered about Iowa and Illinois and stayed there, afraid to venture to the sinful Republic of California. She had one uncle, two cousins, a stepdad and half-brother for family, if she didn't count her mother, and she wasn't sure if she had burned that bridge or not. He didn't understand at all.

"So, I convinced my dad to let me go to Oregon and log, before I got hitched and settled down."

Sapphire looked away from him, toward the dancers. Leaving your family at twenty-five wasn't the same as losing your dad at ten. Trying to hide the rage she felt inside, she took a deep breath and tried to sound as nonchalant as she could. "What do they think of how you're living now?"

River rolled his eyes. "Ain't words for what they think. But now, with the baby coming, I'm bummed that my momma don't wanna know Lauren. Dad's mad as hell 'cause we ain't married." He stepped closer, placed his hands on her shoulders, and kneaded the back of her neck. "Your shoulders are in knots," he mumbled.

She felt his fingers press into a tender spot that she didn't even know existed, and it hurt. She listened to the words coming out of his chest and his heart beating and could picture Lauren's disgusted outrage, and it felt nice to stand here not talking and just feeling each other be.

"Hey, River."

Sapphire's cheeks flushed, and she twisted free of River's hands and turned to face him and an older man with short gray hair.

The older man said, "Just trying to rustle up some folks to lend a palm up at the bakery."

"What's going on?" River asked.

"They're trying to make three thousand rolls for Dinner Circle, and they could use some more bakers."

Sapphire was finished with being everyone's punching bag. Let someone else make dinner rolls.

"Yeah," River said. "Let's go bake bread."

"I'm going to take a nap." She turned and headed toward her tent.

He grabbed her arm. "Don't go. It will be fun."

She yanked her arm away from him.

"What?" he asked.

"I'm busy."

River asked, "Doing what?"

The gray-haired man said, "Let her be, River. If she doesn't want to help feed the family, she doesn't have to."

She didn't want to be that selfish bitch who wouldn't help others. She wanted to be part of the team, not just part of the labor force.

"We'll help," River told the older man.

"I didn't say I'd go," Sapphire said.

"Have you even been there? It's a wicked setup. They've got ovens made of metal drums and a killer wash station. You got to check it out."

"I'll walk up there with you, but I'm not promising I'll stay."

River ran his hands across his head. "Deal."

☮ ♥ ☮ ♥ ☮ ♥ ☮ ♥ ☮ ♥

River rambled on and on about plans for the upcoming direct actions that were destined to save the redwoods forever. He had been arrested during an action, for climbing onto a logging truck hauling the cut bodies of once-giant redwoods that had been growing since the Declaration of Independence.

At nineteen, Sapphire had backpacked the Lost Coast with her mom, just the two of them. The silence had been so complete, her body absorbed it, and peace settled in her toes and fingers. The light. Her mom looked so young and happy in the light filtering through the redwoods. Sapphire imagined Mom had been this full of light when she first came to California, leafy hopes and feathery dreams taking root in the shade of the majestic redwoods. Their destruction made her angry. Maybe she should go up the coast in a few weeks and get involved. If she ever found her father, he would want to go with her. Together, they would figure out how to help each other and the majestic trees.

As River expounded on the dependencies between redwood trees, salmon, and the culture of the Mattole Nation, they climbed a slope toward a flag, cerulean with a corn-colored moon, flapping in the afternoon breeze. In front of the tree line, five huge earthen mounds rested on the hillside, the prehistoric burial sites of some not-yet-ancient culture. The yeasty smell of baking bread mingled with the acrid pine smoke, and piles of cut wood were stacked to the left of the path that took them past the mounds. River went straight for the ovens. "Aren't they cool?"

Sapphire paused next to him as he studied the mud-covered fifty-gallon metal drums, resting on rock boxes with little metal doors. River opened one, and the heat slapped her in the face. Tiny stovepipes stuck out of the center, like slate gray oil paint on unsanded wood. She imagined painting the scene after dark, when the hot air escaping from the ovens would be visible in the cold mountain air: tiny puffs of brown-gray floating through purplish-black night sky. Such faith people had, coming out here and going to all this work to bake bread. It sure would be cheaper, or at least less hassle, to haul in day-old bread from town.

After a few moments, they continued up the trail, past a clump of sugar pines and into a clearing, where, to her amazement, there were rows of metal cooling racks lashed to poles, filled with loaves of dark bread.

"Hey, Vince," River called out.

"Yo, River," he responded. They hugged short and hard, and the lanky man with multi-colored hair wraps slapped River on the back. "What's happening?"

River seemed to know everyone, even though this was his first gathering too.

"Nothing much," River said. "Sapphire and I thought we'd help out for a bit."

"Sweet," Vince said. "So, where's Lauren?"

"At Womyn's Space," Sapphire offered.

River raised his eyebrow at her.

Vince said, "I haven't seen her all gathering. I hear she's pregnant?"

"Yeah, man." River smiled and rubbed his chest.

"You stoked?"

"You know it."

Sapphire said, "They're gonna have the baby in a tepee." As soon as the words came out of her mouth, she wished she could grab them with a butterfly net and destroy them. She wasn't part of their baby birthing plans, and she needed to butt out.

"Sweet," Vince said. "So, listen, guys. We're making dough. You ready to dig in?"

River hooted. "No pun intended."

"That's why we came," Sapphire said. "To help make bread."

"Sweet. Hey, Kalmia. River and… and…." Vince paused and leaned toward her. "What's your name again?"

"Sapphire."

He repeated, "River and Sapphire are here to work."

Kalmia appeared from behind a plywood table covered in flour and mounds of tan dough. "Hand wash is over there." She pointed at a huge metal sink. "Hello, Sapphire. What happened to Lauren?" Then, she spotted River. "Who's your friend?"

"River," Sapphire said. "Lauren's boyfriend."

Kalmia groaned. "So, you're the daddy."

River grinned like a kid with a huge pumpkin full of Halloween candy.

"Well, I hope you're planning on sticking around after her baby's born."

River pursed his mouth and wrinkled his forehead. "What shit you talking. I'm going to care for this baby all my life."

"So says you," Kalmia said.

Sapphire studied Kalmia's round face, her pursed lips, and waited for the woman's outburst on how sisters were treated by brothers.

River stared at both of them and then hastily retreated to the hand wash station.

Kalmia confided in Sapphire. "I don't know about him. He thinks it's some kind of crazy game of pregnant direct action, and Lauren's his shield."

The night before, Kalmia danced around the fire in the persona of an ancient goddess; now, she turned up as the bread-baking mama. Rumor had it she was working on her Ph.D. in math. Awestruck by the woman's many talents, Sapphire believed in her judgment, yet feared seeming stupid by opening her mouth to comment on the situation. "I'd better go wash my hands."

Kalmia called after her, "Please tie your hair back, so you don't shed in the bread."

Laughter burst out from the kitchen. "Get it?"

At the wash station, Sapphire pressed the stick pedal with her foot and clean water squirted across her dark brown hands. A pump of soap, and she lathered the dirt until it rinsed off, leaving them pinkish tan. Then, a quick squirt of bleach water for good measure. Shaking her hands dry, she ambled back to the others at the plywood tables, where La Abuela stood on a split log humming as her wrinkled arms caressed and pummeled the flaxen dough.

Kalmia asked, "Have you done this before?"

"Maybe as a kid." Sapphire couldn't remember for sure, but her parents had been into making everything themselves, so she might have.

"Okay. Here's the secret: dough needs to be pushed and pulled or the yeast won't stretch and grow. But push it too far and the fibers break."

Like people, Sapphire thought, as she scooped a pile of dough out of a bowl and plopped it down in front of her. The gooey wetness stuck to her fingers. Irritated, she tried to wipe the dough off her fingers, but the more she tried to remove it, the more it stuck. So much of life resembled dough; the more you struggled to free yourself from something, the harder it held on.

She cringed at the thought of that damned Womyn's Healing Circle and at her outburst. She had made a complete ass of herself, but no one here knew about it, yet. She needed to learn to keep her mouth shut. She began to mimic the others and tried to be graceful with sprinkling flour on her pile of dough and folding it in half, but her fingers dug in and when she pulled them out, sticky pieces of dough covered her fingers.

"Use your palms," a woman said.

Sapphire tried it and gained a bit of control over the dough. "Thanks for the tip."

On her right, a couple of young sisters were talking to the marshmallow man, who didn't seem to recognize Sapphire from the previous night. He told them about this young brother he'd met at last year's gathering in the Colorado Rockies. The kid had been so excited to be home that he'd pitched his tent and run off to check out the scene, thinking he'd be gone for an hour. One thing led to another, and by midnight he was stumbling around in the dark with no jacket and no flashlight, wearing only a t-shirt and jeans.

Sapphire pushed the mound of dough away from her and folded it back against itself. She sprinkled flour on the counter and folded the dough again.

A sister with short spiky purple hair, a nose ring, and baggy jeans, said in a ragged voice, "It was cold as hell in Colorado at night."

"Yup." The marshmallow man nodded his head. "So, the kid finally shows up at INFO asking for help. After wrapping him up in a raggedy old blanket, I went with him to help him find his gear."

Sapphire asked, "Had he ever been camping before?"

The purple-haired girl giggled. "Hell, at least he brought a tent and sleeping bag. So many kids show up with a blanket and flip-flops."

"If you've never been camping before, it's hard to know what to bring." Sapphire found the rhythm, and the bread started to come alive under her hands, growing stronger with each push and pull.

"We must have hiked around for hours, looking for a gray dome tent behind a kitchen that served coffee."

The table burst into laughter. "There's a thousand tents like that at every gathering, and twenty coffee kitchens."

Sapphire's hands moved in the rhythm, a slow dance with a strong backbeat, and she realized she was kneading bread.

"And when we finally found his tent, it was dawn, and the damn tent was behind a popcorn kitchen." The old man hooted so hard, he started choking and stepped away from the table hacking, as a sister pounded him on the back.

Sapphire giggled at the punchline a bit after everyone else and watched the old man doubled up, his joy infectious. This was fun. Just hanging out, baking bread, telling stories. "He must have been totally embarrassed."

"If I had a dollar for every person who lost their tent."

"I'd be a rich woman,"

And as if in unison, everyone started laughing, and Sapphire joined in and laughed until she was holding onto the side of the table, hunched over with tears in her eyes.

"What are you people doing?" River stepped up to the table and took the spot on Sapphire's left.

She glanced up at him. "He couldn't," she giggled, "find his tent." She tried to stop laughing long enough to tell River the punchline. "And it was there all along."

River shook his head at her silliness, grabbed some dough, and started kneading.

She caught her breath and straightened her body. After a few seconds, she resumed work on her mound. River matched her rhythm, and together they pushed and pulled at the spongy dough.

"So, Lauren told me you lived in Hollywood during the sixties?"

Sapphire nodded. "Sort of. I was born in Topanga Canyon, but I think when I was three, we moved to a bungalow on North Poinsettia just south of Sunset. That would have been in 1968."

"Must have been wild."

"That's what people think." She sprinkled flour on her dough, folded it in half, and pushed firmly down with her palms, stretching the dough away from her. Letting it grow. "It was creative."

River raised his eyebrows.

"We had a garden with flowers and a giant old oak tree, and people would hang out, and we painted everything. Flowers, suns, elves. Each other."

"So, it's true," River said.

"What?"

"Your parents were hippies?" He said, "You're a real hippie kid."

She shrugged her shoulders, burying the hurt of being different, as she had done so many times growing up.

"I think that's what intimidates Lauren."

"What?"

"Some friends of ours accused her of slumming."

"What's that supposed to mean?"

"When she's too hungry or tired of me, she'll head home to her rich parents and become a lawyer, or at least marry one."

In some ways, Mom had done that, traded experimentation for stability, when she dumped Dad and married Brandon. At the time, all Sapphire knew was that she was leaving her entire life, all her friends, Dad, and the amazing oak tree in the backyard, and she had been furious with Mom, angry at leaving everything she knew. And all Mom ever said was that she loved Brandon, but that his job was in San Francisco, so they had to move to where he lived.

Behind her, someone played a guitar and sang, "We was only kids living in America, only kids searching for a pot of gold. Pinning our hopes on the rainbow and the oak leaves blowing in the wind. We was only kids believing in a revolution." The song reflected the music of her childhood, rejecting all that had gone before, but the future required just as much effort as the past, only it was harder to see.

River stared at her. "Earth to Sapphire."

"Just thinking." She pushed down with her hand on the dough and stretched it away from her. People kneading dough in the mountains was a start on creating a different world. She hoped it was a better one.

The purple-haired sister said, "Last year we were on Dead Tour and blew an engine outside of Lubbock, Texas."

A woman at the far side of the table called out, "Sara, are you talking about that split-seat '66?"

Sara nodded. "Elijah had dreads down his back, and we hitched into town looking for a Volkswagen mechanic. The cowboy that picked us up was this good ole boy. I thought he was going to flip at Elijah's dreads." She paused to take a hit off a joint and then passed it to Sapphire. "I was scared."

Sapphire took a hit, slow and deep, until her lungs were drowning and her mind was silenced. Then, she let the vapors escape slowly at first, then coughed as she turned away from the table and the last traces disappeared.

River slapped her on the back and took the joint out of her hands.

Sara kept talking. "So, it turns out he's not only a cowboy, but a Baptist, and we ended up staying at his house for a couple of days, while the cowboy and Elijah worked on the van."

Sapphire folded her pile of dough, pressed the heels of her hands into the mound and pushed it away from her, then doubled it over and pushed it away. She sprinkled flour on the bread and repeated the motion.

"Except for reciting scriptures after dinner, they were real cool people."

The joint made its way around again, and this time, she held the smoke in her lungs without coughing. She found a rhythm with the bread—forward up, sprinkle down—the rhythm sailing her through the universe, mimicking the ever-present drums. *Boom, thump, thump, whap. Boom, thump, thump, whap.*

So many happy faces around the table. No arguing, no judgments, just working together to feed the family. The people at the table inhaled together, exhaled together. La Abuela, Sara, River, the marshmallow man, and the other women all cradled flour in their hands and sprinkled it on piles of dough. Then, they folded their dough in half, pushing it toward the center of the table. Yellow pines surrounded them. One table in the center of the world, and Sapphire painted it with smiling faces and hands on the creamy dough, and the trees rising up behind them. Brown strokes and green slashes toward the ground. The tree pulling against itself. The trunk stretching up toward the sky, and the leaves stretching down toward the earth. What a revelation! Even trees were struggling between realms, as she did in yoga practice when she was told to stretch her spine and head up, up, up, and at the same time press her buttocks and legs down, down, down. While all these thoughts were swirling in her head, a man walked past the table with an armful of wood. A tall man with long, brownish hair and a beard.

She asked who he was.

A few women shrugged, but the marshmallow man replied, "That's John. He's been a fixture at the Bakery for a few years now."

"John," Sapphire whispered. "John."

"He's from LA."

John from LA. She knew it was fate. She had the fight with Lauren, so she'd leave Womyn's Healing Space and connect with River, who brought her to the Bakery to reconnect with Dad. Then, River didn't say anything, just let her spot him on her own. This time it was real, not wishful thinking, or her twisted fantasies. She told Sara she was going to pee and that she would be right back. Then, she sauntered in the direction her dad went. This time, it was simple. No confusion. Just unfolding in a low-key manner. A little trail down to the right. He was chopping wood, and she stopped five feet in front of him. "Are you my dad, John Larson?"

He gazed at her. "Your dad?"

"John Larson. You used to live in Hollywood with my mom, Carol?"

He shook his head and pursed his lips. Then, he sputtered, "I don't have no kids. My name is John McIntire."

Stunned. Her legs wobbled as she tried to process what he said.

"Will you take some wood back to the fire?" asked the other John.

The John who wasn't her father, wasn't the actor, wasn't the wise man come down from the mountains. This John, who was just a man named John at a gathering, chopping wood and piling it by the fire for later. She held out her arms; he handed her five split logs, and then she turned and shuffled back to where the guitar player strummed around the not-yet-lit fire. The smell of baking bread filled the air, until even the dust and the pines smelled yeasty. She put down the wood and sat on the bench and listened to the music. Blue and green notes flowed in clockwise circles, and then the tune changed directions and blew counter-clockwise in purple strands.

She stretched out on one of the logs circling the fire pit and tucked her pack under her head for a pillow in the deceptively familiar surroundings. She had seen pictures of their tepee nestled among the sycamores and live oaks along the mostly dry creek in Topanga Canyon. Mom and Dad and all their friends, dressed in what masqueraded for traditional Indian buckskins, flashing the peace sign for the camera. Photos of her as a toddler, playing naked in the dirt.

She had been born in that lodge off Muerdago Road, when the canyon was still at the ends of the earth, and anything and everything was welcomed, including her.

She started getting it all mixed up with River and Lauren, and then she was waiting to be born. North Coast, Los Angeles, along the ocean. Along the river.

Then, she was baby Sapphire lying on a blanket along a cold Northern California river, and her mommy was Lauren and her daddy was River, and they really loved each other. Lauren was trying to be a good Mommy and trying to save the giant trees, and she got arrested and went to jail for a long time, and then it was just Sapphire and Daddy River. Then, River turned into a turtle and went off into the ocean with Sapphire on his back, and they crossed the ocean for days and days on end, until they got to the land beyond, which was a land of coconuts and palm trees, and the ocean water was very, very warm. Then, Daddy put her on the beach with all the other little kids and swam away.

GREEK PHILOSOPHY AND FESTERING WOUNDS

Friday, July 6, 1990
(Days Eleven of Sapphire's Gathering)

True wisdom comes to each of us when we realize
how little we understand about life, ourselves, and
the world around us.
—Socrates

SAPPHIRE

Sapphire woke up with the taste of cold metal and sand on her tongue. It was dark. The aroma of baking bread drifted past, and she realized she was still at the Blue Moon Bakery. The solitary guitar player had morphed into a quintet with two drummers as accompaniment. The split log benches were full of people, and other people stood around tapping their feet to the music. Everyone seemed to be talking and laughing with friends. Across the fire, a dark-haired woman swayed to the music while nursing her baby. Her breasts were huge and beautiful and brown, and the baby looked pale against her skin.

A flush of tenderness warmed Sapphire's chest, as she gazed upon the mother and child with compassion. Pulling a sketchpad and pencil out of her pack, she lightly outlined the woman and the baby cradled in her strong arms. Curves and swirls filled the page. Even as she drew, she thought about who Lauren had been before. Flipping the page, she sketched Lauren starting college, long wavy hair cascading down her back, gold earrings dangling, pink-polished fingernails writing on notepaper, as a professor gestured toward the chalkboard. College. Then, a dready with dirty jeans, chained to a giant redwood, transforming the echoes of a mother's life unfolding. Taking on the world. Then, life changing so totally, so completely. Such faith these women had. Faith to leap into the unknown and be the change they wanted to see in the world, or at least accept the path life had offered them.

The twang of the guitar rang through the trees, while two drummers supported the melody with a simple rhythm: *fommm, thud, fommm, fommm,* and Sapphire set down the sketchpad and savored the fragrance of weed, wood smoke, and bread that swarmed across her body.

Spotting Vince, she walked around the fire to speak with him. He forgot her name again, but when she asked if there were enough rolls for dinner, he said most folks got at least half a roll. She still couldn't believe Vince was a firefighter. With his long hair and laid-back attitude, she would never have imagined him driving a fire truck and following orders, or that he came alone. "Your wife really doesn't mind that you come without her?"

"I don't go to her mother's in Florida, and she doesn't come to the gathering. A fair trade, I guess." He shrugged his shoulders.

That seemed sad to her, to agree to disagree about what was important in life. She wanted a boyfriend who was passionate about art in one form or another. They sat there staring at the fire for a few minutes. "I've got to get going."

"You're not sticking around for pizza?"

"Pizza?"

"Every Friday we do late-night pizza. We'll start in an hour or so. We could use your help."

"My help?"

"You're pretty good with dough."

She flushed with pride. "I'd love to stay, but I'm trying to find my dad."

"What camp's he with?"

She briefly explained why she had come to the gathering.

Vince said people come and go from the gathering. Change their names. Their look. Who they hang out with. "Keep looking. Best bet is to hit all the small camps in the evening, when people are hanging out."

"That's what I've been doing, but no luck so far."

Vince held out a brown grocery store bag. "Take a couple of rolls for later."

"Thanks." Sapphire grabbed three, tossed two in her pack, and bit into the third. "I missed dinner."

"Catch ya later then, sister."

She bit into the roll, chewy and tasting of yeast and wood smoke, requiring time to break it down, but it hit her stomach as food, and for that, she was grateful. On the hillside, the ovens glowed orange against the black sky behind them. Halfway down the slope, Sapphire paused for a moment and gazed at the stars shimmering overhead. A shooting star flashed across the night sky. *The sign she had been waiting for. He was here.* She stared at the spot in the sky where the star had disappeared. It didn't even leave a mark.

The after-Dinner-Circle tripping and exploring portion of the evening was in full swing, and the trail bustled with people, dogs, and the occasional kitten perched on a shoulder. A sister passed her on the trail with a purple Mohawk and a face full of piercings. After a few days here, Sapphire had learned that the way people looked at the gathering bore no necessary resemblance to how they lived in what some called

Babylon and others called their *other life*. The Mohawk sister could be a nurse, a stock broker, or a street kid. Sapphire wandered up to a fire, where a dozen people sat on the ground. "How you all doing tonight?"

"Awesome." "Just chilling." "How are you?"

They were all a little older than she was, but not near old enough to be Dad. "Do you know what camps are up this trail?"

A brother said, "Uh, there's the Coffee Hut, and Whole-in-One."

"Peace Pig," another guy added.

Sapphire said, "Peace Pig?"

"Yeah. They brought a potbellied pig with them and painted a peace sign on him."

Sapphire laughed.

A sister said, "There's a bunch of camps up that way, but most of them don't have names."

"Okay, thanks," Sapphire said. "I guess I'll head up there and see for myself."

One of the sisters at the fire called after her, "Create a beautiful evening."

Sapphire smiled as she left the glow of the fire. If she were going to create her evening, she would manifest hanging out with Dad, listening to him play guitar, and drinking a cup of tea.

Up the trail she saw the banner for "Peace Pig," but the camp was dark so she kept going, swinging in and out of camps, where small clusters of people sat on logs or folding chairs around campfires. At one camp, a discussion of the secret ingredients of Krishna cookies; at the next fire, drummers. Then, singers; then, a twelve-step meeting in progress; and later, a bunch of muddy teenagers hitting her up for tobacco when she appeared in the light of their fire. At the next camp, she found a dozen or so kids huddled around the flames in shorts and t-shirts. "We thought California was just like Florida," one said.

Sapphire laughed. "It's probably warm in LA right now." Tourists didn't know there were so many Californias. The sophisticated and fashionably rundown streets of San Francisco; the country-twang oil fields of Bakersfield; the oak-covered hills of the Central Coast; the broiling-hot desert to the east. If you wanted to fit in, you lived a chameleon life, changing colors and clothes to blend in with the diverse cultures. She unzipped her hoodie and let the heat from the fire soak into her belly.

"Are you from LA?"

She nodded. "I'm living in San Francisco these days."

"Cool. San Francisco is so rad."

She scanned their young faces, as they talked about their first day at the gathering. "If I'd known we'd need to lug our gear so far, I'd have brought less crap and more clothes." They rambled on, and after a few minutes, Sapphire said, "You have a wonderful evening," and turned to walk off.

One of the sisters asked, "Are you okay?"

"I'm fine, just tired."

"You're welcome to stay here."

Sapphire shook her head.

"We've room in the supply tent."

"I'm looking for someone."

"Trust your instincts, and I'm sure you'll find her."

The temperature dropped twenty degrees once she left the fire, and Sapphire zipped up her hoodie and shoved her hands into her pockets. The trail looped around, and she wasn't too far from her tent, so she decided to make a last stop at the Tea Kitchen for something warm to help her sleep.

Rastaman was behind the stove. She never could remember his name, but with black dreads and a "Jah, man" style of talking, Rastaman was as good a description as anything. He seemed to exist for the sole purpose of helping others pause, take a deep breath, and sit around a fire so old, it felt as if the elders had been circled here for generations, ladling steaming liquid into cups. He asked her, "Ever read Heraclites?"

"Her-ak who?"

"Heraclites. Ancient Greek philosopher."

Sapphire really wasn't up on Greek philosophers, or any philosophers for that matter.

"Nuh true? He wrote, 'You cannot step twice into the same stream, for fresh waters are ever flowing upon you.'"

She wasn't sure what it meant, stepping twice into the same stream, but thanked him for the tea. She clasped the warm mug in her hands, and then gently placed the cup on her cheek, feeling the warmth of the silky ceramic. She loved this time of slowing down before bed with tea and philosophy—even if she didn't always understand what Rastaman meant. From the fire pit, she heard Garth's voice and wondered why he was hanging out here. He didn't strike her as a philosopher, or a tea drinker for that matter. She figured him for a cup of *mud* all the way. Garth perched on a white plastic chair, leaning over someone, who was half-lying on the ground and half-leaning against a log.

"You're done, brother," Garth said, pouring the liquid out of a small bottle. "This is killing you." He put a cup into the man's hands. "Drink your tea."

"Man, you just don't get it. Don't know what I did." The drunk sipped at his tea.

Sapphire sat down on a folding chair at the opposite side of the fire. Her tea steamed in the night, and the peppermint opened her dust-clogged nostrils.

Garth jutted his chin at her. "We all did, PS." He rubbed his nose. "We all did, brother."

"I'm just trying to forget."

Garth said, "Forgetting ain't the answer."

Puzzled by the conversation, Sapphire stared at the shy flames dancing on a red-hot bed of coals.

PS leaned against the log, his face red and splotchy.

Garth said, "PS, listen to me."

PS looked up.

"We all did it."

Sapphire had no idea what *it* was.

"Not you. You's one of the straight guys. No, Garth. Not you."

Garth leaned forward, eyes closed, voice flat and speaking slowly, as if the words were being pulled out of him. "We'd been in-country for weeks."

Sapphire blinked her eyes a couple of times: Vietnam. She could see the orange bursts of napalm dropping in *Apocalypse Now*. Images from movies flashed through her head, and it was always men in a jungle and planes flying overhead, and always the orange bursts. Bright orange against the green of the jungle. Not California gray-green, but tropical green, so green, it oozed.

Garth said, "The vines wrap themselves around your lungs and squeeze. We were tracking Viet Cong through the mud, slashing our way through the jungle."

His words pulled her closer, and Garth nodded ever so slightly at her, before turning back to PS.

"There was this hut. Just an everyday peasant house covered in dried leaves. The kind of place they lived. We surrounded it, yelled, '*Giao nộp,* surrender!'"

He was talking about what she had seen on television and heard people talk about late at night, when she was supposed to be asleep.

"Smitty yelled something in Vietnamese. I think it meant, 'Come out with your hands up.'"

She held her breath, gripping the mug so tightly that her fingers were turning numb.

"And waiting. The sweat dripping down the crack of my ass. Smitty crawled toward the hut, and we covered him. My rifle up and my finger ready to pull. A bang came from inside, and I unloaded. Bam. Bam. Bam."

Sapphire recoiled as if she had been hit.

"We all opened fire. Smitty ran like a rabbit. We kept shooting and shooting 'til my shoulder ached."

She fell back against the chair, stunned by the image of Garth killing people. Everything grew silent; the entire world stopped moving.

PS moaned, tried to pull himself up to the log but slid off. "Don't say it. It ain't true until you say it out loud."

It was a war, she told herself. People shoot each other in a war.

Garth put his hand on PS's shoulder. "I was the first one inside. Dead. An old gray-haired woman." He leaned back into his chair and closed his eyes, "And a baby. A baby girl."

Sapphire's head swayed and she felt woozy. She knew it happened, had known the facts, but it had always seemed so

217

far away—out of a book or movie. Until an everyday person was crying in the woods. Until someone she knew was guilty.

Garth continued, "There were piles of guns in there. Chinese AK-47s. Empty Mat-49s and Simonov SKS rifles."

PS said, "It weren't your fault."

"We was ready to roll, get out of there before the Viet Cong showed up." Garth rubbed his hands on his pants, his voice rolling across a gravel driveway. He confessed, "She was only a few months old."

Sapphire recoiled. Turned away from the images of bleeding children and burned grandmothers. From the photos in Brandon's old copies of *Life Magazine* that she had studied as a teenager, trying to reconstruct her childhood. Nevertheless, she couldn't tune out her own brain any more than she could tune out Garth.

"I picked her up. She didn't weigh nothing. Round chubby thing with fuzzy hair. Wrapped her in a piece of cloth. Buried her in the garden."

A gust of wind blew through the trees and a couple leaves drifted down, got caught in the updraft of the fire and hovered for a bit, before falling to the ground.

Sapphire could see her. See the little girl laughing and playing with a rattle, until the baby fell backwards, again and again in slow motion repeat. Then, the camera angle cut to a high shot of baby on the ground bleeding.

"I put a leaf on her grave and left."

She was just a kid then. During Vietnam. Kids weren't supposed to be killed by soldiers. Listening to Garth, it all came rushing back. But it wasn't a memory, like Latisha at the roller rink, or Brian playing pool in the Tenderloin district surrounded by glowing transvestites. It was a memory in her blood. The entire country's blood. Everyone had been angry.

A huge crowd had formed. Mom said they had to show their support for peace. But Mom was yelling. Everyone was yelling and shouting, the opposite of walking in the hush of the redwood forest or sunrise in the desert, when the silence is huge and the colors melt into each other.

She clutched on to Mommy's leg. Mommy ignored her and waved a sign. The black asphalt had been hot under her feet, and she had longed to be sitting in the garden, listening to Daddy tell a story.

Garth turned toward her, tugging on his beard.

She couldn't see the expression on his face. "You murdered them?"

"I have to live with it every day."

Garth was supposed to be one of the good guys. He was the one that was supposed to catch the bad guys and find the lost children. Not murder them. She stood up and started to back away. "I'm trying to make it right," he said.

"But you can't."

Garth looked at her, eyes pleading for something she did not understand.

PS rolled onto his side and started snoring.

They both looked at him. Then back at each other.

"Don't judge," he said, turning to toss a blanket on PS.

"How can I not?" she asked, as she stumbled away, trying to leave the dead body behind her.

"Sapphire," Garth ordered. "Wait."

Shaking her head, she ran down the deserted trail, trying to escape the image of the baby girl dead on the ground. Garth's sad eyes. She gasped for breath in the thin mountain air.

Behind her, Garth yelled, "Sapphire, wait up. We need to talk."

She sensed him behind her, a wild animal trying to claw her apart. Even the trees seemed to have arms that reached out to grab her. His face exploded in her mind, ears long and pointed. Fangs bared. She darted off the trail, cut through a patch of tents, and plunged into the woods.

"Sapphire!"

Through the woods' dark dust, she tried to find a path, but there wasn't one. His voice boomed through the silence, but she couldn't make out the words. She walked away from the sound. The dark surrounded her, and then there was silence. By this time, she couldn't even tell which way the trail was. She squatted down and listened. Held her breath. Waiting.

She had never imagined him as a solider in camouflage with a rifle slung over his shoulder, even though she knew he had been in Vietnam. She had never thought about what that meant; it was just a fact about him she had memorized. Now, she had the evidence smashed in her face and burning her eyeballs. He had murdered a baby. The image replayed itself. A plump child falling and then bursting into slivers of a porcelain figurine she would be stepping on for years.

Catching her breath, Sapphire tried to focus on the bark and her red canvas high tops. Every time she blinked, she saw the baby exploding in blood, her mother's heart trailing blood up and down the coast of California. *Dad was sleeping with all of them.* He was different now. No longer the heroic legend of tales told around campfires late at night.

The silence in the woods failed to block out the voices in her head. Her mother yelling, "You can't change the world by meditating and talking. You need to get off your butt and do something."

"Harmony," Dad would respond in a quiet gentle voice. "Bringing harmony to the world is a full-time job. I'm living in accord with the peace vibration, and you, my dear wife, are fighting it."

"How can you create peace in the world, if you can't create peace in your own family?"

He replied, "Peace happens when we create peace in our hearts." The crowd around him would nod their heads in agreement and tell Sapphire she was lucky to have such a wise father. Yet, when Dad left, so did Mary Moss and Bob and Ananda Rose. They moved on to find the next happening scene, leaving her waiting for something or someone to fill the chasm in her heart.

She gripped the tree. Betrayal had been passed from Dad to Mom to daughter, and she wanted it to end. The night chill washed over the disoriented feeling in her brain. The ideas swirling. Love. Trust. Forgiveness. Dad holding the baby. Her mother shooting Garth. Garth kissing Ananda Rose. The secrets were unraveling. The stitches of her world tearing, and the stuffing inside spilled onto the ground.

For the first time all evening, Sapphire couldn't hear anything, not even the drums. She yanked the flashlight out of her backpack and turned it on the shadows, following the slope downhill. Pine cones and branches crunched under her feet. The canopy of trees made the stars invisible. She followed tiny rainbow-colored streamers tied to branches, until she reached a trail.

She started walking, hoping the path would lead her to where she needed to be.

MONSTERS LURKING IN THE DARK

Saturday, July 7, 1990
(Day Twelve of Sapphire's Gathering)

You gain strength, courage and confidence by
every experience in which you really stop to look
fear in the face. You are able to say to yourself, 'I
have lived through this horror. I can take the next
thing that comes along.' You must do the thing you
think you cannot do.
—Eleanor Roosevelt

SAPPHIRE

On the trail ahead of Sapphire stood Sara from the bakery,
her purple hair rising above a bulky camouflage jacket. Next
to her, a man wearing a jester's cap shook his head beside a
blonde woman in a blue, gray, and purple Mexican serape and
a couple of the ubiquitous guys her age in dark hoodies. They
all stared at the ground.

Sapphire half-wanted to turn around and scuttle the
other way. At just that moment, Sara caught her eye and
beckoned. Though they only knew each other from kneading
bread, that was a connection, and in desperate situations, even
the most fragile thread became a lifeline.

"We love you," the blonde said to a plaid-shirted man
on the ground. The hoodie brothers shook their heads in
agreement. "Yo, bro. It's all cool." "Chill out man." "Loving
you."

The plaid-shirted man arched his back and let loose a scream that penetrated Sapphire's stomach; she staggered backwards. He flipped over and slammed his forehead into the ground, the thud like a cantaloupe dropped on a kitchen floor, splattering pale orange flesh on the wooden cabinets. He pushed himself off the ground and raised his head. The thick dark eyebrows, the deep-set brown eyes. For a moment, she held her breath. Not yet ready to exhale. Not yet ready for it to be true. The burnt trees, the ridge.

She felt the hungry jaws of the universe open wide. The entire world churned up in a blender, and reality as she knew it evaporated; this had to be fate. "Why me," she whimpered softly. She had met plenty of people who had been coming to gatherings for years without ever having to deal with a crazy guy. She pushed into the circle. Dropped to her knees. Mole smacked his head against the hard-packed dirt. She grabbed his stubbled head in her hands, trying to protect it.

"Why do people treat me this way?" he wailed.

Sara crouched down beside him, her hands pressing down on his shoulders.

The others just stood there staring, as if watching a movie preview created for their entertainment. She glanced up at the man in the jester's hat, his scraggly gray beard hanging down to his stomach, hoping for wisdom or suggestions from an elder, but got nothing.

Mole squeezed his eyes shut. He sobbed, "Why me? Why does bad stuff always happen to me?" He kicked the ground.

She grasped his hand and took a cleansing breath. Tried to warm his chilly fingers. She stroked his arm. "Take a deep breath and count to ten."

He screamed and flipped sideways. Knocked the jester to the ground. She gripped Mole's arm. "Hold him," she shouted.

Sara leaned on Mole's thighs and the blonde grasped at his other arm. Sapphire planted her ass on his shoulder. He arched his back and flung the blonde off him. Sapphire slid to the ground and yelled at the jester, "Help us!"

"His karma is causing him to suffer," the jester said, shaking his head. "If we try to hold him, we'll be interrupting the flow of the universe."

Sara flung herself across Mole's chest. "Songbird, are you okay?"

Rubbing her elbow, the blonde nodded.

Sapphire glanced up at the small huddle of men. "Help us, you morons."

The jester laughed and shouted, "Someone do something!"

Two of the hoodie brothers squatted on either side of Mole and pinned down his shoulders.

Clueless on how to deal with this mess, Sapphire massaged Mole's temples and tried to calm herself down. His stubbled hair felt rough under her fingers. "It will be okay. Please, Mole. Please trust me. We're here with you," she said, mostly to convince herself. Her right arm began to quiver as her fingers circled his scalp. Sara and the blonde Songbird on his legs. The two brothers on his shoulders. They held him down. Sapphire chanted, "Earth our body, water our blood."

Sara joined in, "Air our breath, and fire our spirit."

The others raised their voices. "Earth our body, water our blood."

She turned her gaze back to Mole's dilated eyes. "We love you." She rubbed his temples, while trying to come up with a plan. They couldn't stay here all night. She looked up at the faces peering down at her. There was quite a crowd now, and at least she wasn't alone this time. A middle-aged man with a shirt too short to cover his large belly took notes and said, "He got stressed out, up in the parking lot."

The jester said, "This young brother has ingested too much LSD."

Sapphire thought, *No shit,* but remained silent. They needed to find a fire with some sane people. That's what had worked with Mole last night. She would worry about the rest later.

"It's always crazy energy in the parking lot with everyone coming and going," a woman added.

"I hear ya, sister. The peace-love energy down here will mellow him out."

Sapphire continued to stroke Mole's head, her fingers moving in small circles. She pressed deeply into his scalp, hoping to calm him. She felt the struggle melt out of him. His breaths became even, but his teeth began to chatter.

Sapphire called out, "Is there a fire nearby?"

A voice in the crowd said, "Kid Korral is just up the hill."

"No," Mole cried. "I want to stay here."

"Shush. It's freezing here, and a nice warm fire up there," Sapphire said.

"Mole, don't you want to be warm?" Songbird asked.

Mole looked at Songbird, as if the idea of being warm had not dawned on him. "In the hospital, we had fires just like on a camping trip."

His comment hung in the air—a loud fart at a cocktail party. Everyone heard it, but no one would acknowledge it.

Sapphire grabbed his arms. "You need to stand up. One. Two. Three. And up you go."

Together, they stood him up and started walking. "I'm never gonna trip again," he mumbled between his clattering teeth.

That's the least of his problems, she thought, although she had no clue what problems he had. "We're going to the fire, Mole. I need you to walk."

Mole took a step forward and stumbled.

Sapphire grabbed his belt.

"I've got this side." Songbird peeked around his chest, her long blonde hair hanging across her face. "On the count of three, we start walking. One, two, three."

They half-pushed, half-dragged this human sack of problems up the clearing, toward the glow from the kitchen. It might not have been smooth, but together, three sisters were doing what no one else seemed able to handle.

Mole hollered, "He got it for Christmas and wouldn't let me ride it. I wanted a dirt bike way before my stepbrother, and my mother gave it to him and not me."

A man stuck his head out of a tent. "Keep it down. We've got kids sleeping here."

☮ ♥ ☮ ♥ ☮ ♥ ☮ ♥ ☮ ♥

At the Kid Korral kitchen and bliss fire, a Coleman lantern hung over the serving area, hissing its existence into the silence of the night. Kalmia stood on the far side of the fire, a purple velvet robe cascading off her shoulders, her unruly bronze hair springing off in all directions.

"We've got a brother who needs a warm, safe space to mellow out," Sapphire said.

"Please." Kalmia swept her hand through the air toward them, jangling the multitude of bracelets on her arms. "Bring the brother in."

Sapphire ducked under the branch railings. She tossed a sleeping bag off a bent-aluminum beach chair and pulled the chair towards the stove, until she felt the heat from the fire. Sara and Songbird guided Mole into the kitchen, and Sapphire pointed at the chair. Then, she sunk onto the ground. Hunkering down, she gripped the hard-packed soil with her bare hands and took a few deep breaths.

Kalmia smiled. "Hi, Mole. How are you this magnificent evening?"

Mole lowered himself into the chair as calmly as if he just came to drink tea. He rubbed his hands together and stretched his fingertips toward the fire.

Sapphire leaned toward Kalmia, keeping one eye on Mole, afraid he was going to explode again. "This guy is out there."

Kalmia nodded; her bronze hair sparkled in the firelight. "He's a good soul."

"I'm not sure what to do with him. Every time he seems like he's mellowing out, he turns up some place else even more freaked out."

Unfurling her statuesque physique, Kalmia rose and lifted a soot-blackened pot off the stove. She poured the hot liquid into a cup, added dried flaxen-looking flowers, and then stirred the tea with a spoon.

Sapphire rolled her eyes. Mole needed more than a cup of tea.

He slumped in his chair, rocking ever so slightly front to back, his hands stretched toward the fire.

Kalmia reached into her pocket and held out her hand to Mole, a small glass pipe in her long fingers. "Mole, do you want to smoke a bowl? I've got some real mellow herb."

Mole rolled his head in her direction. He reached out and took the small glass pipe from Kalmia.

He put the end of it in his mouth, and Kalmia struck a match, cupping her hand over the flame and the bowl. He inhaled once and coughed, sending the pipe flying into the stone stove, where it shattered.

Kalmia took the cup of tea from the stove, mixed in liquid from a canteen, and held the cup of tea in front of him. "Drink this."

Mole obediently took the tea and poured it into his mouth.

Sapphire glanced around at the others, who were laughing and chatting in that friendly late-night-around-the-campfire way. She sagged against the log. Getting him stoned wasn't the answer, yet when she opened her mouth to suggest an alternate plan, no words came forth. She studied Mole.

His lips hung loose, his pupils black saucers, and he stared at something in the woods.

All Sapphire could make out was the wood railing and the trees beyond. And that was the problem. The world he inhabited seemed different from her own, but she had no words to explain the cloud hanging over his head to Kalmia, and she wasn't sure how much of what she knew she had imagined herself and how much was real.

Kalmia cleared her throat. "How old are you, Mole?"

He rubbed his hands back and forth on his jeans, then dug the tips of his fingers into his thighs. "Eighteen. I turned eighteen while I was hitchhiking to the gathering. I'm from Kentucky."

Kalmia leaned toward Mole. "Are you here with anyone?"

"I don't know where my dad is." He frowned. "We left him a long time ago."

Sapphire closed her eyes, trying to forget her own pain and focus on Mole.

"What about your mother?"

"I don't like it there. Her boyfriend is mean to me."

Songbird stood behind Mole, massaging his shoulders.

Tears began to trickle from Mole's eyes. "Everyone told me I'd fit in at the gathering."

Sapphire curled herself up into a ball. The longing in his voice vibrated through her chest.

Mole cried, "I don't know why Dad left me."

His words pierced her heart, and she curled up, hugging her stomach as if squeezing the pain in her gut would mute the question she had asked herself every day for fifteen years. The question that she needed to clear from her life, if she was ever going to break free.

"How old were you?" Sara leaned against the railing, her arms crossed over her army fatigues.

"I think maybe ten. He was supposed to pick me up, but my mother showed up instead and said Dad was gone."

Sapphire's mother had been sitting under a gigantic oak tree on the school lawn, wearing faded hip-huggers and a purple paisley halter-top. Santa Ana January hot: the sky painted in peacock blue, but the horizon brown. The greasy stench of smog coating her nostrils. Sapphire ran across the lawn and plopped down next to Mommy in the shade. Mommy had a cold tub of caramel ripple and two spoons. While Sapphire savored her ice cream, Mommy said, "I have something to tell you." Sapphire had never eaten caramel ripple again.

Sara held Mole's hand. "Have you heard from him since then?"

Sapphire shook her head.

Mole said no. "But when I was sixteen, I got in trouble for starting a campfire. They told me I was bad. I wanted to be a Boy Scout. I wanted to get a badge for helping old people."

Sapphire let her head fall into her hands. "Did you start the fire at a campground?"

"In our garage."

All the energy drained out of Sapphire. She wiped her clammy hands on her jeans. He was a pyromaniac, probably tortured cats and chopped the tails off lizards. "Mole, do you still like starting fires?"

"That's bad," Mole muttered. "Mom said Dad was a bad man. She told me he was mean and hurt her, but my dad was gentle."

"It's sometimes hard to see things the way grownups see them, when you're little." Songbird crooned.

The words hit Sapphire like a right hook, mimicking the words her mother had uttered the day she confronted her. A fog of damp grief clutched at her heart and had been growing mold for years. Missing dads, scrambled brains, and lost children. Sapphire's mother had said the same thing when Sapphire was a kid. That when she was old enough, she would understand.

Mole said, "It was my fault he left. He didn't want me anymore. He thought I was dumb. I wouldn't shoot a gun 'cause I didn't want to hurt the bunnies."

Sara said, "It's not your fault, Mole. Your dad loved you. What happened between your parents was their business."

Sapphire's eye twitched, and she started to fidget with her coat.

"Mole. There was a reason your dad disappeared, and we can't judge what happened without knowing all the facts. Many children whose parents are divorced feel abandoned by the alienated parent." Kalmia pontificated as she stood up, lost her balance a bit, and grabbed onto the counter to steady herself.

Sapphire sighed. *Reading books isn't the same as the lump in your chest that never goes away.*

Kalmia flung her hair behind her head and leaned forward with her hands pressed against her heart.

The fire crackled and popped, and Sara said, "This is the first time I've hung out here at night. The vibe is mellower than when the kids are around."

Kalmia said, "There's an energy of peace in the midst of sleeping babies." She offered Sapphire a cup of tea.

Sapphire took the mug and sipped the hot liquid, which slowly dissolved the constriction in her throat.

Mole gulped his tea, oblivious to Kalmia's sermon. "Even Bob left without saying goodbye."

Sapphire asked, "Who's Bob?"

Mole turned toward her, "He's my big brother. Dad used to take us fishing and hunting. Dad liked Bob better than me."

Kalmia sang, "We love you, Mole."

"He just disappeared, and no one ever told me why he went."

"I know. Believe me, I know." Sapphire sighed and sipped her tea.

"We love you!!!" Sara and Songbird sang in unison.

Sapphire leaned toward Kalmia and lowered her voice. "I'm worried about Mole."

"In the morning, his body will be weary, but his mind clear."

"I think he has other problems besides the drugs."

"Oh, dear sweet Sapphire. For ten years, I have seen my brothers and sisters in this condition. But each time, they sleep and then awake reborn."

Mole wiped his face. "All I want to do is make things nice for people and be like everyone else. I don't want to be lonely anymore."

"What if this time it's different?" Sapphire asked Kalmia.

Kalmia patted her on shoulder and moved closer to Mole. "Remember when you had the puppy that was very sick?"

What fucking puppy and who cares? Sapphire swallowed the words she wanted to spit at Kalmia. *He was puppy-less last night.* She didn't know exactly what was wrong, but clearly, he had issues.

Kalmia's hair enveloped Mole, as she hugged him. "You devoted yourself to that puppy. You loved it and took care of it and gave it food. Do you remember that?"

Sapphire couldn't believe they were talking about a puppy, when so much was at stake.

"Yes." Mole solemnly raised his head.

Kalmia continued, "I remember how you took care of that sick puppy. Even though it woke you up all the time, you had endless patience with that puppy. You have a lot of love to share."

Sapphire finished her tea and set the cup on the ground beside her. Mole couldn't even take care of himself, let alone a puppy. Why couldn't the others see this?

Mole said, "I loved my puppy. It was like me; it had no one. I wanted to keep it, but a nice sister who lived on a farm in Tennessee said she'd take him home with her." He looked at Kalmia. "I didn't want to give her my puppy, but I figured she could take better care of it than me."

The jester entered the kitchen and deposited himself on the log next to Kalmia. Regally, he raised his staff to the fire. "You have the energy of Pluto and Saturn in your heart. That is hard energy to balance. Be wary you don't confuse the energies."

Sapphire rolled her eyes at his proclamations.

Songbird hugged Mole. "I knew there was a kind brother in this body somewhere. It just took us a while to find you."

Mole chuckled and rocked his head side to side, a tethered elephant at the circus.

Maybe she was the one who was confused. The others seemed to agree that Mole was a good kid who had tripped too much. After all, he had the wherewithal to worry about the puppy.

Kalmia smiled, "Mole, I'm glad laughter has re-entered your heart. You had us worried for a while."

Mole smacked himself on the side of his head. "Thanks."

The Jester and Sara smacked themselves upside the head, and everyone laughed.

The consensus seemed to be that Mole was saved, taken into the light, and reborn. Sapphire wanted to believe it was that easy. The wind blew through the trees, shaking the aspen leaves. Sapphire stared at the fire, changing shapes and colors before her eyes. One minute a temple, the next moment a riot. At Womyn's Healing Space, she had told others not to judge, so now she needed to take her own advice. Next to her,

Mole laughed and told them about the trucker who picked him up hitchhiking in Oklahoma.

Kalmia asked if anyone had been up to the parking lot in a few days.

The Jester pulled a harmonica out of his pocket and began to play. Songbird started to sing. Sapphire started to nod, feeling sleep welling up in her head.

The conversation drifted on, and she stopped paying attention to the words, just the sounds of voices. The pauses between words grew longer and longer. Perspective changed everything. Near or far. Atmospheric perspective, division of space. Values changing, depending on the composition. The story changing, depending on one's point of view. In her paintings, she controlled the viewer's gaze. In these woods, she had become the lost pilgrim on a dusty road or no road at all.

Sapphire jerked her head awake. Mole seemed half-asleep and barely listening to the conversations around him. He was the moment. He was peace. The birds began to chirp. The tops of the trees, which had been invisible in the night, took shape against the pink sky.

Songbird said, "Mole, you can sleep in our tent. We have an extra sleeping bag."

Sleep. Sleep was all they needed. A warm tent and dissolving into nothingness. It was cold. That was all. Cold and lonely, and he couldn't find the right way.

Sara, Songbird, and Mole said goodnight and ambled down the trail, with Sara and Mole clasping hands, pretending to be old friends at the end of a long night.

Sapphire lifted her palms up and stared at her hands.

Kalmia said, "He'll be fine."

"He just did too much; it was probably his first time," added the Jester.

"No doubt," Kalmia nodded.

Sapphire stood up, "I'm heading for bed, too."

Kalmia smiled. "Let the daybreak guide you to your tent."

Sapphire stumbled down the empty path, the sky a faded indigo overhead. Down below, human and canine bodies lay strewn in the meadow, fallen asleep around the smoldering remnants of the fire. White buckets of water and shovels, the only ones still standing.

With a wadded up jacket for a pillow, she slept. She dreamt of a crazy swordsman, roaming through the woods in the dark, slashing at trees.

She hid behind a tree, hoping to escape. The swordsman turned, looked at her, and laughed. "It's a video game," he yelled and swung the sword wildly above his head. His deep-seated eyes and pronounced eyebrows glared at her. "Do you want to play?"

INSIGHT IS EVERYTHING

Saturday, July 7, 1990
(Day Thirteen of Lauren's Gathering)

Family Picnic to Raise Funds for Roof Repair

Join Feather River Methodist Church this Sunday afternoon for a family picnic at Pioneer Park. Pastor Smithson invites everyone, Methodist or not, to join this family-friendly event from 11 a.m. until 5 p.m. Enjoy a game of softball, try your hand at horseshoes, or join in the volleyball tournament. There will be bunnies, goats, and sheep on hand for town kids who want to pet them. Pony rides and other games will be available, with all proceeds going to repair the roof on the church office building. When Pastor Smithson was asked if he was concerned that the hippies might show up, he laughed and said, "All are welcome to break bread with us." Stay tuned for a recap of the picnic in Monday's paper. *(Quincy Herald,* July 6, 1990)

LAUREN

Lauren roamed the post-dawn stillness, energized by the morning sun peeking through the pines. Ten hours of uninterrupted sleep, and she felt the remnants of her pre-pregnancy self flexing and stirring. *What a beautiful day,* she thought, happy to be at the gathering. Her skirt hung low on her hips. She had tied a red scarf over her chest and the diagonal end hung down over her belly button. Under her breasts in the spot where skin met skin, she felt the first traces of sweat. She could feel the cool morning air around her, but inside she was hot. Always hot, it seemed these days.

A brother smiled and waved. "Good morning, Mama."

She swallowed her response. *I'm not a Mama. Yet.* She put her arms around her belly and hugged the baby. Mamas were grown-up women who had finished college. When her older friends turned twenty-one, those who were old enough had gone bar-hopping, but by the time her birthday came in two months, she would not be able to drink, *because of the baby.* The future shapeless. Only with the past can anyone truly create meaning.

Thud. Something bounced off Lauren's shoulder and landed on the ground. She stopped. A small pine cone lay on the trail in front of her. She gazed up at what looked like a Jeffrey pine stretching over the trail. "Are you trying to tell me something?" A gust of wind shook the branches, and a few pine needles floated slowly to earth. "Oh!" The trees had known it all along. Freefalling through life, without knowing if you have a parachute.

For the first time, she grasped the fear the loggers felt at the prospect of their lives changing. The only difference was she could feel her baby growing, and they had nothing tangible to hint at where their future lay. She stared up at the trees, branches fluttering against clear blue sky. Her own fear of the future created magic goggles that revealed the fears of others—not just the loggers, but even her own mother, who had dragged Lauren to France during her senior year of high school, trying to figure out who she was, as a new phase of life reared up to consume her. Mother had talked about going to graduate school, studying history.

That autumn, Lauren got up at dawn every day and ran along the beach before the crowds packed the sand, and past the old man with the parrot, selling muffins and rolls, who would wave at her. That autumn, she returned to the apartment Mother had rented on a crooked alley in Nice, one block from the beach. Her energy melting as she climbed three flights of stairs. That autumn, Mother sipped tea and wandered aimlessly through the city streets, while Lauren soaked in bubble baths drinking lemonade. Mother had seemed unsure of herself, and that was exactly how Lauren felt now.

When she had called her mother to tell her about the baby, Mother said, "That's nice, dear. What about money? Are you coming home?" Lauren had wanted to ask her how she felt when she found out she was pregnant. Was it part of her life plan? But Mother had to run, meet with the caterers for the charity ball. She had said, "I'll think of something to tell Father."

Trying to keep her on the phone, on the other end of the line, connected for just a few more minutes, Lauren had said, "Mother?"

"Yes, dear."

"I didn't plan things this way."

"Of course not, dear."

"I'm not sure…"

"Sorry, dear, I have to run."

When Lauren had hung up the phone with her mother, she felt abandoned in the middle of a busy intersection. Wanting still to be sitting on her mother's lap reading a bedtime story. Now, she could see her mother's fear of being a grandmother, losing her looks, losing the envy of others. Lauren sighed. She had not just changed her own future, but Mother's as well, and they were both moving into the unknown without supporting each other on the journey.

As rudderless as her mother was, the cult-of-motherhood recruiters were hyper-focused on perineums and placentas. They dismissed Lauren's contempt for their proclamations on the joys of giving birth as raging hormones. She resented their orchestration of her pregnancy. She didn't need an hour-long discussion on the drawbacks of an episiotomy. Her body needed to revel in the redwood forest by moonlight, watching the owls glide fearlessly through the dark woods. If only people could leave her alone to discover for herself what she was unfolding inside, instead of smothering her seedlings of this new life. Alone in the woods, she found the mental space to tend her garden.

Lauren wandered the trail, peeked into kitchens where sleepy-eyed crews were sipping their first cup of *mud*. Luckily, the trail was still empty, and she walked, briskly, until her breath started to come hard, heavy. Birds chirped. The sun shone out of the east. Patches of sunlight glowed through the valley, and the ridges sparkled bright. The trees sang to her, the mountains hummed, and the dirt underneath her bare feet had a rhythm that propelled her, pulled at her heart. A rhythm no one else seemed to hear.

She grabbed a piece of bush and smelled it. Dry and musty. Too many dead branches under these pines. Must have been a long time since a wildfire came through here. Unhealthy. Years of fire suppression created a hot, fast burn when the forest finally went up in flames. The science of forest management that she studied in school was at odds with what happened on the ground, the politics of dividing the trees based on human needs, instead of sustainability.

Lucky for the gathering, they had been blessed with sporadic showers, which kept the immediate fire danger low. Unfortunately, other dangers kept popping up. On the trail, heading towards her was La Abuela. Lauren shuddered as she thought about the night before. All the other women were blissfully pregnant, and her acrimony in the midst of their joy created a separation between them, leaving her feeling even more isolated. Now, La Abuela would want to relive the entire nightmare. Lauren tried to find a path that would lead her into the trees and let the forest swallow her, leaving her a woman alone, rambling in nature.

"Ah, *mi hija.*" The old woman exclaimed, as she hugged Lauren.

Lauren turned and braced herself for more flowery monologues on this special time of her life. "Good morning," she said, hands hanging at her sides.

La Abuela finally let go and stepped back. She raised her hands as if to celebrate. "You go in peace. *Entre en paz.*"

"I slept well last night."

"This is good," La Abuela said. "The healing of the circle protected you from the shadows."

If being kidnapped by a bunch of old women who chanted over your belly and laid hands on your heart was good. Lauren shrugged her shoulders.

"You must create the space that fills you with love. Babies must be born with love."

"We are working it out."

"*Es muy importante.* If you are uncertain, then you have not found the home for your baby's spirit to enter into this world."

Lauren dutifully nodded. "Yes, Grandmother."

"*Muy bien.*" The old woman placed her hands on Lauren's forehead. "Not so much here," she said, moving her hands to the bottom of Lauren's right rib. The top of her hands pressing against Lauren's right breast, lifting it up slightly. "Here. Your liver."

Trapped between an old woman and a baby to be born, Lauren backed up, trying to elude the taste of liver and her increasing queasiness.

SAPPHIRE

Sapphire perched on the log in front of her tent, sketching and watching the activity on the trail below her. It had been cold the night before, and her body still had a bit of a chill. Wrapped in her heavy coat, her knitted gloves limited her dexterity, as she drew in the shade of the trees, the sun struggling to reach her. Finally, sunbeams hit the trees on the far side of the trail, creating intertwined shadows that she sketched, ignoring the actual trees. On the page, she drew the shadow of her father dancing to the sunrise. Two young women wandered down the trail, wrapped in multi-colored Mexican blankets that dragged in the dirt, kicking up dust. She grabbed a piece of charcoal and roughed out the dust. The blankets she drew floating down the trail, human-less. Dad enchanting the world by creating dancing blankets on a cold mountain morning, just to make her laugh. At just that moment, the sun reached through the trees and stroked her cheek.

She stretched her arms overhead, fingers grasping for the radiant sunlight. *Today,* she thought. Today he would appear with the ease of the sunrise over the mountains. The soft clicks and chucks of a bird floated up the hill towards her, sounding like some sort of blue jay. She scanned the trees and bushes but couldn't see any birds at all. A squeal of laughter burst out of the woods.

Startled out of her morning reverie, Sapphire spotted Lauren on the trail below her, sauntering down the trail without a care in the world. La Abuela joined her and they stopped on the side of the trail. Lauren and that baby-to-be got all the attention. She was probably telling La Abuela about the over-emotional basket case who stomped out of the Womyn's Healing Circle yesterday. Well, so what if she had. Lauren had blown her off, so it didn't really matter what she said.

Sapphire shoved a sketchpad and her pencil box into her daypack and zipped up her tent. Scrambled downhill. Slipped and slid a few feet, smacking her ribs against a rock. The pain jolted the fog out of her head. Made her realize she wasn't even sure what she was searching for anymore. Scrambling to her feet, she tried to choose which direction to go. Woods to the right, a meadow to the left, and her tent back up the hill.

☮ ♥ ☮ ♥ ☮ ♥ ☮ ♥ ☮ ♥

At the Tea Kitchen, Sapphire heard the now-familiar shout, "We love you!" followed by the much-coveted call to "Come have some pancakes." By the time she reached the kitchen, the line was thirty-plus people deep. She took her place in line and pulled out her bowl. Around her, small groups of friends talked as they waited for food.

"I was so cold last night."

"Did you hear that wicked guitarist at 411 Camp last night?"

"No way, dude. I missed it."

"Ping pong at Evelyn's tonight."

"Ping pong?"

Sapphire pulled out a fork, covered with dried tomato sauce. She poured some water on it and wiped it on her shirt.

"She couldn't find it."

"Did Taylor ever make it in?"

"Three days at the front gate."

The line moved forward, and Sapphire was closing in on pancakes.

"My arms are killing me from drumming all night."

"Go to First Aid and get that toe looked at."

"Gross."

Sapphire shuddered at the pus oozing from his toe. "Yuck." He needed to get that mess cleaned up.

When she reached the counter, a guy slid a pancake into her bowl. "Maple syrup and walnuts are on the counter." She nodded.

"Tea?" a kind sister asked.

"Yes. Please."

Everyone else sat with a friend or two or three, sipping tea, and laughing over pancakes. She sat alone. This is how things had ended up with Mole last night, leaving her with a bad taste in her mouth. The others had seen laughter in Mole. Kalmia thought she was making too much of the situation. It wasn't what Sapphire saw in him, but what she didn't see that made her wary. Two flip-outs in two nights. At the very least, he failed to learn from his experiences.

Next to her, two thirty-something women wearing clean jeans and t-shirts ate pancakes and sipped from blue enamel cups. One wore a red bandanna on her head. The bandanna woman said, "So, my ex-husband disappeared a year after we were married."

"He left?" her friend asked.

"I came home from work, and all his stuff was gone."

"Was there someone else?"

She shrugged her shoulders. "Well, the rub was he never said why he left."

"Did he file for divorce?"

"I did after six months." She took a sip from her cup. "His lawyer gave me the condo."

Sapphire interjected, "How long had you known him before you got married?"

"Three years."

"Wow." Sapphire asked, "What was his trip?"

The bandanna sister shook her head. "I have no idea. One day, we're having a romantic dinner on the pier. The next day, he was gone." She sipped her tea.

Sapphire said, "Sometimes people vanish."

The friend nodded.

"It probably had nothing to do with you," Sapphire said.

The bandanna woman nodded. "Uh-huh. I obsessed over it for two years, before I could finally let it go."

Sapphire said, "But it wasn't your fault." It wasn't the bandanna woman's fault at all. It wasn't anyone's fault, or so people told her. Of course, that had nothing to do with how she felt.

The other woman said, "It was about him and his choices."

That's the same line Sapphire's mother had fed her, when she was twelve and fifteen and twenty-one. She didn't know what to believe anymore.

The bandanna sister and her friend stood up. "Later, sis."

Left alone, she noticed the dirty plates lying on the ground around the fire and a couple of ratty shirts draped over a chair. She felt paralyzed. She had no control over any of it. That was the thing. They did it to her. No one even asked her what she wanted. She sipped her tea and watched Rastaman heading her way.

"Hey there, sister." He sat down next to her. "How goes life?"

She gazed up at him. "Life?"

He rubbed his beard. "The day. Breakfast. Your morning shit."

"How come you're not serving tea?"

He laughed. "That's not the only thing I do."

"Serve tea?"

"Well, what do you do besides drink tea?"

"Today?"

"Just in general."

"Sketch people. Try to see how they're put together."

He took a slow sip from his cup. "Nuh true, you're a philosopher?"

"An artist."

"Same thing."

She shrugged.

"You're always so lonely."

"No, I'm not."

"Then, how come you're always alone?"

That was the very question she was trying to figure out. "I don't know."

He took another sip from his cup, then set it on the ground. "Do you whittle?"

"Whittle?"

He pulled out a small knife and a piece of wood. "Like this?"

She shook her head.

"Whittling's about the opposite of life."

She scooped up the last pieces of walnuts from her bowl and chewed on them.

"I'm making a fish," he said. "I can make this fish be whatever I want it to be. Skinny. Round. Blue."

"You been doing it long?"

He nodded. "But life is what it is. Got a mind of its own. Stubborn that way life is. Old woman stubborn."

She contemplated this as she chewed and swallowed. "Don't you think you can influence life, change your path?"

He commenced whittling, and tiny bits of wood landed in the dirt. "Changing the world is tricky business."

"Oh, you don't even try?"

"Didn't say that, young lady." He pulled a small metal rod out of his pocket and began to press it into the sides of the wood.

"Can't you just say what you mean?"

He shrugged. "I thought I was."

He was crazy. She stood up. Stepped over the log.

"It's simple, sister. You can't change the world, only your response to it."

She lost her balance and fell back against the log. Her eye twitched. "I'm not the one who left." How could her perspective change her parents' lives or her own? "How I feel about things won't change what happened."

He just kept whittling. Started humming a tune.

"It wasn't my fault, but I'm the one who's suffering."

He glanced at her. "Yup. You're the one who's suffering," he repeated.

⊛ ♥ ⊛ ♥ ⊛ ♥ ⊛ ♥ ⊛ ♥

Sapphire huddled by her tent, breaking twigs into pieces and tossing the chunks down the hill. She preferred being hidden from the world but still able to see what was happening. No people in your face telling you what was wrong, who pretended to care and then disappeared. Watching left her in control. Able to choose when and where to reveal herself.

A voice called out from Lost Souls' kitchen, "Kitchen needs water."

On the trail below, a small boy pulled a puppy along behind him on a rope. An older girl scooped up the puppy, and the boy reached for it. Sapphire wondered if they were brother and sister, destined to be at odds with each other, yet as attached as the puppy was to the little boy; the destiny of being a big sister and her little brother. Sammy was thirteen now and taller than Sapphire. His dad was there every day, but all that could change if Brandon disappeared, and then she and Sammy would be both be fatherless. She couldn't imagine Sammy feeling lonely. He was like an overgrown retriever, happy to play ball with anyone anytime.

The call from the kitchen rang out again. "Who wants to make a water run?"

Some days Sapphire tried to believe that she could shake off her past and dance into her future. Today wasn't one of those days. She sighed as she walked over to the kitchen.

The guy in bib overalls holding the two jugs called out, "Who wants to make a water run?"

"I'll go."

"Water's awful heavy."

"And I'm strong." Sapphire glared at him.

"Alrighty then."

She grabbed two blue five-gallon jugs with "Unboiled Spring Water" printed in black marker on the side and headed for the spigot.

Taking the shortcut through the rows of scraggly Douglas firs, she picked up the trail to the spring as it twisted back into the canyon, past a stand of gigantic incense-cedar and toward the creek. White PVC pipe jutted over the boulders and should have brought clean unspoiled water from the spring on the hillside above. Today, the stones that lined the basin were dry.

She checked the signs: "Don't touch pipe with hands or containers." "Boil water for five minutes or filter with a 1-micron filter." "Water is life." "No soap within 300 feet of water sources." She set the water jugs on the rocks and wiggled the pipe. No water. Either the spring had gone dry or the pipe was broken. She glanced around hoping to find someone who knew what to do, but it was clear she was on her own.

She tracked the pipe upstream, staying as close to the line as the terrain allowed her. At every joint, she stopped and checked the connection between the pipes. Picking her way between the smoky granite boulders surrounding the creek, she spotted two ends of white PVC pipe. The bottom one had a connector on it. Water poured out of the other end onto the bank and sloshed into the creek.

She grabbed both ends and tried to force the bottom one into the connector. Using her body weight to hold down the upper pipe, she managed to leverage the lower pipe into position. It leaked a bit but seemed to hold.

Proud of her work, she headed back to fill the jugs; she leapt over boulders and twirled on the grass. The sun was shining, and the sky was bluer than cerulean. Her arm would swoop across a giant canvas, spreading cobalt blue from one end to the other, and still not be able to capture the expanse of sky shimmering overhead. As she came down the hill, she saw Edgar filling water jugs at the tap. It was easy, she thought, so easy to fix things when she went with the flow. She giggled at her pun.

She called out, "Hello, Edgar. How are you today?"

"How long has the water been back?" he demanded, as he switched out one jug from under the pipe and replaced it with a second one.

"I just fixed it."

"Who authorized you to fix it? We have a water crew. We can't have twits like you messing things up."

She staggered backwards. "I was just trying to help."

"Hell. Now I'm going to have to redo everything."

"I fixed it, you moron. What is your problem?"

"You don't see the problem?" He shook his head, then grabbed his water containers and marched into the woods.

Fucking bastard! She collapsed on a rock and sobbed, gulping for air, wishing Sammy's childhood face was gazing into hers and saying, "What's the matter, big sister." He always called her big sister even though she was the only sister. She had made a mess of everything.

A robin landed on the grass and bobbed toward her, singing a cheery tune.

"Hi there, robin. Are you the same robin I saw before?"

The robin stabbed at the grass, then cocked its head and glanced at her.

"What? Haven't you ever had a bad day?"

It trilled at her.

She wiped her nose on her shirtsleeve and stood up.

The robin squeaked at her and flew away.

No doubt, it was off to find another worm somewhere. "Sorry," she called after it, feeling a bit guilty about scaring it away.

Finally, she could do what she came to do. The water boomed as it hit the sides of the empty plastic container. There weren't supposed to be leaders here. At least that's what the flyer said, "Ignore all rumors of organization. We are all equal." *Equal until she stepped on someone's toes.*

She filled the second jug, then grabbed both of them and headed back to camp. By the time she was halfway back, her muscles were trembling. After a brief rest, she dumped a little water from each container into the grass and followed the trail back toward the kitchen. As she approached the opening in the trees that led back to the kitchen, her arms began to tremble with the strain. She set the jugs down and shook out her arms.

She rolled her shoulders, trying to loosen her muscles, picked up the jugs, and staggered down the trail. Edgar's ugly words echoed in her head: *How the hell do you know anything?* Maybe he was right. All she was doing was making enemies with people who wanted to be her friends. She stopped again to rest her load. The sweat soaked through her shirt and stuck to her. Then, she heaved the jugs off the ground and kept going. The sound of the dinner conch floated up out of the valley. Was it first call already?

The clatter of people shouting and banging pans announced the kitchen. Mickey coordinated a handful of cooks and a dozen or more helpers. He screeched, "Wash your hands." A deeper voice shouted, "Dogs out of the kitchen."

Exhausted, Sapphire set the jugs down under the counter. "Here's water if you need it."

"It's about time," said the same irritating guy in bib overalls. "We've been waiting for hours."

She sighed. It hadn't been hours. A bit over an hour. Insulted, she glared at him: his eyes glassy from smoking weed. She wondered if he had done anything today besides getting stoned. "You're just lucky I brought back any water."

"We needed that water to boil pasta for dinner, and now there's not enough time."

Sapphire's eye began to twitch. "I had to fix the damn pipe. You should be glad you're getting water at all."

"Well, I hope you remember that comment the next time you get fed."

She never managed to get food here anyway. Half the time, they ran out before she got anything. She huffed, "What are you tripping on? You've got your water, let it be."

He grabbed one of the jugs, "Hey, it's half empty." He rattled the other one and the water sloshed around inside. "Why did you take them if you weren't going to fill them?"

Her lower back spasmed, and she grabbed onto the railing to steady herself. "They're three-quarters full."

"Barely."

"They weighed fifty pounds each."

He emptied the jugs into a huge pot. "If that was all you could carry, you should have only taken one jug. We'd have gotten someone else to fill the other."

"It's ten pounds to the gallon," she said.

"Eight." He turned away from her and yelled, "We need someone strong to do a water run."

Humiliated, she yelled, "If you didn't wait until the last minute for everything." From the meadow, the call of the conch shell rolled up the hill, as if to rub it in.

The guy turned his back to her and mumbled, "What's that supposed to mean."

"Nothing," she mumbled. *Absolutely nothing.*

He slammed a pot onto the metal locker with a clang.

She kicked an empty bucket and watched it bounce across the dirt. *Fuck you,* she thought, and stomped back to her tent. Ripped open the fly and yanked her stuff out, throwing things on the ground. When she had emptied the tent, she jerked up the stakes and slid the poles out of their casings. Wrenching the poles apart at the joints, she folded them, end over end.

Then, she shook out her tent, snapping it in the air, and crammed it into a sack before stuffing her gear into her backpack. Grabbing a downed branch, she swept the site where her tent had been and the small path her feet had made over the last week or so. Then, she threw an armful of duff into the air. She tossed the branch onto the spot, hoisted her pack onto her back, and set off down the trail.

She did not need this any more than she had needed her stepdad, Brandon, pulling strings after she got busted spraypainting the bridge at China Basin. Sentenced to community service and probation, Sapphire had wanted to pick up trash in the park, but Brandon had gone to law school with the judge and got her assigned to some stupid art therapy program they were running for rape victims at the crisis center on Polk.

Brandon had driven that first day. Double-parked in front of the doors. Watched while she rang the bell and they buzzed her in.

She shuffled into the room, afraid to meet their eyes, staring at the floor, trying to hide what she thought was their shame and returning to them a sense of dignity, until she realized she was trying to hide her own shame.

Mrs. Brenton, the therapist who organized the class, paired her up with a woman a few years older. Sally was nineteen, only she seemed more like ten, so hunched inside herself she almost disappeared. Sapphire floundered for the right words, hating having been sent here to help with art therapy. Whatever that was. She was supposed to teach the practical aspects of painting, while Mrs. Brenton guided them in uncovering their emotions, putting feeling on paper, symbolically shedding fear or loneliness or rejection. Some of the women were bright and cheery, painting blue skies overhead or a girl flying a kite along the ocean, hoping that a pretty picture would solve their problems, as if painting had solved anything in her life.

Speechless that first day, Sapphire babbled on about mixing color and the difference between oils and acrylics and squeezed a rainbow of colors onto Sally's palette. She taught her Impasto strokes, using wooden Popsicle sticks and impressionist dabbing techniques that created pixilated trees and fences.

But Sally. She was charcoal gray and black with dark red. Red the color of dried blood. Red that conjured up Sally's own blood where the knife had slashed her throat ever so slightly and the blood dried before he was done with her. Or so she told Sapphire. She never mentioned the other, just the scar on her neck. The fine white line about three inches long. The line that separated them. The line Sally's father drew with a knife when she was sixteen. The age Sapphire was then, when she hadn't seen her own dad in six years.

By the third week, Sally was blending shades of gray with an occasional foray into blues, and Sapphire felt comfortable enough to talk to her. To ask her what happened next. After demonstrating a brush stroke and letting the question hang in the air, Sapphire remained silent. Left the space open for Sally's words or her tears.

Sally painted the answer. A black canon with a child's bloody carcass draped over the top, and an eagle swooping down from the upper right-hand corner. Only the eagle looked more like a duck; the canon, like a penis; and the only light in the corner came from a waterfall cascading down a rock face. A light blue waterfall with a rainbow in the corner.

Sally never had said much, and Sapphire had not either. But after those sessions, Sapphire had gone home to her corner of the garage and had painted fallen angels, torn-apart dragons, ballerinas with knives in their backs. Trying to figure out what was wrong with her.

Sapphire stumbled on a tree root and grabbed the trunk to steady herself. Enough about the past, already. She focused on getting out of this Mad Hatter's Tea Party before she lost her mind. In the meadow below, the dinner conch blew again, louder. She hustled along the trail, dodging people, hoping to make it to the parking lot before dark or someone else yelled at her. She squinted at the sun starting to dip toward the west, toward the Pacific Ocean and home. She probably had two hours.

The seventy bucks in her wallet would get her a motel for the night and dinner. All she needed was a ride into town. At the crest of the trail, the crowd spread across the meadow. Her right eye twitched. There were five thousand people in the meadow, and she was alone. Looking for Dad was a mistake. If he wanted her, he would have found her. She had been dreaming about him for longer than she had even known him. She was such an idiot. All that time wasted on him. *What about me? Don't I deserve to be the star of my own life?*

If she found him, she would throw rocks at him, throw glass bottles. Make him bleed. Leave scars on his arms and cheeks, indistinguishable from the scars he had left in her heart. She marched down the trail, furious at everyone.

"Safe journeys, sister."

"See ya next year."

"Happy trails."

An old man waved a stick of burning sage in front of her face. She side-stepped him, only to end up face-to-face with three teenage girls who waved scarves in the air and started to dance.

"Excuse me."

The girls burst into giggles and stepped aside.

A woman her mom's age called out, "Darling. Eat before you go."

Many kitchens had already brought food, which was sitting in the center of the meadow in coolers and five-gallon buckets. Her stomach growled again. Cutting through the meadow would be quicker than the hike around. She plunged through the crowd, heading for the trail on the far side of the meadow that would take her to the parking lot and out of this nut show.

In the center of the meadow, the grass had been worn down to bare soil from the daily gathering for dinner, and the people wandering around kicked up the soil, creating a low-lying haze. She picked her way through the crowd, avoiding loose dogs, sleeping babies, and trying not to run into anyone she knew. A man by the servers yelled at the top of his lungs, an announcement swallowed by the vastness of the meadow and muffled by the sheer number of people.

The air behind her burned hot. She clenched her fists and gulped air, struggling to stand upright as a wave of impending doom covered her. She stepped sideways, trying to catch her balance, and turned just a bit.

Black trench coat.

Mole.

THE PAST IS ALREADY GONE, THE FUTURE IS NOT YET HERE

Saturday, July 7, 1990
(Day Twelve of Sapphire's Gathering)

Always trust your gut; it knows what your head
hasn't figured out yet.
—Anonymous

SAPPHIRE

Standing in the middle of the Dinner Circle circus, surrounded by people dressed in pink, orange, and purple hippie garb, Mole stood motionless, a mannequin in a black coat. Sapphire crumpled to her knees, clutched the ground, and dug her fingers into the dirt. She gasped and choked on the dust being kicked up. Her eyes spasmed. Everything around her blinked on and off, as if under a strobe light. Not again. Desperately, she searched the crowd hoping to see someone she knew: Kalmia or Bumblebee, even Lauren. When she glanced back at Mole, he was just broad shoulders holding up a black trench coat, staring at the performance that was Dinner Circle.

"It's time to circle up."

A man reached down for her hand, and Sapphire pulled back, dazed.

"Circle up, family!"

The huddles of people melted into rows, and then the lines started to curve. Mole vanished. Sapphire clasped the outstretched hand of the man next to her, and he pulled her to her feet.

Around her, people joined the Om, but she couldn't manage a deep breath, or even a proper exhale. Couldn't manage much more than a hum. A sense of dis-ease lodged in her bowels. Her eye twitched and she scoured the circle, trying to spot the black coat and whatever was going to happen next.

After the Om, the food servers made their way around the circle. She filled her bowl with bean stew and vegan linguini and shoveled the food into her mouth, barely chewing before swallowing, in her rush to get the food into her stomach. Someone she didn't recognize from the Blue Moon Bakery handed her a roll, and she stashed it in her bag for later. As she ate, she scanned the crowd for Mole, preparing herself for the moment of impact.

"Hey, Sapphire," a voice boomed.

Great, now Grizzly Bear Garth shows up. Where was he twenty minutes ago?

He lowered himself to the ground and leaned back on his arms. "How's dinner?"

She scooted around to face him. "I was about to pass out from hunger."

"How come you got your backpack down here?" Garth asked.

"I'm heading out after dinner."

Garth grabbed his beard and tugged on it. "I thought you were staying till cleanup."

"Changed my mind."

Garth lit a cigarette and stared at it with disdain. "I'm trying to quit, but…"

Sapphire continued searching for the black trench coat. "Garth, I need to talk to you about this guy." Sapphire yanked a clump of grass out of the ground.

Garth pushed his gray cowboy hat back on his head and laughed. "I don't really deal with boy problems. That is, unless he did something to you."

She shook her head. "I think there's something wrong with him. Every night he trips, flips out, and it turns into a movie."

"You'll have that."

"That's what everyone keeps saying, but I think there's something more going on. I think there's something wrong with him."

Garth leaned towards her. "How do you mean?"

She shrugged her shoulders. "He's here at the circle. Or at least he was twenty minutes ago. Stubbled blonde hair, tall, wearing a black trench coat."

"Well then, if you spot him, point him out and I'll talk to him."

Her stomach rumbled from eating too fast, and she felt the urge to go find him, go find him accompanied by Garth, and maybe then Mole wouldn't scare the bejesus out of her. She fiddled with the withered stalks of grass she had yanked out of the ground. "Do you want to look for him now?"

Garth took a couple of drags off his cigarette and then smashed it out in the dirt. "I'm heading up to Mad Hatter's," he said. "PS told me they're serving cookies at dark-thirty, and I don't want to miss out." He looked at the sky. "I never can figure out when dark-thirty is, anyway."

Overhead, the indolent clouds stretched across the sky, erasing the last moments of blueness from the day. Sapphire shivered a bit and realized she needed to leave if she was getting out before dark. She packed up her meal gear and then slipped into her sweater.

Garth heaved his body up until he towered above her. "Why don't you come with me, and we'll talk for a while before you leave?"

Sapphire gazed around at the people eating and talking. Her right eye twitched, and she wiped her damp forehead with her sleeve. If Mole was crazy and she didn't get Garth involved, then something bad was bound to happen, and it would be all her fault for not speaking up. If she was clueless, then it was better she just split. She fiddled with the zipper on her daypack, trying to sort out what she was feeling, trying to make the right decision for once in her life. "Can we, um, find this guy first? Um, I really need for you to meet him, the guy."

Garth bent down, grabbed her pack, and swung it onto his shoulder. "Cookies first, then we find the guy, and then I'll get you a ride into town."

Sapphire stood up. "It will be midnight by then."

She shook her head and stared as the last remnants of sun vanished in the trees. "I don't need your help with my gear; I need it with this guy."

Garth swaggered towards the trail and hollered over his shoulder, "Let's get a move on, and we'll discuss this guy while we eat."

"Come back here!"

"No time, if we're gonna get cookies."

Sapphire stood her ground. "You're stealing my pack."

Garth kept walking.

She ran after him. "I can't go with you—I have to find this guy."

"We'll find him."

"All night he flips from stoned to insane, and every time I ditch him, he reappears even worse than before."

"That's the way it happens. Too much LSD, and they think Jesus and the shitter are one and the same."

"That's what Kalmia said."

"They're all that way. Three days later they're fine."

"But you don't know this guy."

Garth asked, "What did he do?"

The things that had seemed so terrifying the night before didn't seem that crazy now. "He scared me, and then smacked his head on the ground and blathered nonsense."

"Trust me on this," Garth said. "I've been dealing with this shit for almost twenty years,"

"But," Sapphire stomped her foot. "It doesn't feel right to me." She crossed her arms and opened her mouth to speak, but the words got all twisted up. She wanted to tell Garth about the burnt trees and marshmallows, and Mole's mom who wasn't even here, but that all sounded so melodramatic and she didn't want Garth to think she was hysterical. She pushed the stray hairs out of her face and tucked them into the thick braid that hung down her back.

"How about after cookies, we'll go find this guy. What's his name?"

"Mole." Then, Sapphire started to second-guess herself. She had completely failed to distinguish her own father from other aging hippies. After fifteen years, she couldn't tell anymore where her imaginary dad ended, and her flesh-and-bones dad began. Maybe it was the same way with Mole.

"Rumor is, almond chocolate chip."

Everything was junked up in Sapphire's head, and she couldn't think straight. Her thoughts had become a painting that just wasn't working, and no matter how many layers of paint she applied, everything got worse, not better. Finding Mole by herself probably wouldn't solve anything better than last night and the night before. Shuddering at the thought of another encounter with Mole on her own, she realized that Garth was the only person she knew that would know how to deal with the flip-outs.

Garth cleared his throat. "Are you coming?"

Too exhausted to argue anymore, she followed him.

Garth said, "Man, this day has been crazy. The Forest Service movie at Main Gate was getting out of hand."

Sapphire sighed as she floundered after him, half-listening to his stories in the hopes that he would deal with Mole and get her a ride to town. If eating cookies was the price to pay for all of it, then that's what she had to do.

"Sometimes I don't know if I get more exasperated with our people or theirs. I worry someone will take a swing at them, and then I'll have to break up a riot."

A tall man rushed toward them. He called out, "Grizzly Bear. Grizzly. Man, we've been looking all over for you."

Garth straightened up on point, reminding her of her best friend's Labrador who got all stiff-legged and bold when men wearing hats entered the house.

"Jack's up at Welcome Home, screaming at everyone."

Feeling utterly deflated, Sapphire turned around to look back towards the darkening meadow. Garth was going to abandon her again to deal with something more important. She'd have to go back to the meadow and find Mole on her own.

Garth stroked his beard. "He been drinking?"

"Sure seems like it. Edgar sent me down here to get you."

She tensed up. Not that jerk, Edgar. Well, at least she wasn't going to have to deal with him.

"Well, hell." Garth shook his head. "Isn't there anyone else can deal with Jack?"

"Grizzly, you know Jack listens to you."

Sapphire tried to remember just how far an uphill hike it was to the parking lot.

The brother said, "If I go back up there without you, Edgar is going be all over my ass."

"Let Edgar handle him this time," Garth said. "I'm going to get cookies at Mad Hatter's. If it don't work out, send word down later."

Resentment gripped Sapphire's chest. She was sick of being tossed aside when something more interesting came up. She snapped, "Don't let me get in the way of your important life."

"Me and you eating cookies. That's what's important."

She tried to gauge whether he was serious or bullshitting, but his facial expressions hid behind his graying beard. She couldn't figure him out.

"Come on, girl." Garth meandered up the trail and told her that yesterday afternoon, the Forest Service had promised they would wait twenty-four hours before they started towing cars off Old Mill Road. Then, at dawn this morning, they started towing and he had to go up there and stop it.

The first stars began to flicker. Trying to change her attitude, Sapphire asked, "Why is everyone so angry at the Forest Service?"

"They don't like that we gather without asking permission." Garth tugged on his beard. "Hell, the First Amendment is the only permit we need. They just can't deal with a non-organization that's disorganized and gets all this done."

In the twilight, the trail grew crowded with parents carrying their kids back to their camps, and Sapphire had to keep stepping off the trail to allow the larger groups to pass, but Garth kept ploughing ahead. She said, "I think that's why guys hate Womyn's Healing Circles so much. They just can't understand that women don't need a guy to solve all their problems."

"They don't bash men?" Garth asked.

She forced a laugh. "You think you're all that important?"

They approached the kitchen and the scent of fresh-baked cookies hung in the air. She squeezed through the miniature doorframe into Mad Hatter's Kitchen, while Garth stepped over the small branch railing. She could have bribed Mole to come here using the promise of cookies—a temporary solution at best. Garth completely ignored the people waiting patiently in line. A voice called out, "Hey, Grizzly," and Garth nodded his head. He sauntered to the counter and grabbed a handful.

Garth handed her two cookies. She inhaled the vanilla and chocolate and the familiar smell brought back memories of baking cookies with Dad in the house in Hollywood and licking the bowl clean. She cradled the cookies in her hands. The soft chocolate left dark brown spots on her palm.

Garth chomped on a cookie. "Do you want to sit down?" he asked, pointing toward the campfire.

She nodded, and they drifted toward the small group of people sitting on logs around the blaze. A man strummed a meandering rhythm on his guitar, and another accompanied him on an ocarina; the hollow ceramic ball created a lilting melody as he blew into it, and his fingers danced across the multiple holes.

Garth deposited the pack on the ground and sat on a makeshift bench. Sapphire took the spot next to him. "I keep running into this weird guy."

"You told me." Garth took another bit of a cookie. "Where you from?"

"California."

"Me too. I grew up in Elk Grove. Near Sacramento."

Sapphire glanced around. On the other side of her, two men talked about Old Testament values versus Jesus-as-social-worker Christianity.

"But the church is hung up on the rules of the past."

"Jesus loved the street people. The down and out. That's why we're washing feet at our camp."

"I dig it, man. That was how Jesus showed his love."

Sapphire smiled at them, wondering if they had washed the feet of that guy with the infected toes, before asking Garth, "Did you grow up on a ranch?"

"Tract house in the suburbs."

"Do you ride horses?"

He laughed. "I didn't ride my first horse till I was twenty-five, and the damn thing dumped me and broke my foot."

"Did you try again?"

"Not that day. I ended up in the emergency room, but I can ride a little bit now, if the horse is gentle enough."

"Can you rope?"

Garth shook his head. "I'm strictly a dude ranch cowboy."

"So, why do you dress that way?"

"What way?"

"The cowboy hat, Lee jeans, and a button-up shirt. Most guys I've seen dressed like that are at the rodeo, riding a bull and chewing tobacco."

"I don't know. Seems to be a pretty normal way of dressing where I'm from." Garth stroked his beard. "So, where 'bouts in California are you from."

Sapphire pictured Mom in the backyard of the bungalow in Hollywood, weeding flowers, and her parents kissing while she watched. She wanted Garth to take her seriously. "I was born in Topanga Canyon in a birthing yurt by the creek."

Garth stared at her and then turned his head toward the flames. "Your folks are hippies?"

"I guess."

"Miles away from the tract I grew up in." Garth took another bite out of his cookie. "I never even heard the word 'yurt' until I came to the gathering with some buddies from my platoon." His eyes crinkled up, and that was the only way Sapphire could tell he was smiling under his beard. "I lived in Hollywood until I was ten," she said.

"Lots of crazies there."

"Then, my mom and I moved to San Francisco."

"What about your dad?"

"When I was a kid, he would take me to see him in the movies." She unzipped her jacket, letting the heat from the fire sink into her chest, the knots in her shoulders softening, the memory of the past comforting her. "How long have you been coming to gatherings?"

"Since I got discharged from the Marines in my early twenties."

"Doesn't it ever get to you?"

"Vietnam?"

"The gathering," she said.

"Sometimes. But I can't stay away."

Sapphire wiped the crumbs off her hands. "I thought it was about making peace and harmony."

"After all these years, I still don't know what it's about."

"What about making a place in the world for everyone to feel loved?" She rubbed her palms against her worn denims. "All I see are people arguing with each other or getting stoned out of their minds." She heard her father's voice echoing in her head. *Peace in our hearts creates peace in our world.*

Garth cleared his throat. "Sounds like things ain't going your way."

Sapphire's eye twitched. No one saw Mole the way she did or understood why she needed to find her father. She kept peering through a glass door. Inside, people laughed and ate, but no one heard her banging on the door. "It's not about my way. It's about changing the world and making a difference."

"It takes a long time to understand how the gathering functions. There's a lot going on beneath the surface."

"I grew up going to the Griffith Park Be-Ins, seeing what was left of Jefferson Airplane play at Marx Meadows in San Francisco. Dad was always telling Mom to go with the flow and be one with the universe or nothing was going to change. And Mom would say, 'That's great, but what about today? Who's going to feed us?' They never listened to each other. So, it's the same shit here, and eventually half the folks are going to disappear."

"How long has it been since you seen him?"

"Garth, that's not the point. Instead of people respecting differences, they just yell at each other until someone leaves. I don't need to be here for this. I can find this bullshit anywhere."

Garth unbuttoned his jacket and took it off. His belly hung over his pants just enough to strain the buttons on his shirt.

"At any rate, that's why I'm taking off tonight. What I need isn't here."

"Like your dad?"

Sapphire stood up and straddled the log bench.

"What are you really looking for?" he asked.

She tried to swallow the thoughts but failed. *I want love.* Sapphire held her breath until her chest hurt, and then exhaled. A guy threw a log on the fire and the flames erupted. "I'm not. Looking for anything that's here."

Garth munched on his cookie, brushing crumbs from his beard.

Sapphire held her breath again, hoping if she choked down the thought, it would be forgotten. Even if Dad didn't love her, she wasn't sure why no one else seemed to love her, and it seemed awfully pathetic to tell other people you wanted love.

"Anyway, I seen you hanging out with Lauren a bunch."

"Not so much."

"You ain't friends?"

She shrugged.

"Lauren's a good egg. First, I remember her she was working parking—might have been the '88 gathering."

She shrugged her shoulders, not wanting to say anything bad about Lauren.

Garth took another bite. "She loves your drawings."

Sapphire broke a piece off a cookie and put it in her mouth. "I'm supposed to be grateful that she bestows her blessings on my work?"

Garth leaned over to the guys sitting near them and asked for a swig of their water. After pouring it in his mouth, he put the lid back on and returned it.

"I have water." Sapphire held out her water bottle.

"Seems to me that she might be a little scared of becoming a mama."

"Lauren? Scared?"

"Hell, even I get scared. It's why I get mean. Sometimes, it just seems safer to punch first and ask questions later."

She couldn't even imagine what would scare Garth. He was big and strong and dominated everything he did. She unscrewed the lid from her water canister and took a sip, before closing it up and sticking it in the side pocket of her pack. She didn't know what to say.

"Just 'cause we're here, don't mean we got it all together. We're all just traveling on this road, trying to find a better, more peaceful way of living." Garth laughed. "At least that's what we tell ourselves."

"He was living it."

"Your dad?"

"He was trying to change the world, make a place where the human spirit was celebrated, not crushed."

"Sounds like a good man."

"Mom didn't think so. She kicked him out when I was ten, and I haven't seen him since."

Garth shifted his weight around on the log. "That was a damn good cookie."

"Unless you consider watching old movies as seeing your dad."

"I knew a guy once who claimed he was a movie star, but I never really believed him."

Sapphire sat down, stretching out her legs, and busied herself with rearranging stuff in her daypack.

"Said he was in Butch Cassidy with Robert Redford."

Her heart froze and, just as she felt a lack of oxygen, her heart kicked into high gear, pounding.

"I was working construction." Garth laughed. "I mean, how many movie stars do you know swinging a hammer in Albuquerque? So, one day, he has us all over to his apartment and we watched a couple of B-rated movies on video, and sure enough, he was in them."

The chain link between the past and her memories vanished, and Sapphire could see herself in a pea-green rain poncho, walking in the park with Dad, holding hands and blowing bubbles, singing nursery rhymes.

"In some of those old movies, he'd been really sharp-looking, but that winter he was trashed. Track-marks all over his body and barely able to stay awake. We figured the only reason he had a job was 'cause someone owed him something. He sure didn't do much work."

This couldn't be the father of her future. "His name?"

Garth looked up at the stars. "John," he said. "John something. It was Scandinavian, I think. Lofgren, Lars, Larson. Something like that."

Suffocating plumes of smoke covered Sapphire's face. Time became bare feet on broken glass. She pressed her palm into the log until blood dripped onto her shoe. She pushed harder, searing the pain into her memory like a daguerreotype image of something she should have felt long ago.

"This guy John was a real trip," Garth said. "Told us he was one of the horsemen chasing Butch Cassidy across the desert. In the film, you can't see their faces. I was never quite sure if he was bullshitting, but he was an old hippie all right. Some things you just know."

She pictured a beige couch, springs busted. Courtyard motel littered with broken-down cars and tumbleweeds. He never even sent her a birthday card.

Garth shook his head. "I've lost a few good friends to dope." He took off his cowboy hat and scratched his forehead, then firmly wedged the hat back on his head. "I never could figure out why they want to sit on a couch all day long, nodding in and out of life."

She stood up and staggered. He grabbed her elbow. The long brown beard streaked with gray moved up and down as he talked.

Sapphire yanked her arm free and fell toward the trail. She crawled through the dirt, grabbed hold of a tree, and pulled herself upright. Darkness enveloped her. Silence seeped into her pores. She smacked her shoulder on a branch. Trail. Out. Away from here. From him. Blinded. Despair swelling her belly.

She heard thudding footsteps behind her.

Dad flopped on a threadbare couch, telling everyone what could have been, *if only.*

Garth grabbed her.

"Leave me alone."

"Hold still, little girl. What's going on?"

Her dad dissolved into a scrawny cur with shifty eyes and pus-filled lesions on his back. Her stomach knotted up and her shoulders heaved. She fell to her knees, pressed her hands into the earth and hunched her back. The scream locked in her belly came rumbling out, all mixed up in beans and rice and chocolate chip cookies.

The mess steamed in the brisk air. She shivered. Felt the looming night piercing her chest. Mud on her hands. Hulking body squatted beside her.

"Hey," Garth asked. "What in hell is going on?"

Sapphire shifted her weight off her left arm and brought it up to wipe her mouth. "Are you getting me a ride out of here?" She leaned to her side and collapsed onto her right haunch.

"You're not going anywhere, until you tell me what's up. Folks just don't go stomping up trails and puking their guts out for nothing."

"I want a hot shower and a mattress."

He squinted at her. "Are you pregnant?"

Pregnant! She'd have to be having sex for that. He didn't have a clue. "Just 'cause you knew some junkie actor don't mean he's my dad."

Garth took a deep breath and exhaled, loud and loose. "Wow."

Sapphire slumped to the ground. Clutched onto a piece of bark to keep herself from floating away. "My dad was in *Butch Cassidy and the Sundance Kids.* He was one of the guys on horses chasing Butch across the desert."

"You're sure you're not pregnant?"

His eyes pinched together, and Sapphire could see he was worried about her. She rolled her eyes at him.

"Why'd he run off?"

"My mother kicked him out."

Garth lit a cigarette and smoked it in short quick puffs. "Harsh."

"He was cheating on her." That was the first time she had said the words aloud. Waves of nausea rolled through her body; then, she heaved again. *Shit.* He could have told her this the night she arrived at the gathering. Wiping her mouth with her sleeve, she said, "Why didn't you tell me you knew my dad?"

"Didn't remember John until you started talking about Hollywood." Garth rolled back off his heels and sank onto his left side. He stretched himself out and pushed his hat back off his face. "You never told me your dad's name."

"How'd he end up in New Mexico?"

Garth shrugged his shoulders. "People change. Life changes."

"Not like that."

"Yes." He paused, then rubbed his eyes. "I did. And I didn't want to."

Sapphire glanced up at him and thought she might even see tears in his eyes. "Vietnam?"

"That's what some people called it."

She stared at the creases inscribed on his face, his punishment for murdering a baby and carrying that weight around with him every day. "Do you think he's still there? In Albuquerque?"

Garth's radio crackled and exploded with electronic sounds. "First Aid to Grizzly Bear Garth. First Aid to Grizzly Bear. Come on back if you're out there."

Sapphire flopped onto her back and closed her eyes. Dad should have been one of the gnarly gray drummers lost in the trance of the rhythm, not puking in a dirty toilet and passing out on torn yellow linoleum. Yellow-faded in splotches by sun streaming through uncurtained windows. Watercolor yellow. Watercolor dreams. Translucent images.

She remembered him playing a pale beige acoustic guitar around a golden bonfire on the beach, while she ran through the briny air flapping her arms—a seagull flying along the beach. She had painted Mary Moss kissing Dad in the park and left the canvas piled in the back of her mother's garage, next to the guitar Dad had given her for her eighth birthday. A bass drum throbbed in her temples, and she could smell the rank vomit on her breath.

The radio crackled again. "Rich to Garth."

Garth responded, "If it's about Jack, deal with him yourself."

The transmission garbled for a few seconds. Finally, the words broke free. "Rich at First Aid. We've got a possible Peanut Butter Sandwich."

"I'm on my way." Garth got up.

"What's a Peanut Butter Sandwich?"

He leaned down and spoke softly. "Sexual assault."

Garth was going to leave her lying in a pile of her own vomit and she didn't even have a shovel to bury it. Now what? He had ripped the scab off her wound, and now that it was bleeding, he couldn't just abandon her, again. "Let me come," she begged.

He stared at her. "I need someone who knows what he's doing."

Sapphire thought about Sticky and the rape center and how blurry the lines were between her and Sally. "I do."

Garth muttered, "Everyone's always on my case to get more sisters involved."

"And?" she pleaded. She had no idea what was going to happen next, and she didn't really care. Just so she wasn't alone. Just so she could stay with Garth and feel safe.

"Then, let's go." Garth marched off. The trail snaked along the edge of the valley, and Sapphire could see the twinkles of light bobbing through the murky meadow.

AWAKENING

Saturday, July 7, 1990
(Day Twelve of Sapphire's Gathering)

It's your road and yours alone. Others may walk it
with you, but no one can walk it for you.
—Rumi

SAPPHIRE

Half-dazed, Sapphire hurried to keep up with Garth as
he barreled down the trail toward First Aid. The trail was
crowded with people who paraded across a movie screen,
enunciating their lines, while the monster crept up on them.
Her stomach spasmed again and she bent over, hoping
to vomit, and instead the dry heaves worked her stomach
muscles—not that she had anything left in her but a rotten
feeling.

Garth's radio exploded with static. "I'll be there in five
minutes!"

The radio sputtered back, "Copy, Garth."

"Keep this off the radio until I get there. We don't ..."

His voice disappeared in the conversations going on
around her. The empty hollow of Sapphire's stomach clenched
up, stomach wall pressing against stomach wall. Afraid to be
left behind, she ran after him until she caught up. As they
barreled past the pile of boulders that marked the beginning
of First Aid, Coleman lanterns and tiki torches lit up the area.
She squinted against the brightness.

"Where's Rich?" Garth's voice crashed through conversations and echoed off the boulders, silencing everyone.

People rushed out of the tarp structure and swarmed Garth. She recognized Rich, Bumblebee, and Kyle. The others were eyes and mouths swaddled in bulky sweaters and faded blankets worn as ponchos. They all seemed to be waiting for the mighty Grizzly Bear Garth to solve their problems. Everything reeked of wood smoke and medicine, while Sapphire craved pungent piney crispness.

Doubting her ability to contend with all those people, she held back and grabbed her water bottle from her daypack. She swished her mouth and then spit, trying to erase the putrid taste lingering in her mouth.

Rich said, "Grizzly, it's about time you got here."

Bumblebee pushed toward Garth. "Will y'all keep it down? We got sick folks trying to rest."

Garth leaned toward her. "How's the sister doing?"

Bumblebee grimaced. "What kind of question is that?"

The crowd pushed Sapphire back, until she bumped into a hand-painted cardboard sign: "Welcome to First Aid." Someone shouted, "We've got to find this creep!" She slipped away until she was standing alone. The cold penetrated her bones, her teeth started to chatter, and she wandered toward a small fire. She didn't understand why she felt so cold; she was still breathing hard and sweating. She stretched out her fingers toward the gold and burnt-sienna flames, rising and falling under the slight breeze that came down the hill.

They had been finger-painting at the kitchen table. Dad's big hands and her little ones covered in satiny yellow and creamy blue, as they had swirled the colors around on the sheet of paper. He had helped her sculpt a tree trunk rising up next to the lake. She had felt the bark rising under her fingers, as they dipped and pressed, dipped and pressed, each thumbprint a chunk of bark on the tree. Then, they had created an orange sun and she stared at her hands, wet with orange finger-paint, only now they were wet with tears. She gasped for breath, trying to swallow her sobs, trying to erase the image of the little hand and the big hand creating a tree out of nothing, as she shivered by the fire. She could go to Albuquerque and find him, get him into rehab.

"Sapphire." Garth's voice thundered through the camp. "Where are you?"

She flinched. "At the fire!"

"Get over here!"

She circled the crowd and ducked under the sagging edge of the tarp, towards Garth's voice. A Coleman lantern hung from the cross-pole, illuminating faces but not feet. Bumblebee, Kyle, and Rich stood next to two scared and confused kids in their late teens.

Garth glanced at her. "If you're going to be with me on this, you need to stay with me."

"I'm here already."

Garth grunted and lit a cigarette.

She stepped sideways, trying to avoid the smoke.

Bumblebee introduced the people who had found Daisy: Paul and Jessica.

"Thanks for stepping up, guys," Garth said. "I know you've already told folks what happened, but it would sure help me out if you could tell it again."

Paul took a deep breath. "It was just past dark-thirty, and we were walking down by where the llamas are camped, when we heard a scream. Then, this dude comes charging up the path. But he stopped when he saw us."

Jessica said, "I asked him was he okay. He said, 'I think I might have done something really bad.'"

Paul took Jessica's hand. "'What's happening, bro,' is exactly what I said to him, but he just walked past us."

Sapphire shifted her weight from leg to leg, suspicious of them, then immediately felt guilty. She took a deep breath, trying to calm down and stay grounded in what was happening instead of what she thought.

Paul continued, "We walked up the path a bit, until we heard a woman crying inside a tent."

Under the tarp, everyone was silent.

"Jessica went up to the tent and called out to the woman to see if she was okay."

"But she wasn't." Jessica started to cry. Paul put his arm around her and pulled her close.

Jessica pressed her cheek into Paul's chest. "She'd been raped."

"Well, you done right by bringing her here," Garth said. "I'll need a description of this creep."

Paul and Jessica looked at each other and parted a few inches. Jessica said, "He was almost Paul's height and had a chunky body."

"He was our age," Paul said. "Nineteen. Maybe even twenty."

"Light brown hair," Jessica added. "Or maybe dark blonde. Very short."

Sapphire folded her arms across her chest and kicked at the ground. That description fit hundreds of guys at the gathering.

Bumblebee said she had done a partial rape kit on the victim.

Garth said, "Sapphire, what do you think?"

All eyes on her; he wanted her opinion.

Sapphire straightened her back. "We need to talk to Daisy." She thought about Sally and the thin white line, and how Sally never could talk about what her dad did to her in the dark bedroom.

Garth nodded in agreement.

Bumblebee approached them. "Garth, I need a word with you."

Sapphire jumped in. "I can do it. I used to volunteer at a rape crisis center."

Garth and Bumblebee stepped a few feet away from Sapphire and the others, before Bumblebee turned her back on Sapphire and faced Garth.

His voice rang out, "I know you've talked to her, but if I'm gonna hunt down this creep, I need someone to come with me who got a statement from the victim. You're stuck at First Aid."

Stung by the lack of faith Bumblebee had in her, Sapphire racked her mind for what she had done so terribly wrong to turn a woman, who she thought was her friend, against her. She would have thought that finding Dakota would have proven herself to Bumblebee.

Garth's right hand grasped his beard, and as he nodded his head up and down, his beard alternately stretched and loosened.

She couldn't tell if Garth was defending her or selling her down river, so she inched closer until she could hear what they were saying about her.

Garth said, "I respect your feelings, but I've been down this road before, and it's been a dead-end more often than not."

Kyle butted in. "Garth, don't you trust us?"

"It ain't about trust, Kyle. It's about running a proper investigation." Garth stepped back to let Kyle in. "We need to sort out the he saids / she saids."

Sapphire moved closer. "I spent six months doing art therapy with rape victims. Helping them process what happened through art."

"Teaching art ain't the same as getting a young woman to tell you what happened," Bumblebee said.

Sapphire stepped back a few feet. "I know how to listen. To hear what's not spoken."

"That's not what I saw yesterday."

"I know I overreacted," Sapphire said. "I was caught off-guard."

Bumblebee crossed her arms.

"But this. I have experience with this. I can help. I need to help." Sapphire told Bumblebee about Sally and the thin white line and the guilt they were all trying to shed.

"I always figured you for an uptown white girl."

Sapphire shook her head. There was so much they didn't know about each other; how could she possibly explain it all to Bumblebee. "Trust me, please."

Kyle laughed. "Hell, if it was me, I'd be to the next county by now. Last thing I ever want to do is end up in front of Garth's kangaroo court."

Garth grunted.

"Okay." Bumblebee turned around and strode off. "She's over here."

Sapphire followed close behind her, until they came upon a small tepee, maybe ten feet wide.

Three old guys sat cross-legged on the ground smoking cigarettes near the tepee, their long beards peaking out from the mud-stained blankets draped over their shoulders.

Sapphire's eye twitched and her legs trembled. Now, she had to prove herself. No room for any more failure. Not for her. Not for any of them.

Together, she and Bumblebee approached the flapped portal of the tepee. Bumblebee lifted up a corner. "Daisy," she crooned, "I've brought a sister to talk to you. Can she come in?"

"I think so."

Sapphire crouched down and entered. Inhaling and exhaling, she tried to match her breathing to the rhythms inside the tent.

Daisy's left eye was swollen, spreading purple across her left cheekbone. She raised a mug to her lips, pressing her bottom lip against the edge, and stared into the cup as she sipped. A trickle of tea escaped and ran down her chin.

Sapphire swallowed; her throat, raw and scratchy. Her skin prickled; each time she shifted her leg or moved an arm, she heard the rasping of her clothes in the otherwise silent lodge.

Candles flickered against the canvas of the lodge and sweet sage smoldered on the altar to her right. A woman in a long blue cape played a bamboo flute. Daisy leaned against a pile of blankets. A golden shawl covered most of her auburn hair. One hand clasped another young sister's in embroidered jeans. Now, Sapphire had the opportunity to learn the truth. For too long, she had been scared to know, afraid that if she demanded the truth, some unspeakable horror would befall her. Nevertheless, the gates had been opened, and truth was raining down on her. She tried to be one with it.

"Hi," she said. "I'm Sapphire." She waited for Daisy's reaction and her own courage to continue. Daisy's hand trembled, as she lowered the cup and handed it to the attentive sister at her side. Pain had plunged into Daisy's heart.

There was nothing Sapphire could say to make that hurt go away on a cold mountain night, in a white man's lodge. Over time, it would transform into a throb or an ache, just as Dad's disappearance formed the background of her life. "Can I ask you some questions?" Sapphire's chest rose and fell, as she tried to ground herself. She pulled a small sketchpad out of her coat pocket. Her hands shook and the paper rattled. Laying the sketchpad on the ground, she wiped the palms of her hands on her jeans, before scooting closer to Daisy. Then, she sank cross-legged onto the tattered Oriental rug. "Are you ready to start?"

Daisy sighed. "I already told Bumblebee what happened."

"I know, sweetie. But she didn't write it down, and if we're going to catch the man who hurt you, we've got to get a statement." Sapphire leaned over and grabbed her sketchpad. She scribbled the point of her pen against the paper until the ink began to flow. "Please. Just one more time." She held up the paper. "I'll write it down, and then you won't have to tell it anymore."

The sister in embroidered jeans brushed Daisy's cheek with her fingertips and smiled. She lowered her head and whispered into Daisy's ear.

Daisy nodded, pulling the gold scarf forward until only her eyes, nose, and mouth were visible. "I'd been at the drums and was trying to find my camp. I knew my tent was near the llamas, but it was really dark. So, this brother with a flashlight comes along and I ask him to help me find my tent." She paused and then said, "We're all family, aren't we?"

Sapphire listened intently as Daisy spoke. She scribbled on the pad, strangling the pen with her fingers and trying to

capture the story. Her middle finger pressed so hard against
the pen that a lump started to form. She set the pen down for
a moment and rubbed her finger to restore circulation. She
wished she knew shorthand and could preserve every word.

Daisy spoke.

Tall with short hair

Had a stick

Gave his puppy

Cold

Mushrooms

Gave her a flannel

Found tent

Daisy closed her eyes.

Sapphire recorded Daisy's words and ignored their
meanings, blocked the images from her mind, even though
they were echoes of words she had already heard. Sketched
a puppy and mushrooms in the corner of the page. Tried
to shut down her brain and become nothing more than an
instrument. Daisy continued.

In her tent

Started (startled) kissing

Trees dancing

Wouldn't stop

Ripped clothes

Head hit rock

Hit me

Hurt.

Me.

Sapphire drew lines between the words. Wiped tears from
her face. Scribbled arrows and added comments, and Daisy
spoke.

Ripped my clothes. Kissing.

Daisy stopped. She clasped her hands together and pressed her thumbs against her lips. She rocked side to side and began to hum.

As Sapphire inhaled, she knew. She knew who it was and how it happened and saw him lost and lonely in a black trench coat and didn't want to hear Daisy say his name. She was tired of finding lost children, weary of being lost herself. "Did he tell you his name?"

Daisy nodded.

"Mole." Daisy squeezed her eyes shut. "He said his name was Mole."

Sapphire dropped her pen. Swallowed hard. Right eye twitching. Pressed her fist into her stomach. She had betrayed Daisy. Instead of tackling Mole's problems at Dinner Circle, she had wallowed in her own self-pity. Scorched by guilt, she struggled to stay focused, to put her personal feelings aside.

The light from the stubby candle in a glass jar flickered on the canvas tepee. Tears trickled down Daisy's face, and the embroidered jeans sister blew into the flute, causing it to tremble to the rhythm of Daisy's timid breathing.

Sapphire wanted to return to the world she had constructed with canvas and oils, the life she had colored with gold ochre, viridian, and indigo blue. "Do you want to press charges?" she asked.

Daisy turned her wide eyes from Sapphire to the embroidered jeans sister on her left, and back, until they bored into Sapphire's skull. "What will happen to him?"

Daisy looked like a six-year-old Tinkerbell, whose luminous white wings had been torn. If Sapphire could forget who destroyed Daisy's freedom, it was easy to know what should happen. "If you want to press charges, we'll turn him

over to the police. You'll have to give the police a statement."
She paused. "If there's enough evidence, there'll be a hearing
and a trial. You would probably have to testify."

Daisy asked, "What should I do?"

"I don't know," Sapphire said. Outside, the trees stood
guard over them. "I don't know what's right for you."

"He hurt me."

Sapphire nodded. *And himself.*

Candlelight glimmering on her golden shawl, Daisy
lowered her head. "I don't want to hurt anyone."

"If you don't, he'll do it again." Sapphire imagined Mole
smothering Daisy with his body. Burning sage clogged her
lungs. "To someone else."

"But I'd have to keep telling people. Reliving what he did
to me."

The embroidered jeans sister began to softly sing, "Earth
our body, water our blood...."

"You don't have to decide right now." Sapphire hesitated.
"If there's something. I mean I know there's nothing that I
can do to help, but I." She abandoned her attempt at words—
such meaningless gadgets masquerading as love or friendship
or empathy. Instead, she crouched next to Daisy, trying to
share energy with her. Passing time. Sensing breath. Until she
needed to pull back, move out of the womb they had created
and finish her journey. "I'll be back in a few hours." She got
to her feet and ducked out the doorway.

The night air slapped her across the face. Her throat
tightened, and she inhaled a shallow breath. Afraid to let it
out, afraid when she exhaled, she would explode into sobs.
She choked on her breath, coughed, and swallowed, but a few
tears escaped her eyes. Tears for Daisy. For her own family.

For the children they all had been once upon a time. When she had swallowed her grief, she stood up.

WITHIN THE ILLUSION IS REALITY

Saturday, July 7, 1990
(Day Thirteen of Lauren's gathering)

Dare to declare who you are. It is not far from the
shores of silence to the boundaries of speech. The
path is not long, but the way is deep. You must not
only walk there, you must be prepared to leap.
—*Hildegard of Bingen*

LAUREN

"**H**ot pans!" rang out through the kitchen, as Lauren leaned
into the dough on the table, a few feet away from the path
between the ovens and the cooling racks. A cacophony of
voices roared from the Bliss Pit, where chords of twelve-bar
blues lilted through the crowd in bits and pieces during lulls
in the conversations. The heat from the ovens was just far
enough away to feel nice in the cool night air, but even here,
Lauren used her t-shirt to wipe the sweat from her brow. Pizza
night at the Blue Moon Bakery had drawn what seemed like
half the gathering, and the fatty joints being passed around
probably drew the rest.

"Hey, Lauren."

"Hi, Vince." Lauren smiled. "I'd hug you, but ..." She
held her flour-covered hands in the air.

"I see what ya doing."

"We're trying to serve up all the food tonight. Kitchen's
breaking down in the morning." She wiped her face with her

sleeve and pulled her t-shirt away from her chest, fanning it back and forth a couple of times. "How was your gathering?"

"Sweet. It's been sweet."

Even though Lauren could sense the cool air around her, she could not cool herself off.

"I'm gonna check out that smokin' blues over at the fire. Do you want to come?"

She shook her head. "I'm going keep kneading for a bit longer."

Vince smiled and disappeared into the crowd.

Lauren folded the dough and gave it a quarter turn, before leaning into the mushy pile, pushing it away from herself. Again, she folded and turned the dough, using the heels of her hands to push the bread-to-be away from her.

A brother held out a joint on her right side. "Do you want to hit this, sister?"

She pointed at her belly. "Trying to keep it clean for the baby. I even quit coffee." Laughter broke out around the table, and she cringed, not sure if they were laughing at her or something else. The truth was coffee was making her nauseous.

The brother moved on to the next person, who turned away from the table, hit the joint, and bent over coughing. Across the table, two giggling sisters were telling a brother how they lost their tent the first night they arrived. A kind brother who had a great flashlight walked with them until dawn when they finally found it.

Lauren shook her head, silently laughing. Seemed like every year tents were lost and found again in the morning, after lots of drama and all-night searches; people were always reunited with their camp once the sun rose. She chuckled to herself and worked her dough. The constant leaning forward to push the dough away from her started to create twinges in her back, and she stopped to twist and then stretched forward, trying to relax the muscles in her lower back.

"Are you getting tired, Lauren?" Kalmia asked.

Lauren swung her head and arms side to side, nodding her head up and down before standing up. "Leaning over the dough causes a stitch in my back."

Kalmia pointed towards the Bliss Pit. "Take a break. Go listen to the music."

"We've got peppermint tea over here, and I can grab you a slice," said Grandma Star.

Lauren pressed down on the dough, feeling it turn silky under her hands. "I'll finish this pile, and then I'll take a break."

Wandering over to the Bliss Pit with tea in one hand and a slice of pizza in the other, Lauren looked for a place to sit down and get off her exhausted feet. A young brother in remarkably clean clothes offered her his seat in a folding chair and she took it, stretching her feet out in front of her. Normally, she would have sat on the ground, but the chair felt good, back from the fire far enough, allowing the cold night air to waft over her. She finally started to cool down.

From here, the muted notes and the lowered pitch wormed into her lower body. The languid guitar-work seduced her. The riff sank into Lauren's belly, and her hips wiggled in the chair. She began to tap her achy feet and bob her head. Slowly wailing, grounded, sinking into mud, the endlessly suffering slide guitar matched her mood. She asked the brother who'd given her his seat the name of the band,

and he replied, "The Kentucky Possum Posse." The lyrics rang out in that slow Mississippi Delta style.

The Blue Moon Bakery say loving ain't bad,
But my baby ate all the pizza.
The sisters done told me loving ain't bad.
My woman done ate three slices of pizza.

Everyone burst out laughing at the gathering-version of a classic blues song. Surprised at her own gaiety, Lauren took great pleasure in this moment of elation. Perhaps, even the blues could lighten one's day. She kept letting her pregnancy get her down, and this sense of defeat was new to her. Her whole life, she had been encouraged to smile and think positive, look good and achieve, and now, she felt like she had a hangover. An "over-achiever, forest-defender, able to leap into giant redwoods in a single bound" hangover. Going through the withdrawals of living on adrenaline-fueled direct action, to being just a pregnant woman, one among many, nothing special. Grasping at the faint beginning of an idea, she needed time to herself to approach this growing life.

River barged into the crowd, next to her. "There you are. I've been looking all over for you."

Irritated, Lauren didn't look at him. "I left you a note."

"Yeah, that you'd be at the bakery, but this place is a zoo."

"It wasn't a zoo two hours ago," she pointed out.

River sat down at her feet and gazed up at her. "I worried about you, is all. I thought …"

Lauren interrupted, "You thought I was doing something you don't want me to do."

River shook his head. "Listen, I saw Sapphire at Dinner Circle."

"And?"

"She's packing out tonight."

The people around Lauren turned into a slow-motion tilt-a-whirl, their movements rolling and spinning along with her chair. She grabbed onto the seat to steady herself. "What's the big deal?"

River said, "I thought you were friends?"

She muttered, "I don't know. She's okay, but she's a bit melodramatic."

"Well, did you know she was leaving today?"

"Nope. She told me she was staying for cleanup," she said with a twinge of guilt. They had made plans, but then she had lost her patience with Sapphire's woe-is-me mentality and brushed her off. No doubt, Sapphire had connected with her father, making their relationship superfluous anyway.

"Well, maybe we can connect up after the gathering."

Lauren shrugged her shoulders.

River turned towards the band. "They're really good."

Lauren nodded.

For a few minutes, she and River quietly sat while the band tugged at her heart. Bittersweet blues fit her mood perfectly. The gathering was ending; everyone was leaving; this gathering would never happen again. Another gathering would, but the special moments from this one were gone, relegated to stories to be told around future campfires with other people. Next year would be different.

River stood up. "I'm going to head back to camp for a bit, and then I'll come back here. Are you ready to go to bed?"

"Not at all."

River disappeared into the crowd.

After he left, Lauren's breath slowed down and she relaxed into the chair, grooving to the music.

Not five minutes later, an older woman made her way through the crowd, carrying a child, and sank down on the log bench beside her. The woman set the child next to Lauren and took off her pack, then gazed around the crowd.

The older woman sighed. "That's quite a hike up the hill to get here."

Lauren nodded. "Totally worth it. This band is killing it."

The woman looked towards the band and then pulled a cup out of her pack and handed it to her son, who promptly sipped out of it. Turning towards Lauren, she said, "I'm Catherine, but most people call me Cat."

"Hi, Cat. I'm Lauren. Who is that next to you?"

"Cody. He's four. My youngest."

Lauren waved. "Hi, Cody." The band stopped playing, but the conversations kept going.

"Darn! I wanted to hear the Possum Posse. Someone told me they're awesome. I just love blues, don't you?"

Lauren nodded. "I'm sure they'll play another set. It's not that late."

The woman smiled. "How far along are you?"

"Five months."

"Being pregnant is awesome. But I'm done now. Besides Cody, I have a nine-year-old, Camilla, who's with her dad. And my son, Indigo, is nineteen, but he's not here."

Lauren's belly fluttered. Delighted, she put her hands on the baby. *Hey, baby. I bet you love blues too.* Her legs felt like dancing, expressing this sudden lightness in her heart.

"Have you made birthing plans yet?"

Lauren shook her head. "The father wants the baby to be born in his tepee in Mendocino."

Cat laughed and pulled Cody close to her. "That's how I had Indigo, but it was rough."

Trying to hear Cat over the other conversations, Lauren leaned closer, desperate to learn more.

Cat told her about the magic of birthing in a tent, but of missing the comforts of running water and a flush toilet. She had the other two in a house, taking warm showers in between contractions to relax. "Plus, after Camilla was born, I realized having people who love you be part of the birth is what's most important."

Lauren sighed. "The father and I haven't exactly worked things out."

"You still have time."

Lauren nodded, curious about how Cat's life turned out, but not wanting to pry.

Cat looked down at Cody. "He's out now."

"He sure is." Lauren had an urge to kiss that angelic face, rock his body against hers, hold a baby in her arms.

"Just keep going to school. Don't let that go; that way, you'll have something that's all your own."

"I'm planning to."

Cat slowly stood up, holding Cody in her arms. "I'm going to bed. He'll be up at the crack of dawn."

"Nice meeting you, Cat."

"Have a blessed night." Cradling Cody, she wandered down the trail.

Cat had Lauren thinking more practically of her future. There was no way she could do the practicum in fall quarter. Once she got home, she would need to see how to rearrange her courses and see how to stay enrolled for fall semester.

"Lauren," River called, as he made his way around the fire. "I need to talk to you," he said, crouching by her side.

"Well?"

"In private."

River grabbed her pack, and they walked away from the soothing music and the crowd. As they melted into the dark woods, Lauren shivered.

River pulled her sweater from her pack. "Here, put this on."

She pulled it over her shoulders. "What's so important?"

He put his arm around her shoulders. "A sister was raped."

"No way!" Lauren pulled back. "Are you sure?"

"I overheard it on the radio at INFO."

"What happened?"

River rubbed his forehead. "All I know is it happened over by the llama camp."

"And? What about the sister?"

"I don't know. I couldn't hear anything else. Goofy plugged the headset in his walkie-talkie."

She had always felt so safe at the gathering. She hugged her belly with both hands, protecting her baby from what she couldn't even say aloud. "Okay. Let's head over to INFO and find out what happened?"

River stared at her. "Are you sure you want to get involved in this movie?"

Lauren wanted to erase it from her mind or make sure whoever hurt one of her sisters paid a heavy price. Nevertheless, if the sisters didn't stick together, then Womyn's Healing Circle was just a feel-good moment, not a sacred bond to look out for each other. She nodded.

He said, "You know I would never let that happen to you."

She stopped. "Let that happen? What, am I your property now?

"No, babe. I just mean. Well, I love you and I want to protect you. Is that so bad?"

She paused for a moment and glared at him, before continuing up the trail. She heard him following her and they trudged in silence.

INFO was buzzing and lit up by Coleman lanterns and candles. Bodies crowded around the counter, voices raised and laughing. Just as loud as at the bakery Bliss Pit. Lauren spotted Goofy sitting quietly near the INFO supply tent, holding the radio in his hand. Merry Mary sat on his left. Lauren sat down in the empty chair next to Goofy.

She leaned over and whispered in his ear, "I heard a sister was raped."

He nodded and pressed his left finger to his lips.

She leaned back in the chair.

River plopped himself down on the ground facing them. "What's the scoop?"

Goofy glanced at her and shook his head.

Lauren said, "River, can you work the counter for a bit."

"Why?"

Goofy growled, "We need this to stay quiet."

River shook his head. "Lauren, I'm the one who told you. I already know."

Lauren nodded to Goofy. "He overheard it on the radio when he was here earlier."

Goofy muttered and pulled the ear bud out of his left ear. "Hang tight for a bit. We're still trying to sort out the situation and determine what our next steps are going to be." He put the ear bud back in his ear.

River asked, "What now?"

Merry Mary said, "We sit here until we're needed to do something."

Lauren envisioned herself knocked down on the trail by a man she could not see in the dark. Trying to scream. His hand over her mouth smothering her voice. Would she be brave enough to try to bite his hand, kick him in the balls? Would she be a simpering fool hiding in the bushes, too scared to come forward? Her fear of her own response morphed into anger, righteous indignation that some random man had the right to force himself onto a sister, make her afraid of walking by herself at her own gathering. At a peace and healing gathering? At a place where she had come to be loved and supported?

She protected her belly and leaned forward, whimpering softly. What about her baby? Suddenly, River was kneeling in front of her, holding her arms, kissing her forehead.

He murmured, "You're safe, Lauren."

She shook her head and sniffed. "How can this happen here?"

Merry Mary moved her chair to Lauren's right and lightly stroked her back. "Sweetie, this isn't some nirvana where everyone behaves perfectly. We all bring our shit here, and some of our shit is pretty bad."

Lauren pulled back from River and sat upright, still cradling her belly. "A sister was raped," she said.

Merry Mary nodded. "It happens from time to time. What makes the gathering different is not what happens, but how we respond to what happens."

"And how the fuck do we respond to this?"

SEA LEGS

Saturday, July 7, 1990
(Day Twelve of Sapphire's Gathering)

When Pandora opened the jar and let all the
good and evils created by the Greek gods and
goddesses escape onto the mortal realm, "only
Hope remained there in an unbreakable home
within, under the rim of the great jar, and did not
fly out at the door."
—Hesiod, "Works and Days"

SAPPHIRE

Sapphire shivered in the cold night air, outside the tepee,
where Daisy's journey in life had been towed after she had
crashed into a ditch, leaving bits and pieces of her former life
scattered on the road and embedded in her arms. Sapphire
wondered if Daisy would be successful at finding a path
forward. Sapphire shivered. Teaching art to women who
had survived rape a year ago was completely different than
dealing with the raw and gaping wounds when they were
still bleeding. In the art therapy program, she was trying to
help women find a way to express emotions they had buried,
sometimes for years. What Daisy needed now was trauma care
and love. Sapphire had no idea what she needed.

Bumblebee stood on the path ahead of her, tapping her
foot, arms folded tight.

Sapphire's arms hung loose at her side. Her shoulders slumped forward. "She's only eighteen." Her shoulders weren't big enough to carry all of this. "Now what?"

Bumblebee pointed towards the fire where the others had stayed. "You go with Grizzly and find this son of a bitch."

The road in front of her was a dirt trail in the murky woods with no visible horizon line, not a yellow brick road in front of an artist's rendition of an idyllic countryside. Nevertheless, Sapphire needed to finish what she had started. "Let's go," she said to Bumblebee, as she strode back to the others.

Garth sat in a folding chair, surrounded by a huddle of people Sapphire did not recognize. She touched his arm and pointed to a tree about twenty feet away, and he followed her.

"Physically, she's not hurt too bad," she said. "A black eye and some scrapes." She sighed, unable to fathom the extent of Daisy's emotional trauma.

"When I catch that scumbag," Garth muttered. "He'll probably be happier in jail than he will be with me."

"She isn't sure she wants to press charges. She doesn't want to hurt him."

"Piece of shit."

Garth was an action figure hero—long on action, short on feelings—so how could she explain to him that there was more to this situation than he was grasping? "Slow down, Garth." Somehow, she stripped Daisy's story of its shading and was able to lay it out in primary colors.

Garth nodded. "Get me a description and a name. Then, we'll catch this piece of shit."

Trepidation coursed through her body in jagged brushstrokes caught on a rough canvas. "It's Mole. The guy I told you I was looking for at Dinner Circle."

Garth looked at her in complete disbelief. "Mole—what the fuck—sounds like the type of dude who slinks around in dark corners. What's his legal name?"

She shrugged her shoulders and tried to put words to the intuition she had ignored. "I don't think he's normal."

They glared at each other. She couldn't tell what he was thinking, but his eyes pinched and his brow furrowed.

"You're coming with me." Garth pulled his radio out of his coat pocket.

She was an idiot, no more intelligent than her still life drawings. Even with people in them, they were static. "He's tall, maybe six-foot, blonde hair—real short, as if he shaved his head and it's growin' out. Deep set eyes and a pronounced brow. He wears a black trench coat."

Garth called in the description on the radio. "The witnesses said he was heading for Bus Village. Search the area and hold him until I get there." He lowered the radio and turned toward the tent. "Richie! Richie! Get a ride to meet me at the end of the supply road. I'm heading to Main Gate."

It was all moving too fast. Garth wasn't giving her a chance to explain that Mole processed the world with a ten-year-old's cognition.

"Sapphire!" Garth shouted, as he set off into the darkness.

She grabbed her daypack and ran after him. Five minutes past First Aid, they reached the hill trail that wound through spicy sage scrub and granite rocks. Garth set a fast pace, and the nine-thousand-foot elevation coupled with the steep incline of the trail sucked her breath away. She glanced back and saw shadows of people trailing behind them. She couldn't figure out who they were or why they were coming. Garth ignored them.

She picked out the jagged trail by the feel of hard-packed soil under the soles of her shoes and couldn't paint over the images that cycled through her mind. Mole rolling on the ground crying, a flopping fish. Her dad dancing in Griffith Park. She inhaled sharp bits of cold air into her lungs. Daisy's tears. Mole standing alone at Dinner Circle. Her dad puking in an alley. The look of disgust Lauren had given her.

Headlights crept along the road above them. She passed Garth in the last stretch, as he huffed his way up the hill. The beam from his flashlight flickered on the trail, on the rocks, on the trees above them. At the top, she stopped and waited, as Garth and the others joined her on the dirt road whose vanishing point led to the Main Gate.

A rusty old truck pulled up, and Garth yanked the door open before it had come to a stop.

"Mole's at Main Gate," Edgar shouted from behind the wheel.

Garth swore, "Well, it's about fucking time." He climbed in the truck and slammed the door. Leaning out the window, he yelled, "Whoever's in on this movie, stop jabbering, and get in."

Sapphire scrambled into the back of the truck, along with the others. The truck slowly turned around and inched along the twisting dirt road, pulling over periodically to avoid people wandering in the dark. Sapphire listened to the others tell stories about other nights at other gatherings, and who did what and how cool they were for having done it. It seemed terribly cold to be laughing in the midst of tragedy.

Finally, the truck swung around a horseshoe bend, and the lights from Main Gate burst into view. Voices shouting, radios blaring, frantic activity in all directions. A boombox spewed forth garbled noise, while engines raced and rumbled.

Empty cans of beer lay scattered around the fire, and a scrawny man toasted the sky with a bottle of whiskey. From Sapphire's perch in the truck, she spotted PS sitting with Mole on the outside of the fence.

Edgar pulled the rattling truck alongside a makeshift fence. Grabbing onto the tailgate to steady herself, Sapphire leapt out.

Garth hollered, "Sapphire. Where are you going?"

She pointed at Mole and PS.

A loud bang ricocheted through the camp. Sapphire cowered by the truck. Silence engulfed the camp. A sputtering car drove past, and she exhaled, peering around the truck.

Her eye twitching, she edged toward PS and Mole, squatting down. "Hi, Mole. Remember me?"

"You were at Kid Korral?" His eyes looked directly into hers. "How come I gotta be here?"

Trying to avoid telling him what was happening, she asked if he was hungry.

He nodded his head and wrapped the blanket tightly around his body.

Two skinny men with ragged beards left the crowd around the fire and stumbled toward her. "Is that him?"

"The guy who raped my sister."

"That fucker." The shorter one lifted his right arm, and the shiny metal of the pipe reflected the firelight. "I'll knock some sense into you, motherfucker."

Sapphire pressed her body into Mole's, as Garth moved toward them.

The drunks stepped closer, and she could see the pipe carrier's bloodshot eyes.

"Blue!" Garth yanked the pipe out of his hand and stepped between Sapphire and the drunks.

She gasped for air.

"Outta the way," Blue said. "My turn."

Garth shoved him back so hard he crashed into his buddy, who fell down. "He's off limits to you."

The yelling around the fire stopped. Only the boombox continued to blast for a few more seconds, before it too went silent.

"Leave him alone. And the girl too." Garth tossed the pipe behind him and stepped forward toward the mob.

Sapphire froze.

Out of the dark, bodies materialized. Lined up behind Garth. Edgar and PS. Some of the faces she had seen in the back of the truck. Other men and a few women she didn't recognize.

Huddled against the log with Mole, she trembled.

Blue glowered and paced in front of Garth.

A man by the fire waved a bottle. "Hey Blue, wanna shot of Jack?"

Blue's friend scrambled to his feet. "I don't want no trouble, man."

Arms shaking and heart pounding, Sapphire crouched against the fence, unable to move.

From the fire, someone shouted, "Come on, man. You're wrecking the party." The music resumed its crackly rendition of *Sunday Morning Regret*.

No one said a word as Blue's friend put his arm around Blue's shoulder and pushed him back toward the fire.

Mole tugged on her jacket. "Can I have spaghetti?"

Flabbergasted by his cluelessness, she tried to clear her head. Manifesting marshmallows was one thing, but spaghetti? She rummaged through her backpack. "How about a roll?"

His trembling hand took the bread. He ripped off a chunk. Chewing slowly, he kept his face turned toward the fire. The flames danced in his pupils, revealing fear. When he looked at Sapphire, she saw herself reflected in his eyes, and she stared until Daisy's auburn hair danced in his pupils, and the images bounced off each other like sunlight and clouds bounce off glassy water.

Mole gnawed on the roll and swallowed.

They huddled together, backs pressed into the old fence, their eyes on the drunks yelling around the fire. She cringed. One of them could be her father, broken and destroyed after years of drug abuse. PS scowled, arms folded across his chest. Garth and Edgar stood behind him. Garth asked PS how they found Mole.

"The call come out over the radio, and I asked around for Mole. This young bro turns to me and says, 'I'm Mole.'"

Garth shook his head. "Is this guy the village idiot or what?"

"He's a strange one, alright."

Then, Garth and PS stepped away from Sapphire and she couldn't hear what they were saying over the blaring radio. Edgar stood there glaring at her.

This entire mess was all her fault. She had known something was wrong with Mole. She pulled her knees to her chest and hugged them. *If only.* Her refrain, and she was tired of it. No wonder Lauren was sick of her. She glanced back toward the road, and the number of hangers-on had grown. They parked themselves on the ground in small groups, talking, passing cigarettes back and forth, as if the sharing of tobacco were sacrament.

Shouts sprung loose from the fire. "Smash in his head!" "Dead!" "Not right!" "The sisters need us!"

Being here was lunacy. Sapphire had no idea what they were doing and how long this was going to go on, but she would not let Daisy come to this madhouse. Garth marched up and down, smoking furiously; the drunks on one side, Sapphire and Mole huddled on the other. She stood up and walked over to him. "Give me one for Mole."

Garth scowled. "I'm not sharing cigarettes with scumbags."

"You don't know everything. And you won't let me explain. He's my dad." Sapphire stumbled over the words, trying to separate their images. "He's my friend. Mole. Mole was my friend. Sort of. Or something. Besides, a cigarette will help him chill, until we can get him somewhere with professional help. Do you want him flipping out?"

From the safety of the fire, Blue hollered, "This ain't over, Garth."

Garth glanced at Blue, then pulled on his beard. "You're right." He handed her a cigarette.

She took it, while keeping her eyes on his face. They stood there. Eyes locked. "Thank you." Her words broke their stare and they both turned away. Maybe her opinion counted for something around here. She handed Mole the cigarette.

"Do you have a light?" he asked.

She rummaged through her pack and fished out a box of matches. Striking one, she held the flame, as he sucked hard on the cig until the tip glowed red. Once he started puffing, he ignored her as if he were alone. Her dad had been that way sometimes, so inside himself that he was oblivious to her very existence. Perhaps that was the only way he could deal with life's craziness—just turn inside, and pretend. She shut her eyes and leaned against the stump, wanting to gesso over the canvas and start all over again. When she opened her eyes, she was gazing at the sky, black and sparkling overhead.

"What does everyone want with me?" Mole asked.

"We're trying to keep you warm and protect you. Remember last night? Remember how we hung out at the fire and things got better?" Mole's life was sliding downhill fast, and Sapphire couldn't change his direction or his speed; all she could do was provide a cushioned landing. "Remember last night; remember how you trusted me, and it was okay?" She shuddered at the way she had treated Mom, screamed at her, blamed her, when really, they were all doing the best they could in life.

The fire exploded, as a couple of logs landed on it. Mole lunged sideways, hitting the stump with a thunk, then curled into a ball and gripped his body tight.

Sapphire wrapped her arms around him. "It's okay, Mole. Just a log on the fire. Everything's okay." She stroked his head, rubbed his back, and breathed as the tension evaporated from him. Softly, so that no one but Mole could hear, she began to chant, "Earth my body, water my blood. Air my breath, fire my spirit," while Daisy's tear-streaked face loomed in the corner of her eye, and she imagined the girl whispering, "It was all your fault."

PS said, "Quit fussing over him. He's going to jail, and what happens next is his own problem."

"How does letting him get hysterical help anyone?"

"The sister he raped is the one you should be fussing over."

Sapphire would have been much happier fussing over Daisy, drawing with Daisy, staying in that cocoon of love and protection in the tepee, but.... She slumped towards Mole, pulled her knees into her chest, allowed her body to collapse against his. She rocked forwards and backwards for a moment, refusing to cry. The voices at the fire shouted and yelled drunken words that exploded on her fatigued and broken heart. Changing the energy here was hopeless. They needed a tranquil spot. She leaned the tranced-out Mole against the stump and stood up.

She looked at PS. "I'll be right back." She wasn't sure where they could take him, but any place had to be better than this madhouse.

Sapphire marched up to Garth and Edgar. "We have to move Mole someplace quiet so we can figure out what we're doing."

Edgar said, "Why coddle him? Too bad that he's scared. He deserves it."

"Let him stew," Garth said. "He's going to jail and that's the end of it."

She staggered backwards, upset by their lack of compassion. "Can't we care for him until then? Try to find out what happened?"

Garth nodded and looked at Gideon. "She's right. One thing at a time."

"But what about…" Edgar broke in.

Garth shook his head. "I can't hear myself think here— too much noise." Garth turned his head. "Vince," he shouted.

Vince stood up out of the crowd of hangers-on and swung his legs in long strides as he approached.

"Can we use your camp?"

Vince looked around the circle and stared at her before he spoke. "It's your party, Garth. We'll put it wherever you want."

They gathered up Mole and his bedroll, following Vince back through the parking lot and leaving the chaos behind.

They ducked behind a white step-van. Mole shivered, and Sapphire pointed to an overstuffed recliner. "Mole, why don't you sit here?"

He flopped into the chair, sinking into the broken springs as if the chair were clasping onto him. PS threw Mole's bedroll onto the ground next to the chair.

Kyle sent a young brother to get some wood while he lit what was left of the previous fire. She grabbed a plastic chair and pulled it alongside the recliner, before crumpling into the wobbly chair. Gripping the handles tightly, as if her will could steady this floundering boat, she stared at the fire pit, waiting for the flames to warm them all. If she had pursued Mole at Dinner Circle and taken care of him, none of this would have happened. Only she realized her culpability.

"Why isn't the fire warm?" Mole asked.

Vince tossed a blanket onto his lap, and Sapphire wrapped the blanket around him.

Mole rubbed his forehead. "I'm tired. When can I go to bed?"

Exhaustion gripped her heart. Lauren pregnant with no home. Her dad a junkie in a cheap motel room. Alienated from her mother who loved her. Mole, a child in a man's body. Daisy raped and bruised. She didn't have the energy to deal with any one of these situations, let alone all of them. Let alone herself. She sighed. "I'm exhausted too. It feels like I haven't slept in a month."

A disheveled bunch of hippies perched on upturned buckets and squatted in the dirt. Cold and dirty, tired and hungry, their patience rapidly draining from them, and outside the circle was darkness and cold. Overhead, a blue tarp stretched between the white van and a pickup truck, blocking the stars from view.

Forcing herself to stand up on her weary legs, Sapphire said, "I'm going on a quick water run. Be right back." She asked Garth where she could get some filtered water. He pointed up the path, told her to find the blue Ford camper-van with a bubble top, and there'd be boiled water sitting on a table.

She plodded in the direction Garth had indicated. A dog barked as she passed a Volkswagen van. Its tiny face pushed aside the green, red, and purple curtains made from Guatemalan fabric, reminding her of dad's tale about the indigenous peoples in Central America, who wove stories into their fabrics. He had spun his own lies about what was possible, and now, she struggled to inhabit the real world, the world that had nothing to do with her father's make-believe reality. Her dry tongue lay heavy in her mouth, and thirst motivated her to keep going. Ahead of her, she spotted the Ford van in just a few more feet.

Edgar burst out from behind a truck and blocked her path.

She jumped back.

He hissed, "You need to stop coddling that scum. What about the sister who was raped? Don't you care about her? I'm sick of people treating—"

"Don't you dare tell me how to act!" Sapphire's fists clenched, she exploded. "I've been dealing with this situation for days. You! Don't. Know. Shit!" Heart pounding, she sidestepped him and tried to go around.

Edgar grabbed her arm and yanked her back.

She jerked free. "What's your problem?" she shouted.

He charged after her. His tobacco dragon-fire breath attacked her, and she gagged on the stench of stale sweat and overripe clothes, as she dodged him. He said, "What do you know about dealing with this shit?"

The realization flushed over her face; he wouldn't attack her this way if Garth were here. He was scared of her, scared she was going to take his importance away. "What the fuck do you suggest?"

Edgar hemmed and hawed and finally spit out, "Not keeping him warm and hugging him."

"Mole's not dealing with a full deck. I doubt there's anything else to do," she replied, surprised by her own self-confidence.

Edgar said, "You think it's that easy?"

"Nothing is easy," she said. "I'm learning as I go along, and I'm doing okay." She spun around and left him sputtering in the dark. Once she was clear of him, her body trembled and she gasped for breath. Trying to regain her composure, she ducked behind the blue Ford, gripping the table to steady herself. When her legs stopped shaking, she filled up her jug with filtered water and gulped water repeatedly, trying to quench the thirst that had left every cell a shriveled outline of itself. Finally satiated, she refilled the jug. The silence was huge and overwhelming; even the drums were hushed. The sound of her own breathing boomed in her ears.

Back at Vince's camp, the light of the fire flickered orange, and a tangy mixture of tobacco and patchouli filled the air. Half a dozen people huddled around the small fire, more asleep than awake. Garth sat in the plastic chair. Kyle intensely guarded Mole to prevent him from escaping, as if Mole had the nerve to try.

Sapphire plopped down next to Mole and handed him the water. "You need to drink."

He stared at her and then reached for the jug, lifted it to his mouth and poured, and half the water cascaded down his cheeks and shoulders, wetting the blanket wrapped around his shoulders. He didn't even notice—that's what she found so odd. Things happened around him, and he was oblivious. Could he really have failed to notice he raped someone? Inconceivable. "Mole, do you remember what you did tonight?"

Mole stared at her. "I was tripping. I don't remember."

"No shit he was tripping." Garth's "whisper" boomed across the circle. "He's guilty and he's going to jail. Why are we wasting all this time and energy on a scumbag?"

"Okay, Mole." Kyle's haggard face looked even worse in the firelight. "You were tripping. Do you remember what you did? What were the trips like?" He looked off into the darkness and then returned his gaze to Mole's face. "Hey, bro. Let's think about this."

Garth said, "We have the victim's statement. We don't need his."

Mole put his hands up to his face, covering his eyes and scrubbed his hands against his eyebrows, the skin on his face rumpling and crumpling beneath the pressure. "I think they were pink with purple flowers. Or purple with pink flowers."

Mole turned to Sapphire. "The sisters I was with last night. You remember, don't you?"

"Sarah and Songbird?"

"We wanted to. They had this idea. To get dosed. Well, we found them. I mean, they found this guy and he gave us some."

Kyle nodded.

Garth grumbled, "Fuck this shit."

Bewildered, Sapphire looked around the circle, trying to gauge her behavior from other perspectives and wondering what she should be doing. "Are we doing something wrong?"

Garth shook his head. "Usually, the hardest part of a rape is finding the suspect. This was a slam dunk, so why the fuck am I still up to my eyeballs in this mess?"

She shrugged her shoulders.

Garth stood up and stomped away from her, but she could hear him talking to someone. "The girl is worried about the son of a bitch. She knows him. Thinks he needs our sympathy."

Stunned, Sapphire stood up. She thought she was handling things okay. She left the circle and made her way toward Garth, who was leaning on a blue pickup truck talking to an older man.

Garth continued, "There's no point in wasting a bunch of energy on this. I'm tired."

Sapphire stood next to him, waiting for a break in his tirade.

Garth looked at her. "Now, what's the problem?"

"What?" she said. "You think I'm messing things up?"

He groaned. Ran his fingers through his beard. "You've got a good heart, and I'm sorry as hell about your dad."

"But?"

"Don't take it personally. You don't have much experience."

The older man said he was going to bed and disappeared into the night.

"You think it was a bad idea to move?" she said.

Garth ignored the question. "I'm really sorry about your dad and all. I know you're upset."

Her eye twitched, and she folded her arms across her chest. Raising her voice, she blustered, "You're damn right I'm upset. I'm upset that no one listened to me when I asked for help. I'm mad at myself for not trusting my instincts. I knew Mole was trouble before this happened." She gulped for oxygen. "I fucked everything up!"

Garth rubbed his forehead. "Your dad's probably not as bad as I made him out to be."

"Yeah, yeah, yeah," she said. "You're not hearing what I'm trying to tell you."

"We should feel sorry for him 'cause he's retarded."

"Garth, will you shut up and listen for once."

He exhaled loudly. "Hell, girl. Quit telling me you're gonna tell me, and spit it out."

"He's not all there."

She told him how she had met Mole in the burned-out woods on the ridge. Then, last night he had flipped out, tried to bash his brains into the ground, and everyone else thought it was the LSD. Everyone except her. She thought there was something else, something broken inside him, and she had done nothing. "Remember when I asked you about him?"

"You never told me about Mole."

"At Dinner Circle. The guy I needed to find."

"I thought you were looking for your boyfriend."

"Don't you even listen to what I'm trying to tell you?"

He took off his hat and scratched his head. Then put it back on. "Hell," he said. "Kids like that are generally nothing more than pains in the ass."

"You didn't fucking listen to me when I asked for help."

Garth was silent.

"Now, I have to live with this guilt." Light-headed, she swayed, and Garth grabbed her arm. She leaned into him, hurling into a tunnel of her past: Mole in the black forest, Lauren at Womyn's Healing Space, her mother on the floor of the kitchen, Sticky in the old warehouse. The images opening up and then disappearing so quickly, she couldn't register them all. Her body flying through the past, swooping to the left, and then the right, deeper and deeper, until it all rewound and she came back out, struggling to maintain her balance and catch her breath.

Garth steadied her. "Do you need to sit down?"

She shook her head. "Deep down, I knew."

"Hell, you can't go around arresting people for something they ain't done yet."

She gripped onto Garth to steady herself.

He leaned back against the truck and sighed. "At this point, there ain't a lot we can do. Besides, I sent Vince into town for the sheriff an hour ago."

Vince into town for the sheriff. For the sheriff. I sent Vince. She gasped for breath, and her stomach churned. Calling the cops was so desperate, so final. But then again, what did she think was going to happen?

She exhaled deeply. She couldn't recreate this in another way; she couldn't gesso over Mole's mistakes and start again. She had seen the bruises on Daisy's face. Sometimes, you had to send someone away to protect others. She kicked at a rock. It scuffled a few feet and landed hard. A few wisps of dust floated toward her. The rock lay there in the middle of the night, oblivious to drunks, rapists, and lost children.

THE WISDOM OF THE GODDESS

Sunday, July 8, 1990
(Day Thirteen of Sapphire's Gathering)

There was in the midst of the city [of Athens]
an altar belonging to no god of power; gentle
Clementia (Clemency) [Eleos] had there her seat,
and the wretched made it sacred; never lacked
she a new suppliant, none did she condemn or
refuse their prayers. All that ask are heard, night
and day may one approach and win the heart
of the goddess by complaints alone. No costly
rites are hers; she accepts no incense flame, no
blood deep-welling; tears flow upon her altar, sad
offering of severed tresses hang above it, and
raiment left when fortune changed. Around is a
grove of gentle trees, marked by the cult of the
venerable, wool-entwined laurel and the suppliant
olive. No image is there, to no metal is the divine
form entrusted, in hearts and minds does the
goddess delight to dwell. The distressed are ever
nigh her, her precinct ever swarms with needy folk,
only to the prosperous her shrine is unknown.
—Statius, Thebaid

SAPPHIRE

The silver shimmer of the lopsided moon peered over
the treetops, and only a few people remained around the
dwindling fire. The interrogation had been going round in
circles without getting anywhere. Vince had gone to call the
sheriff hours ago and had yet to return. Garth said it was at
least thirty miles on rough roads to town, and he couldn't

remember if it even had a pay phone. Once contacted, Garth said it might take hours for the sheriff to respond. Impatiently, Sapphire jiggled her leg, eager for the sheriff to come and end this stalemate. Garth paced behind Mole, supervising the situation to make sure no one was hurt. He smoked cigarette after cigarette, tossing his butts on the ground, and PS promptly picked them up and tossed them in the fire. Kyle grilled Mole with questions.

"Why do you want to know?" Mole cowered in the chair. "Why are you asking me this? Did I do something wrong?"

Sweating in the cold night air, Sapphire clenched the chair, trying not to scream. The next moment she slumped, sunk by despair at whatever was wrong with him. Wavering between anger and empathy, her guts twisted into knots.

Kyle droned on with his interrogation. "No one's saying that you did anything. We're just trying to find out what you did."

Sapphire sighed, unsure of what justice could look like in this mess.

"I don't know. I tripped. I smoked some stuff. Some," Mole searched for the right word. "Up, Op, Opium."

They all dutifully nodded their heads.

PS growled, "Are you still high, Mole?"

Mole ignored them, hands rubbing back and forth against his jeans.

Sapphire's shoulder knotted up and her eye twitched. She recognized Mole's expression from the other nights when he turned inside himself before exploding. She scooted her chair a few feet away. "Please," she pleaded. "Try to remember your evening."

"We went to the creek and smoked a joint." Mole swung his gaze around the circle.

He seemed to be expecting confirmation of what he had told them. "Then what?" Sapphire shuddered.

"I was at Bus Village. Some guy asked for Mole. I said, 'I'm Mole.'"

Sapphire prodded, "That was a long span of time. You must remember something in between."

"No," Mole yelled. "No, I can't. I can't remember. I was in the trees. I don't remember."

"You were in the trees and what happened?" Kyle asked.

Mole started crying. "I don't know. There were trees and they were moving, and I started hitting them."

Sapphire's empty stomach heaved again, and she pressed her hand against her abdomen, hoping to calm herself.

He looked up at her. "But I knew they were trees. I was hitting the trees," Mole whined. "I was only hitting trees."

Kyle nodded, "Okay, brother, you're remembering."

Mole leaned forward in his chair. "I was sitting in the dark, and Sunflower and Sara were gonna take off. They tried to get me to come with them." He looked around the circle, as if he had just remembered the most important point of all. "I was tripping too hard. I told them to leave me there." He giggled.

His misplaced laughter sent a shiver down Sapphire's spine. Paralyzed in her chair, choking on guilt. Her failure to act caused this madness.

"Don't you understand?" Mole raised his voice. "I want to remember. I'm trying hard!" His left hand pressed against his head, and his fingers began to curl, digging into his scalp.

Garth edged in, as Mole remembered hanging out with a friend and then sitting in some trees. He remembered his friend going for coffee, and the clouds rolling across the sky, and people walking by laughing at him.

No one helped him, she thought. She messed up big time.

Mole leaned forward in his chair. "All I did was some LSD and hit trees with sticks." Mole stared at her. "I didn't hurt no one."

The fire hissed, flames moving slower and slower, until the red, yellow, and blue hardened into a painting of a fire. The pungent smoke left a bitter taste on her tongue. A chunk of charred wood broke off the fire and rolled toward her. Sapphire had to ask the question. "Did you rape a sister named Daisy?"

Mole screamed, "I would never hurt anyone like that." His head jerked back and forth, as Sapphire watched his mouth open wide. He collapsed into the easy chair for a moment, and then he screamed, "What did I do?" His hands went to his face; his fingers dug into his eyes.

Stunned, she stopped breathing.

Garth yanked Mole against the back of the chair. "Crazy motherfucker. Sit still!"

Sapphire shifted her gaze between Mole and Garth, the sound of her heart booming in her head.

Mole screamed jumbled words of nonsense.

Garth grabbed Mole's hands. Yanked them from his face. Blood trickled out of Mole's left eye.

"You think I did it." Mole thrust himself back and forth, struggling to break free of Garth, and repeatedly being shoved back into the chair. "I must have done it, or you wouldn't say it. Let me go." He lunged towards the fire.

Shrunk into her chair, all Sapphire could do was stare, mouth open wide.

Garth shoved him back into the chair, and Mole began to cry, his face red and crumpled. For a moment, everyone stared at Garth, the only sound the whispered crinkle of the fire. Garth shook his head and stomped out of the circle.

Sapphire gasped and started to breathe.

Kyle and PS stood watch on either side of Mole.

Mole bent over, choking on his tears, swinging his head wildly from side to side.

In agony, Sapphire squeezed her eyes shut, trying to reconcile the anguish in Daisy's face with the torment in Mole's. What would she feel if she awoke from a nightmare and realized it was real? That she had done what she had never meant to do. She remembered the tremble in Daisy's hand as she lifted a cup of tea to her lips. Daisy hiding herself under the shawl, hiding herself from the shame, hiding from something that she had no control over. Sapphire had been hiding too. Blaming herself for something that was out of her control. She was only a child when Dad left, and it wasn't her fault. It wasn't Daisy's fault she was raped, and Sapphire wasn't even sure if it was Mole's fault either. If only someone had stayed with Mole. If only she had....

Mole curled up in the chair, sniffling.

Sapphire had to get away from the smoldering haze hanging over them, had to breathe clean air, had to breathe. She sidled away from Mole and the fire, and toward the trees, gulping in the crisp pine air.

"Are you okay?" Garth followed her, as she stumbled to a log.

Speechless, she sank onto the rough bark.

"Was that wild?" he asked. "He didn't blame it on the woman."

"Where's the sheriff?" She gulped.

"It's long haul from Quincy." Garth lowered himself onto the log and draped his arm around her shoulder. "I actually feel sorry for that kid."

His arm felt comforting, probably as close to her father as she was ever going to get. "What'll happen to him?"

"Jail. Prison. Maybe an institution." He shrugged his shoulders. "Life sure is easier when you can blame someone." He pushed his hat back on his head. "There's supposed to be a bad guy."

She nodded. "I blamed my mom." She whispered, "I blamed her for everything." For Dad's absence. For running away with Sticky. For the gaping abyss in her heart that she hid from everyone she met.

"I didn't believe you at first. About Mole, I mean. I thought he was trying to weasel out of a rape charge."

"What made you change your mind?"

Garth bent over and snubbed out his smoke in the dirt. "He was horrified at what he'd done." He mashed the cigarette until it crumbled into nothing. "What a night. The whole gathering was mellow until the last day, and then all the crazies came out of the woodwork. First, it was the weirdo smearing grease in everyone's hair and now a rapist who doesn't know what planet he's on. Sometimes, I don't know why I do this."

Sapphire looked at the dark sky above and the shimmer of stars peeking through the clouds. "'Cause the stars always come back."

Garth glanced at her and then turned his gaze towards the sky. "I never thought about it before, but you're right. The stars always come back."

"Daddy told me that when I was a kid. Sat me on his knee on the front porch and we stared at the sky, waiting for the stars to come out. And they did."

They sat there for a few minutes, watching the flickering stars slowly stretch out across the black canvas and the dying moon loitering overhead.

Garth said, "I'm sorry about your dad."

What her dad hadn't told her is that people don't always come back. "Sometimes not knowing is worse than the truth."

When the sky bled orange across the treetops, Sapphire spotted La Abuela climbing the hill toward them, with Lauren in her wake. River trailed behind, lugging a djembe.

The grandmother stayed on course until she sat down on the arm of Mole's chair, inhaling and exhaling, until her breath synchronized with his. *"Ah, mi hijo,"* she exclaimed. *"Pobrecito,"* she cried, pulling him into her arms as if he were her long-lost grandson. Sapphire yearned for that hug. "We've let you down, my son. We didn't guide you when you needed our guidance." She grabbed his jaw with her fingers. "Let the tears out. You need to cry. I will cry with you." The tears ran down her cheeks and she rocked Mole in her arms as if he were a toddler who had skinned his knee. The grandmother tilted her head to the sky and wailed, "Mother of all the world."

As Sapphire watched them, her skin tingled and her eyes watered. She rubbed her nose against the right sleeve of her jacket. Something touched her left hand, and she glanced down, seeing a hand in hers. Her gaze followed the arm up until she realized it was Lauren's. She gave Lauren's hand a small squeeze

The grandmother cried, "The grandmothers and grandfathers do not talk to our children. We are too isolated. We failed you. We, who must listen to your hearts, share our wisdom, guide you when you need it. Oh, how we have failed. *Lo siento,* I am sorry, my son."

Lauren whispered, "When I heard what happened, I asked La Abuela for her help."

Puzzled, Sapphire remained silent.

"We were with Daisy before we came here. La Abuela held a healing circle for her." Lauren whispered, "I can't handle this. Not now." She rubbed her belly.

Sapphire stared at Lauren's face.

Lauren asked, "Are you okay?"

Sapphire nodded and shrugged her shoulders. "What about Daisy?"

"We sent Kalmia to call her mom. But when we left, Daisy was asleep."

Sapphire asked, "How are we going to support Daisy once the gathering ends?"

"I don't know."

Sapphire nodded and searched the circle for signs that the others were glad to see La Abuela. On her right, PS sat with his arm around his girlfriend, hugging her. Kyle sat with his arms folded across his chest, knees spread open, and leaning back with the front legs of the chair off the ground. She saw tears on his cheek. Garth's eyes pinched together, but she couldn't tell if it was the morning glare or his own emotions overtaking him.

"How long have you been here?" Lauren asked.

Sapphire hung back just a bit. "Since the beginning."

"I know Daisy. We took a couple of classes together at Humboldt."

Sapphire said, "Oh, I'm so sorry." Lauren's eyes were swollen and red from tears. Sapphire tried to force a smile onto her own sad face.

Lauren whispered, "About yesterday. I wanted the circle to be healing, like it was…"

Sapphire nodded. "I'm the problem, not you. I'm the one who messes everything up."

"Not true. I'm floundering, trying to find a path forward."

"You're stressed about the baby." Sapphire glanced at La Abuela leading Mole away from the fire and out into the open. "I'm sorry; I was out of line yesterday."

Lauren stroked Sapphire's hair. "I need to ask you…"

"Later." Sapphire held back all the things she wanted to say. Now was not the time to tell Lauren about her junkie father or her own self-pity. Now was not the time to tell Lauren she failed to deal with Mole. Now was not confession; there was still work to be done.

"*Ahora,* my child," La Abuela said as she stood up. "It is time to heal. For you to accept what you have done. Ask forgiveness from the Great Mother. Most importantly, you must ask forgiveness from your sister. The sister who you have hurt." She led Mole to the edge of the hill, overlooking the blanket of trees rolling into the distance, and the gathering hidden beneath them. Sapphire, Lauren, and everyone else trailed behind them.

"I'm sorry," Mole said.

"Louder, my son."

There had been photos of the three of them, Daddy playing guitar and Mommy singing while she danced. And a photo of a whole bunch of people hugging, and Sapphire was on Dad's shoulders and Mom was hugging him and everyone was hugging Mom. Then, there were no more photos. The next time she painted Dad, he would be on a worn beige couch with a dazed look on his face. The painting would be gothic, dark blues and blacks, and him in gray.

"My sister," Mole screamed, "I'm sorry."

"Mi hermana," La Abuela echoed. *"Lo siento."*

"Forgive me, my sister."

Their voices echoed off the hills and bounced back to Sapphire, disembodied sorrows trying to find their way home. A string of Stickys and Manuels and Zachs lay scattered on the trail like dried leaves. And Lauren was a green leaf floating in front of her. Sapphire reached for Lauren's hand.

La Abuela put her arms on Mole's shoulders and turned him gently toward a group of sky-high pine trees. "Now, you must ask the trees for forgiveness because you have dishonored them." She tilted her head back, opening her face to the sky and the sun rising in the east.

Mole yelled, "Please forgive me, beautiful trees."

"Por favor árboles magníficos, forgive my son who violated his sister."

Sapphire wondered if trees could forgive or if they stood above her passing judgment on her humanness, her inability to live in harmony with others. Could she forgive? Her mother had once told her that trees accept the rain and the sun as equals. Her breath deepening, Sapphire watched La Abuela asking the universe to forgive Mole, knowing that she needed forgiveness too. Not just forgiveness, but mercy. She needed to feel mercy in her heart for herself and her parents. For the paths taken and avoided. For a future that was better than the past. Lauren's hand was warm, and Sapphire glanced at her friend, who whispered the words the older woman uttered under her breath.

Mole sunk to his hands and knees, but his body was stiff and his head did not touch the earth.

Sapphire knelt down to embrace the earth. Pressed the palms of her hands to the ground. Her tears sprinkled the soil. She shouted, "I'm sorry." The rising sun cast shadows of the trees on the grass in front of her. Shadows that reminded her of Dad and Mom and the child she once had been, dancing in the park surrounded by other moms and dads trying to create a new future, reaching for lavender and magenta dreams and the pale cool sliver of the moon that controlled the ocean's tides. A moon that she had inherited from her father, before he fell. The moon whose pale image in the sky danced above treetops to the west. She pressed her forehead into the grass and let her tears water the ground.

Again, and again, La Abuela made Mole yell his apologies into the earth. Each time, he cried. The Grandmother cried. Sapphire cried. Lauren whimpered. Around her, everyone but Garth cried. La Abuela rose, as if she were a tree growing out of the soil, toward the sun. Mole turned over and lay on his back, looking up at her, his face covered in dirt and tears, a snot-nosed, sandbox-playing kid.

Sapphire stood up and went to La Abuela. "My grandmother, for the healing to be complete, Mole must ask forgiveness from his brothers and sisters."

"You are right, child." La Abuela bent down, took Mole's hands in hers and pulled him to his feet.

Sapphire trembled, as the older woman placed Mole's hand in hers. La Abuela touched her cheek gently. "You shall guide the others, my child. Embrace the pain and discover the world that awaits."

EYES WIDE OPEN

Sunday, July 8, 1990
(Day Thirteen of Sapphire's Gathering)

Each night, Ra, the king of Ancient Egyptian gods, embarks in a solar barque to Duat, the Ancient Egyptian otherworld of lands like ours and not like ours. Peopled with grotesque beings, Ra battles against serpent monsters and returns. Returns from the journey through the dark. To rule at dawn.
—Ancient Egyptian myth

SAPPHIRE

The brilliant gold sun climbed higher above the tree line, and the sky turned crystalline blue. Sapphire surveyed the area. Scattered clumps of people stood on the perimeter of the tree line and among the cars, watching. She called out, "Circle," and beckoned. "We need fresh energy, rested souls." People shifted towards her. "The circle must be closed to complete the healing." Slowly, the circle formed. Kyle and PS, River and Lauren, fresh faces with bewildered expressions, a wearied Blue. La Abuela and Mole stood on her left. When the circle had formed, Sapphire looked to La Abuela.

The old woman smiled at her. "You are ready." She left the circle.

And Sapphire was. Ready, that is. Willing to move on. Stepping into the center of the circle, she brought Mole with her. The worn faces of the crew that had been together all night stared at her. New faces, drawn to the power of the moment, seemed unsure of what was happening. She was lightyears away from that motel room, or her dad for that matter—but exactly where she needed to be. The sun warmed her back, and she felt the vibrations of the mountain under her feet, the power pulsing through her legs. The rumble of drums in the distance grounded her, the rhythm woven into a warm blanket. "Good morning, sun. Thank you for warming our faces; thank you for healing our hearts." She led Mole to Kyle. "Now, ask your father for forgiveness."

Staring at Kyle's face, Mole's arms hung at his side. "Father, forgive me for what I did. I didn't mean to do it."

Kyle grabbed Mole's shoulders, and said, "Brother, what you did was wrong." He gave Mole a quick hug. They stared at each other.

Sapphire's bones dripped with sorrow, the weight of her head heavy on her shoulders. She inhaled to the count of four, exhaled to the count of six, breathing deep into her belly, into the earth, into the integral sorrows of life.

Mole stepped sideways until he faced PS. "Brother, help me fix it. Help me undo last night."

PS shook his head. "No can-do, little brother. No going back. Only forward. You can only go forward." PS shook Mole's hand and slapped him on the back. "Go forward with your heart, and you will find the light."

Sapphire guided Mole around the circle, prompting him to apologize to all present, to her newly discovered patchwork family. One by one, they chastised him, schooled him, and hugged him.

On the ridge, the flashing red and blue lights of a four-door jeep signaled the arrival of the sheriff. An unmarked white sedan pulled up behind it. Two men got out of the black-and-white, and Garth hurried toward them.

Sapphire placed her right hand on Mole's back. "It's time to go."

River and Lauren dropped their hands and stepped back, opening the circle. Sapphire guided Mole towards the sheriff. She paused, took a deep breath, and exhaled. Behind her, the circle exhaled and joined their voices in an Om that trembled in the morning breeze, soft and mournful. In silence, they approached the sheriff. This wasn't the way she had imagined the story would end, but at this point, the possibilities were few. She looked at Mole. She had spent three of the most intense nights of her life with him, and now he was disappearing. He had to go because of Daisy's black eye and his own wounded spirit and the lines he had shattered.

Garth and the sheriff stopped talking as they approached.

Sapphire shook the sheriff's hand. "This is my friend, Mole."

The sheriff nodded. "Hello, Mole."

Mole shuffled his feet.

"Do you have a legal name. A first and a last name?" he asked.

"My name is Walter Johnson."

"Okay, Walter." The sheriff smiled. "Do you understand what's happening here?"

"You're taking me to jail?"

Sapphire released Mole's hand.

Lauren caught up with them and handed Mole his bedroll.

The sheriff nodded. "Do you know why?"

"I did something very bad, and my friends want me to go." He hugged his bedroll, pants hanging low on his hips, rumpled and streaked with dirt. "I hurt my sister."

"You're not under arrest at this time. We want to place you in protective custody. This is totally voluntary on your part." He jotted notes in his little book. "Do you consent to come with me?"

Mole looked at Sapphire, and she nodded. Then, he said, "My friend thinks I should go with you."

She hugged him, hard and long and kissed his cheek before stepping back. A hawk shrieked, *kee-eeeee-arr. Tilting her head back, she spotted it soaring* in the endless sky. Snow-capped mountains reflected sunlight that shimmered through the trees. A dab of brown ochre against a million dabs of cerulean blue on a reused canvas, layering her future onto her past. *Kee-eeeee-arr. Kee-eeeee-arr. The hawk spoke wisely. Knowing the old truth created a path forward.*

Garth moved closer. "I've caught a few rapists over the years, but this is the first time I ever felt bad about it."

Remembering her mom picking up pieces of the carousel picture shattered on the floor and the angry words they had spoken, Sapphire nodded. "Sometimes, things don't work out the way you want them to. Sometimes, all you can do is make someone leave to protect someone else."

Garth scowled. "Maybe there's something to this forgiveness crap after all."

Sapphire gazed up at Garth. He pulled his cowboy hat down low on his face, creating a slanted shadow. Light and dark. Good and bad. Black, white, and the infinite colors in between created the image, created life. Both her parents were multi-hued people. She imagined Mom wearing a lavender sundress, dancing in a field of daisies, her blue eyes sparkling with joy. Mom had nursed her and had grown her with light, water, and love. Mom who had been there for her every day of her life. She sighed. "Do you think my dad's still alive?"

Garth stared at her. "He could be dead. He could be clean. Honestly, I don't know. After the gathering's over, I'll call some of my friends in Albuquerque and ask around."

"Maybe." Sapphire watched the sheriff drive off with Mole. The jeep kicked up dust that settled on her skin and in her eyes. She blinked several times. Overhead, the sky was crystal clear and the sun golden in its radiance. She should have felt bad, but really, life was a sunflower growing and unfolding on a summer morning. Her mother had given her that. Her dad had given her a dream. If he were alive, she would find him, but first she needed to make peace with Mom.

Lauren put her arm around Sapphire's shoulder.

She leaned into Lauren's body. "Dad's not here."

"When I heard you were leaving, I thought maybe you found him."

Sapphire shook her head. "Turns out he's a junkie in New Mexico." She whispered, "I think."

Lauren took Sapphire's hand in hers and squeezed it gently. "I'm afraid I can't do it." Lauren cradled her protruding belly.

"Do what?"

"Be a mother. Raise a child."

As if any of them had a roadmap for where they were headed. Sapphire knew that now. "You will do the best you can do. That's all any of us can do. Life doesn't make any promises, but love will guide you." Love was really all any of them had.

"River wants me to live in a yurt two miles from the nearest road."

"What about River's folks?"

Lauren laughed. "They're down-home Baptists. When River told them about the baby, they disowned him for living in sin and…."

"Come home with me."

Lauren rubbed her belly.

"You can stay with me. River too. My mom will help. She's always helping other women. She had me in a tepee in Topanga Canyon."

Lauren pressed her hands together. Right thumb to left thumb. Right fingers to left fingers and brought her hands to her chest until her thumbs were pressing into the space between her breasts. "River wants us to have the baby along the river, surrounded by tree-covered mountains in a wild place. He wants to have a wild child." She smiled.

Up on the hillside, a couple of djembes started up. *Thump wap boom.* Sapphire felt the pulse in her heart. "My mom is pretty cool. She'd help you have the baby anywhere you want—I didn't turn out so bad." She smiled.

Lauren looked over her shoulder to where River and Garth stood.

Sapphire said, "It's up to you. Wherever you feel comfortable, I'll be there."

Lauren wiped at the corner of her eyes and forced a smile.

Sapphire wrapped one arm around Lauren's shoulder, pulling her close, and placed her other hand on Lauren's belly. She felt a soft thump under her palm and squealed with delight. "The baby's kicking!"

The End
Safe journeys and happy trails, my friends.

ABOUT THE AUTHOR

Karin E. Zirk earned her doctorate in Mythological Studies with an emphasis in Depth Psychology from Pacifica Graduate Institute in 2016. Her collection of poetry, *Notes from the Road*, chronicled her years traveling the USA in a Volkswagen camper van. Her poetry and short stories have appeared in numerous small journals. When she is not at work in the technology industry, she is trying to save Rose Creek and attending peace and healing gatherings.
This is her first novel.

ACKNOWLEDGMENTS

A huge thank you to my sister, Tina Childers, for caring for our mother on Sunday mornings so I could write; Jennifer Simpson for reading untold drafts, providing feedback, and endless discussions on the meaning of life; Dawn Sperber for her intuitive editing; Deborah Johnson, Roxanne Michaud, Carletta Chadwell, and Cyndi Cannady for providing feedback on multiple drafts; the San Diego Writing Center and its progeny, San Diego Writers Ink, for helping me hone my craft; Tony Bond for book design and layout.

With gratitude to The Elizabeth George Foundation for providing a generous grant to unpublished fiction writers. We all need more time to write.

To all the scarecrows, tin people, cowardly lions, and wizards I have met along the journey, each one of you have shaped this work.